SPIDER
SEASON

SPIDER SEASON

JOHN MORGAN WILSON

ST. MARTIN'S MINOTAUR

NEW YORK

SPIDER SEASON. Copyright © 2008 by John Morgan Wilson. All rights reserved. Printed in the United States of America. For information, address St. Martin's Press, 175 Fifth Avenue, New York, N.Y. 10010.

The excerpts quoted from Benjamin Justice's autobiography are from *Simple Justice,* by John Morgan Wilson. Copyright © 1996 by John Morgan Wilson. Reprinted by permission.

www.minotaurbooks.com

Library of Congress Cataloging-in-Publication Data

Wilson, John Morgan, 1945–
    Spider season : a Benjamin Justice novel / John Morgan Wilson.—1st ed.
        p. cm.
    ISBN-13: 978-0-312-34148-0
    ISBN-10: 0-312-34148-2
    1. Justice, Benjamin (Fictitious character)—Fiction. 2. Journalists—Biography—Fiction. 3. Los Angeles (Calif.)—Fiction. I. Title.
    PS3573.I456974S65 2008
    813'.54—dc22

                                                                          2008028965

First Edition: December 2008

10 9 8 7 6 5 4 3 2 1

For my beloved aunt, Betty Lou Dean

And in memory of Uncle Bud, Irv Letofsky, and

Barbara Seranella

ACKNOWLEDGMENTS

Many thanks to my agent, Alice Martell, who has handled all eight Benjamin Justice novels, as well as other books of mine; Keith Kahla, my invaluable editor at St. Martin's Minotaur; Pietro Gamino, who makes it possible in so many ways for the writing to get done; John Langley, for his remarkable generosity and support; Gary Cotler, Detective, Retired, Los Angeles Sheriff's Department, and his wife, Cathryn Cotler, Deputy, Retired, LASD, for their input on police matters; painter-sculptor-photographer Christopher Oakley, for his insights on art; and Larry Kase, my good friend and uncomplaining research whiz.

Once again, I must also thank a number of friends for lending their names for characters in this novel. With the exception of Topper Schroeder, Billy Avarathar, and Noel Alumit, who "play themselves," they bear little or no resemblance to the characters depicted. These brave souls include the aforementioned Cathryn Cotler, who allowed me to use her maiden name, Conroy, for a particularly venal character; and Judith Zeitler, Dave Haukness, Bruce Steele, Jan Long, Larry Kase, Lance (whose last name must go unmentioned here to avoid a spoiler), and Steven Reigns, all of whom fared better. (Please note that all the characters in this novel are purely fictional, except as cited earlier.)

Over the years, I consciously patterned only one major or recurring character after someone from my life. Irv Letofsky, my editor and mentor at the *Los Angeles Times* for more than a decade, served as the sole inspiration for Harry Brofsky, the editor who was so important to protagonist Benjamin Justice in the early novels (albeit with some adjustments in my depiction for dramatic purposes). Irv passed away on December 23, 2007, and I've included him in my dedication. Like so many writers, I was blessed to know and work with him.

ONE

Despite all that would follow that summer, it's the crows I remember most vividly. It was as if they were sending a warning signal, an omen that the darkest of days lay ahead.

They began screaming in the early afternoon. Not just a few, but dozens. It was late June, a warm month of severe humidity that was unusual for Southern California. For more than a week, the sultry weather had hung on everyone like wet laundry, dragging us down, leaving us worn-out and on edge. For years, the climate had been changing in odd ways that were worrisome—more than worrisome for those who understood the science—but no one in Los Angeles could recall an early summer quite like this one.

I was in my small apartment over the garage, wrapping up a call with Jan Long, my editor in New York.

"Hang in there, Benjamin," she said, in her wise and motherly way, even though we were both pushing fifty and I had the lead by several months. "Keep a tight lid, dear. Just a few more weeks, and you can slip back into anonymity." She added coyly, "Unless, of course, there's more writing in your future, and more work to promote. I wouldn't count that out if I were you."

My first book had been published earlier that month, a memoir laying out in shameful detail my spectacular fall from grace not quite eighteen years earlier. It was my chance to do some public atonement, make a little money, and possibly get back in the writing game, if things went reasonably well. Now I was back in L.A., winding up a grinding, twelve-city publicity tour during which I'd faced the same accusatory questions again and again about why I'd done what I'd done and why anyone should believe my version of events now. I deserved the scrutiny and condemnation, no question. But I also have a notoriously short fuse, and there wasn't much left. Jan's message was intended to pacify me: Thick skin, stiff upper lip, the worst of it will soon be over. Little did we know that the worst was about to begin and that a few tough questions from the media would soon be the least of my problems.

"Don't give too much weight to the reviews," she added. "The attacks haven't focused on your writing, but on you personally, on your character and credibility. Not much surprise in that, given your history."

"Thanks for the encouragement," I said. "My writing's okay. It's just me they want to string up by my testicles."

As she laughed and clicked off, I was drawn to the front window by the collective shrieking of the crows. They were perched on telephone wires and tree limbs, with more descending from the sky on their broad, black wings. As they came, their shadows passed ominously across the small house below, where my elderly landlords, Maurice and Fred, were comfortably ensconced. I'd never seen so many crows bunched together at one time, certainly not in West Hollywood, a bustling little city not exactly known for its wildlife, unless you count the late-night crowd at the crazier clubs along Santa Monica Boulevard and the Sunset Strip.

Then I saw what had drawn the flock together and triggered its hysterical chorus: On the narrow driveway that ran alongside the house, a muscular black tomcat was stalking a weakened crow that was apparently too sick or injured to fly. It flapped its wings ineffably, while the feral cat slowly drew closer on his coiled haunches and the crows above screeched their alarm in a futile effort to drive the predator away. I knew how much Maurice was troubled by the spectacle of violent death among animals; even Fred, his burly partner of nearly sixty years, had become protective of the squirrels and winged creatures that populated their modest property. So I trotted down the rickety wooden steps to the drive, clapping my hands and hollering at the crouching cat. He hissed at me before I stomped my foot in his direction. Then he fled, while the disabled crow disappeared into a bank of ivy and the frantic cries above gradually diminished to the occasional uneasy squawk.

Maurice emerged from the house in pink bunny slippers, his long, white hair bound up in a damp towel, his slender frame clad in a lavender satin kimono. Behind him, I could hear a scratchy old record on the turntable, something mournful and French by Edith Piaf. Maurice glanced upward, his rheumy eyes widening, to see the crows lining the telephone wires like a scene out of *The Birds*.

"My goodness, Benjamin! What attracted so many of them? And whatever got them so upset?"

I explained about the cat and the crow and Maurice looked about for the grounded bird, thinking he might rescue it. But it was nowhere to be seen. As large as it was, it had completely vanished; not a leaf of the ivy was stirring in the muggy air. He commented about how one so rarely sees a dead bird, while the numbers that expire each day of natural causes alone must be staggering.

"I suppose they find a private place to die," I said, "where they won't be a bother to anyone. I can understand that instinct."

No sooner were the words out of my mouth than I realized how insensitive they were in the presence of a man in his early eighties, whose older partner was on the frail side. Maurice stared pensively at the ivy for a moment before smiling painfully and turning silently toward the house. I was headed back to my apartment, cursing my thoughtlessness, when he called out to me.

"Benjamin! A young man just climbed into your car."

I followed Maurice's eyes out to Norma Place, where my '65 Mustang convertible was parked at the curb with the top down. It was a classic I'd restored to cherry condition years ago, the only thing of material or sentimental value that I owned, with the exception of a couple of photographs. Sure enough, there was someone sitting behind the wheel, his hands set casually at ten and two o'clock, as if he intended to drive away. As I started in his direction,

I watched him run his fingers appreciatively over the tuck-and-roll upholstery, which I'd selected to complement the Mustang's lustrous red paint job.

Behind me, Maurice called out, "Benjamin, don't do anything rash!"

I barely heard him as I hit the sidewalk and dashed across the street, already feeling a surge of adrenaline. For two weeks, I'd endured the barbed questions and barely veiled insults of interviewers, gritting my teeth as they grilled me like a choice fillet. Intentionally or not, they'd made me feel small and defensive. Suddenly, I was free to stand up for myself, or at least my only possession worth defending.

As I closed in on the punk behind the wheel, I got a better look at him. He appeared to be in his late twenties, and in decent shape. He was shirtless, on the wiry side, with a cleanly shaved dome and a blond soul patch bristling between his lower lip and cleft chin. Colorful tattoos decorated the sunburned skin on his back and upper arms. I went straight for him, seizing him by the back of the neck and grabbing him under his left biceps, which was inked with the legendary Marine Corps slogan: *Semper Fi.*

In one explosive motion, I pulled him up from the seat and dragged him over the door frame, flinging him to the rough pavement.

"Stay down," I said, hoping he wouldn't.

He studied my face a moment before sizing up the rest of me. Then he rose slowly but purposefully to his feet, keeping his eyes on mine. I made a quick evaluation of my own: He stood roughly an inch under my six feet, carrying a good twenty pounds less on his lanky frame. But his shoulders were nearly as broad as mine and his muscles sinewy and taut. Not once did his piercing blue eyes flicker or blink.

In some ways, I felt like I was looking at a younger version of myself, back in my college wrestling days—blond and blue-eyed like this guy, lean as a racehorse, and chomping at the bit for some action, something physical and challenging that would bring some momentary focus to my fractured, confusing life. The problem lay in the thirty years that had passed since, when my physical prowess had gradually diminished along with my hairline. I'd recently rebuilt some lost muscle, but my waist had thickened and my sharp reflexes were mostly a memory. My eyesight was another issue. I'd lost my left eye several years ago in a violent encounter I should have avoided, if overweening male pride and machismo hadn't overcome reason. Now I wore a plastic prosthetic in its place. The fake eye looked perfectly real—it had been shaped and painted by the finest technicians—but my depth perception and peripheral vision were marginal at best. I was in decent shape for my age but long past my prime.

If the skinhead had been a Marine—his *Semper Fi* tattoo and camouflage pants suggested as much—then he was almost surely a serious threat. As he stood firmly in a pair of heavy black boots, there was a sense of recklessness about him, and maybe a deeper anger forged by pain and punishment, the kind that chronically leads a certain type of man to trouble. The kind that had haunted me most of my life. I relished a confrontation, but I didn't underestimate him, either.

His lips curled into a small, enigmatic smile that I took for a challenge. I felt my heart race a little faster and my vision narrow. It was a potent and exhilarating moment, dangerous and unpredictable, the kind I hadn't experienced in years. I wondered if the anticipation was as pleasurable for him as it was for me.

He glanced at the vintage Mustang. "Cool car." Like he was there to buy it, not steal it.

"You had no business being in it."

He shrugged his knobby shoulders. "I just wanted to sit behind the wheel for a while."

He spoke matter-of-factly, like he'd done nothing wrong, like I was making too big a deal of it, which didn't fit the circumstances. I figured he might be high on something—crystal maybe—one of the meth heads one sometimes encountered around WeHo, tweaking for days with their brains rewired over time by the insidious drug and their perception about as close to reality as Mars. Yet his pupils didn't appear to be dilated; his fierce blue eyes were clear and steady. He stared at me implacably for a few seconds more. Then he took a step forward. I held my ground.

"I told you to stay down," I said.

"I stopped taking orders when I left the Corps."

I braced for a strike, maybe a sucker punch or some combative move he'd learned in the military. But what he did next I could never have foreseen. He reached up and touched my face.

My reaction was defensive, automatic: I shot low to my right, sweeping his left leg near the ankle, taking the leg out from under him the way I'd done hundreds of times in takedown drills and competitions decades ago. Often, an untrained man will go down immediately, especially if his momentum is moving forward, the way a table topples if it loses a leg at its weighted corner. But the skinhead didn't fall that easily. He resisted just enough to balance on one foot, leaning into me in an effective sprawl, as if he might have had some wrestling in his own past, or picked up some useful countermoves in boot camp. He reached out and clung to me, clinching my upper body to his, until my face was buried in the web of golden hair that spread across his hard chest. I could smell his sweat, taste his salt, feel the solid structure of his torso as he clung to me and strained to keep me there. I slid my encircling arms higher up his leg, between his thighs and deep into his crotch. I bent my knees and lifted him upward until his heavy boots came off the ground, giving me more control.

Briefly, we were frozen like that, locked in a violent embrace. With both hands he pulled my face to his rippled belly, clutching me tight, like a desperate lover trying to hang on to someone leaving for the last time. Then, as I felt his heart pounding behind his ribs, he surprised me again. He suddenly went slack, as if he was giving in to me, allowing me to do with him what I wanted.

I seized the opportunity, slamming him facedown to the street and falling on top of him. I straddled his hips and tied up his legs with mine, flattening him and grinding his face into the rough pavement with my left forearm, while I used my other hand to cinch his right arm in a hammerlock. He wasn't resisting at all now. His head was turned, one side of his face pressed firmly to the gritty asphalt.

His forehead and the bridge of his nose glistened with blood, and his mouth was bruised and torn. Yet despite the thrashing he was taking, he bore a passive expression, like a long-battered child who'd grown callous to pain.

At some point I'd cut the inside of my mouth. I savored the tangy taste of my blood and the adrenaline high I was riding. It had been years since I'd experienced the thrill of a brawl. I realized how much I'd missed it, how alive it made me feel.

Dimly, as if from a great distance, Maurice's voice penetrated my consciousness, like a hypnotist calling a subject back from a trance. He was telling me that the police were on their way and pleading with me to show restraint, insisting that the young man no longer posed a threat. Hearing Maurice gradually drew me out of my euphoria. My heartbeat began to slow and my tunnel vision gradually opened up. Little by little, I sensed the larger world around me again. For a minute or two, everything had been a slow-motion blur, but now it all became remarkably clear and sharp.

I lifted my forearm from the stranger's neck, testing his will. He remained prone and still. As a precaution, to keep him down, I placed the flat of my hand near his left shoulder, over a tat of an eagle clutching a sheaf of arrows in its claws. In the sudden stillness, I became aware of the skinhead's powerful shoulder muscles, the warmth and moisture of his flesh, the steady heaving of his breath, a few scars here and there on his lean body, possibly from battle. My face was pouring sweat, which mingled with his as it dripped onto his glistening skin. The intimacy between us was palpable. I wondered if he sensed it as keenly as I did.

That's when it dawned on me how little fight he'd put up, even from the outset. A vainglorious part of me wanted to believe I'd overpowered a dangerous young man in his prime. But a more objective voice suggested something else was going on, something I didn't understand.

He shifted his eyes to stare at my hand on his shoulder, reminding me of what had triggered my reaction in the first place—the movement of his own hand toward my face, which I'd taken as a threat. He'd touched me, but I realized now that it hadn't been quick or aggressive. It had been gentle, almost tender. Our eyes met, and I tried to find something in his that might explain his odd behavior, whether he was innocently out of his mind or something else was going on. But the conflicting emotions I saw were impossible to sort out. Then his gaze fell forward again, passive and calm, toward a crowd of onlookers gathering on the sidewalk.

Sirens wailed through nearby streets, approaching fast. As they grew louder, I continued to study the stranger, searching for some sign of remorse, or at least anxiety, since he was about to be arrested. But all I saw was a bloodied young man lying facedown on the pavement, literally in my hands and under my control, his battered face a mask of seeming contentment.

I had the strange feeling that this was what he'd wanted all along.

TWO

"Benjamin, are you all right?"

Maurice unwrapped the terry-cloth towel that bound his damp hair and folded it neatly into quarters. He gently lifted the young man's head and placed the makeshift pillow beneath. The skinhead accepted the kindness passively, without a word.

For a moment, I didn't know if Maurice's question pertained to my physical or mental state; perhaps it was meant for both.

"A couple of scrapes," I said. "Nothing serious." I glanced across the street to the old Craftsman bungalow where Maurice and Fred had lived for more than fifty years. "Where's your other half? Ordinarily, he'd be out here, backing me up."

"Napping," Maurice said, sounding oddly stern. "He must have slept right through it. Just as well. He needs his rest." Maurice scolded me with his eyes, before they darted sympathetically to the injured man beneath me. "Really, Benjamin, what's gotten into you? I thought you'd put all this frightful violence behind you."

The sirens reached a crescendo and two black-and-whites turned into the street, speeding toward us from opposite ends. No more than three minutes had passed since I'd yanked the skinhead from my car, which meant the radio call had gone out from dispatch seconds after Maurice had called 911. Within a minute, three more patrol cars were on the scene, the kind of prompt response you get in a tightly knit community like West Hollywood, with thirty-six thousand residents packed into less than two square miles. Two uniformed deputies separated me from the skinhead while the others set about questioning witnesses, including Maurice. A female deputy who seemed to be in charge asked me a few questions, put the skinhead in handcuffs, and sat him across the street on the curb. A minute or two later, an ambulance arrived and two EMTs began attending to him, checking his vital signs and cleaning up the abrasions on his face and upper body.

Finally, an unmarked detective's car rolled up. A tall, lanky man in a western-style jacket and snakeskin boots climbed out leisurely, like he was on his way to a down-home Texas barbecue. His salt-and-pepper hair was clipped short in a crew cut, but a Pancho Villa mustache added a flourish to his narrow, bony face. The military-style haircut had probably been stylish fifty-odd years ago, around the time he was born, if the lines in his craggy face were a useful gauge. His jacket was open, and I could see a nine-millimeter Beretta in a clamshell holster on his left hip. His gold shield was displayed nearer his big belt buckle, a tacky piece of pseudo-silver jewelry shaped like the Lone Star State. I didn't know whether to admire his ballsy taste in clothes or laugh.

The female deputy, who was now questioning Maurice, stepped away to confer with the detective. She pointed in my direction, then returned to Maurice, while the detective ambled toward me in his showy boots. Without extending his hand, he introduced himself in a southwestern drawl as Detective Dave Haukness. He let me know right off that he knew who I was and that I came with a past.

"Benjamin Justice," he said, in a voice that conveyed no judgment, but no warmth, either. "I believe we've had dealings with you before." His mild green eyes were as hard to read as his taciturn manner. "So why don't you tell me what happened here?"

I tried to keep it simple and to the point. I explained that I'd caught the suspect behind the wheel of my car, apparently intending to steal it, pulled him out, then defended myself after he'd faced off and made a threatening move.

"He assaulted you?"

I hesitated. "He raised his hand to me."

"He struck you?"

"He made contact. I took it as aggression."

"Open hand or closed fist?"

"Open."

"Right hand or left?"

"Right."

"Where did he make contact?"

I pointed to my left cheek, which Haukness briefly examined.

"I don't see any marks or unusual coloring."

"I reacted quickly. He never landed a blow."

"You said he made contact."

"He touched me."

"Touched you?" Again, the flat, neutral tone. "That's it? And you threw him to the ground?"

"We engaged each other physically. I was fortunate enough to put him in a prone position and gain control."

"How exactly did you accomplish that?"

I explained how I'd managed it, though I made it sound less violent than it was.

"He fought back?"

"He resisted a little."

"Why didn't you call nine-one-one, instead of tangling with the man?"

"My landlord, Maurice, took care of that." I turned and pointed toward Maurice, who was tying his long, white hair back in a ponytail. "The older gentleman in the lavender robe."

"About the suspect," Haukness went on. "Did he have keys in his hand when you confronted him?"

"Not that I noticed."

"Implements of any kind, something he might have used to switch the ignition?"

I saw where Haukness was going and felt myself tighten. I'd been arrested once before for assault, not two blocks from where we were standing now. There had been other incidents, although

I'd always managed to skate without a formal charge or a conviction. Alcohol had usually been involved, something I'd given up years ago.

"I didn't really take time to look," I said evenly. "It happened quickly."

"So you don't really know that he was attempting to steal your car."

"He was in my car without permission."

"Did you ask him why?"

"Eventually, after I'd subdued him."

"And what did he tell you?"

"That he wanted to sit behind the wheel."

Haukness raised his graying eyebrows. "Sit behind the wheel?"

"That's what he said."

"Did it occur to you to wait at a safe distance and let the deputies handle it?"

"Car thieves don't usually wait around for the cops to show up."

"Did he appear to be in a hurry to be gone?"

I hesitated again, fashioning a reply that wasn't exactly a lie.

"I had the impression that he liked the car and might want it for himself."

Haukness was silent a moment, looking thoughtful. Then he said, "Witnesses are giving us a different story." I didn't say anything, so he added, "They see you as the aggressor, Mr. Justice. Even your landlord feels you overreacted."

"Maurice said that?"

"Not in so many words. But he's concerned that your response was out of proportion to the threat."

"The guy was in my car, Detective."

Haukness glanced over at the skinhead. The EMTs were applying bandages to his wounds.

"You're sure you don't know the suspect?"

"Never saw him before."

"A casual acquaintance, maybe? Someone you might have forgotten?"

It wasn't that strange a question, in a city where gay men comprised nearly a third of the population. Still, under the circumstances, I resented it.

"Someone I picked up, you mean? A one-night stand lost in a blur of drugs and alcohol? Something like that?"

"I didn't suggest that, Mr. Justice."

"I never saw the guy until he got in my Mustang about twenty minutes ago."

"You certainly got the best of him. You're what—late forties?"

"I'll turn fifty in September."

He ran his eyes over my upper body, which I'd been diligently working on in recent months.

"You're in pretty good shape for a man your age."

"There are a lot of men in the neighborhood who are in pretty good shape for their age. It's a gay ghetto. What can I tell you?"

He studied my eyes closely. "You take any drugs, Mr. Justice?"

"A few, for HIV."

"That's it? Nothing else?"

"Psychotropic, you mean?" He nodded. "Only prescriptions related to HIV, Detective."

"You need any medical attention?" I shook my head. "A deputy will take your full statement and contact information."

I nodded in the direction of the skinhead. "What happens to him?"

"He'll be checked out in the ER, then booked in at the sheriff's substation."

"For attempted GTA?"

"I'm not sure the evidence supports a felony like grand theft auto. We'll have to sort it all out." He dug in a pocket of his jacket and handed me a Sheriff's Department business card with his name and extension on it. "If you have anything to add, I'd appreciate it if you'd give me a call. That number will only be good for another few weeks. After that, I'm headed downtown to work homicide."

"Congratulations on the promotion."

"Call me if you want to clarify anything."

"I'm quite clear about what happened, Detective."

He left me to speak with the female deputy. A neighbor had brought Maurice two bottles of water, one of which Maurice handed to me. I unscrewed the cap and drank it down all at once.

"That was quite an ordeal you went through, Benjamin." He paused as worry lines creased his forehead. "Although the young man clearly got the worst of it, didn't he?"

"I have a right to defend my property, Maurice. I have a right to defend myself."

"Yes, of course." His troubled eyes flickered in the direction of the house. "Why don't we check the mail and then I'll make us a nice lunch. I'll wake Fred. He needs to eat something."

We crossed the street as the EMTs helped the skinhead to his feet. His wrists were handcuffed in front of him, and with his bandages, he looked like any other punk who'd made a bad choice and was about to pay for it. He glanced over, but I looked away before our eyes met, unwilling to waste more time on him.

Maurice opened the metal mailbox at the end of the drive, which he'd painted years ago in rainbow colors. He removed a stack of mail, sorted through it, and handed me a letter from my publisher, a couple of bills, and a plain postcard hand-printed on the front. Whoever had sent the postcard had used an odd variation of my name: *Benjamin In Justice.*

I turned it over to find a message in the same handwriting:

Read your book. Long and boring. I did enjoy the part in which you describe killing your father when you were 17, after you caught him diddling your little sister. He must have been a real bastard. That would explain why you turned out to be such a prick. Happy Father's Day, faggot.

The postmark was dated the previous Saturday, the day before Father's Day. The message was anonymous, no signature of any kind, and no return address. It wasn't the first piece of negative mail I'd received since my memoir had been published, but it was certainly the nastiest. All the others had been addressed to my publisher for forwarding to me. Whoever had sent this one obviously knew where I lived.

"Benjamin, are you coming in?"

I looked up from the postcard, feeling weary and distracted. "I think I'll catch a nap first, Maurice. This heat and humidity—I guess it's gotten to me."

"Sounds prudent, dear. I'll bring up some lunch for you later, after I see to Fred."

"Thanks, Maurice. That's very kind."

He turned into the house, leaning on a handrail for support as he mounted the steps. I was about to head up the drive when a clatter of wheels caught my attention. Out on the street, the EMTs had the skinhead strapped down on a stretcher and were loading him into the back of their ambulance, while a deputy stood by. When the suspect was in, sitting halfway up, he stared out through the open doors. His look was as indecipherable and his blue eyes as riveting as ever.

I could still feel them fixed on me long after the paramedics shut the ambulance doors and drove him away.

THREE

Upstairs, I turned on a ceiling fan, soaked a washcloth at the bathroom sink, and lay down with the wet cloth over my eyes. Not quite an hour later, I was awakened by the phone. Judith Zeitler, a thirtysomething book publicist I'd hired at the suggestion of Jan Long, was on the line. She was in her usual mood—energetic, upbeat, irrepressible.

"Which do you want first, Benjamin, the good news, or the good news?"

I sighed deeply, trying to shake off the lethargy of sleep. "Why don't you start with the good news, Judith?"

"I've set up an interview with Cathryn Conroy from *Eye!*"

It took a moment for the name to register. When it did, I said, "Not to spoil your party, Judith, but Cathryn Conroy would just as soon spit on me as shake my hand."

"What? Why?"

"It's a long story that goes way back."

"Maybe she's gotten over it."

"Did you approach the magazine, or did she bring the idea to you?"

"Actually, she came to me with it."

"Why am I not surprised? She's on the hunt for a kill."

I explained that Cathryn Conroy and I had been up for the same plum position at the *Los Angeles Times* nearly twenty-five years ago, when we'd both been young reporters on a fast rise in the journalism world. I'd gotten the job, which Conroy had blamed on misogyny and gender discrimination at the *Times*, which in those days had far more men than women working the high-profile investigative assignments. Conroy had been voluble about the hire and had vowed never to work a staff job again. She'd channeled her anger and frustration into a successful freelance career and was now a regular contributor to *Eye*, the popular biweekly out of New York, known for its investigative pieces and probing, pull-no-punches profiles. Conroy must have been salivating at the chance to have at me all these years later, after I'd turned my great opportunity at the *Times* into one of the trade's more notable scandals.

"If Cathryn Conroy writes a feature on me," I said, "expect nothing less than a hatchet job, with plenty of my blood on the blade."

"Benjamin, *Eye* is a very influential publication. Anyway, there's no such thing as bad publicity."

"Maybe not to a publicist," I said.

"You'll do the interview, right?"

"I'll think about it."

In fact, I knew I'd do the interview. My book wasn't exactly flying off the shelves, and I had a lot riding on its success. It was probably my last chance to forge some kind of career as a writer, though in what direction I wasn't sure. When you've won a Pulitzer Prize for a front-page newspaper series that later gets exposed as fabricated, as I had eighteen years ago, editors don't come clamoring with offers of assignments.

"If Cathryn Conroy was good news," I said, "I'm not sure I want to hear more."

"Believe me, this is even better. Are you ready?"

"Standing against the wall, blindfolded."

"*Jerry Rivers Live!*"

"The TV guy?"

"The highest-rated evening talk show on cable. The place where every author of a potential bestseller wants to be interviewed. At every commercial break, Jerry holds the book up to the camera and repeats the title. He always says what a great book it is, even when he hasn't read it."

"Sounds like a very serious show."

"Benjamin, an hour with Jerry Rivers and you can sell enough copies the next day to put your book on the *New York Times* Best Seller List. It's huge!"

"When do I have to do this?"

There was a pregnant pause. "The booking's not actually confirmed. But it's looking like a real possibility."

From everything I could see, Judith was a terrific publicist, hardworking to a fault, but she wore me out.

"Judith, do me a favor. Just tell me when it's a done deal, okay?"

"I'm just trying to be encouraging, Benjamin, to let you know I haven't stopped working for you, even though your book tour is winding down."

Now she sounded hurt.

"I know. It's just that I'm on overload. It's been a rough day."

"What happened?"

"Personal stuff. Nothing to worry about."

"I'm working on more print and radio interviews. I'll let you know when they're solid."

"That'd be great."

"And we've still got three more bookstore readings, plus the West Hollywood Book Fair in late September."

"You're doing a bang-up job, Judith. I really appreciate it."

She suddenly had someone on call waiting, apologized, and abruptly ended our conversation. As I hung up, I noticed the unpleasant postcard on my desk, where I'd tossed it. I dropped it into the top drawer and headed for a shower.

As I toweled off afterward in front of the bathroom mirror, checking my scrapes and bruises, I made a quick study of the muscles I'd redeveloped in recent months. The medicinal cocktail I'd been taking the past couple of years had kept my virus in check but had led to wasting and lipodypstrophy—the serious loss of muscle mass and unsightly redistribution of fat common to many HIV positives. My doctor had put together a new drug combo that promised fewer side effects, but we wouldn't know until my next blood test if it was continuing to suppress my virus and protect my immune system. In the meantime, he'd prescribed artificial testosterone to combat my loss of muscle mass. The results had been dramatic: After only a few months of steroid therapy and pumping iron at the gym several times a week, I'd gained twelve pounds of solid muscle, most of it in my upper body. I was due for another injection, and there was no better time than now, right after a shower, when my flesh was warm and soft.

I prepared a sterile syringe with 200 cc from the vial and swabbed a spot on my upper thigh with alcohol, where the muscle wasn't too thick. I stuck the needle in with one fast motion, the most efficient and painless way. All that was left was to push down on the plunger and empty the syringe. Instead, I held up, staring at the needle embedded in my leg.

I suddenly realized why I'd reacted so violently out on the street, after years of working hard to keep my temper in check and avoid physical confrontations. It was the testosterone coursing through my system, triggering my rage and aggression, fueling my need to beat my chest and show the world how tough I was. A bit of the old "roid rage," suddenly surfacing. Pumped up with the steroid, I'd reverted to my old ways, beating a young man nearly to a pulp.

Part of me felt guilty and embarrassed. The other part marveled at what I'd done, recalling how good it had felt, how empowering. I could easily withdraw the needle, I thought, empty the testosterone into the sink, and let my prescription expire without renewing it. I'd regained sufficient strength and then some. But I liked the sense of virility I'd experienced that day, facing down a younger man who'd challenged me. I was about to turn fifty. But thanks to the steroid, I'd been reborn with the vigor, muscularity, and libido of a man half my age. I wasn't about to give it up.

I pressed down on the plunger, slowly forcing the clear liquid into my system. When the syringe was empty, I withdrew the needle, used a cotton swab to dab away a spot of blood, and covered the needle prick with a small adhesive bandage. There would be some stiffness in my thigh for a day or two, a minor ache, a tiny bruise.

A small price to pay, I thought, for cheating time.

FOUR

"Not in the shade, Benjamin." Maurice pointed to a more open section of the backyard. "For healthy blooms, a gardenia needs sunlight."

I was helping Maurice with his gardening, while he ordered me about like a benevolent drill sergeant. Not one to bear grudges or nag interminably, he'd left unmentioned my violent behavior of the previous day. He paused to close his eyes and sniff the air, letting his imagination inhale the perfume that would come with the opening blossoms.

"I can't tell you how many evenings Fred and I have sat out here, listening to one of our favorite records and enjoying the sweet smell of gardenias." He smiled, calculating in his head. "Hundreds, I suppose. Hundreds of evenings spent with the same man, doing the simplest things. Others might be bored silly, I suppose. But you know what? I wouldn't trade one moment of it."

I began digging another hole for the new gardenia bush, while Maurice hovered closely.

"Be sure to dig the hole so there's plenty of loose soil at the bottom," he said. "We'll mix in some coffee grounds, for the acid. It helps loosen up the harder soil beneath, and invites the earthworms."

Maurice turned into the house while I prepared the hole to his specifications. He returned carrying a plastic bowl with the coffee grounds and with Fred on his other arm, moving slowly down the back steps. I hadn't seen Fred for nearly three weeks, since just before my book tour started, and I was shocked by how gaunt and pale he'd become in such a short time. For much of his life, he'd been a long-haul truck driver, a burly, robust man who drove an 18-wheeler for a living, until he retired in his sixties to spend more time at home with Maurice. Now, in his mideighties, he was a frail shadow of that once vital man. I understood immediately why Maurice had seemed so preoccupied lately about Fred's health.

Maurice tried to help him into an Adirondack chair, but Fred fended him off, grabbing a rake instead.

"I'm not dead yet," he grumbled.

Maurice glanced painfully my way but said nothing. Fred began raking weakly at small leaves in the grass. Maurice handed me the bowl and I spaded the coffee grounds into the freshly turned soil. I set the gardenia into the hole, covered up all but the top of the root ball with soil, and wet the roots from a watering can.

Nearby, Maurice kneeled to lift a stepping-stone that needed leveling. He suddenly shrieked, dropping the concrete square as he rose to his feet.

"A spider!" He closed his eyes and waved his upraised hands, as if trying to shake away the sight of it. "I do believe it's one of those horrid black widows. Benjamin, take a look. You know how I am about them."

I kneeled, gripped the edge of the stepping-stone, and raised it at an angle. Nestled in a small crevice of the flattened soil was a black spider with a bulbous body. Inches away were three egg sacs spun in silk, probably close to hatching in the late June heat. I used a hand spade to flip the spider over. Its belly bore a red, violin-shaped mark, identifying it as a common black widow. It wasn't the most dangerous of spiders, but I knew that its venom was considerably more potent than that of most types of rattlesnake. Not something you wanted to experience if you could help it.

Maurice had covered his eyes with both hands but was peeking through his fingers. When the spider started squirming he yelped and backed farther away.

"It's just a damn spider," Fred said. "One of those sacs can produce a hundred spiders or more. If we turned over enough stones, we'd find plenty more."

"Thank you for your support, dear," Maurice said. "Please, Benjamin, do something. Before it comes after us."

I laughed. "They're not aggressive, Maurice. Quite the opposite."

"Just the same, get rid of it, will you? I hate to do harm to an innocent creature, but I can't work out here knowing it's there."

While he averted his eyes, I used the hand spade to crush the black widow against the packed soil. Then I destroyed each of the egg sacs. After digging in the soil to loosen and level it, I set the stepping-stone back in place and put my weight on it to firm it in the earth.

"All gone," I said. "Out of sight, out of mind."

Maurice sighed audibly, and began to relax.

"Spiders are the only part of yard work I don't like." He turned to Fred, clutching his arm. "I've always relied on Fred to handle them." He stretched to peck Fred on the white stubble of his cheek. "My big, strong, reliable man."

Fred grunted good-naturedly but wobbled a bit as he resumed raking, and finally agreed to sit. Maurice went into the house and returned with a cold drink for him. I was washing up with the hose when a visitor appeared from around the corner of the house, stopping at the edge of the patio.

It was Alexandra Templeton. Maurice brightened the moment he saw her.

"Fred, look who's here!"

Maurice embraced her as he might a favorite grandchild.

"We never see you anymore," he gently scolded. "Haven't you time any longer to come visit a fussy old queen?"

"I'm here now," Templeton said amiably, bending to kiss Fred on the forehead. She glanced in my direction, smiling awkwardly.

"Indeed you are, dear, and we couldn't be happier to see you." Maurice nailed me with a sharp look. "Isn't that right, Benjamin?"

"It's been a while," I said.

"I'm sorry," she said. "I—I've been busy with a long-term project."

Templeton was her usual gorgeous self. Her tall, lithe frame was draped in a light, flowing dress of vibrant colors that beautifully complemented her lustrous dark skin. She'd changed her hair since the last time I saw her, several months ago on her thirty-eighth birthday. It was drawn back and braided, with colorful string beads falling among the braids along her slender neck. I sensed another change in her too, but couldn't quite put my finger on it. The explanation came soon enough.

"I'm getting married," she said, beaming. "In September, to Larry Kase." Her eyes found mine again. "You remember Larry, don't you, Benjamin?"

Indeed, I did remember Lawrence Kase. I'd known him for years by reputation—a top county prosecutor who'd once harbored political ambitions and still cut an imposing figure in the courtroom and before the cameras. The first time I'd met him he'd been out with Templeton and I'd been on a date of my own. Templeton and I had run into each other by accident, and she'd introduced us. Kase had been chilly, and I'd sensed right off that he didn't like me. Maybe because of my unsavory past, I'd surmised, or maybe because I was homosexual and unapologetic about it. Or maybe both.

"Lawrence Kase, of course." I worked up my best smile. "Terrific news, Templeton. Congratulations."

I'd seen less and less of her over the past two years, assuming she was on special assignment for the *Los Angeles Times*, where she worked as one of its more prominent reporters. Now that she was getting married, I figured, we'd drift apart even further. I knew what a heterosexual marriage could do to an outside friendship between buddies, especially when one of them was gay. But Templeton's impending marriage, it turned out, was only the half of it.

24

"We're going to start a family," she said. She grinned happily and laid a hand on her stomach. "In fact, I'm already expecting. I found out this morning. I wanted to tell the three of you right away."

Templeton mentioned that she and Kase were to be married on the third Saturday in September, and Maurice promised that all of us would be there. Then he told her that he and Fred had just been married themselves in a civil ceremony, following the state supreme court decision validating gay marriage. Of course, he added, it could all be for nothing if voters passed an anti-gay marriage amendment in the November election. Templeton was ecstatic anyway, and hugged Maurice again.

"We wouldn't miss your wedding for anything," he assured her, and sliced me with another glance. "Would we, Benjamin?"

"As long as the groom wants us there," I said, with a taut smile.

"Of course he wants you there," Templeton said, sounding stung.

Maurice asked her in for refreshments, but she declined, apologizing for being on a tight schedule. Then she grew silent and glanced tellingly in my direction. Maurice picked up the cue, suggesting to Fred that they join the cats inside for naps. I helped Fred up—Maurice could no longer get Fred to his feet from such a deep chair—and Templeton and I watched them shuffle slowly across the patio, Maurice gripping Fred by the arm to keep him from falling.

When they were inside, Templeton wandered out into the yard, commenting on how lovely the garden looked. She glanced up to a flutter of wings near the top of the stairs. Under the eave, a mother dove huddled over her nested eggs as her male partner stood watch nearby, from the stair railing.

"They come every spring," I said, "returning to the same nest. Or maybe it's a new pair of doves, we can't tell. We see two or three hatchings every season, through the summer. This will be the second."

"They must feel safe here." Templeton smiled tentatively. "It's like the Realtors say—location is everything."

"You've got something on your mind," I said.

She took a deep breath, found my eyes. "Benjamin, I've written a book."

I cocked my head in surprise. "You've done what?"

"I've worked on it for the past two years. Last year, I took a leave of absence from the *Times* to finish it."

That explained why I'd missed her byline for a while, although a lot of bylines had been missing lately, as the *Times* steadily downsized on its way to obsolescence, like so many other newspapers.

"So when's it being published?"

"Next month."

The news staggered me. "You never said a word about it."

"I know. I feel bad about that. But it's hush-hush. It's very provocative stuff."

"Hush-hush—even from me? Templeton, we used to share everything."

"My publisher insisted."

"You can't even tell me what it's about?"

"The title is *The Terror Within*. It's nonfiction, investigating the threat of domestic terrorism in the U.S. That's really all I can say."

"Sounds impressive."

She brightened. "My publisher thinks it's going to get a lot of attention. They're planning a big promotional push. All the major newspapers, a bunch of talk shows. *Newsweek* might do a cover. It's all a bit intimidating."

"Wow, next month." I laughed uneasily. "It's coming right on top of my little memoir."

She stepped toward me, touching my arm. "I couldn't control the timing, Benjamin. I wanted to warn you about it, but—"

"It's okay, Templeton. I understand. It's great news; it really is."

"You're sure?"

"You've worked incredibly hard. It's the right time to take the next step. I always said you should be writing books."

"I couldn't have gotten this far without you, Benjamin. You've been a generous mentor all these years." Her eyes fogged up a little. "More than that."

Up above, the male dove flew off, making a squeaky musical

sound with his wings, leaving the female to watch over the eggs. He did this from time to time, disappearing for a day or two, possibly to mate with another bird. When the eggs hatched and the downy babies were sprouting feathers, he'd return for longer periods, to begin teaching the chicks how to fly.

"I should go," Templeton said. "With the book coming out next month, and the wedding in September, it's getting a little crazy."

"And the baby," I said. "Let's not forget the baby."

I walked her to the street, we hugged good-bye, and I watched her zip away in a new Porsche, one of the pricier models. Templeton had been born into money—her father was a top corporate attorney—and she supplemented her salary at the *Times* with a monthly stipend from the old man. He also tossed in a new automobile every other year on her birthday, all of which allowed her to dress and drive like a movie star. With her stunning looks and family wealth, I thought, it was a miracle she'd turned out so well, hardworking and successful in her own right, and an unselfish friend. She raised a slim, brown hand out the window and waved as she turned the corner.

As I stood staring down the empty street, still digesting her news, the mail carrier was arriving behind me. I heard the familiar jingle of keys on the long chain at her side and turned to see her approaching briskly down the walk. She greeted me, handed me the day's mail, and moved on to the next house. As I sorted through the various pieces, I found the usual bills and brochures. Also, one plain postcard, addressed to me.

The handwriting on the front was the same as yesterday's, although the variation of my name had been changed: *Benjamin HIV Justice.*

The unsigned message on the reverse side was brief:

Did I ever tell you that I deliberately infected your lover Jacques with the virus? (I've slept with lots of famous people too, not just poor, pathetic faggots like Jacques.) Gosh, I hope he didn't suffer much. (Nyuk, nyuk, nyuk.) Too bad he died, but you're still alive.

I stared at the postcard in disbelief, feeling clammy and ill. Jacques had been dead for eighteen years, his death precipitating the series of articles I'd written that had led to my downfall as a journalist. A day didn't go by that I didn't think of him. His was one of only two photographs I owned; the other was of my little sister, Elizabeth Jane, taken on her eleventh birthday. Over time, I'd accepted his death from AIDS at an early age, when the disease was killing gay men by the thousands. It had taken me a while to absorb the crushing reality that he was gone, but I'd finally come to terms with it and moved on.

Or so I'd thought. Seeing his name invoked like this, in such a bizarre and hateful context, was a shock to my system. Who could have sent me a message like this? What kind of person would write these words? And why?

Trembling, I scanned the message again:

Did I ever tell you that I deliberately infected your lover Jacques with the virus? (I've slept with lots of famous people too, not just poor, pathetic faggots like Jacques.) Gosh, I hope he didn't suffer much. (Nyuk, nyuk, nyuk.) Too bad he died, but you're still alive.

I slipped quietly in and out of the house, leaving the rest of the mail for Maurice and Fred on their kitchen table. Then I climbed the stairs to my apartment, feeling an indefinable uneasiness settle over me. The mother dove sat perfectly still on her nest, staring implacably at me with her dark, beady eyes, ever watchful.

FIVE

That evening, Judith Zeitler showed up at half past six in her shiny new hybrid to transport me to a downtown café for my first interview with Cathryn Conroy.

I wasn't keen on having a publicist present—something I'd never tolerated as a reporter—but I didn't want to drive that far at rush hour and Zeitler didn't mind. She didn't seem to mind anything that was part of the job, and didn't appear to have much life beyond it, as far as I could tell. So I agreed to include her in the first of two scheduled interviews, as long as she promised to stay out of the way, even if Conroy and I started throwing food at each other across the table.

Zeitler arrived chattering like an excited squirrel, a salon-tanned gamine clutching a sixteen-ounce Starbucks cup in one hand and the latest *Publishers Weekly* in the other. She was wearing a pale blue pants suit and heels, and she'd tinted and permed her hair into a blond Afro. I tried to get a word in, but she chatted nonstop while urging me to get a move on. We were down the stairs and on the road in a minute or two.

We hadn't driven three blocks when we hit the rush-hour glut on Santa Monica Boulevard and turned east into a flow that moved glacially, when it moved at all. I wasn't in a great mood after getting the vicious piece of hate mail that afternoon, and slogging through L.A. traffic didn't lighten me up.

"You seem awfully quiet this evening," Zeitler said.

"Pensive, I guess."

"The Conroy interview?"

"That must be it," I said.

Judith reached over and patted my knee. "You've faced tougher challenges than Cathryn Conroy, Benjamin."

"You must have read my book."

She laughed and swung right, just before we reached West Hollywood's burgeoning Russian neighborhood. She seemed to know all the shortcuts, punching the accelerator down side streets, working her way over to Third, where we turned left, heading east again. We reached downtown L.A. at half past seven, having covered nine miles in an hour. Zeitler was ecstatic.

"We made great time," she said, and got on her cell to tell Conroy we'd only be a few minutes late.

Conroy was waiting for us at a bistro at Fourth and Main, sitting at the bar and ordering another Johnnie Walker on the rocks. After the obligatory introductions, she asked us in a whiskey voice if we wanted a drink. Before we could reply, she said quickly to me, "That's right, you don't drink these days, do you, Justice?"

"Not for some time."

"Didn't like it?"

"Liked it too much," I said, "which I thought I'd made clear in my book."

"I always like to get it straight from the horse's mouth."

She'd been attractive when I'd last seen her nearly twenty years ago, and still was, although she had a face with plenty of mileage on it. Her hair was brown with a reddish tint, medium length, modest curl, and swept back from her face. Despite the alcohol, or maybe because of it, her golden eyes seemed especially keen and alive. She wasn't a big woman, but her posture was erect and the set of her chin was strong. You got the impression that she knew who she was and what she wanted.

"Shall we get a table," Zeitler asked, "before we lose our reservation?"

"They know me here," Conroy said. "We won't lose our reservation."

The restaurant, which Conroy had chosen, was a comfortable place, with lots of dark wood, unvarnished wrought iron, and the original white tile on the floor, complete with old cracks that had probably been underfoot for a century or more. It had what the guidebooks refer to as ambience and character, the kind carefully preserved for people with money who want to pretend that their lives are less orderly and sanitized than they really are. It was on the ground floor of a vintage building recently renovated as part of the ambitious revitalization of the downtown area, which meant luxury loft and penthouse apartments above and trendy cafés, clubs, and galleries at street level, the city's latest Mecca for credit card bohemians.

A block west of the restaurant, Broadway was still ground zero for downtown Latino shopping and culture. It was a vibrant, cacophonous mix of working-class people and garish merchandise, but the wealthy developers were gradually buying up and renovating the old buildings and the Latino businesses were living on borrowed time. Most of the *vendedores* had disappeared in a crackdown to clean up and beautify the area, replaced by elegant restaurants where "*haute* dogs" went for fifteen bucks and steaks for three times that, soup or salad not included. Now that affluent whites were moving in, police patrols had visibly increased, and civic leaders had decided it was finally time to sweep away the hundreds of homeless people who slept on skid-row sidewalks every night. Little by little, the riffraff and the hardworking poor were being pushed farther east or into other low-rent communities, where gentrification hadn't yet taken hold.

"We'll be sitting outside," Conroy announced. "I smoke." She glanced at Zeitler. "Were you leaving soon? Not to be rude, but I don't conduct interviews with publicists hovering about."

"I told Judith she could sit in on this first meeting," I said.

"I don't recall being consulted," Conroy said.

31

"Then I'll take the blame. Anyway, she's my ride home, so she stays."

"I can drive you home, Justice."

"Thanks, but I don't ride with intoxicated drivers."

Conroy showed us a steely smile. "Then you owe me two more interviews instead of one. Agreed?"

Zeitler glanced at me plaintively.

"I can live with that," I said.

Conroy's smile was transformed into one of triumph. She emptied her glass and signaled the hostess. While we followed, Conroy headed through a side door to a string of tables along the sidewalk, protected by a metal railing and potted foliage. Dusk had settled over Main Street, which was relatively quiet, but we could still hear the traffic surging like a huge beast to the west, where the corporate towers rose up nearer the freeway. It occurred to me that the big *Los Angeles Times* building was only a few blocks away, to the north, and I suddenly realized why Conroy had chosen to meet here. We were dining in the shadow of the most influential newspaper on the West Coast, where I'd begun to make my mark as a reporter before crashing so spectacularly only seven years later, at the age of thirty-two.

"I imagine this neighborhood has a familiar feeling," Conroy said, as if it had just occurred to her. "These were your stomping grounds for a few years, weren't they?"

"And very nearly yours," I said, "if memory serves."

Our eyes met across the table.

"Memory can be a tricky devil, can't it?" She paused, then hit me with the zinger. "I imagine you discovered that while writing your book."

"Are we skipping the softball questions," I asked, "and going straight for the jugular?"

"Why don't we order first?" Zeitler said helpfully.

"I recommend the rib eye, with a good cabernet," Conroy said. "At least for those with some hair on their chest."

Zeitler, who was always on a diet, selected an appetizer of crab cakes on a bed of spring greens, with a bottle of Pellegrino water. I ordered the pan-seared salmon.

"A glass of pinot noir would go nicely with that," Conroy said.

I ignored it and told the waitress to bring a large bottle of the fancy water and that Zeitler and I would share it. Conroy chose the steak, cooked blood rare, and a half bottle of cabernet to wash it down. When the waitress was gone, Conroy lit a cigarette and took a hit before she placed a pint-sized audio recorder on the table with the external microphone pointed in my direction.

"You don't mind, do you?"

"Not at all," I said.

She dropped her first question like a bomb.

"Now that your book's written and published, do you feel less burdened by the guilt of what you did? Or is that something that never goes away?"

"I assume you're referring to the Pulitzer business."

"We can start there."

"With diligent reporters like you around, Cathryn, I doubt that I'll ever be allowed a complete reprieve."

"You aren't suggesting that we abdicate our responsibility to get at the truth, are you?"

"Why don't you define truth for me, from the perspective of someone who specializes in hatchet jobs?"

"Oh, look," Zeitler said brightly. "Here come the drinks!"

And so it went. Conroy and I sparred with each other, just short of drawing blood, while Zeitler darted in now and then like a referee, determined to ward off any low blows. Finally, her steak half-eaten but her wine gone, Conroy pushed back her chair and abruptly stood.

"Enough of this," she said, grabbing her cigarettes, recorder, and purse. "Next time, no publicist. Understood?"

I smiled benignly. "Whatever you say, Cathryn."

She dabbed at her mouth with a cloth napkin, imprinting it with red lipstick before tossing it rudely to the table. "I'll leave you to handle the check."

"Of course," Zeitler said. "Our treat!"

When she was gone, Zeitler said perkily, "It's always good to get the first one out of the way, don't you think?"

"This was your idea, Judith. I won't take the blame on this one."

"My crab cakes were quite good. How was your fish?"

I gave her a look and raised my hand for the check.

Out on the sidewalk, a well-groomed, white-haired gentleman in expensive clothes was walking a small dog. He eyed a good-looking Hispanic boy standing nearby under a street lamp. The kid was slim and brown, with a soft, dark mustache that had probably never seen a razor. The older man stopped to chat and then they walked down the block, turning into an elegant building with a uniformed security guard out front. Along the gutter, a disheveled-looking woman whose age was masked by grime pushed a shopping cart in our direction, the wheels clattering along the asphalt. The cart was piled high and teetering with all kinds of trashy castoffs. She stared straight ahead as she passed, mumbling to herself, not ten feet from where we sat.

Zeitler eyed Conroy's abandoned plate. "Would you mind if I asked for a doggy bag? My Pomeranian loves rib eye."

"By all means," I said. "No one likes to see good steak go to waste."

SIX

Friday came and went without a new hate message in the mailbox, but the harassment resumed on Saturday. This time, the postcard was addressed to *Benjamin Poz Justice*.

I turned it over and scanned the words:

AIDS was made for the likes, or hates, of you. I realize your dead lover boy, Jacques, probably didn't deserve it like you do. But we all have to die sometime, don't we? (Some hopefully sooner than others!) Anyway, he's better off without you. See you in hell, faggot.

The first time I'd read the hate mail mentioning Jacques, I'd felt tremulous and sick, like someone in the grip of a bad chill. Now I trembled with rage. The problem was that my anger had nowhere to go. I didn't know the name of the sender, or why he was doing this—if indeed it was a man—or where I might find him. Which was probably a good thing, given what I might have done if I'd found him at that moment.

"Benjamin, what is it? What's the matter?"

Maurice had come from the house, apparently concerned over the look on my face. I didn't answer right away, just kept staring at the ugly words, trying to make sense of the whole thing. I wasn't sure I wanted to involve Maurice in it; he had enough to worry about with Fred. But Maurice moved closer, raising his voice sharply.

"Benjamin, I asked you a question."

I looked up to see him standing with his hands on his hips, colorful bracelets decorating each of his narrow wrists, his eyes hawkish under their white crowns. I knew there was no putting him off.

"I've been targeted with some strange mail." I described the contents of the other messages and handed him the new one. "I don't know who's behind it. This is the third one."

As he scanned the scurrilous lines, his mouth fell open. When he'd finished, quiet outrage crept across his face and tears brimmed in his eyes.

"Who could be doing this? To say these kinds of things about Jacques, a young man who never harmed so much as a fly. And to address you in such a hurtful manner. I'm so sorry, Benjamin."

"It beats getting kicked in the teeth."

"Are you sure about that?"

I laughed a little. "No."

He studied the message again.

"Do you really think this person—?"

"Deliberately infected Jacques? Jacques died eighteen years ago, so he would have been infected years before that. Given the time frame, and the fact that this fellow's still alive, makes it highly improbable. Still, it's theoretically possible. There are people who have lived well over twenty years with the disease."

"Or he could just be a very twisted individual," Maurice suggested, "writing these things to needle you. But why?"

I shrugged, clueless. Maurice turned the postcard over to study the printing on the front, looking thoughtful.

"Benjamin, I believe I might have seen this handwriting before."

"Seriously?"

He looked up, nodding. "Among your old documents and

papers, the ones I helped organize when you were writing your book. There was a letter—I believe it was written eighteen years ago, or very nearly, not long after your problem at the newspaper."

"Why would you remember something like that?"

"The letter itself was typewritten, but the signature at the end was big and grandiose, just like this handwriting. I particularly recall the letter *J* in the name—it was drawn just like the *J* in your name on this postcard, with the same flourish. I only glanced at it—I don't recall the contents. But the signature was quite outlandish, the mark of someone very taken with himself."

"Frankly, when I was writing the book, I didn't pay much attention to the personal correspondence. There was so much other material to go through."

"Unless you've thrown things out, it should still be there."

"I put it all back in the garage, in the same file boxes."

Maurice placed a hand on my shoulder. "Do you want to know who's been writing these notes to you? Would that be useful?"

"I wouldn't mind."

"And if you found out, what then?"

"Confront him, I suppose." I smiled mildly. "Suggest that he stop."

"You could file a complaint with the authorities. It's clearly harassment, which is against the law. And I wouldn't be surprised if sending hate speech like this through the U.S. mail is a federal offense." He handed the postcard back to me. "As soon as I can find the time, I'll begin digging for it."

"If it's not too much trouble."

He waved that away as if it were a pesky insect, causing his big bracelets to jangle.

"In the meantime," he said, "I want you to forget all about these nasty notes you've been receiving. You have a reading at A Different Light tonight and a party afterward back here at the house. The world's full of unhappy people who have nothing better to do than make others as miserable as they are. You mustn't let them get to you, dearest."

At a quarter past seven, while Fred stayed behind to welcome early arrivals for the party, Maurice and I strolled down the hill to A Different Light. Out front, volunteers were registering sympathetic voters for the November election, when the anti-gay marriage amendment would be a crucial issue for the community.

The bookstore was modest in size, set among the ubiquitous clubs and cafés along Santa Monica Boulevard, where untold millions were spent on alcohol and gayety but relatively few dollars for books that explored gay history, politics, and culture. A Different Light still sold books, but more and more of its display space seemed devoted to CDs, sexy magazines, and rainbow tchotchkes and less and less to gay literature, as the store struggled to survive the onslaught of the discount chains and online booksellers.

Not surprisingly, Maurice knew the manager personally, and he'd urged her to give my memoir a featured spot in one of the store's two windows. My book—*Deep Background: The True Story of a Disgraced Journalist and the Pulitzer Scandal That Destroyed Him*—was prominently positioned among titles by authors far more notable and deserving than I: Edmund White, Michael Cunningham, Alison Bechdel, Armistead Maupin, Michelle Tea, Eloise Klein Healy, Bernard Cooper, Manuel Muñoz, Katherine V. Forrest, Mark Doty, Radclyffe, Adrienne Rich, Clive Barker, Christopher Bram. It pleased me to see my book among those of such luminaries, although I felt a bit like a beggar who'd sneaked into a fancy dinner party.

"Benjamin, look at the crowd!"

As Maurice and I stepped inside, I was stunned to see a packed house. Billy Avarathar, the events coordinator with the soulful dark eyes and V-shaped torso, had pushed aside racks and display tables and was setting up more chairs to accommodate the overflow.

"This is your doing," I told Maurice gratefully. "You must

have invited everybody in your phone book. Warned them they'd better show up or else."

"Nonsense, Benjamin! They've come because they want to hear your story. With this book, you have a chance to explain things, and to put the problems of the past behind you."

I slipped my arm around his narrow shoulders and drew him close. "It's been a long road to this point, Maurice. Without your support, I'm not sure I'd still be around."

"But you are, Benjamin! And you have so much to look forward to." He pushed me gently toward the podium. "Now get up there and share your fine book with us. That's what we've all come to hear."

As I made my way forward, I ran into Judith Zeitler, who was complaining to the manager that she hadn't ordered enough books, although there appeared to be several tall stacks of them on a side table, ready to be signed. Alexandra Templeton was also there, near the front, next to Lawrence Kase. He was a tall, broad-shouldered, barrel-chested man who wore his thick gray hair in a wavy mane and his salt-and-pepper beard carefully trimmed. For all his famous bravado as a prosecutor, he looked uncomfortable in this little bookstore filled with queers, sitting stiffly on his metal folding chair like someone dragged along against his will, who hoped he wouldn't have to buy a book. Sitting on Templeton's other side was Cathryn Conroy, her notebook already open and her lethal pen poised for duty.

Most of the crowd was older, fifty and up, and well represented with activists, all friends of Maurice, who'd been out of the closet and working hard for gay rights for decades. Then my eyes fell on a handsome man sitting in the back row, whom I hadn't seen for several years but whose face was imprinted indelibly in my memory. Ismael Aragon had been a compassionate Catholic priest when I'd become involved in a disturbing investigation of child molestation and murder that had led me to the Los Angeles archdiocese, for which Ismael oversaw a small church on the Eastside. He'd be close to forty now, but the intervening years had done nothing to diminish his tawny Aztec beauty; if anything, there was a new radiance about him that I hadn't seen five years ago. I could have easily fallen in love with Ismael back then—or Father Aragon, as he'd been known—but he'd made it clear that his vow of celibacy and devotion to church and God were absolute. He was without his cleric's collar tonight, dressed more casually in a loose-fitting cotton shirt and khaki slacks. Seeing him again after so long triggered a rush of unexpected emotions.

The store manager, a sturdily built woman with close-cropped hair and handsome, square-jawed looks, took the podium and welcomed the audience in a husky voice.

"There's more testosterone in this crowd than your average professional football team," she joked, looking around at all the activists. "And that's just the women."

As the laughter faded, she introduced me and I stepped to the podium with a copy of *Deep Background* in hand. Before I'd written my memoir, I'd read a dozen that Jan Long had recommended. Some had been composed in a terse, detached style, perhaps to suggest distance and objectivity. Others had been less a memoir than a long string of entertaining anecdotes, organized with clever chapter headings but without much depth or meaningful reflection. But the ones I'd admired most had been novelistic in approach, which had seemed to give the authors more freedom to call up memory and detail in a deeply felt and sensory way. For better or worse, that was the style I'd chosen for my book.

For my reading that night, I'd selected a long passage from my lengthy epilogue, which I'd added at Jan Long's suggestion. She felt the bleakness of the main narrative—the scandal that had engulfed me and the events leading up to it—needed some light at the end of a dark tunnel, a note of hope and possible redemption at the end. As an editor, she might also have wanted to leave the reader with the hint of a possible sequel, should my first book sell enough to warrant another. My epilogue began roughly twelve years ago, as my old editor, Harry Brofsky, came back into my life six years after I'd been forced to give back my Pulitzer, a visit that would draw me out of self-imposed seclusion and dramatically change my life.

I cleared my throat, sipped from a bottle of water, and began reading.

"'Billy Lusk was murdered on a Tuesday, shortly after midnight, and Harry Brofsky came looking for me that afternoon.

"'It was mid-July. Hot winds that felt like the devil's breath blew into Los Angeles from the desert, rattling through the shaggy eucalyptus trees like a dry cough.

"'The city was golden, blinding, blasted by heavenly light. It was one of those days that made nipples rise and minds wander and bodies shiver with sensuality and inexplicable dread. The kind of day when the heat wrapped snugly around you but sent an ominous chill up your back at the same time, like the first sexual touch in a dark room from a beautiful stranger whose name you'd never know.

"'Harry found me in West Hollywood, bobbing my head to an old Coltrane tape and trying not to think about alcohol.

"'"Look who's caught up with me," I said to the empty room, when I saw Harry's car pull up. "My, my, my."

"'I was staying in a small garage apartment in a leafy neighborhood known for its irregular shape as the Norma Triangle, where quaint little houses crowded cozy lots and lush greenery crawled unrestricted over the rotting corpses of old wood fences. My single room was up a wooden stairway at the deep end of an unpaved driveway, which ran alongside a neatly kept California Craftsman, one of those finely beveled, wood-framed bungalows that sprouted up by the thousands during the building boom of the 1930s and 1940s. Through the kindness of the owners, Maurice and Fred, I was able to live in the apartment rent-free, in exchange for performing odd chores. It wasn't the most dignified arrangement for a former reporter, but how and where I lived didn't matter much anymore. Nothing really did now, except somehow getting through another day, until all the days were mercifully used up.

"'Through the unwashed window of my room, I looked down on the rear yard, where a loose-limbed jacaranda swayed like a lonely dancer in the restless breeze. Three plump cats lounged in the tree's shade, their tails barely twitching in the oppressive heat, watching a hummingbird dart among syrupy pistils of honeysuckle while I watched them.

" 'In the three months since Maurice and Fred had installed me in the apartment, I'd spent most of my time at this window, where I could see down the narrow driveway to the street without anyone clearly seeing me. When Harry finally showed up, unannounced, I felt as though I'd spent most of those hours waiting for him.

" 'I watched him wrestle his Ford Escort into a space at the curb and struggle wearily out. He mopped his round face with a handkerchief, found a cigarette, and adjusted his bifocals to check a scrap of paper for the Norma Place address. When he'd confirmed the numbers, he glanced up at the apartment, just long enough for me to see what the years had done to him, and to feel the gnaw of guilt.

" 'I briefly wondered how he'd found me after all this time. Then I remembered that Harry had once been a reporter too, and a good reporter knows how to find people who don't want to be found.

" ' "Oh, Harry." I listened to Coltrane blow the final jumpy notes of "My Favorite Things," the fourteen-minute version, then heard the machine click off. "I do wish you'd left well enough alone."

" 'As he crossed Norma, came up the drive, then mounted the stairs, I listened to his hacking smoker's cough. He'd always had trouble with warm weather, and by the time he reached the top, oily sweat pebbled his forehead, and his pale face was blotchy. It was the first time I'd seen or spoken to Harry Brofsky in six years.

" ' "You can't afford a phone?" He squinted at me through the screen. "Things are that bad?"

" 'For a moment, I considered asking him to leave. Jacques had lived in this apartment when I'd first met him ten years ago. He'd stayed through the years until the virus got him and he became too sick to take care of himself, moving into my apartment the last months of his life, in his twenty-ninth year. After he'd died, Maurice and Fred had never rented the place again. They'd loved Jacques like a son, and I think they missed him nearly as much as I did. I could feel his presence in the room, fragile and fading with time, like my memories of him, and I didn't want intruders.

" ' "Hello, Harry."

" ' "I have to stand out here like a salesman?"

" 'I felt the guilt again, flushing through me like a sickness coming on. I opened the screen door and stepped aside to let him pass. He took a final, nervous drag on his cigarette, crushed it underfoot on the landing, and shuffled in. His sad gray eyes, bright and mischievous not all that many years ago, surveyed the small room. There wasn't much to look at, except for a framed photo of Jacques on a shelf, next to one of my sister, Elizabeth Jane, snapped at her eleventh birthday party, smiling for the camera with a sadness I'd been too blind to see.

" ' "Lovely," Harry said, looking around. "Early Salvation Army, if I'm not mistaken."

" ' "What's on your mind, Harry?"

" ' "Where the hell have you been?"

" ' "Around."

" ' "Doing what?"

" ' "Living in the backseat of the Mustang. Trying not to drink myself to death."

" 'Harry had never had much time for self-pity. "I guess you fucked that up too."

" ' "I guess I did."

" 'I could have told him more: That Maurice and Fred had rescued me from the backseat of my old Mustang convertible, just as they'd once rescued Jacques as a troubled teenager from the streets. That they'd moved me into the apartment and shamed me into pulling myself halfway together, telling me that I owed Jacques at least that much after he'd fought so hard for so long to hang on, before slipping away from us.

" 'But that was intimate stuff, and Harry and I had never been too comfortable with intimate stuff.

" ' "Cut to the chase, Harry."

" 'He perched himself on the only chair in the room and asked for a glass of water. Then he told me he had a young reporter he was bringing along who needed mentoring he didn't have time to handle himself. She was exceptionally bright, he said, extremely ambitious, and had the chance to go all the way, like I'd once had before I'd committed my infamous act of fraud, taking Harry down part of the way with me. She was investigating the murder of a young man named Billy Lusk outside a gay bar in Silver Lake, Harry said, but she was in over her head. He wanted me to come around to the *Los Angeles Sun*, the second-rate newspaper where he was forced to toil now, and take Alexandra Templeton under my wing.

" ' "Not a chance, Harry." The idea of leaving the safety of my little apartment, venturing back into the world, being around people again, filled me with dread. "I'm sorry, Harry. I can't."

" 'I saw muscles tighten along the jawbone of his soft face, and his eyes turn to cold stones. "You're going to do this for me," he said. "For one simple reason."

" 'Then he spoke the words that for nearly six years I'd hoped I'd never hear from Harry Brofsky.

" ' "You owe me." ' "

I stopped reading, and closed the book.

A moment later, applause erupted that ranged from polite to enthusiastic. I saw Templeton clapping harder than anyone, tears streaking her lovely brown face. After the applause had ended and I'd sipped more water, I mentioned the contentious and combative relationship Templeton and I had shared at the beginning, and how we'd overcome our differences and grown close over the years. I introduced her and insisted she stand, which she did briefly, laughing with embarrassment and brushing away her tears. Next to her, Lawrence Kase smiled like a puppet with tight strings.

The questions that followed from the audience were generally genial and inoffensive. One woman asked if I thought I would ever work as a journalist again, and I told her no, and that I didn't feel I deserved to. A man asked how I was coping with the loss of my left eye, and I said I'd become so accustomed to the prosthetic I was rarely aware of it. Another man asked what had been the most difficult part about writing the book, and I said it had been deciding what to put in and what to leave out, along with the general worry that the writing was awful and no one would want to read it.

The exception to these respectful questions came from a slender, effete fellow standing at the back. His hair was died an unconvincing blond and his narrow face had been so cosmetically carved up that gauging his age was difficult.

"Do you feel any shame," he asked, in a pointedly superior voice, "making money off such an egregious act of deception?"

"After my agent takes her fifteen percent and the government gets its cut," I said, "I'll barely make enough to cover the two years I spent organizing and writing the book."

I turned to point at another raised hand, but the man jumped in again.

"Did you write the book yourself, or is that just another of your lies?"

I offered him a diplomatic smile. "I wrote it myself."

He started to blurt another question, but the manager stepped quickly to the podium, announcing that it was getting late, and that I had a lot of books to sign. She thanked everyone for coming, escorted me to the table where the books were stacked, and handed me a Sharpie with black ink and a fine point. She'd already flapped each book—marked the title page with the front edge of the dust jacket—a thoughtful gesture that allowed the signing to move more quickly.

Everyone I knew personally purchased a book—Templeton took five—and quite a few strangers bought copies as well. I dutifully signed each one, adding "creative inscriptions" when they were requested. It was nearing nine o'clock when the end of the line finally drew near.

The unpleasant man with the unfortunate blond hair and obvious cosmetic surgery stepped forward. His pasty face had a taut and unnaturally smooth quality that gave him the appearance of a burn victim, apparently from multiple nips, tucks, and peels. His eyes were a washed-out yellow, set close together in his narrow face. Up close, the blondness of his fine hair looked like it might have been accomplished at home, with a bottle of cheap peroxide. Yet he carried himself as if oblivious to his ghastly appearance, with a manner that conveyed more conceit than insecurity. He thrust forward a copy of my book with a small, pale hand.

"I bought it earlier this month online," he said tartly. "It was cheaper that way. But they let me bring it in, anyway, to have you sign it."

"Would you like it personalized, or just my signature?"

"Personalized, of course. Just put 'To my dear friend, Jason, All my love, Benjamin.'"

"That's awfully personal, since we don't know each other."

His prissy smile turned smug. "Oh, but we do."

I studied his face more closely. "I'm sorry. You've got me at a disadvantage."

"Jason Holt—the actor?"

"We've met before?"

"A long time ago, before I changed my name. I was Barclay Simpkins then."

"I'm sorry, I'm drawing a blank."

His yellow eyes flared. "Or maybe you just don't want to remember."

I didn't know what kind of game he was playing, but I'd had enough, and jotted a routine inscription:

To Jason Holt, All My Best, Benjamin Justice

When I handed it back, he was clearly displeased with what I'd written. But the chill in his manner quickly gave way to a self-satisfied smile.

"Now that we've been reunited," he said, "perhaps we'll be seeing more of each other."

He turned on his heel and waltzed blithely out, his pointy,

reconstructed chin held high, as if he were quite above everything and everyone around him.

Ismael Aragon had waited patiently at the end of the line, and now it was his turn to face me. As he handed me his book, I found myself riveted to his expressive brown eyes, which regarded me with a frankness that surprised me. As a seriously lapsed Catholic, I'd long ago dismissed my feelings for him as confusing and impractical, given his vow of celibacy and allegiance to a church I'd grown to loathe for its hypocrisy and abuse of power.

"Benjamin."

"Father Aragon."

"Just Ismael now." He briefly dropped his eyes. "I've renounced my vows and left the Church."

The news came as a shock, but I can't say I was unhappy to hear it.

"That's quite a decision."

"Yes." He smiled bravely. "I suppose we're both making new starts in life, aren't we?"

Nearby, the manager glanced my way and tapped her watch.

"Listen," I said to Ismael. "We're having a little gathering back at the house. It's only a short walk. Why don't you come?"

"I'd like that."

He handed me his book, and I inscribed it:

To Ismael, Who Gave Me Comfort and Understanding When I Needed It Most, Benjamin Justice.

Beneath my name, I jotted the date.

He thanked me and turned away to stand near Maurice and a group of others who were waiting to walk with me back to the house. Maurice had seen me and Ismael talking and engaged him immediately in conversation, introducing him around. As that happened, my eyes were drawn away to the front window where my book was on display. In the background, the Boys Town crowd, mostly young men, streamed past on their way from club to club, as carefree as kids at Disneyland. But in the foreground, close to the glass, was another young man who seemed altogether out of place.

It was the tattooed skinhead with the blond soul patch with whom I'd brawled earlier in the week, his forehead and nose still scabby from our confrontation. He stared at me, unblinking. I wondered how he'd gotten out of jail so quickly, and how long he'd been standing at that window tonight, watching me.

"Mr. Justice?"

It was the manager, holding open a copy of my book to the title page so I could begin signing the remaining stock. I flattened the book on the table, scrawled my name with the Sharpie, closed the book, and set it to one side. As she handed me the next copy, I stole another glance out the window, but the tattooed young man was gone.

SEVEN

There's nothing quite like the experience of being single and lonely when someone you've never forgotten unexpectedly comes back into your life.

It can suggest the possibility of a relationship that might be healthy and lasting. It can trigger boundless optimism and hope. It can be heady, thrilling, and disorienting in the most wonderful way. But it can also be dangerous, a romantic fantasy built on need and desperation that can lead you blindly into places where you shouldn't go.

As I walked back to the house with Ismael Aragon, just brushing accidentally against his shoulder sent a shiver of pleasure and expectation running through me. Suddenly, the night ahead didn't seem quite so trying and the days beyond so empty, as if one man, the right man, could transform everything in an instant. Maurice apparently noticed the change in me; he'd discreetly raised his eyebrows for my benefit, as if to tell me he was pleased for me, or perhaps that he'd taken quick stock of Ismael and approved. Or maybe, in his wisdom, he was warning me to take it slowly and be careful.

We passed one of the more popular clubs, where the music pounded and the shirtless bartenders poured drinks as fast as they could take the orders. I could see the go-go boys dancing up onstage, fondling themselves in front to stay mildly aroused and pulling down their bikinis in back to show off their perfect butts, while leering men stretched up to stuff dollar bills into the waistbands along their washboard stomachs and cop a feel of pubic hair. Ismael glanced over for only a second before looking away in seeming embarrassment. In any other gay man, I might have found such prudishness silly. In Ismael, it seemed endearing.

I wanted to know everything about him, past and present. I hung on his every word, and couldn't take my eyes off him. I learned that he'd gone back to school, earning a graduate degree in social work, that he was living at an old hotel in East Los Angeles, and that he'd joined a gym for the first time in his life, which explained his trim, firm physique. We turned the corner at Hilldale, heading up to Norma Place, where we turned again. As we approached the house halfway down the block, I remembered that he'd been here once before, years ago. He'd come up to my apartment, where I'd punched him in the mouth and knocked him down because I'd wrongly suspected his involvement in a cover-up of child molestation and murder by high officials within his archdiocese.

"I'm surprised you'd want to be friends with me," I said, "after the way I treated you five years ago."

"You were in a lot of turmoil, Benjamin, a lot of pain."

"Still, I behaved abominably."

He rubbed his jaw, grinning. "You did pack quite a punch." More seriously, he added, "It was the first time I'd ever been struck by anyone, ever. It was quite a shock."

"If I didn't apologize then, I am now."

"Apology accepted."

Maurice reappeared, beckoning from the front door.

"Benjamin, everyone's waiting for the guest of honor. I believe Alexandra wants to make a toast."

"Coming, Mother," I said, as Ismael and I turned up the walk.

I've never been particularly fond of organized parties. They always struck me as overly orchestrated gatherings for people who didn't know how to enjoy one another's company and have fun otherwise, without the arranged atmosphere and requisite alcohol. But I must admit I thoroughly enjoyed myself that night and the party seemed to be a rousing success. Even Fred was up and about for much of the night, seeing to drinks and food. Maurice kept the music playing, mostly disco classics and old gay anthems. Half the crowd was dancing at the first beat of a Gloria Gaynor tune, with Maurice leading the way.

He urged me to circulate and I reluctantly let Ismael drift away. I made a beeline for Templeton, to thank her for taking time from her pressing schedule to join us, and for her touching toast that got the evening going. She was sipping a glass of white wine and chatting animatedly with Cathryn Conroy, who was imbibing her trademark whiskey. Listening to them, I quickly realized they'd been acquainted long before tonight. It made sense—two tough-minded female reporters, both operating out of L.A., no doubt crossing paths from time to time. Templeton was effusive and Conroy polite, but Lawrence Kase didn't even pretend to be happy to see me. I was beginning to think his animosity had to do with more than just my checkered past or sexual orientation— that jealousy might also be behind it, since I'd known Templeton much longer than he had and shared an easy familiarity with her, an intimacy between close friends that some couples never manage to achieve, no matter how long they stay together.

The four of us hadn't been chatting five minutes when Kase glanced at his watch and said to Templeton, "We really should go."

I laughed. "The party's just started."

"We arrived at the bookstore two hours ago. Alex insisted we be there early." He extended a hand and shook mine perfunctorily. "Congratulations on the book, Justice. It's nice to see you turning things around." Then he was facing Templeton and saying firmly, "We really do need to get going."

As I saw them out, I bumped into Bruce Steele, a spectacular physical specimen as dark skinned as Templeton who'd brought along his bearish white boyfriend. Steele was a former collegiate and AAU wrestling champion in the upper middleweight classes whom I'd pursued romantically off and on for years, without success. These days, he worked as a successful investment broker but stayed in shape running the West Hollywood Wrestling Club. He'd pestered me for years to drop by one of the club's Saturday workouts and conduct a clinic. He pressed me again that night and I finally agreed, feeling obligated since he'd shown up for my reading and even purchased a book.

Maurice grabbed me and dragged me off to meet friends of his and kept me moving after that, while I tried with great frustration to connect again with Ismael. Fred retired early, to a bedroom down the hall where the cats were hiding. While I circulated, Judith Zeitler chatted up anyone she could find who was connected to writing or the media, handing out business cards. Conroy drank enough whiskey for several people and grabbed smokes in the backyard, flicking the butts rudely onto the lawn. The music played, the drinks flowed, the aroma of marijuana permeated the air, and everyone seemed to have a fine time. Then it was after midnight and people were drifting out. The party was finally over.

Ismael hung by the front door until I spotted him, and I walked him to the street. I told him how great it was to see him again, and that we had to stay in touch. We exchanged phone numbers, and promised to get together for coffee. I wanted desperately to kiss him good night but didn't; I had no idea what his romantic experience had been after he'd given up celibacy, or even if he'd been with another man, or a woman. But when we hugged, I sensed no awkwardness on his part. Quite the opposite; it felt as warm and natural as embracing an old friend.

As Maurice and I cleaned up the house, listening to a Haydn symphony, he told me how much he liked Ismael, that he had a good feeling about him. We talked about what a fine evening everyone had had and how the reading had gone so well. Candles flickered in the living room, where the cats had curled up on the sofa. A sense of calm and contentment settled over the old house, which had been my sanctuary for so many years, and the same for Jacques in the years before he died.

Maurice paused as he washed glasses in the soapy water.

"Try to enjoy this special moment in your life, Benjamin. You have a tendency to see the glass as half-empty. But you have so much ahead of you, dear one. Try to embrace it, won't you?"

I was about to tell him I was feeling better about things, more optimistic about the future, when the phone rang. It was nearly one, and I couldn't imagine who might be calling at this hour, unless it was someone who'd left their keys or cell phone behind. Then it occurred to me that Ismael might be calling to say something more, to put a final cap on the evening, and my heart gladdened at the possibility. In the living room, I turned the music down, picked up the receiver, and pressed it to my ear.

"I've killed before, just like you." The voice sounded vaguely male, but it was barely more than a whisper, so I couldn't be sure. "So, you see, we have more in common than you might realize. You've always loved a good mystery, haven't you? Sniffing about like a bloodhound, sticking your nose where it doesn't belong."

"I've unraveled a few. So what?"

The caller laughed smugly. "Perhaps, if you're curious enough, you'll unravel mine."

"Why would I want to do that?"

The voice turned petulant but also sounded hurt. "We could be such good friends, if you weren't such a cold, heartless prick."

I was about to ask for a name when the caller hung up. I hit the star key on the phone, then a 6 and a 9 to reconnect, but the number was blocked.

"Who was it?" Maurice called out from the kitchen as I hung up.

"Wrong number."

I've killed before, just like you. So, you see, we have more in common than you might realize.

Someone who knew at least a little about me knew enough to call me at this number at this moment. I stood staring out the front window, across the broad porch and small yard to the tree-lined street, studying it for some sign of suspicious movement or prying eyes. All I could see was a mosaic of meaningless shapes and shadows, shifting almost imperceptibly as the air moved slightly

53

or nocturnal rodents crept about. The neighborhood, alive with the laughter of departing guests such a short time ago, had grown as still and quiet as a funeral parlor after hours.

I drew the curtains, turned the music up, and retreated to the kitchen to help Maurice finish the dishes.

"Be sure to lock your doors tonight," I said.

"I always lock up, Benjamin. You know that."

"I know." I kissed him on the cheek. "Just be sure, that's all."

EIGHT

Several days passed without incident—no violent confrontations, no hate mail, no mysterious phone calls—and the unpleasantness of the previous week began to recede in my mind. With the publicity push for my book winding down and Judith Zeitler on to her next author, my life felt like it was returning to its usual aimlessness.

That's one reason, I suppose, why Ismael Aragon carried so much weight in my thoughts. There wasn't much going on in my life, nothing to give it focus or purpose. Ismael's job as a social worker had taken him to Mexico, where he was trying to reunite immigrant families torn apart by deportation, the foreign-born parents forcibly separated from their American-born children by the laws, politicians, and courts. While he was away, I couldn't stop thinking about him, couldn't stop hearing his voice and seeing his face, and remembering how it had felt to hold him close in that brief moment when we'd hugged good night. Before leaving, he'd told me he'd be gone for at least a week, possibly longer. The days stretched ahead like a gaping chasm, so unnervingly that I applied for a new passport so I might accompany him if his work were to take him out of the country again. It was a silly notion— we barely knew each other, after all—but that's how desperately I needed someone like Ismael in my life.

As I waited to see him again, I kept myself as busy as possible, helping Maurice tend to the yard and house and get Fred to his medical appointments, which were becoming more frequent.

Then there was the nest under the eave to keep watch over. Two dove chicks appeared, their eyes still closed, their bodies scrawny, their downy feathers matted with mucus from their gestation period inside their shells. By stretching up on our tiptoes at the top of the stairs, Maurice and I could look over the edge of the nest and see them beginning to stir and discover the world. During the day, the mother disappeared from time to time, returning to drop food into their gaping mouths. At dusk, she settled over them, patient and alert, to protect them and keep them warm through the night. The nest was up high enough, and far enough away from the railing, to keep it safe from marauding rats and cats. It was like Templeton had pointed out: Location is everything.

At midweek, I spotted the skinhead again. He was astride a big motorcycle, an older Harley-Davidson, as I walked home from the supermarket with a bag of groceries in each hand. He was there only long enough for me to see him before he hit the throttle and rumbled off, quickly disappearing into the narrow residential streets of the Norma Triangle. It bothered me enough that after delivering the groceries to Maurice I sauntered back down the hill to the sheriff's substation to have a chat with Detective Haukness. I asked for him at the front desk and got lucky; he'd just returned from the field. He kept me waiting a few minutes but finally appeared from a back room, the ends of his big mustache twitching as he strode to the counter in his snakeskin boots.

"What can I do for you, Mr. Justice?"

He was as laconic as ever, his taciturn manner seemingly at odds with his good-old-boy attire and Texas drawl. I mentioned that I'd seen the skinhead outside the bookstore the previous Saturday night and again this morning in my neighborhood, and wondered how he'd gotten sprung so fast from county jail. Haukness provided some basic information, cut-and-dried: Given the witness statements and the suspect's clean record, the district attorney handling the case didn't feel that grand theft auto and misdemeanor battery charges were warranted. Those charges were dropped, and the suspect pled guilty to misdemeanor trespass. He'd been sentenced to three months but was out of jail in two days.

"Catch and release," I said.

It was the term the press had given to the Sheriff's Department policy of quickly discharging criminals convicted of minor or non-violent offenses because there wasn't enough space in county jail to hold them all. The county jail system was teeming with more than eighteen thousand prisoners on any given day, reportedly the largest jail population in the world. For convicted lawbreakers who weren't considered predatory or dangerous, it was a turnstile operation—in and out in days or even hours—except for the unlucky ones still awaiting trial, who couldn't cut a deal or afford bail and might languish behind bars for months, if they were lucky enough to survive. There'd even been violent convicts released well before their mandated terms were up; one of Templeton's investigations had revealed that some had killed new victims on days when they should have still been locked up.

"As I said," Haukness repeated, his delivery as flat as a Texas plain, "he served two days before release."

"And now he's back in West Hollywood, stalking me."

"It's a small city, Mr. Justice. Two sightings of the guy could be coincidence."

"I also got a strange phone call the other night."

I told him what the caller had said. Haukness seemed unimpressed.

"You're certain it was the suspect calling? You recognized his voice?"

"I can't say that, no."

"He hasn't approached you, or come onto your property?" I shook my head. "Mr. Justice, you're certainly free to file a complaint if you wish. But what you've told me so far doesn't remotely rise to the standard of a crime."

"Can't you tell me something else about this guy? Since I was the victim."

His eyes narrowed. "Were you?"

"I'm the victim of record, Detective. That should count for something."

"There's something you need to know, Mr. Justice. Two days ago, I received a CD in the mail. Someone with a high-tech cell phone videotaped the incident in which you alleged assault at the hands of the suspect."

I hesitated, digesting this new information. "So you have the entire incident on video?"

He nodded. "You might be the victim of record at the moment, but that could change."

"Meaning what?"

"We're currently reviewing that video, along with witness statements, and weighing possible charges against you."

"What kind of charges?"

"Assault, giving false information to a police officer. Those are the two under discussion. The video leaves no doubt that you were the aggressor."

"He had no business being in my car. Or coming back here, trying to intimidate me."

"This bookstore event was a private affair?"

"Of course not."

"It was promoted in some way?"

"Probably."

"He's got a right to be wherever he wants, Mr. Justice, as long as he's not threatening you or trespassing on your property."

"The guy's got a screw loose, Detective."

Haukness clammed up as two men came in, seeking temporary parking permits for a dinner party they were having that night. A young deputy took care of them while the detective led me a few steps down the counter, where he lowered his voice.

"I'm going to go out on a limb here, Mr. Justice. Apprise you of a few facts you might not be aware of."

"That's why I came down here, Detective. To get some information."

"He's a veteran, Marine Corps. Lance corporal, served three

tours of duty in Iraq. Got himself involved in some pretty horrific stuff over there."

"This excuses the fact that he's stalking me?"

"If that's what he's doing."

"Maybe his military background makes him more dangerous, puts me in greater jeopardy. Have you considered that, Detective?"

Haukness set his jaw firmly. Color seeped into his neck, where a vein had begun to bulge. So the man wasn't unflappable after all.

"Before playing the victim with such sanctimony," he said, his tone finally taking on some feeling, "you might want to consider the possible consequences."

"Meaning I've got charges hanging over my head and if I ruffle the wrong feathers my ass could land in jail."

"I'll let you interpret it any way you see fit."

"Anything else, Detective?"

"I guess that does it."

I started to go, but a hunch stopped me. I turned to face him again.

"One more question."

He glanced at his watch. "What is it?"

"You wouldn't happen to be a former jarhead yourself, would you, Detective?"

"As a matter of fact, I am."

I gave him a small salute. "Semper Fi."

He didn't smile as he turned on his heel to disappear back into the station's inner sanctum. I wasn't smiling, either, and left feeling less at ease about things than when I'd arrived.

NINE

That evening, I was scheduled to meet Cathryn Conroy at a Beverly Hills restaurant for the second of our three interviews.

My plan was to make our meeting a long one, being as congenial and forthcoming as I could, and then try to wiggle out of my promise to meet her a third time. I'd grown weary of serving as a punching bag for writers with axes to grind and egos to feed. Anyone who seeks publicity as I had deserves what they get. You put yourself out there, seeking attention, you'd better be able to handle the flak. But given all the critical problems in the world, she seemed to be wasting an awful lot of time on a washed-up reporter with a name most people outside L.A. wouldn't recognize and whose transgressions were old news.

The restaurant she'd picked out was roughly a mile west of my apartment. To make my small contribution toward ending U.S. dependency on fossil fuels, I set out on foot. The enervating humidity we'd been experiencing had largely subsided, and the early evening was pleasant for a stroll, with a fitful breeze taking the edge off the heat. I followed the trail through Beverly Gardens Park, the narrow, green strip that runs along Santa Monica Boulevard through the flats of Beverly Hills and past the opulent architecture of City Hall, with its vintage mix of Spanish magnificence and fanciful Art Deco. Fitness-minded joggers and power walkers were coming and going beneath a canopy of eucalyptus, along with brown-skinned nannies walking pedigreed dogs or pushing strollers carrying well-fed Caucasian babies.

The steak house was a few blocks south on Beverly Boulevard. Like the downtown site of our previous meeting, it was not an accidental choice on Conroy's part. It had been a favorite weekend haunt of my late editor, Harry Brofsky, in the old days when we'd both worked at the *Los Angeles Times* before my sins had ended my career and seriously damaged his. For Conroy, I surmised, the location would serve as a nifty device to turn our conversation toward a past that she wanted to probe and I would rather forget, as well as a useful reference point in the article she'd eventually file. As I stepped inside to the cooled air and long, polished bar, I was reminded, once again, that she was an old pro, calculating and clever.

"Right on time," she said, peering at me over a tumbler of Johnnie Walker straight up.

She'd reserved a booth close to the bar, where her drinks could conveniently keep coming. As we settled in, I put her on my right, since my blind side was on the left and I wanted to look her in the eye without getting a stiff neck. As I glanced around the restaurant, I couldn't help but remember the good times I'd shared here with Harry, drinking hard, digging into a juicy cut of prime beef, and celebrating some big story I'd just broken under his guidance. I'd been young, full of piss and vinegar, in love with my bylines and in love with Jacques. It was a long time ago that seemed like yesterday.

"Brings back memories, does it?"

Conroy had her audio recorder ready, but with a notebook and pen to back it up, so she could jot down atmospheric detail and random thoughts and observations her recorder wouldn't pick up. The same way I'd handled interviews, and later taught Alexandra Templeton, when she was still green and Harry had me teaching her the trade.

"That's why you got me here, isn't it, Cathryn? Harry's favorite hangout?"

A waiter placed a fresh whiskey in front of her and took our orders: Caesars to start, two fillets, blood rare, with sides of sautéed spinach and rosemary potatoes that we'd share. Conroy ordered a bottle of cabernet that came with a sixty-dollar price tag, and asked for two glasses.

"One glass will be sufficient," I said. "For the lady."

"Come on, Justice. A nice cab with your steak. Just a taste. Can't hurt, can it?"

"One glass," I repeated, and the waiter departed.

Conroy sipped her fresh whiskey and asked casually, "Whatever happened to Harry Brofsky, anyway?"

"He died nearly a decade ago. I think you know that."

"It wasn't in your book."

"My book ended before he died. But I dedicated it to him. I imagine you know that too. Why not get to the point, Cathryn?"

"He must have died a broken man, working at the lowly *Los Angeles Sun* just before it collapsed."

"Thanks to me, you mean?"

"It's obviously an uncomfortable subject for you."

"Is it?"

"Isn't it?"

"What I did to Harry was unconscionable. In my book, I was up-front about that. Use whatever you want from it."

"One can never put everything in a book, Justice. You know how I work. I'm looking for something fresh, something you left out, an angle no one else is likely to run with. Otherwise, what's the point?"

"I didn't hold much back, not anything that mattered."

"Maybe readers should be the judge of that. Or reporters like me, who aren't satisfied with only part of the story."

"I included everything I felt was relevant. To the best of my knowledge, I was accurate and truthful. That's all one can do."

"Frankly, I'm more interested in what you left out than what you put in."

"Like you said, one can't include everything. Choices have to be made."

"Let's look at some of those choices, shall we?"

We'd gotten off to a bad start, so I tried to get the conversation back on a more productive track. I even smiled with my best fake sincerity.

"If you feel it's useful, Cathryn."

"Let's go back a few years, before the scandal. To your high school and college days."

"I don't see the importance of that. But if I can clear something up, I'll try."

"You were apparently quite the ladies' man in high school."

"That would be overstating it."

"You dated good-looking girls. You slept with a number of them."

"I felt that section of the book should focus on what my father did to my little sister, his death, and how it affected our family."

"How you killed him when you discovered him abusing her."

"She was eleven. It was rape. Yes, I killed him. It's well documented in the book, as you know."

"Justifiable homicide. I believe that was the ruling."

"Correct."

"Let's go back to your girlfriends, shall we?"

"If you feel it's necessary."

"You were quite the athlete, quite the stud. You even wrote angry poetry now and then, to show off for the more impressionable girls and get them into bed. Or into the backseat of your Chevy Impala, depending on the circumstances." When I said nothing, she added, "I've done my own research, Justice. Found some fresh sources."

"Congratulations." I put up the saccharine smile again. "Anything else?"

"You're admittedly gay—"

"*Admittedly* would be your word, suggesting there's something wrong with it."

"Excusez-moi. You're *openly* gay, and have been for many years."

"About half my life, yes. Since coming to L.A."

"But through your senior year in college, you slept exclusively with women."

"Yes, and exclusively when I was drunk."

"Is that an excuse?"

"An excuse for what?"

"For lying to so many women. For deceiving them, exploiting them sexually, using them to help maintain your charade."

I glanced at her tape recorder. "It's more complicated than that."

"Oh, really?"

"I was young, still finding myself. I was in deep denial about my sexuality."

"An identity crisis." She said it like the term was a joke.

"More or less."

"You were a college senior in 1980," she went on. "The gay revolution was in full swing. Homosexuals were coming out of the closet in droves. Yet you were still lying to women, using them as both a cover and a sexual outlet."

"I'm not proud of that part of my life, if that's what you want me to say."

"What I want is the truth."

"I just told you the truth."

"You must have been very attractive to certain women back then. Crusading student reporter, captain of the wrestling team, and probably a very decent fuck when you'd worked up your courage with enough alcohol."

I glanced at the drink in her hand. "Is that where your courage comes from, Cathryn?"

She flinched but came back at me tougher than ever.

"I'm not the subject of this interview, Justice. You are. You're the one beating the publicity trail to sell your book. My job is to fill in some of the holes you conveniently dug while writing it, burying some inconvenient facts."

Our Caesar salads arrived and I started in on mine. Conroy ignored hers, having at me.

"You were even engaged once, weren't you?"

"For about two minutes, my senior year in college."

"To Cheryl Zarimba—attractive brunette, Polish-American, English major, one year behind you. Rather high-strung, from what I gather."

"I don't see the point of—"

"The point is that the two of you were to be married and you didn't even bother to mention it in your life story."

"I'm not sure it was really headed toward marriage. That was more her fantasy than mine."

"So it *was* deliberate deception on your part? She was in love with you, and you led her on, bought her an engagement ring. That was just part of your heterosexual act?"

"A lot of men were confused about themselves back then, unsure of who they were, what they wanted. For some of us the idea of suddenly acknowledging our feelings for other men, of leading a gay life, didn't seem remotely possible."

"Because you were too cowardly to face the truth?"

"Because of a lot of things."

"Do you know how many women have been deceived by men like you?" The tone of Conroy's voice had become sharp and accusing, a far cry from her usual ironic cool. "Do you realize how many women have sacrificed years of their lives, suffered terrible confusion, been irreparably hurt, even blamed themselves, because men like you didn't have the balls to be honest with them?"

I'd heard that Conroy had been married, many years ago. I glanced at her right hand but saw no ring.

"Is it possible that you're one of those women, Cathryn? That that's what all this is about?"

"Don't try to turn this on me, Justice. This is about you. You and Cheryl Zarimba, your old college flame, the last woman you slept with before you decided that you preferred cock to pussy."

I slowed down, took a deep breath, then said quietly, "I'd appreciate it if you'd leave Cheryl's name out of your article. It's been nearly thirty years since I saw or spoke to her. Yes, she was hurt when I broke off the engagement just before graduation. I felt lousy about it. I'd change the way all of it went down if I could, but I can't."

"How noble of you."

"But I don't see the point of hurting her again after all these years. So if you'll promise to leave her name out of your article, I'll be as forthcoming as I can about anything else you want to know. Just not her name, that's all."

Conroy finally put down her pen and picked up her salad fork, spearing a leaf. The anger went out of her voice, replaced by bemusement.

"Oh, I don't think she'll mind if I mention her by name."

"You spoke with her?"

"Spoke with Cheryl? Not possible. Cheryl Zarimba languished for years, brokenhearted and bitter about what you'd done, before she finally committed suicide ten years ago. I don't know much else about her, but I still have more phone calls to make."

The news hit me hard. I must have blanched, because Conroy smiled a little.

"You're certain about that?" I asked. "That Cheryl took her own life?"

"Oh, yes. Quite certain. I even have a copy of the death certificate, if you ever want to see it."

I hadn't thought about Cheryl Zarimba in years, except in passing as I wrote my memoir, before deciding to leave her out of it. Suicide, Conroy had said. One more casualty strewn along the path of my reckless life. And Conroy was surely going to use it for all it was worth, condemning me for ignoring Cheryl in my book.

I stood, tossed some cash on the table, and left just as the steaks were arriving, still sizzling on their iron platters. I could hear Conroy's smoky voice behind me.

"You still owe me an interview, Justice. I've got more questions, if you've got the gonads to answer them."

I strode back up Beverly Boulevard, furious with Conroy for nailing me with such calculated and cruel effect. But I really couldn't blame her. She was a certifiable bitch, no question of that, about as nasty a journalist as I'd come across. But I'd written a book and was cashing in on my ugly past and she had every right to probe and question and judge. Cheryl Zarimba, dead—at least partly because of me. I walked faster, pounding the pavement harder.

I crossed Santa Monica Boulevard into the dark, narrow park and turned east toward home. I'd walked for a minute or two when the steady rumble of a nearby motorcycle caught my attention.

To my right, I saw a figure in a leather jacket but without the required helmet cruising slowly in the nearest lane, which put him on the wrong side of the boulevard, facing oncoming traffic. The lanes ahead of him were clear for the moment, but he didn't seem concerned about them at any rate; his eyes were fixed on me. Even in the dark, I could recognize the rider, with his strong jaw and cleanly shaved head. There was no doubt now that he was stalking me. He must have been watching my apartment, I thought, and followed when I left for my dinner meeting.

He continued riding parallel to me, slowly enough to match my pace. As I emerged from a maze of hedges, his eyes never left me. We kept on like that, our eyes locked, as the seconds ticked away. As I broke eye contact and glanced ahead, a traffic light changed from red to green and vehicles began moving in our direction. I saw a municipal bus coming straight at the skinhead in the same lane. Still, he stayed his course, seemingly oblivious to the danger he was in. More vehicles were approaching from behind, as eastbound traffic caught up with him. If he was even slightly concerned, he didn't show it.

As the westbound bus bore down on him, catching him in its headlights, he turned his front wheel to the right and hit the throttle. More headlights struck him and horns blared. At the last moment, he shot into the eastbound lanes, squeezing between cars, as if to show me I wasn't the only one who had a taste for recklessness and danger.

TEN

The next morning, I called Detective Haukness to complain about Motorcycle Boy and his attempt to intimidate me the night before. I didn't like going to the cops about such matters; I'd always preferred handling them myself. But Haukness had warned me I was already on thin ice. I couldn't afford to tangle with the skinhead again, not with a possible assault charge dangling over my head.

Haukness was out in the field, so I left a message on his voice mail. He got back to me that night, just before he went off-duty at eight. He was abrupt, and sounded vaguely irritated.

"I can't arrest a guy for riding past you on a motorcycle," Haukness said. "It's like I told you—"

"I know, Detective. He has to approach and threaten me."

"He does that, call nine-one-one and report it. Anything else I can do for you, Mr. Justice?"

"I'd like a copy of the police report on the original incident."

"Why would you need that?"

"To learn as much about this guy as I can, since you don't plan to do anything about him."

"I'll think about it," Haukness said.

"As the victim of record, I'm not entitled to a copy?"

"It's not pro forma, no."

"Do I need to make a stink about this, Detective? Go over your head to get a copy of a police report that led to a conviction?"

"I'll see what I can do."

He hung up before I did.

Over the next few days, the baby doves grew surprisingly fast, and began to stretch their fragile wings. By week's end they were perched on the edge of the nest, their beady eyes big and dark in their skeletal heads, their matted down starting to fluff and grow into feathers. The father returned more often and for longer periods, sitting on a nearby power line where the chicks could see him, flapping his wings until they began to raise and lower their own in imitation.

Fred and Maurice were careful to keep their two cats inside, worried that a baby bird might fall from the nest, which sometimes happened. They'd learned long ago from the experts to gently pick up the grounded chicks and place them back in the nest, that the old caveat about a human smell scaring away other birds is just a myth. Over the ensuing days, Fred took to sitting on the patio for hours, watching the rite of passage taking place at the top of the stairs. He'd witnessed it countless times in springs and summers past but seemed more intrigued this year. He often dozed off in his patio chair. Maurice would appear from the house to check on him, looking weary and worried. As it turned out, he had good reason.

"His heart's quite weak," Maurice confided to me privately, one morning when Fred had nodded off. "He needs a quadruple bypass, but he's too frail to qualify for the operation. Don't mention that I told you, Benjamin. He doesn't want anyone to know. Too proud and all that. Doesn't want anyone feeling sorry for him."

More and more often, I looked out my upstairs window to see Maurice sitting beside Fred as he snoozed on the patio, quietly holding his hand and gazing pensively into the yard. I didn't know how to comfort either of them, feeling caught between a secret and the truth, and never much good during times like this at any rate. So I just helped around the house the best I could, acutely aware of how the atmosphere had subtly changed, as if all the bright colors had slowly drained away, leaving only somber shades of gray.

Toward the end of the week, I opened the mailbox to find a few items for Fred and Maurice and a single plain postcard for me. This one was addressed to *Benjamin BJ Justice*, in the same florid handwriting as the others:

> *HIV comes to the promiscuous, who by definition are shallow and self-destructive. (Yes, there is a God!) Just remember: HIV now, AIDS tomorrow. Don't linger too long, and don't forget your pills! (I keep looking for your book on the Fag Bestseller List but have yet to see it. With any luck, you'll be dead before that happens.)*

So it had started up again. At least this one didn't mention Jacques, I thought, which made it less offensive. Maurice appeared from the house to get his mail and I tucked the postcard away where he wouldn't see it. He'd mentioned something about a letter in my files, dated eighteen years ago, that might have a connection to the hate mail I was receiving now, and had promised to find it for me. Given the situation with Fred, I wasn't going to bring it up, and decided to forget about it.

Maurice reached out and touched the old mailbox lovingly, as if remembering the day Fred had installed it decades back, and how Maurice had later added the rainbow colors, which had since begun to fade.

"Do me a favor, will you, Benjamin? Let Fred get the mail from now on. He's written out a list of chores he wants to do—collect the mail, rake the yard, feed the cats. Little tasks that allow him to stay active, to feel useful."

"Of course, Maurice. Whatever he wants." I handed Maurice his mail. "How are you doing, by the way? You look a little worn-out yourself."

He smiled for my benefit. "I'm doing fine, Benjamin, but thanks for asking."

I watched him trudge back into the house with sagging shoulders, and my problem with the hate mail seemed less significant than ever. If there was a jerk out there so desperate for attention that he had to send me messages like this, I figured, he deserved my pity more than my anger. I'd just ignore him, and go about my life.

Besides, at that moment, I had something considerably more important on my agenda: Ismael Aragon was finally back in town, and we were meeting for coffee that afternoon.

At the appointed time, I found Ismael waiting for me down on the boulevard at Tribal Grounds. We dispensed with the handshake and hugged straightaway, and I even managed a quick kiss on the nape of his neck that he didn't seem to mind.

"It feels like you've been gone forever," I said.

"To me as well," he said. "It's good to be back."

Inside, I ordered my usual dark roast, drinking it black, while Ismael chose herbal tea. We settled in at a small table by the window, facing each other. Sonny Rollins was playing in the background, a slippery tenor sax solo on the easygoing side.

"You look great," I said. "Your work must suit you."

"It can be heartbreaking at times, trying to help families torn apart by borders and immigration laws. But it's important work, I think. I feel blessed to have the opportunity to do it."

He told me he'd begun working with undocumented immigrant families as a priest—more than seventy percent of the Catholic population in Los Angeles was Hispanic—and he'd continued after leaving the Church. It had given him a sense of continuity and community, he said, that had helped in his transition.

"Still," I said, "your break from the Church must have been painful."

His eyes grew somber. "It was agony, Benjamin. I felt like I was being ripped from my own skin."

I could hear in his voice that much of the pain was still raw. I reached across the table and took his hand.

"I'd like to hear about it," I said.

And so we talked, a lapsed Catholic and an ex-priest, sipping from our heavy porcelain cups and getting refills as first an hour passed, and then another. Ismael spoke about the anguish he'd suffered as he'd wrestled with the decision to renounce his vows and leave the Church he'd served since he was a teenage acolyte. He was not one to wallow in self-pity and his narrative had more to do with the substance of his decision than the pain it had personally caused him. His disillusionment, he said, had begun with the hypocrisy of the Church in the wake of the scandal that had exposed thousands of priests and former priests as sexual predators and thousands more children as their victims, while covering up the complicit crimes of its highest officials. He'd been deeply troubled by the unwillingness of certain bishops and cardinals to turn over potentially incriminating records, particularly within the Los Angeles archdiocese, which he'd served so loyally for so long.

Yet his problems with the Church, he said, went much deeper than its recent sex abuse crisis, to the violence it had committed centuries ago in Christ's name, its shameful history of anti-Semitism, and the rigid dogma that, in his view, fostered intolerance, suspicion, and hatred. Ismael likened the flawed doctrines of the Catholic Church to those of the evangelical Christian movement and the fanaticism of Muslim extremism, the kind of irrational mass thinking that had led to the Crusades, the Spanish Inquisition, and the Holocaust, an us-versus-them mind-set that was now leading the world toward a terrible conflagration that would ultimately be waged with weapons of mass destruction in the name of God.

"I was so naïve to have never seen these things," Ismael said. "How could I have been so blind? How could I have been a part of it for so long?"

He grew increasingly passionate as he spoke, reminding me of the fire I'd once felt for crucial causes, a flame that had nearly sputtered out. I wanted to be more like Ismael, I realized. I wanted to be close to his goodness and his selflessness, to share it, to somehow be made better by it. Much the way I'd once felt about Jacques.

Ismael laughed. "You want to know what's so ironic about my work? The immigrants I try to help—most of them are as devoted to the Church as ever."

"I suppose their faith is all they have."

"And the Church counts on that," Ismael said, "on their poverty and their ignorance."

"Yet you don't give up," I said. "It's one of the things I admire about you."

"I still have my spiritual faith," Ismael said. "That hasn't changed. But I'm learning a new way to worship, one that's more compassionate and inclusive, and less condemning. If we could just get back to that, to that essential principle of loving one another, without judgment, we could do so much good in the world."

"Sometimes," I said, "you seem too good to be true."

He dropped his eyes, embarrassed. "Please don't say things like that."

"It's how I see you, Ismael. I can't help it. You inspire me."

"It works both ways, Benjamin." He squeezed my hand. "You might not realize this, but you were the catalyst that helped me change my life. Five years ago, when we met, I found myself drawn to you in a very powerful way. I'm not sure exactly why. Your anger, your passion—it was like an earthquake in my placid world. It stirred feelings in me, made me face truths about myself I could no longer ignore."

"That last day I saw you," I said, "when you took my confession in the church garden, I reached out and stroked your face."

"You also kissed me."

"Chastely," I reminded him.

"Yes, but I've never forgotten that moment."

"Nor have I."

"And here we sit again, all these years later." He shook his head. "It doesn't seem possible."

"And your break from the Church—you're sure you're okay with it?"

"It feels like grief. Like I've lost someone I expected to have with me for the rest of my life."

"I know the feeling."

His eyes were steady, but they couldn't hide his suffering. He clasped my hand even tighter.

"It's a lonely feeling, isn't it?"

"The loneliest feeling in the world," I said.

ELEVEN

Early that evening, I was completing a workout with free weights at Buff when I glanced out one of the big windows to see a familiar figure across the street. Motorcycle Boy was leaning against a palm tree in front of Starbucks, staring up in my direction.

At that moment, flush with testosterone, I snapped. Within seconds, I was racing down the stairs and out of the gym, still in my workout gear. As if anticipating me, the skinhead strode east, passing a courtyard tapas bar as he left the glitzier section of Boys Town behind. He had more than a block on me and I began to trot, closing the gap. It was still the rush hour, but he dashed pell-mell into traffic, causing drivers to hit their brakes and diners at outdoor tables to look up as tires squealed. He weaved through traffic until he was on my side of Santa Monica Boulevard—the south side—and moving east again, picking up his pace. He caught a green light at La Cienega and I sprinted after him as it turned to yellow, chasing him several blocks past City Hall and Hamburger Mary's. The venerable Gold Coast came into view, with its rugged bartenders, strong drinks, and a pool table that was always busy. Just before we reached the bar, Motorcycle Boy turned right down La Jolla Street and out of my sight.

When I rounded the corner, he was gone. I dashed to the alley at the next corner and scanned the adjacent public parking strip to my left, where men sat in their idling cars or drove slowly through, cruising for a pickup. A few hustlers lingered about, one eye out for clients, the other for cops. A ragged homeless man dug through the big Dumpster behind Out of the Closet, picking through discards that weren't even good enough for the thrift shop. The skinhead was nowhere to be seen.

I was seriously winded and took a moment to get my breath. Then I glanced in the other direction down the alley, to my right, and caught sight of the skinhead again. He stood at the end of the block, hands on hips, waiting for me. The moment I saw him he took off, south down Kings Road in the direction of the famous Schindler House, clearly daring me to follow him.

I quickly reached the street and saw him a few hundred feet away. He glanced back before turning into Kings Road Park, and I went after him again. The park was a small green space carved from the surrounding landscape of condo and apartment buildings, which blocked out most of the light that was left in the deepening dusk. When I reached the cast-iron fence and turned in at the gate, the park looked dark and empty beneath its heavy canopy of pine and eucalyptus.

On my right, where one often saw parents and nannies with small children, or elderly men and women chatting or feeding the squirrels, the benches were empty. I followed a short path that opened to a small lawn ringed with trees and dense foliage. I didn't see him. I scanned the rear of the park, wondering if he'd made his escape through the back gate. Logic told me he hadn't. He wanted me here, where it was private and the shadows were deep.

The path wound to my left, around a small grove of banana palms, twisting vines, and other leafy foliage, where a narrow stream of water cascaded down a rock formation into a small lagoon. Except for the titters of small birds high in the trees, the sound of the falling water was all I could hear. I continued along the trail as it circled the dense grove. As I reached the far side, I stopped to listen again, aware of the insistent beating of my heart.

The faint light of street lamps failed to reach this side of the fountain and towering banana palms. Darkness enveloped me.

"Benjamin Justice."

I whirled to find him standing a few feet away in a small alcove, in front of a slatted wooden bench. He was close enough that he could have put a knife in me if he'd wanted to.

"You move quietly," I said. "You know how to sneak up on a guy."

"When I need to."

"What do you want from me?"

"Who said I wanted anything?"

He was wearing a faded tank top with the logo of a heavy metal band I hadn't heard of in years, snug-fitting Levi's that showed off his package, and the same menacing black motorcycle boots he'd worn the first time I'd encountered him. Dark blond stubble was thick along his jaw and chin, accentuating the ruggedness that made him so attractive. His blue eyes blazed, even here, beyond the reach of the streetlights, where the dusk was quickly becoming night.

"You're the one who followed me," he said. "So maybe it's you who wants something."

"I want to know who you are, and what it is you're after."

"My name's Lance. Does that help?"

"It's a start."

"And you're Benjamin Justice. The faggot who wrote a book about stuff he did a long time ago and how bad he feels about it now."

I raised my eyebrows skeptically. "You read it?"

"Yeah, I read it."

"Why?"

"Because I wanted to learn more about you."

"For what purpose?"

"Not because I want to suck your cock, if that's what you're thinking."

"Why would I be thinking that?"

"Because you're queer, and that's what you guys like to do."

He said it straight out, like a simple statement of fact. If there was malice in his words, I didn't hear it.

"I understand that you're a jarhead," I said. "That you served in Iraq."

He pulled out a pack of unfiltered Marlboros, lit one, took a long drag.

"Yeah, I was over there. What's it to you?"

"Couldn't have been much fun." When he didn't say anything, I asked, "You from around here?"

He pulled deeply on the cigarette again, holding in the smoke. When he finally let it out, he said, "You know how many packs a day I smoked when I was over there? Six. Six fucking packs a day, and when I went over I was trying to quit."

"That's a lot of tar and nicotine."

"So how come you don't smoke?"

"How do you know I don't?"

"I know plenty about you, and not just from your book."

"What's so interesting about me, Lance? Why do you follow me around, trying to get under my skin?"

He took a final drag, dropped the butt, crushed it with the toe of his boot. Then he took a step closer and studied my face a moment with something more than just curiosity, some emotion I couldn't name. He repeated what he'd done the first day we'd met, just before I'd grabbed him and slammed him to the ground. He reached up with his right hand and caressed my face. This time I didn't stop him, or move away. I felt him run his fingers over my rough beard, around the contours of my jaw, down my neck, along a biceps still swelling and hard from my workout. Then he pressed his hand to my left pectoral and kept it there, while my heart beat faster.

Nearby, someone cleared his throat. I glanced over to see a uniformed city worker with a set of keys in his hand, looking faintly embarrassed. He told us the park was closed for the night, that it was time for him to lock the gates.

Lance kept his hand over my heart a moment longer, peering deep into my eyes, before removing it and stepping back.

"Maybe I'll see you around," he said, making it sound like both an invitation and a threat.

Then he was gone, back down the path and across the park. I followed to the edge of the street, where I saw him ride off on his Harley. It was a stylish FXST Softail, the seminal 1984 model with the V-2 engine that had saved the company from financial ruin. As Lance roared away on his gleaming hog, I realized he'd kept it in mint condition, the way I'd restored and maintained my '65 Mustang. He'd had it parked at the curb, right out front, which meant he'd had this encounter planned all along, right down to the privacy of the location. Whatever was going on with him, I thought, he wasn't stupid.

The city worker locked up the park and drove off. I stood alone as night closed in on the neighborhood, trying to figure out what kind of game Lance was playing but no closer to knowing than I'd been an hour ago, or yesterday, or last week.

Back at Buff, I showered and changed into my street clothes, then dropped in at the sheriff's substation on my way home to inquire about the copy of the police report I'd requested. When I asked for Detective Haukness at the front counter, a deputy informed me that Haukness had been reassigned to the homicide division, working out of department headquarters in East L.A.

"I'd still like my copy of that report," I said.

The deputy slid a form in front of me, asked me to fill it out, and told me my request would have to go through channels.

TWELVE

By the second week in July, five weeks after its publication, *Deep Background* had managed to sell enough copies to warrant a modest second printing.

Although it was barely a blip on the BookScan radar screen, it would have been a great excuse to celebrate with Ismael. I even entertained fantasies of getting him drunk on champagne and having my way with him. The problem was he was roughly twenty-six hundred miles away in Washington. He'd been called out of town again, this time to help organize a new effort to get an immigration amnesty bill before Congress as early as possible in the next presidential term. He knew such legislation would face stiff opposition from Americans who appreciated the benefits of slave labor from across the border as long as the workers didn't ask for too much, like decent health care and education for their children. He wasn't sure when he'd be back. We'd never even managed to meet for dinner before he left.

My book turned up briefly on the *Los Angeles Times* bestseller list, peaking at number three, for which Judith Zeitler deserved most of the credit. She'd set up readings at key bookstores around Southern California that were thought to be on the *Times* survey, a routine ploy by savvy publicists and authors that could make a modest seller look more successful than it really was. I could now claim to be a "best-selling" author, though only regional in scope. Southern California was a big book market, to be sure, but the truth was that if an author sold a mere few hundred copies at the right bookstores in a brief enough time span, his or her book could jump on a regional list and warrant the bestseller label. One notorious author, a game show producer with buckets of money, had even run around to key bookstores buying up armloads of his own poorly reviewed love story. The strategy had worked and, ever since, his publicity materials had referred to him as a best-selling novelist.

I was more clear-eyed about my own success, or lack of it. *Deep Background* hadn't shown up on any of the major national bestseller lists, and hadn't sold anywhere near the number of copies needed if I was to earn back my advance. That made it one of thousands of books released around the same time that barely caused a ripple at the cash register, let alone in the public's consciousness. With only a few promotional events remaining, my memoir's shelf life was quickly running out, like a fish flopping on the dock and gasping its last breaths.

"We've got to get you on *Jerry Rivers Live*," Zeitler said, during a quick phone call as she raced around town, escorting her new client to readings and interviews. "Trust me, Benjamin, I haven't given up. I want that booking!"

"If anyone can get me on *Jerry Rivers Live*," I said, "it's you, Judith."

Ismael called in mid-July to tell me he was coming home, and my heart soared at the news.

While he'd been gone, I'd stayed busy painting my apartment and refinishing the hardwood floor, something I hadn't done in the eighteen years I'd lived there. Maurice found new curtains to replace the faded ones, and I'd purchased my first full set of dinnerware, after eating for years off a mix of thrift store bargains. On the day Ismael was to arrive home, I took delivery of a new queen-sized mattress and box frame, anticipating the moment when we'd make love for the first time.

The deliverymen were departing as the postal carrier arrived with the day's mail. Following our new routine, I waited while Fred shuffled from the house to retrieve the items from the mailbox and dispense them accordingly. He handed me the latest issue of the *Lambda Book Report*, a bill from my credit card company, and a plain postcard.

It had been weeks since I'd received a piece of hate mail and when I saw the card I felt myself clench up, despite my vow to not let the taunting messages get to me. The new card was addressed to *Benjamin Virus Justice*. I checked the postmark, which, like the others, indicated a 90046 zip code a few miles northeast, within Los Angeles city limits.

I turned the postcard over to read the message, but there were no words. Just a crude graphic: my photo, cut from the dust jacket of my book and pasted down, with the word *AIDS* drawn in red ink across my face. Most people probably thought AIDS was no longer a serious health crisis, but I knew better. It was still spreading, particularly among minority communities, and was a raging epidemic in the third world. Each year, several hundred people died in L.A. County from AIDS-related complications and an unknown number from the side effects associated with the toxic drugs used to suppress HIV, deaths that rarely showed up in the HIV mortality statistics. So to see the word *AIDS* scrawled in bloodred ink across my face meant something.

Maurice appeared on the front porch, urging Fred to come in out of the sun. When Maurice saw me seething as I studied the postcard, he suspected what it was and joined me, asking to see it. I held the card up, showing him the graphic on the back.

"This has gone quite far enough, Benjamin. It's got to stop."

He took the card and studied the familiar handwriting on the front.

"I should have gotten that old letter for you," he said, "the one I promised to find weeks ago. I'd forgotten all about it. Let me get Fred some lunch and then I'll attend to it."

I told Maurice I'd begin looking for the letter myself, and he said he'd join me as soon as he could.

The boxes containing the research material I'd saved through the years were stacked neatly in a far corner of the double garage, sharing space with a 1960 turquoise and white Nash Metropolitan convertible.

Ever meticulous, Maurice had marked each box by topic—story files, article clippings, correspondence, and so on—with the papers inside separated into individual files, where they were arranged alphabetically. He'd salvaged much of the material on my behalf during the years following Jacques' death and the collapse of my career, the lost years I'd spent drinking obscene amounts of tequila, before Maurice and Fred had intervened to rescue me from myself.

I kneeled and started in on the box marked "Correspondence," but hadn't gotten far when a file slugged "Pulitzer" caught my eye. Inside were three formal letters sent to me in 1990 by the Pulitzer committee. None pertained directly to what I was looking for, but I couldn't pass by them without at least a glance. The first was a letter officially notifying me that I'd won that year's Pulitzer in the feature-writing category, for my series in the *Los Angeles Times* chronicling the devotion of two gay men for each other as one died slowly from AIDS complications. The articles had been based loosely on my own experience with Jacques, but with the names changed and essential facts altered to create a rosier version of the truth, one that I might live more comfortably with. The second letter came a few weeks after the first, informing me that the committee had been tipped by an anonymous source that the two men featured in my series of articles did not actually exist as depicted, that many other elements in the story had been made up, that an investigation was under way, and that my full cooperation would be appreciated. The third letter had arrived not long after the second, thanking me for my cooperation during the investigation, expressing regret at the outcome, and informing me that my Pulitzer had been rescinded, with a public announcement soon to follow. By then I'd already informed my editor, Harry Brofsky, of my unforgivable betrayal, quit the *Times,* and gone into seclusion, anticipating the news coverage soon to follow.

As I reread the letters now, it wasn't difficult to envision the first line of my obit when it was eventually written. It would go something like this: "Benjamin Justice, who turned his life around after killing his father in self-defense at age seventeen to become a respected investigative reporter, only to destroy his career in a scandal involving the Pulitzer Prize, died yesterday at the age of . . ."

My fiftieth birthday was less than two months away. And what was there to show, I asked myself, for the half century I'd been granted? Not much. It felt like time had blown through my life like a storm wind, breaking and scattering nearly everything and everyone I cared about. Fifty years—how could it have gone by so quickly? How could I have made such a mess of things?

"Benjamin? Are you working in here, or daydreaming?"

I looked up to see Maurice approaching through the open garage door, a sticklike figure silhouetted against the glare of sunlight. I shoved the three letters back into the Pulitzer file and the file back into the box.

"I just took a minute to look over some old documents. Nothing important."

"A minute? Benjamin, you've been sitting here for half an hour with those papers, deep in thought. I could see you from the kitchen window."

"I guess I lost track of time."

He kneeled beside me, surprisingly nimble for a man his age.

"Let me in there," he said. "I'll find that letter in short order."

It took him less than a minute to locate the file heading he was looking for—"Letters from the Public"—and a few minutes more to find the one in question.

According to the postmark on the envelope and the date on the letter, it had been written and mailed about a week after the public announcement that I'd been forced to relinquish my Pulitzer. The return address and the postmark indicated a 90046 zip code, duplicating those on the anonymous hate mail I'd recently been receiving. I wasn't surprised that I couldn't remember this particular letter from so long ago; it was possible I'd never even read it, though the envelope had been neatly opened across the top.

"I might have opened it myself," Maurice said, "last year, when I was helping to organize your papers."

It was written on heavy flannel stationary, the expensive, embossed kind that one sees less of now that letter writing has largely been replaced by the convenience of e-mail and the quickie cell phone text message. The fine weave of the paper bore a pinkish tint, faint enough that it wasn't as tacky as it sounds.

At the top of the first page, centered, was an embossed name: *Silvio Galiano.*

"Means nothing to me," I said.

"There was an interior designer by that name," Maurice said. "Well-known in the old days for his Hollywood clientele. I believe he died some time ago."

What followed were several pages, rambling and strangely intimate, as if the writer and I were well acquainted. On the surface, the words were friendly and concerned, but venom seeped from nearly every line.

Dear Benjamin,

I call you Benjamin because that's how you're known now, your name forever synonymous with scandal and shame. Of course, within my small circle of college friends you were known as Big Ben, after we'd glimpsed you in the showers. I suppose, given your recent problems, you're not so "big" anymore, are you? (No offense—just a little joke!)

On that subject, how sad I was to read of your great misfortune regarding the Pulitzer Prize. (I won a number of awards myself when I was younger, mostly for my impressive high school science projects. Fortunately, I didn't have to give mine back!) Caring deeply for you as I do, I wanted to offer my sincere sympathy and condolences. Isn't it tragic how certain people with genuine potential are also deeply flawed, so much so that they destroy any chance they have at greatness? When we attended college together, I always admired your skill and ambition, and tried to tell you so on numerous occasions. (I often think how differently our lives might have turned out had you not been so uneasy about your sexuality and unresponsive to my overtures of friendship.)

Forgive me for not writing sooner, by the way. I've only just returned with Silvio (Silvio Galiano, the acclaimed interior designer; I'm sure you know of him) from a wonderful trip abroad, where we visited with the crème de le crème of European society. While abroad, we were treated like royalty (Hollywood royalty, thank God, not the British kind; they're so stiff and boring, don't you think?) and had the most fabulous time. Because of Silvio's health issues, we don't get a chance to do much traveling (which is probably just as well, since neither of us is fluent in anything but English, although many people insist that I show remarkable verbal acuity; my IQ is quite high—not bragging, mind you, just stating a fact). We especially loved the Continent, which we found so civilized, although it's becoming rather expensive. (I'm thinking of writing a book called *Europe on Five Thousand Dollars a Day*—don't you think that's clever?)

One recent afternoon in London, when I was having tea and the most delightful biscuits at the Savoy (we stay in only the best hotels), I was reading one of the local rags (the newspapers there are so much more catty and sensational, which is kind of fun, don't you think?), and I came across a smallish item about your regrettable behavior and the furor it caused because of the Pulitzer. I mention how small the item was only to point out that while you may be notorious in the States, the rest of the world apparently doesn't know who you are or very much care, which is rather hopeful for your future, don't you think? Perhaps you can start over again in one of the more remote English-speaking countries, like New Zealand (very homophobic there, however, and quite racist toward the Maori, though many of the blond farmboys are to die for, but then you've never been that taken with blonds, have you?). Anyway, when I read the minor news item about your "Pulitzer problem," my heart went out to you, even though you treated me like shit (pardon my language, but it's the truth) when we were in college and I was so devoted to you and told everyone what a wonderful person you were, even though it became quite clear over time that you're not a very nice person at all. (From what I've heard since, someone "tipped" the Pulitzer people about your fabrications. Have you any idea who might have done such a thing? One of the countless enemies you've made over the years, no doubt. What's that old saying—what goes around comes around!)

Getting back to the subject of our ill-fated friendship, I guess I was the lucky one, wasn't I? Things have turned out so well for me. I count among my dearest friends some of the most famous and talented people in the world (did I mention that I had affairs with Sir John Gielgud and Tennessee Williams before I met Silvio? Tennessee insisted that with my looks, I should have no trouble establishing myself in the movies if I should wish it). There's nothing quite like being in a committed, long-term relationship (even though Silvio is many years older than me, don't think for a minute that we don't share a very active and satisfying sex life), and I couldn't be happier. And you, from what I hear, are just an unhappy, miserable queen. Of course, I put no stock in that kind of gossip and truly hope that, despite the rumors, you're adjusting well to your recent setbacks. (By the way, how old was Jacques when he died? Twenty-nine, if I'm not mistaken. What a shame, dying so horribly at such a young age. I glimpsed him once or twice when I was out and about and he was still healthy. I suppose he was attractive, if you go for that type. But I'm sure he was a perfectly nice person.)

Anyway, to return to the subject of your various problems, there's no point in dwelling on the past, is there? I always say look forward, not back—or you might end up with a pain in the neck! (I plan to write a little volume one day of my favorite witticisms and bon mots and those of my famous friends, which would make the most fabulous gift book, don't you think?) Toward that end (looking forward, I mean), I'd love to do lunch sometime soon and catch up. I know a lovely little restaurant just off Rodeo Drive that serves the most delicious crepes (salads if you're more health conscious, as I try to be, but I like to treat myself to something sinful every now and then, don't you?). You needn't worry about my relationship with Silvio; he knows all about you. It would just be lunch, not a date!

Call me here at the house (the number printed below) and we can arrange a time, which shouldn't be a problem for you, now that you're on extended vacation (sorry, just another little joke I couldn't resist; I actually wish you nothing but the best). If I'm out, just leave a message, and I'll get back to you the moment my busy schedule allows.

Your devoted friend,
Jason Holt (aka Barclay Simpkins, back in college)

"My goodness," Maurice said, reading along with me over my shoulder, "the man does go on and on about himself, doesn't he?" Maurice ran his finger down to the signature at the bottom of the last page. "Look at the *J*, Benjamin. It's very distinctive. It's identical to the *J* in your last name that appears on those vile postcards you've been getting."

"Yes, I noticed it myself."

"But who is he, Benjamin?"

I studied the signature again.

"I met a Jason Holt recently. At my reading at A Different Light.

He stood at the back, asked a couple of very pointed questions. Had me sign a book afterward."

"That strange man with the ghastly blond hair and all the facial work?"

I nodded. "He insisted that we'd known each other, long ago."

"He certainly seemed to know a lot about you when he wrote this letter. You don't remember him?"

"Not even remotely."

"Do you think it's possible he's the one who instigated the Pulitzer investigation? That one line—he seems to be taunting you about it, doesn't he?"

"It wouldn't matter if it was him or someone else. I deserved what I got. I came to terms with that long ago."

"There's not much doubt that this Jason Holt is behind those nasty messages you've been getting. What do you think he's up to?"

"I'm not sure." I studied the return address on the envelope, which indicated a house number on Nichols Canyon Terrace. "I wonder if he still lives in the same place."

"I suppose it's possible, even after all these years." Maurice arched his brows sternly. "Benjamin, you don't intend to go up there, do you?"

"I'd like to have a talk with him."

"I still think you should turn this matter over to the authorities."

"I doubt there's enough to connect this guy to any prosecutable crimes. Anyway, the cops don't like me much. Don't worry, Maurice, I won't knock the guy around, much as I'd like to. Just a few questions, that's all."

THIRTEEN

The return address on Jason Holt's letter put the house high in the Hollywood Hills, near the top of Nichols Canyon.

The midafternoon sun blasted the brush-covered hills as I made my way up twisting Nichols Canyon Road. As I neared Mulholland Drive, I saw the street sign for Nichols Canyon Terrace and turned right. The street was short but long on Hollywood history, by the look of it. I felt a bit like Jake Gittes in *Chinatown*, driving up for an appointment with Hollywood money.

The narrow lane ended abruptly in a cul-de-sac, where I found the number I was looking for. It belonged to a vintage Spanish-style house that sat amid lush foliage that hadn't seen a gardener in a while. At two stories, the house wasn't exactly crumbling, but it was getting there. Rounded terra-cotta tiles decorated the roofline and arches, and smaller, decorative tiles had been scattered for accents, although a few were missing, leaving little square craters where the lost tiles had been embedded. Vines clung tenaciously to the walls, allowing stained-glass windows to peek out while giving the weathered house a dank, medieval look, even in the summer glare. It was the kind of place the Realtors would advertise as having "character" if it ever went up for sale, although its condition probably wouldn't matter much up here, where a buyer was likely to tear it down for the lot and the view and put up a more showy monstrosity in its place. Sitting out front in the circular driveway was a bloodred 1953 Ferrari with a cream-colored top, a classic 375 America coupe that caused a car buff like me to swoon but also cringe, because of its neglected state. The paint was worn and coated with grime, the chrome of the wire wheels and oval grille pocked with rust. Like the house, the car had long ago lost its sheen, and in their disrepair they seemed a perfect match. It occurred to me they might even have been purchased around the same time, decades ago, with new money that was long gone.

I pressed the button for the doorbell but didn't hear any chimes. When no one answered I pressed again, wondering if the bell even worked. When I knocked, my knuckles were equally ineffective, so I followed a path of inlaid stepping-stones to my left around the unfenced property, swiping at spiderwebs along the way. I emerged onto a flagstone patio green with moss at the edges closest to the north side of the house. Dilapidated lawn furniture sat forlornly around an empty swimming pool flecked white from peeling paint and choked with dry leaves at the deep end.

Beyond the forlorn swimming pool and across a lawn gone to seed was Jason Holt, hacking awkwardly but furiously with a machete at a dense grove of tall bamboo that pressed against a hillside. He wore long pants but no shirt, a pale, soft-looking man who appeared unaccustomed to manual labor as he gripped the machete's handle with his small hands, grunting each time he raised the heavy blade to deliver another stroke.

He was so absorbed in his work that he didn't notice my arrival. I crossed the dead lawn until only a few yards of it separated us, but still he failed to look over. To my right, beyond a low wall whose columns were partly entangled with morning-glory vines, was an open view of the city, all the way to downtown Los Angeles, where skyscrapers poked up through the pollution. To the northeast, I could make out the Hollywood Sign and the golden domes of the Griffith Observatory, landmarks from a time when the air was clean and the vistas uncluttered and suburban sprawl hadn't yet turned Southern California into a concrete-and-asphalt wasteland. Just below us was Runyon Canyon Park, a rare urban landscape of wild chaparral, palms, pine, eucalyptus, and other vegetation that had survived from the thirties, when a private mansion had been built there. The overgrown ruins of an old Lloyd Wright house once occupied by Errol Flynn could still be found on the grounds, if one knew where to look. I could see hikers and joggers on the trails, and unleashed dogs bounding around with their owners, which was permitted, and helmeted bikers pedaling determinedly up Runyon Canyon Road in their colorful Spandex outfits, the zealous outdoor types desperate for open space and breathing room, if only for a stolen hour or two in their otherwise anxious, overly scheduled lives.

"Quite a view you've got up here," I said.

Holt went rigid from the shoulders down, while his head swiveled in my direction with a startled look. When he saw it was me, the rest of his body came slowly around while his pale yellow eyes grew wide. In the cruel light of day, his surgically enhanced face looked even more grotesque. The peroxide hair didn't help; neither did the makeup he'd applied in a futile attempt to bring some color to his pasty complexion. His undeveloped chest was nearly hairless, with a few wispy strands sprouting around his small, pink nipples. When he was considerably younger, I thought, he'd probably been regarded as appealing by certain older men with money who doted on slim, vaguely pretty types who knew how to ply their ambisexual looks and calculated charm. But that was before time and desperation had transformed Holt into what he looked like now: an aging eunuch obsessed with turning back the clock.

His alarmed reaction didn't last long. He quickly regained control, smiling hospitably.

"Benjamin Justice. What a pleasant surprise!"

"Is it?"

"Of course!" His manner became sly, and a little smug. "An old friend, coming up for a visit. Unexpected, but certainly not unwelcome." He added carefully, "Though I wasn't aware I'd given you my address when I saw you at the bookstore recently. How did you happen to come by it, anyway?"

I decided to lie, wanting to keep him off-balance and hoping he'd forgotten the letter he'd sent me eighteen years ago.

"I found it in the phone book."

His eyes narrowed with suspicion. "That's not possible. I haven't been listed for years."

"It was listed under Silvio Galiano's name. I found it in an old directory, at the downtown library. They keep them archived. It's an old reporter's trick."

That seemed to please him. He perked up.

"You knew about Silvio and me?"

"It wasn't exactly a secret, was it? As I recall, you two were quite an item."

"You went to a lot of trouble to find me. Why the sudden interest?"

"I felt we should have a talk, get to know each other better."

"Nothing would please me more!" He set the machete aside and pulled off his gloves. "I'm single again, you know."

"You and Galiano split up?"

"You didn't know? Silvio passed on, some years ago. Thankfully, we were able to share eight wonderful years together before he died."

"When was that exactly?"

"So many questions, for someone who wouldn't give me the time of day at his book signing." He laughed self-consciously. "Or should I say, the time of night?"

"You aroused my curiosity, Jason. I want to know more about you."

Holt stepped toward me, close enough that I picked up the scent of cologne and powder wafting off him. His eyes roved my face and stole glances at my upper body.

"Silvio passed on in 1997," he said, finally connecting with my eyes. "You must have seen something about it in the papers. I was mentioned in several of the obituaries, although they apparently hadn't done their homework. They could have at least made note of my film career, instead of just 'companion.'"

"Still acting, are you?"

"Not so much anymore. The business isn't kind as we actors mature. Even more difficult for women, of course. My aunt,

Victoria Faith, hardly worked at all as she got older, until she landed a part on the soaps as a dowager."

"Victoria Faith?"

"Surely you've heard of her. She was quite famous at one time."

"I guess talent runs in the family."

"Why, thank you, Benjamin!"

I glanced around at the once opulent property.

"And Galiano left all this to you?"

"The house and everything else. Why not? I was devoted to him."

My eyes strayed to the morning-glory vines creeping along the wall, out of control. He'd placed the machete on top, next to his gloves, easily within his reach.

"You do your own gardening, do you?"

"My gardener wasn't up to my standards. I had to let him go."

"You're sure it wasn't a problem with your finances?"

"Why all the questions?" His manner took another shift, becoming coy. "Are you really all that interested in me, Benjamin? After all these years?"

"I'm interested in learning more about the person who's been sending me some correspondence recently."

His coyness evaporated. His eyes flickered anxiously.

"Correspondence?"

"Postcards, with offensive messages."

I pinned him with my eyes, letting him sweat. A drop of perspiration hung on his pointy chin a moment, then fell and formed a slow rivulet between his fuchsia nipples.

Finally, he said hurriedly, "I have no idea what you're talking about. I certainly haven't sent you anything like that."

"I don't like the weird game you're playing, Jason."

"Game?"

"The little performance you put on the other night at the bookstore. This fantasy you've concocted about being close to me in the past."

His nostrils flared; he raised his moist chin.

"It's certainly no game."

"Listen, Holt. Or Barclay Simpkins, or whatever your name is. I don't know you, and I don't want to know you. Can I make it any plainer than that?"

He shook his head in bewilderment. "You're still in denial, aren't you?"

I felt my jaw clench and my hands ball into fists. I willed myself to relax. "Denial about *what*, Jason?"

He reached out for me, but I brushed his hand roughly away.

"Your feelings for me," he said, "the way you treated me back in college." His voice became urgent, imploring. "I understand, Benjamin. It must have been difficult for you, the position you were in, your prominence on campus. Really, I do."

I was tempted to tell him how pathetic he was. Instead, I asked, "We were in the same class?"

"Actually, I was a year ahead of you. To look at me, you'd never know it, would you? I delayed graduation an extra year, hoping you might—"

"Notice you?"

"You were dating that woman, Cheryl Zarimba, that Polish girl." He said it as if he were spitting poison from his tongue. "She never really cared about you, you know. Not like I did."

"You knew Cheryl?"

"I made a point of meeting her and gaining her confidence. Sure, she thought you were a real catch. But it was just a passing fancy. My feelings were so much deeper."

"Without even knowing me?"

"I knew you, Benjamin, even if you ignored me. I arranged my life to be close to you. My major was zoology, which put most of my classes on the other side of campus from the journalism school. But I volunteered to sell advertising for the campus newspaper, just so I could be near you. When you were on deadline, writing one of your articles, I used to bring you coffee. Black, just the way you liked it. In that heavy mug you always drank from, the red one everyone knew not to touch, because you'd claimed it for yourself."

It was true. I'd always taken my coffee black, and always in the same red mug, which I'd finally smashed against a wall in a tirade over something or other. So he was telling the truth, I thought. He *had* known me, or at least he'd been around back then.

"I'd set the mug on the upper right corner of your desk," he went on, "just where you liked it, where you wouldn't spill it on your precious copy. You'd mumble a thank-you, but you'd barely look up."

"I was a bit full of myself in college. I apologize for that."

I was surprised that I felt a twinge of sympathy for him. He was clearly obsessed and apparently lonely. Hating him suddenly felt petty and wrong, and smacking him around seemed counterproductive.

"I'm sorry, Jason. I simply don't remember you. Why don't we leave it at that, shall we?"

But my softer tone seemed only to spur his hope.

"I went to all your wrestling matches," he said, growing excited. "Afterward, I'd wait outside the locker room until you came out, just to tell you how much I admired you." Again, chameleon-like, he changed his tone, growing bitter. "But you'd walk right past me as if you didn't notice me. I'd hear you and your jock buddies laughing. I knew you were laughing at me, but I didn't care. I loved you, anyway, even though you were unbelievably cruel."

"You can't love someone you don't know, Jason."

"What would you know about love? Your boy toy, Jacques, the disco queen who got the disease he deserved? You call that love?"

No one had ever spoken that way to me about Jacques, not to my face. I smacked Holt hard across the cheek with my open palm, nearly knocking him down. For a moment, it occurred to me that he might go for the machete, even use it. Instead, he placed a hand over his reddening face, narrowed his eyes, and squeezed out his words slowly.

"You haven't changed a bit, have you, Benjamin?"

His hand lingered on his face, as if he savored the sting I'd delivered, happy just to have me touch him. The fingers of his other hand strayed self-adoringly to one of his pouting nipples, in a fondling gesture that repulsed me. He turned his head slightly, lifting his chin, as if to show me his good side.

"Even now," he went on, "you still can't admit that you were enchanted with me, and probably still are."

I shuddered volubly.

"Can you really afford to be so picky, Benjamin? Not many quality men like me care to hook up with HIV positives."

"I'm going now, Jason. I'm warning you, the hate mail needs to stop."

I turned, crossed the barren lawn, and retraced my steps along the overgrown path, ducking to avoid cobwebs. I could hear Holt's footsteps behind me and instinctively glanced back, thinking of the machete.

"Be careful," he said. "The webs are everywhere. There are spiders all over this property. I've always been fascinated by them, you know. In college, they were my special field of study."

I didn't answer him, just kept walking to the street. Holt followed, chatting amiably as I climbed into the Mustang.

"I suppose you could call me if you'd like," he said. "I've kept the same number all these years, only the area code now is three-two-three. Or perhaps I'll call you. We could do lunch. My treat."

I drove away without another word, realizing he'd never asked for my phone number. Probably because he already knew it, like so much else about me.

FOURTEEN

I returned to find Fred sitting alone on the back patio, watching the doves. Maurice was out shopping for groceries, so I pulled up a chair to keep Fred company for a while.

He was shirtless in the July heat, dressed in a pair of old sweatpants that were baggy on him now. I was reminded how much his once beefy arms and chest had shrunk and sagged, how flaccid the muscles had become, how the physical man he'd been was disappearing before our eyes day by day.

Fred rarely talked much, but that afternoon he was thoughtful and reflective. He spoke of all the doves he and Maurice had watched come into the world and then leave the nest over the years. He wondered if the birds we'd seen returning to the same nesting spot year after year were descended from the original pair decades ago, if that was how their instinct worked, the ritual and location imprinted into their DNA.

"I'd like to think they're all related," he said, scratching the white stubble on his jowl. "We've enjoyed having them, Maurice and me. Some people don't like 'em, I guess. They can make a mess. Hell, that's what hoses are for."

"You and Maurice never kept birds yourself, though."

He looked at me with something like reproach. "Cage a bird? Clip its wings?" He shook his head with disgust. "Never did understand how anyone could do that. Birds were meant to fly, not be kept captive in a damn cage for someone's amusement."

He was seized by a coughing fit that left him worn-out and in pain. I went into the house and came back with a glass of water.

"Getting old sucks," he said, and took a few sips.

I sat down again and we watched the doves in silence. Up on the wire, the father flapped his wings while the two chicks, now half-grown, perched awkwardly on the edge of the nest, mimicking his movements. Fred finally dozed off, wheezing audibly. He was still napping when Maurice returned and quietly took my place.

As I climbed the stairs, rising closer to the power line, the father dove flew off until I was inside and the screen door was closed behind me. Then he settled back on the wire and resumed the lesson, preparing the two chicks for the moment when they'd attempt their first flight.

Maurice had made a new file for me, slugged the folder with Jason Holt's name, and left it upstairs next to my computer. Inside the folder was the letter Holt had sent me eighteen years ago, along with the postcards I'd received in recent weeks. I scribbled a few notes from my conversation with Holt that included the names Silvio Galiano and Victoria Faith, added the notes to the folder, and switched on my PC.

I started with Galiano, using his name as my keyword in a Google search. A few dozen links turned up, mostly to Web sites and texts dealing with Hollywood history, which reaffirmed what Maurice had already told me, that Galiano had been a top interior designer in his day, numbering among his clients some of Hollywood's most famous stars. Here and there, photos accompanied the texts, showing a slender, dapper, dark-haired man who grew thicker and grayer as he moved into his later years, without losing his debonair demeanor. I also found a number of news stories and obituaries mentioning his death from a fall at his Hollywood Hills home on April 14, 1997, when he was seventy-nine years old. Holt was mentioned in one piece as Galiano's "companion," in another as his "partner of eight years." According to the news reports, Holt had returned home to find Galiano's body on a rocky embankment sixty feet below the east-facing wall of the house, just off the patio. That would have been the low wall I'd peered over earlier that day, with its smoggy view across the L.A. basin. The accounts mentioned Galiano's age and frail health, implying that he'd apparently fallen while he was alone and unsteady on his feet.

My next search keyed on Holt's aunt, Victoria Faith. According to an entry in Wikipedia, the online encyclopedia, she was not quite the famous actress Holt had made her out to be, though she'd started out with promise. She'd been a starlet in the late thirties and early forties who'd had a few prominent roles in B movies before fading into near obscurity, like thousands of other talented actors who fail to capture the public's fancy or land the key role that turns out to be the break they need. By the fifties she was taking small parts in television, something she continued to do with less frequency. Her career had something of a rebirth in the seventies, when she landed the prominent role on a daytime soap that Holt had mentioned, which probably accounted for her Wikipedia entry. In the late nineties, pushing eighty, she'd retired to the nonprofit Motion Picture & Television Country House in Woodland Hills. There was no mention of a husband or children, so I assumed she'd never married.

Finally, I turned to Jason Holt himself. He'd mentioned his work in movies, so I logged on to iActor, the online casting service of the Screen Actors Guild, where the union's members were able to upload their head shots, résumés, and video and audio clips to create individual profiles. My search turned up a few other actors with the last name of Holt but none with the first name of Jason. Nor was he listed anywhere in the Internet movie database, IMDb.com. So I abandoned the computer and used the phone, calling SAG directly and asking for Holt's credits. After a quick check, the woman on the line informed me that Jason Holt was no longer a SAG member. When I pressed for a lead on Holt's agent, she became terse and a bit sharp, repeating what she'd just told me, and offering no further information.

I hung up, returned to the computer, Googled Holt's name, and came up with numerous links. Quite a few were keyed to the obits on Silvio Galiano that I'd already seen, so I ignored those. But one link in particular drew my attention. Holt's name was included in a partial excerpt from an article attributed to a blog known as DishtheDirt.com, something to do with a scam in which several people had fraudulently gained membership in SAG. I double-clicked on the link and it opened directly to an online investigative piece about the scam. According to the article, which seemed well sourced, a number of men and women had qualified for SAG membership by making brief appearances in movies produced or directed by relatives or friends—scenes that were never used. This allowed the imposters to claim film credits, maintain their SAG standing, and continue to enjoy the generous benefits that came with union membership. The most prominent of the poseurs was a venerable trade paper social columnist, but Holt's name was also mentioned, which explained why SAG had expelled him. He apparently wasn't the successful actor he pretended to be. Given his grossly inflated view of himself, I wasn't all that surprised.

Impressed by the reporting in the article, I hit the link for the home page to learn more about DishtheDirt.com. To my disappointment, it opened to a flashy page overloaded with advertising pop-ups and various headlines promising all kinds of sordid and sensational stories, most of them connected to Hollywood celebrities. As I scrolled down through the graphics, I found a few noncelebrity pieces in the mix, all of them featuring heavy doses of sex, drugs, or violence.

I was about to sign off when I came to a video frame slugged "Shocking Video of the Day" that stopped me cold. I saw my own image on the screen—a freeze-frame from the video a passerby had shot of my altercation with Lance, presumably the same one that had been sent to Detective Haukness. Underneath the image was a brief text.

Benjamin Justice, a disgraced journalist with a new book (*Deep Background*) out about the scandal that ruined him, kicks the crap out of a skinhead in West Hollywood. Exclusive footage from a DishtheDirt.com member, captured with a cell phone. Double-click on the controller button to see this real-life bloodbath from start to finish!

I double-clicked and the video started running. It was on the grainy side, but the identity of the two combatants was unmistakable. I watched Lance reach up to touch my face, then my reaction as I slipped a single leg, held him airborne for a moment, and threw him to the ground. I was like a wild animal, ferocious, out of control. Watching myself like that was like watching another person, a person I didn't want to be. If this was the same video Haukness had mentioned, and it apparently was, I understood why the Sheriff's Department was considering assault charges against me.

I glanced at the posting date: The video had gone up on the blog the previous hour, during the time it had taken me to drive home from Holt's place, which explained why I'd heard nothing about it. I knew how the Internet worked: When the video's time was up on the home page, it would remain in the Web site's archives, virtually forever, uploaded, downloaded, and replayed by other media and countless Internet visitors, replicated like metastasizing cancer cells.

I was watching it a second time when the phone rang. It was Judith Zeitler, reminding me that I had two bookstore readings over the weekend and a final interview with Cathryn Conroy after that. Judith asked me what I was doing and I told her. Within seconds she was connected to DishtheDirt.com on her laptop, shrieking ecstatically as she viewed the video.

"Benjamin, this is awesome! Why didn't you tell me about this when it first happened? I could have gotten you on the evening news! You captured a dangerous criminal single-handed!"

"If this is news, Judith, then we're all in trouble."

"If it bleeds, it leads. Do you know how many hits DishtheDirt .com gets each day?"

"I have no idea."

"Well, neither do I. But it's a lot, I can tell you that. By the time the rest of the cybermafia picks this up, millions of people are going to see it. Do you know what this could do for your book sales?"

"I doubt that many people who log on to these sites are interested in reading a memoir by a repentant journalist."

"Who cares if they read it, as long as they buy it?"

"Judith, you're making me seriously depressed."

"If I'm going to get you a major publicity break, Benjamin, you're going to have to work with me." In the background, I could hear her hitting keys. "I'm e-mailing the producer at *Jerry Rivers Live* as we speak. Jerry loves to build an interview around video, especially if it's violent."

"If it's all the same, Judith, I'd rather not—"

"What's the story on the skinhead you beat up? I see tattoos. This is good. He's probably a gang member, right?"

"Actually, he's an ex-Marine. An Iraq war veteran."

"That's even better! Soldiers are so in right now. Do you think you can get him for the show?"

"Frankly, if I never see him again, it'll be too soon."

"Maybe we can find him through the police department."

"I'm going to hang up now, Judith, before I become physically ill."

"Call me when you get hold of him, will you? Tell him he'll get a free trip to New York out of it, and two nights in a nice hotel. Or else we can put him on the phone, and do a live video feed from here."

"Good-bye, Judith."

I hung up and logged off, unable to watch the video again. Maybe it would account for a few sales, I thought. But at what cost to my privacy and peace of mind?

I was beginning to question whether getting my memoir published was worth the trouble. What's that old saying? Let sleeping dogs lie. With the publication of *Deep Background*, it seemed, I'd stirred up a whole pack of snarling dogs, and I wondered what it would take to get the hellhounds off my heels.

FIFTEEN

As the days passed, one of the baby doves worked up enough courage to perch on the edge of the nest, while its sibling huddled behind, barely visible. The two adult birds were nowhere in sight, which was all part of the plan. Fred, Maurice, and I watched from the patio as we so often had in past years, Maurice serving as the cheerleader.

"Go, go, go," he whispered.

The half-grown bird flapped its wings tentatively a few times. Then it suddenly lifted off, flying as far as the limb of a nearby purple plum. It stayed within the leafy protection of the tree for several minutes, flapping with more vigor as it grew bolder. Then it alighted again, flying up to the power line where its father had spent so many hours serving as a beacon. For a moment, it sat there, exposed and vulnerable, while we thought about the neighborhood hawk that sometimes swooped from the sky to grab a small bird in midair or even a caged parakeet on someone's balcony, seizing the bird with its extended talons and feasting on it through the bars of the cage.

A few tense seconds passed and then the small dove took off again, this time in full flight. Gone.

"One down, one to go," Maurice whispered.

But the other chick stayed where it was, hunkered down in its comfort zone. The father returned later in the day, continuing the flying lessons. The mother replaced him that night, bringing food and watching over the nest. This pattern continued for two more days, until the adults failed to return, leaving the timid chick alone. We thought it might be sick or injured, which caused Maurice no end of consternation. Finally, on Friday morning, forced to fend for itself, the chick gathered its courage and fluttered from the nest, but only far enough to drop softly to the lawn and hop into the shrubbery for cover.

"It's perfectly healthy," Maurice said, "just afraid, poor thing."

There had been a time, many years ago, when Fred would have reminded Maurice that the bird was simply part of the food chain, not to belittle him but to help him accept the reality that the bird might not survive. But Fred had become more sensitive in recent years, and in particular since his health had gone into serious decline.

He urged Maurice to keep the two cats inside the house until the baby bird had finally alighted and taken to the sky. Hour after hour, Fred continued to sit vigil on the patio, until dusk approached and Maurice insisted he come in for the night.

My reading at Book Soup was set for seven-thirty that Thursday evening, my name positioned on the plastic marquee between two Hollywood-connected authors, above the hustle and bustle of the Sunset Strip. Judith Zeitler had reminded me more than once how lucky I was that such a high-profile bookstore had agreed to put me on their events schedule, even if my publisher wasn't willing to pay for a window display.

"Must be a slow week," I told her.

I arrived fifteen minutes early, expecting to face a blast of her usual energy and exuberance. Instead, she appeared downbeat as I approached. I asked her straightaway what was wrong.

"I don't like being the bearer of bad tidings," she said, pursing her lips regretfully. "I wanted Jan Long to be the one to tell you."

"Tell me what?"

Zeitler grimaced.

"Someone's been sending nasty messages in your name to various book reviewers across the country. Very insulting messages."

"How long has this been going on?"

"It started just before your book came out. Jan only learned of it this afternoon. She's planning to call you."

"Wonderful. That might account for some of the more savage reviews, anyway."

"They've turned it over to the legal department for investigation and notified *PW*, which plans to run an article on it, clearing it up."

"Please don't tell me there's no such thing as bad publicity, okay?"

She looked properly chastened. "No, not this time. Benjamin, do you have any idea who might want to hurt you like this?"

"Someone comes to mind," I said.

"Be sure to let Jan know."

We went inside and met the manager, who announced over the PA system that I was about to read from my new book, *Deep Background,* in the annex next door. At half past seven, as I stood behind the podium, my audience consisted of exactly three people: the manager, Judith Zeitler, and a homeless man who'd parked his shopping cart and belongings outside. The manager suggested we wait an extra few minutes for late arrivals and made another announcement over the PA system.

"Don't be discouraged by the small turnout," Judith whispered. "You can't predict these things."

When no one else had shown by a quarter to eight, the manager stepped to the podium and introduced me to the homeless man, who was already dozing. I opened a copy of my book to the epilogue, where I'd marked a passage recounting a Chinese lunch I'd shared with Alexandra Templeton twelve years ago. At the time, we were each deeply suspicious of the other, as she dug relentlessly into my past, attempting to understand me and figure out why I'd self-destructed six years earlier.

" ' "You were seventeen," she said, referring to my fateful last year in Buffalo. "Your name then was Benjamin Osborn."

" 'I reached for the teapot, drew it over, but didn't pour. I just stared at it stupidly, wishing I'd never agreed to be her mentor as a way of settling old debts with Harry Brofsky. When I finally looked over, she had an Eastman Reporter's Notebook open, the same kind I'd used when I worked under Harry at the *LA Times*.

" ' "According to court records in New York City," she said, "you legally changed your name shortly after your eighteenth birthday."

" ' "I took my mother's maiden name, Justice. I thought it would look good on a byline."

" ' "I also came across news accounts from the Buffalo area papers. Accounts of what happened on a Saturday afternoon in late November, in the three-bedroom house where you grew up."

" 'The waitress cleared our plates and disappeared to get the check. Templeton continued scanning her notes.

" ' "Your father was a police detective. Homicide. Quite a good one, when he wasn't drinking."

" ' "So people said."

" ' "Some of your neighbors and teachers thought you might become a cop yourself. If only to please him, win his admiration."

" 'I glanced at a booth across the way, where a little Chinese girl sat on her father's lap, eating chow mein with chopsticks. He was patiently coaxing her, as she repeatedly let the noodles slip back into the bowl.

" 'Templeton continued. "They characterized him as a cold, hard man. He was also violent, mostly at home."

" 'I turned my eyes back to her. "You're stirring up some warm memories, Templeton."

" ' "Your mother was also an alcoholic. But she was a decent person, from all accounts. She tried courageously to keep the family together, took a lot of abuse."

" ' "She believed in keeping up appearances," I said. "Plus, she was Catholic, and considered divorce out of the question. That's not necessarily decency, or courage. Especially when kids are being hurt."

" 'Templeton flipped a page, glancing through her notes. "As you got into your teens, you started fighting back. You were getting bigger, and when you began wrestling in high school, he couldn't beat you up so easily."

" ' "No, it took him a little longer."

" ' "Then, that Saturday, in your senior year, you and your mother went to the store. Your father stayed behind with your little sister, watching football and drinking bourbon while she did her homework. I believe she was eleven at the time."

" ' "She'd just turned eleven," I said. "We'd had a party for her the Saturday before. I've still got a photo."

" ' "On the way to the store, your mother realized she'd forgotten her checkbook. She drove back. As you entered the house, you heard your little sister crying in a rear bedroom."

" ' "So far, so good."

" ' "When you went to check, you found your father molesting her."

" ' "He'd penetrated her. He was halfway in, and still pushing." I saw Templeton wince, which pleased me. "I believe that's called rape."

" 'She swallowed dryly, turned another page, kept going. "You attacked him, pulling him off. Your mother went for the phone, to call the police. He grabbed the phone from her hands, started beating her. Worse than he ever had. He said he'd kill her if she told anyone, kill all of you."

" ' "Correct."

" ' "You tried to keep him away from your mother, but it was impossible. He kept hitting her, while your little sister cowered in a corner, sobbing."

" 'She looked up from her notes, as if seeking my permission to continue.

" ' "Don't stop now, Templeton. You're almost at the best part. The payoff every reporter lives for."

" ' "You ran into the next room." She recited now from memory, abandoning her notes, keeping her eyes on mine. "You grabbed your father's police revolver, raced back, and killed him. You were never charged. It was ruled justifiable homicide."

" 'I smiled grimly. "Don't you just love a happy ending?"

" ' "Four years later, your mother died of cirrhosis of the liver. You were in college then, studying journalism. When she was nineteen, your sister died of a drug overdose. According to an article I read, she was a promising painter."

" ' "Her name was Elizabeth," I said. "Elizabeth Jane. Yes, she was quite a good painter, though she never quite believed it herself."

" 'Templeton slipped her notebook into her handbag. "I'm sorry, Benjamin. I really am."

" 'It was the first time she'd addressed me by my first name.

" ' "Don't be sorry for discovering the truth," I said. "That's what you're trained for. It's the career you chose. You'd better get used to it."

" 'The waitress brought the check, thanking us in broken English. Then she went away again.

" ' "You have no reason to feel any shame about what you did," Templeton said. "You shouldn't have to carry that kind of pain around with you anymore."

" 'She meant well, but I was tempted to laugh; she was so young and saw things so simply. She leaned toward me and covered my hand with hers. I drew mine away.

" ' "He raped your little sister, Benjamin. He almost killed your mother. You had every right to shoot him."

" 'I smiled, which was unfortunate.

" ' "I didn't shoot my father, Templeton."

" 'She gave me a curious look.

" ' "I emptied his revolver into him. Then I beat him with the butt end of it until his face was a bloody pulp and I couldn't stand to hear my mother screaming anymore." ' "

I'd intended to read more but couldn't stomach the rest, so I stopped. Zeitler and the manager looked stunned and sickened. The homeless man snored audibly. Seeing the look on Zeitler's face, I realized she hadn't read the book, at least not all the way through. I suddenly felt bone weary, disillusioned, and painfully ridiculous.

"I'd be happy to sign a copy for anyone who wants one," I said.

The manager suggested I sign only ten copies of stock. I understood the unspoken subtext of that: Don't sign more because we'll probably be sending the rest back.

Zeitler offered me a ride home, but I told her I'd walk, since Norma Place was only a few blocks down the hill and the exercise would do me good.

I trudged home in a deep funk, thinking about all the crap that had come down on me in recent weeks. At one point in my life, when I was young and ambitious, my most fervent desire had been to one day see my first book published. I suppose I'd looked at it as an event that would somehow change my life, a milestone that would catapult my career to a new level, a magic elixir that would make everything right.

Be careful what you wish for, I thought.

I arrived home to find the mother dove in the backyard, feeding her chick on a garden bench. In the moonlight, I could see seed husks and droppings on the velvety lawn beneath the slats. I was approaching the stairs quietly, to avoid disturbing the birds, when I heard the back door open and turned to see Maurice step from the house. He was dressed in his robe and bunny slippers, his white hair contained in a hairnet for the night. He motioned me silently to join him on the driveway.

"I didn't know if I should call the police," he said, "or if you'd want to handle it yourself."

I had no idea what he was talking about, and said so.

"Your car, Benjamin. Didn't you see it as you came in?"

He led me to the end of the drive, where the Mustang was parked at the curb fifteen or twenty feet beyond the house. Someone had vandalized it savagely. The tires were slashed and flattened, the cherry red paint job ruined with acid that was still smoking, the convertible top sliced open, the tuck-and-roll upholstery ripped to shreds. The word *FAG* had been spray-painted across the windshield. I'd bought the Mustang twenty-odd years ago with the first real money I'd made as a journalist, in part because Jacques had considered it such a cool car. He'd loved riding around beside me with the top down on Sunday afternoons while Queen's "We Are the Champions" blasted from the speakers, in those fading years of gay liberation, as a plague descended on us like a mass of locusts from a darkening sky. It wasn't the material value of the car that mattered to me; it was the memories. Whoever had done this, I thought, knew more about me than they had a right to.

Be careful what you wish for.

I thanked Maurice for pointing out the damage and told him I'd notify the authorities on my own.

SIXTEEN

I waited until morning to report the vandalism.

I didn't know if Jason Holt was responsible, or the skinhead named Lance, or someone else entirely. Without a witness to the act, I didn't expect the cops to pin the crime on any one person, or even to investigate it. But there was the matter of insurance, and I knew my carrier would insist on a police report.

I found the same deputy behind the desk who'd given me a form to fill out the previous time. I told him why I was there and that I had two possible suspects in mind, though I couldn't prove that either one had done it. The fact that the word *fag* had been used got the desk officer's attention, since it suggested a hate crime. He took my name and contact information and told me a deputy would call and arrange a visit, to see the damage for himself and take photographs. Before I left, I asked about the copy of the police report I'd requested when I'd been in before, the one involving the incident with Lance. The deputy didn't remember anything about it until I filled him in on a few details.

"It's going through channels," he said, already busy with something else.

I raised my voice. "That's what you told me last time."

He looked up from what he was doing and a moment passed

while his eyes did that cop thing—sizing me up fast, calculating how best to deal with me.

Then he said evenly, "You'll have to be patient, Mr. Justice. We're a busy department."

"I'm being stalked," I said. "Someone's dismantling my life, piece by piece." I slammed the flat of my hand on the counter. "I want that damn report!"

"You need to relax, Mr. Justice."

A sergeant appeared through a rear door to address the deputy, but he had his eyes on me. "Is there a problem out here?"

"It's Benjamin Justice," the deputy said, as if my name was well-known around the station.

"Yes, I know," the sergeant said.

"No offense," I said, "but you don't know crap."

"You need to calm down," the sergeant said.

"You've been talking to Haukness, haven't you? Before he got reassigned, he warned you guys about me. That I'm a hothead, with a troubled past. Something like that?"

"He showed us a certain video." The sergeant spoke without a trace of judgment or feeling, which infuriated me even more.

I started to say something I would have regretted, suggesting an orifice where he could shove the item in question. Instead, I said quietly, "I have a right to see that report. And I need to file a complaint about the vandalism to my car."

"We can certainly help you with that," the deputy said, sounding like an overly polite actor in a sheriff's academy training film. "Why don't you go home, get all your evidence in order, and a deputy will call to arrange a time to come by. If you wish, you can mention this other harassment at the same time."

"I'll do that."

As I turned away, I caught the deputy and his sergeant exchanging a look but decided to keep my mouth shut. I stepped outside to the sound of traffic on nearby Santa Monica Boulevard, embarrassed that I'd behaved like a jackass but still simmering. Not because of the two cops but because someone out there knew how to rattle my cage and was doing a very good job of it.

As I strode up Hilldale, I kept thinking about something the anonymous caller had said late in the night after my reading at A Different Light: *I've killed before, just like you. So, you see, we have more in common than you might realize.*

At the time, I'd assumed it was a hollow boast designed to pique my interest for some reason, or simply trouble or confuse me. A taunt by some nutcase who'd gotten Maurice's phone number and had known about the party. Maybe someone who hadn't been invited and was unhappy about it. Now, I wasn't so sure.

By the time I got home, my brain was churning with possibilities. I called Templeton and told her I needed to meet with Lawrence Kase, that I wanted to look at some LAPD documents going back eleven years and that Kase was the only person I knew who might have access. I figured he'd fight me on it, I said, so I didn't want to ask him over the phone, which would make it too easy for him to brush me off. I added that it would be nice if she could be there, to temper the situation. She said they were both on tight schedules—the actual phrase she used was "terribly busy"—with her book due out shortly and their wedding coming up.

"You haven't got five minutes for an old friend?"

She was silent a moment while the guilt sank in. Then she said, "Come by for lunch. But no promises regarding Larry. He still thinks you're a loose cannon."

With the Mustang trashed, I borrowed Maurice's vintage Nash Metropolitan, which had been sitting in the garage for years, rarely used because of his diminished eyesight and reflexes. It wasn't exactly my style—a turquoise and white subcompact convertible that looked more like a kiddie car than an automobile—but I was happy to have wheels just then. I got the engine to kick over by pushing the Metropolitan out the drive, down the street, and then down Hilldale, jumping in to pop the clutch as it picked up speed. It hiccupped a few times, but the engine turned over and ten minutes later I was cruising out Third Street with the top down, on my way to Hancock Park.

Like Templeton, Kase came from money, although his was older. He owned a big place on South Muirfield in the area where the wealthiest Angelenos had started building their homes in the 1920s. It was just up the street from the stately house the popular singer Nat King Cole had lived in with his family in the late forties, when someone had burned the word *nigger* in their front lawn. The Kase house was one of those brick-and-timber English-style structures with a pitched roof, dormer windows on the second floor, two tall English chimneys, and formal gardens in the front and back. If you wanted to own a home that looked down its nose at the rest of the world without seeming too ostentatious about it, the Kase place would have been a good choice.

Templeton greeted me at the front door and whisked me quickly through the house and into a rear garden. Kase joined us a minute later, moments before a live-in cook began serving lunch. They weren't wasting any time.

"My mother's coming by at two," Templeton explained. "We're going shopping for my wedding gown."

"I'll get right to the point then," I said.

"Alex tells me you need some kind of documents," Kase said, doing it for me.

He had an excellent record as a prosecutor—extremely high conviction rate, no malfeasance that he'd been caught at—and had once been thought of as a potential candidate for the elected position of top D.A., and maybe higher office after that. But the political winds had blown another direction and now he was apparently content to marry a gorgeous woman fifteen years his junior, start a second family after an earlier divorce, and retire as soon as possible. I admired the fact that he had the balls to marry a black woman, given his uppity white background and breeding, but beyond that I didn't like him very much, and it pained me to have to ask a favor of him.

"I've been having a problem with a certain individual," I said, "and I'd like to know as much about him and his past as possible."

Without naming Jason Holt, I explained the onslaught of

harassment that had been directed at me since late June—the ominous phone call, the hate mail, the messages to book critics, the vandalism to my Mustang.

"I've also been having some problems with a skinhead," I said, "a Marine vet who rides a big chopper. Maybe he's involved in some way, maybe not. Either way, I need to get to the bottom of it, starting with what I already know."

Unsurprisingly, Kase suggested I contact the police. I told him I'd already done that but that I wanted to do some investigating on my own.

He paused as his gleaming gold fork hovered above his Waldorf salad.

"What exactly is it that you want from me?"

"I'd like to see the police files from the investigation into the death of Silvio Galiano in 1997."

"That name sounds vaguely familiar," Templeton said.

"You were a cub reporter at the *Sun*," I said. "It wasn't too long after Harry had introduced us. Galiano was a hotshot interior designer, had a lot of celebrity clients."

Kase looked over as he speared some salad, sounding mildly interested. "This was a homicide?"

"It was apparently ruled an accidental fall. There were no arrests or charges, not that I found in old news accounts."

"But you have some suspicions."

"I'm curious to know more."

He dabbed his mouth with a linen napkin.

"May I be frank with you, Justice?"

"Please."

"You have a reputation for trouble. I'm not telling you anything you don't know."

"I've kept my nose clean for several years now."

He glanced over at Templeton. They exchanged a look.

"Except for that incident that was caught on video," I added, "which I imagine you've seen, or at least heard about."

"I've seen it," Kase said. "I'm surprised you weren't charged with assault."

"You checked to see if I was arrested?"

"Alex asked me to make an inquiry."

"For your sake, Benjamin," Templeton said quickly. "In case you needed our help." Then, to Kase, she said, "You could pull the initial police report and the final detective's report, Larry. That wouldn't be too much trouble, would it?"

She reached over and laid her slender hand on his big paw. It seemed to have a transforming effect on him. He smiled at her touch, and I saw his tension ebb a little. He cleared his throat, then sipped some iced tea.

"I suppose I could have someone in my office pull the file. Discreetly, of course."

"And if Benjamin turns up something," Templeton went on, her voice as smooth and sweet as warm syrup, "I'm sure he'd let you know. You could have the case reactivated. Who knows? It might be a nice investigation to retire on, a final feather in your cap."

"I'll see what I can do," Kase said, without quite looking at me.

"I'd appreciate it," I said, and reached for my salad fork.

On my way home, I stopped by Buff for a workout, concentrating on my lats and pecs. After that, I dropped into Capitol Drugs to pick up my HIV meds, along with a renewed prescription of testosterone. From there, I hit Boy Meets Grill for a burger to supplement the light lunch I'd eaten at Templeton's and pack in more protein after my workout. By the time I got back to the house, dusk was settling over Norma Place.

As I reached the top of the drive, adjacent to the rear patio, I saw Fred dozing in his chair. In the same instant, I became aware of a commotion across the yard and sensed instinctively what was happening. I dashed across the lawn, clapping my hands and chasing away the black cat. The baby dove sat hunched and motionless on the grass at the edge of the shrubs. I bent to pick it up and could see that it was still alive, without any visible wounds.

But it didn't resist or try to get away, either, and I knew I was too late.

I lifted the little bird in the palm of my hand. It looked up at me with its dark, round eyes, and blinked once. Then its small, beaked head fell forward on a limp neck to rest against its chest. It didn't move again. I'm sure that had I looked, I could have found puncture marks deep in its feathers, where the cat had crushed it in its jaws, but I didn't bother. I was more concerned with breaking the news to Maurice and Fred.

Fred woke as I was laying the dead bird on the bench, where I felt we should leave it for an evening or two, so the mother could find it and understand that she didn't need to keep returning night after night. Maurice saw me from the kitchen window and came out, helping Fred cross the lawn to join me. I told them what had happened and that I wished I'd arrived home a minute or two earlier.

"If only the little fellow had found the courage to fly when it was time," Maurice said.

The feral cat crept back into view on the back fence, watching us closely. I turned on the hose and gave him a good squirt, sending him scurrying, and figured we wouldn't see him again.

The mother dove returned after dark, bringing more food. She settled in a flutter of wings on the bench beside her chick and attempted to push seeds into its closed beak. After a while, she gave up trying to feed it and simply sat there, patient and watchful and probably confused. Hour after hour she maintained her vigil, never budging, waiting for some sign of life from her chick. Finally, late that night, I heard the squeaking of her wings as she flew off. There would be no more doves in the nest that summer, as if word had gotten out that this place was no longer the safe haven it once had been.

Maurice and Fred buried the baby dove in the morning, in the shade of a hydrangea abloom with globular blue flowers.

I watched from my upstairs kitchen window as they kneeled in the soil, using a hand spade to dig the hole, lay the chick gently in, then cover the grave back up. When they were done, Maurice put an arm around Fred, their heads bowed together, touching at the temples.

I could see their shoulders shaking and suspected they were weeping for more than just that little bird.

SEVENTEEN

My final reading was scheduled for that night at Skylight Books in Los Feliz, on a trendy, bustling stretch of North Vermont Avenue. Ismael was going to be there and we'd planned on dinner afterward, which would be our first real date.

I drove over in Maurice's little Metro and circled the neighborhood a few times before a space opened up in a public lot behind the Los Feliz 3, a venerable neighborhood theater that had gone multiplex to survive. According to the old deco marquee, the theater was featuring a Todd Haynes revival that included a double bill of *Poison* and *Far from Heaven,* films that couldn't be more different in style yet seemed like ideal, if unsettling, companion pieces. Along the sidewalk, animated young people in couples or small groups were noshing or sipping coffee while others sat alone, looking like they wished they weren't. Seeing the self-conscious loners with their faces buried in books or copies of *LA Weekly,* sneaking furtive but hopeful glances at passing strangers, made me glad I wasn't in my twenties anymore.

Judith Zeitler met me in front of the bookstore, took me inside, and introduced me to Noel Alumit, a young novelist with handsome, bronze Filipino looks, who was also Skylight's events planner. I looked around but didn't see Ismael. Alumit and I chatted a bit and I purchased a copy of his latest novel, *Talking to the*

Moon. Zeitler had suggested I buy a book wherever I was invited to read to show my support for the bookseller, but Alumit's bedroom eyes probably had something to do with it too. He signed the title page, asked me to sign a copy of *Deep Background* for him, and introduced me to a decent crowd of about fifteen people. I scanned the rows of folding chairs but couldn't find Ismael.

For my final scheduled reading, I'd selected a particularly pungent passage from the epilogue, but I was no longer sure it was the right choice. It detailed the turning point between Templeton and me twelve years ago as she'd laid out her theory about why I'd self-destructed as a journalist. She'd forced me to finally face the truth that day, not just about the Pulitzer mess but about its connection to Jacques as well.

As I opened my book to the marked page, I felt my gut constrict and my face flush. I suddenly had doubts that I could go through with it, reading to an audience of strangers. Even after all these years, my feelings were too raw. I felt too exposed, too vulnerable. Better to read something safer, I thought.

I was about to turn to another chapter when I saw Ismael hurry in from the street. He took a chair near the back, found my eyes, and shrugged apologetically. Seeing him there buoyed my confidence; I suddenly felt less alone, and reading the passage no longer worried me as much. I would read my words to Ismael, I told myself, and it would be okay. I set up the passage for the audience, filling in some background, and started in.

" ' "When you wrote that AIDS series," Templeton said, "I believe you created the two lovers as a way of idealizing a personal situation that was too painful for you to handle."

" ' "This isn't really the time," I said.

" ' "When will it be time, Justice? So you go on like you are for years, drinking yourself slowly to death, alienated from everyone and everything, because you don't have the courage to face the truth and move on?"

" 'I turned to walk out but she moved around me and blocked the door.

" ' "Jacques' death left you consumed with guilt, didn't it?"

" ' "You didn't know him," I said. "Stop using his name as if you did."

" ' "I think that to this day you feel you didn't love him enough, didn't do enough to save him. That you weren't there for him emotionally the way he'd always been there for you. Because you didn't know how. Because you were too afraid."

" 'Volatile feelings rose inside me, but I knew they were driven more by fear than fury. I worried that I might slap her to make her stop and shoved my hands deep in my pockets.

" ' "Maurice told me you did your best," she went on. "Taking care of Jacques, tending to his physical needs. Feeding him, bathing him, cleaning up his vomit."

" 'I clamped my eyes shut, unwilling to see it all again. "Yes, I took care of his physical needs."

" ' "But you couldn't tell him you loved him, could you?"

" 'Like any good investigative reporter, she'd prepared herself well; she knew the answers before she asked the questions. It was how reporters, like skillful prosecutors and defense attorneys, pushed their prey deeper and deeper into a corner.

" ' "No," I said, "I couldn't tell him that."

" ' "You couldn't hold him the way he needed to be held. You couldn't be his lover in the truest sense of the word. Not in those final months. Getting that close terrified you, because you knew you were losing him."

" 'Bravo, I thought. I've mentored you well.

" ' "But the worst moment was yet to come, wasn't it, Benjamin?"

" 'She recounted the last hour of Jacques' life, almost minute by minute, when he'd known he was dying of Pneumocystitis and continually asked a nurse named Amelia Tomayo where I was, until she'd lowered the oxygen mask over his face for the final time.

" ' "You found Amelia Tomayo," I said.

" ' "She still works at County. She spoke to me, off the record."

" ' "Nice work, Templeton."

" ' "When Jacques died, you were on assignment. At the moment he needed you most, you were in the Hall of Records, digging through documents related to a slumlord case."

" ' "Yes, I was in the Hall of Records."

" ' "You could have been at the hospital. Harry would have given you time off. All the time you needed."

" ' "Of course."

" ' "But you didn't ask for time off."

" ' "No."

" ' "Why, Benjamin? Because you couldn't bear to watch Jacques die?"

" ' "I'm not sure any of us really knows why we make certain choices at certain points in our lives. We'd like to think we do, but we don't, not always."

" 'I felt exhausted, sick. I sat on the edge of the Templetons' plush couch, staring at her spotless Berber carpet.

" ' "You'd planned to write a first-person series about you and Jacques, hadn't you? About one man caring for his dying partner. It was a story you felt needed telling."

" 'I nodded.

" ' "But the truth was too painful. When the time came, you couldn't do it, could you?"

" 'She'd beaten me down. I didn't want to fight her anymore. I wanted some peace.

" ' "No," I said.

" ' "So you wrote it the way you wished it had been. You created two fictional men, working with the real feelings you never expressed when Jacques was alive. That's where the power of the writing came from. And that's why it won the Pulitzer."

" ' "There are couples like that all over this city," I said, "thousands of them. All over this country. Tens of thousands. Helping each other die."

" ' "They say there's sometimes more truth in fiction than in fact."

" ' "Is that what they say?"

" 'She sat down beside me. "It's time to forgive yourself, Benjamin."

" 'I turned to look into those remarkable brown eyes of hers, so full of intelligence, as quick to compassion as to anger.

" ' "Have you forgiven me, Templeton? For my transgressions, for the way I disgraced our trade, for the way I hurt you personally by what I did."

" ' "Is it important?"

" 'I shrugged, smiling a little. "It wouldn't hurt." ' "

As I closed the book, Ismael stood, leading the applause. I swallowed hard to get rid of the lump in my throat.

"I'd be happy to take a few questions before I sign books," I said.

I suddenly felt unburdened, lighter and freer than I had in longer than I could remember. Except for a final interview with Cathryn Conroy, my book tour from hell was officially over. And I'd ended it by reading the most difficult passage in *Deep Background* without being overwhelmed by the emotions it stirred up. Putting them down on paper, getting them outside myself, had been therapeutic. Reading the words that night had been a final catharsis, setting the feelings free like releasing memorial balloons into an infinite sky. Without Ismael there, I'm not sure I could have done it. That's how important he was to me. That's how much I trusted him.

The moment I'd finished signing stock, I grabbed him and was out of there like a rocket. The rest of the night was for Ismael and me, and nobody else.

We drove in his Toyota Camry to a Mexican restaurant in nearby Silver Lake that he'd picked out himself. I was surprised by his choice because he was so new to the scene and the restaurant he'd selected was so obviously gay. When the most popular drink in the house is a "Margayrita," you can be pretty sure that its primary clientele is queer.

"How did you find this place?" I asked, as we followed our sashaying host to a booth, past a group of pink-clad mariachis serenading a female couple.

"I may be an almost-forty-year-old virgin," Ismael said, grinning, "but a man still has to eat." He winked. "And have some fun."

Three colorful flags hung above the busy bar—Mexican, U.S., and rainbow—and the murals on the walls offered gender-bending twists on traditional Mexican village scenes. Each dish on the menu was named for a historic GLBT figure or a gay celebrity, from Alexander the Great—the giant burrito grande—to a whitefish special called the Lance Bass. It was all very silly, very camp, which wasn't usually my style. But at the moment it seemed the perfect choice, a great place to let our hair down, forget our troubles, and share our first dinner together, maybe even a kiss.

We held hands across the table by candlelight, like any other couple falling in love, the kind of simple expression of affection that could have gotten us thrown out or hassled by the cops a few decades ago. Ismael told me how moved he'd been by the passage I'd read at Skylight, and how he wished he had the talent to put his thoughts and reflections into words as I did. In turn, I learned about his family: immigrant parents still alive and still married, half a dozen brothers and sisters, relatives scattered throughout the Southwest but always in touch, with a bunch of nieces and nephews among them, and more on the way. Ismael spoke of frequent holiday reunions, of piñatas and music and dancing and laughter, of elderly grandparents held in high esteem and cared for at home by their children, of a shared sense of family history and ethnic pride. It was the kind of close-knit, warmhearted family I'd never known, the kind that seemed like a fantasy, an impossible dream.

"You've come out to them?" I asked.

He nodded. "I started with my sisters, then worked up my courage and told my parents." He laughed. "Telling my brothers was the hardest part. You know, machismo and all that." His smile dimmed. "It wasn't easy, and some of them are having a difficult time with it, especially my parents. More because I gave up the priesthood than the sexual aspect."

"Any regrets?"

He shook his head. "It was something I had to do. Living a lie, carrying that weight—I just couldn't do it anymore."

As I listened to him, losing myself in his deep brown eyes, I felt a rising current of lust, and wondered if Ismael was feeling the same. I couldn't imagine what it was like for a man who'd remained celibate for so long, contemplating his first sexual experience so late in life. Was he anxious? Afraid? Would the shame the Church had ground into him over a lifetime destroy his pleasure when the time finally came for him to fully express his love for another man?

"It seems like a miracle that you and I are together like this," he said. "I wasn't sure I'd ever see you again. Sometimes I wonder if I'm dreaming."

"You keep talking like that," I said, "and you might just get me into bed."

We laughed awkwardly, but it still felt good, as we gradually became more at ease with each other. After dinner, over small saucers of flan, we seemed on the brink of our first kiss, even if we had to stretch across the table to do it. But the waiter arrived with our check just then, breaking the spell.

With a first kiss, like making love for the first time, timing is everything.

I wanted to take Ismael up to the Griffith Observatory to see the city lights and the stars, if the sky was clear enough. I'd kissed Jacques for the first time up there, and figured maybe the magic would work again.

As we pulled out of the restaurant parking lot, I noticed a familiar-looking car across the street—an old Ferrari similar to the one I'd seen in the driveway of Jason Holt's house. But the lighting was scant and my angle of vision lousy—the Ferrari was to my left, on my blind side—and by the time I craned my head for a better look we were too far down the street.

"See someone back there you know?" Ismael asked.

I reached over to stroke his sleek, black hair, admiring his profile.

"I only have eyes for you," I said, and meant it.

At more than four thousand acres—five square miles—Griffith Park was said to be the largest municipal park in the country, situated at the east end of the Hollywood Hills and rising to just above sixteen hundred feet.

The park's crowning attraction was the Griffith Observatory, an astronomical museum perched on the park's south rim, just above Los Feliz. Originally built in the early thirties, the observatory had undergone a major overhaul in recent years, but its three golden domes had been preserved, along with its two telescopes, planetarium, and grand architecture, which ranked among the best examples of thirties Art Deco design in a city replete with them.

We entered the park just before ten, as the observatory was about to close and a line of cars streamed down. When we reached the top, the parking lot was emptying out.

"I guess we're too late," Ismael said.

I grinned. "We're just in time. Before too long, we'll have the place all to ourselves."

I took his hand as we mounted the steps on the north side. They wound up and around the western portion of the monumental structure, leading us to a series of balconies between and around the three big domes. Various vantage points offered unparalleled views of the city, from downtown to the east, across the Westside, and into the San Fernando Valley to the northwest. When we'd finally picked a spot looking southwest, toward the ocean, we were alone.

With a perfectly straight face, Ismael said, "This place is cursed, you know."

"No kidding." My most personal knowledge of Griffth Park was of its fifty-three miles of trails, which I'd explored as a young man mostly on Sunday afternoons, when gay men came up by the hundreds to tan and mingle in the seclusion of the wild chaparral. I decided not to mention that part of my life to Ismael, at least not yet, until he had a firmer footing in a gay world whose social rituals were sometimes shocking to outsiders, forged as they were in a distant time when meetings between homosexuals could only be clandestine and furtive.

I asked him about this alleged curse he'd mentioned, and he gave me a thumbnail history of the park. It had probably been a hunting ground for Gabrieleno Indians, he said, until the Spanish began settling the area toward the end of the eighteenth century, when the vast acreage became part of Rancho Los Feliz, awarded to one of the soldiers accompanying the original forty-four settlers. The Los Feliz family owned it until 1863, when it began passing through a succession of hands, selling for as little as a dollar an acre. The final private owner was Griffith J. Griffith, a self-made millionaire who bought it despite the curse believed to haunt its hills and canyons after the Indians were driven out. The legend of the curse was so entrenched, Ismael said, that Griffth couldn't find a buyer for the land. So, in 1896, he donated it to the city of Los Angeles, designating that it always be accessible and free to everyone, so the working poor would have a place of recreation and relaxation.

"A noble gesture," I said, and glanced around at the labyrinth of shadowy passages, and out to the dark hills surrounding us. "What about that curse? Anything to it?"

A grin cracked Ismael's face and his dark eyes twinkled. "Why? Are you scared?"

I stepped closer, facing him squarely. I reached up to brush a few strands of hair off his forehead, then traced the outline of his lips with a finger.

"Are you?"

His eyes faltered. "Maybe a little."

He glanced around uneasily, searching the shadows. I turned his face back toward mine.

"We're alone, Ismael. There's nothing to be afraid of."

I cupped the back of his head and drew his face toward mine.

He didn't resist, and, finally, we kissed. Looking back, I'm struck by how easily we can take kisses for granted, especially in L.A., where people dispense them like breath mints, even blowing them through the air when parting with the utmost insincerity. But that first kiss with Ismael was nothing like that.

In that singular, electrifying moment, I felt transported back to a more innocent and hopeful time, when I was discovering my own identity, figuring out who I was, finding my rightful place in the world, as Ismael was doing now. Back to a time when I was throwing off the shackles imposed on me by others, when the future seemed to stretch out infinitely and everything was possible. Maybe it was foolish to invest so much in one man, choosing Ismael to be the catalyst I needed, the one who would help me start over, as I sought one more chance to get it right. But those were the emotions that swelled in me at that moment, even more than the lust that had been heating up inside me since that night I laid eyes on him at A Different Light.

As we pressed our lips together, I could feel him relax as he got comfortable with the notion of kissing a man. Then our kisses became bolder, more urgent. I let him take the lead, not wanting to intimidate him, letting him discover where he was going on his own. As he led and I followed, he left no doubt that this was his natural course as a man; this was who he was, how he was meant to love. I touched him with almost painful tenderness—the fine contours of his face, the startling roughness of his beard, the firmness of his body as I pulled him closer to me, hungry for him. In turn, though more tentatively, he began to explore me, as curiously and innocently as the virgin that he was.

Then we heard footsteps nearby. Ismael separated from me and glanced anxiously around, a man still ashamed of displaying affection in public and terrified of being caught. I followed his eyes and saw a shadow disappear around the base of a dome, where moonlight bathed the white walls. Then I heard scrabbling feet.

"Probably just kids fooling around," I said. "Believe me, Ismael, we aren't the first gay couple to share a kiss up here."

But the apprehension remained in his eyes. So I left him to

take a look, following the descending footsteps. I trotted down the steps and around a balustrade, saw no one, and stopped to listen. The footsteps grew fainter until they were gone.

Ismael joined me. "Who was it?"

"Maybe a security guard who saw us and decided to give us a few more minutes together."

"It's past closing time," Ismael said. "We probably should leave."

I reached for his hand again, but this time he drew it away. We continued down, side by side but no longer physically joined. The steps swept to the right, curving around and down to a landing atop a final set of steps that led to the park grounds. I paused for a moment, realizing where we were: the setting for the knife fight in *Rebel Without a Cause*. An iconic movie, haunted by tragedy. James Dean, Natalie Wood, Sal Mineo—three stars who died before their time, their deaths shrouded to varying degrees in violence or mystery. Mineo, the decidedly gay one in the group, knifed to death in the garage of his West Hollywood apartment building, a murder that had never been solved. The Griffith Park curse?

Somewhere below, an engine started up. I scanned the big parking lot until I saw headlights go on and then a car speeding toward the distant exit. The car was too far away in too little light for me to say for sure what model it was. But not so obscure that I couldn't make out the dark bottom and light-colored top, not unlike the old two-tone Ferrari I'd seen in Jason Holt's driveway, and the one I'd spotted earlier tonight on the street in Silver Lake, outside the restaurant

Or maybe not, I thought. It was dark and the disappearing car was a couple of hundred yards away. I'd been badly on edge lately, given all that had been happening. Maybe it was just my imagination playing tricks on me. Maybe I was starting to see things that weren't there.

I stood staring at the empty parking lot until Ismael said to me, "Benjamin, what is it? What did you see?"

"I'm not sure," I said, which was the truth.

EIGHTEEN

I was so spooked by what I'd seen up at the observatory—or, more accurately, by my confusion about it—that I didn't want to discuss it as Ismael drove down the hill.

An awkward silence crept between us, followed by stilted conversation. The evening's spell had been broken, and I didn't know how to get it back. Ismael dropped me off in the parking lot behind Skylight Books, where I'd left the Metro. I was still badly distracted and kissed him good night only perfunctorily, before driving home alone.

Unable to sleep, I stayed up most of the night reading an Alan Hollinghurst novel that Maurice had passed along to me. As well-written as it was, I found my mind wandering from the story every few lines, back to that phantom Ferrari streaking from the observatory parking lot, if that's what I'd seen. I finally drifted off to a fitful sleep around dawn, only to be awakened a couple of hours later by the ringing phone.

When I picked up, the caller didn't identify himself, but he didn't have to. The snippy tone was unmistakably that of Jason Holt.

"I see you have a new boyfriend, Benjamin."

The last time I'd heard that voice, as I drove away from his Nichols Canyon house, he'd been upbeat and flirtatious. Now he was back in his sinister mode. Keeping up with his shifting moods was like trying to grab mercury. I carried the phone into the kitchen to start water boiling for instant coffee.

"What can I do for you, Holt?"

"He's marginally attractive, I suppose, if you like the swarthy type. Personally, I've always found Mexicans rather dirty looking. Especially the darker ones, like your new boyfriend."

"Listen to me, Holt—"

"They all look like they need a good scrubbing, don't you think? But maybe that's why you find them so appealing, since you're nothing but filth yourself."

"Was that you up at the observatory? Did you follow us?"

"You're making a big mistake, Benjamin, treating me like this. Consider yourself warned."

The line went dead before I could interrupt again and tell Holt that he was pushing me further than was good for him. My hand was shaking as I placed the receiver back in its cradle. I stirred coffee crystals into a dirty mug and took my caffeine standing up, trying to contain my anger.

By the time the mug was empty, I'd decided to drive back up Nichols Canyon for another chat with Holt, and maybe a little more than that.

The circular driveway was empty when I arrived at Holt's place, although the old Ferrari might have been in the garage. I pounded on the front door several times, hard enough to cause some paint to flake off and float to the tiled steps. No one answered my knock.

I followed the stepping-stones around the north side of the un-tended property, brushing cobwebs from my face and hair. I found the patio and rear yard deserted, so I rapped my knuckles against the dirty glass of the old French doors. There was no re-sponse. I shielded my eyes and peered in. Heavy velvet curtains were drawn across the big front windows to my left, leaving the living room in dim light. I squinted but couldn't see anyone inside.

I rattled the latch and lock, finding them shaky, while I weighed how badly I wanted to gain entry and learn more about Holt, maybe even uncover some serious evidence that he was behind the harassment and vandalism that had me so worked up. I glanced around to make sure I was alone, then gave the door handle a few tugs. A dead bolt might have given me some trouble, but this was a standard lock, so old that most of the brass surface had been worn away. The screws were loose and the wood around them was on the verge of rot. I got a better grip and pulled with more force. I felt the lock separate from the brittle wood and the doors came open with a groan.

As I stepped in, my nose caught a musty smell that reminded me of every cut-rate antique store in Canoga Park. I shut the doors behind me, in case Holt had pets that might get out, while keeping my eye open for a dog that might still have teeth. None showed themselves. I ventured farther in.

Deep couches and chairs were arranged in the center of the living room, facing a stone fireplace built into the southeastern wall. On either side of the fireplace was a large, arched window that must have provided stunning views of Runyon Canyon and the city beyond when the heavy curtains were drawn back. Like the drapes, the furniture was plush but faded and worn from decades of sunlight and use.

A single, small light shone in the dimness. It illuminated a large portrait that hung above the mantelpiece and dominated the high-ceilinged room. The artist's name, Charles Wu, a name I didn't recognize, was etched in the lower right-hand corner, along with the year, 1997. His oil painting was of a younger Jason Holt, before all the reconstructive surgery had turned his face into a mask of futile vanity. The features were softer and more pliant, and blond highlights accentuated his darkening hair, apparently an effort to suggest what had once been its natural color. To my untrained eye, Wu's portrait seemed competently executed but undistinguished, without much sense of life or depth. I studied it briefly but closely, trying to see something in it that might remind me of Holt thirty years ago, around the time he claimed we'd known each other in college. If I could remember him, I thought, and acknowledge it, then maybe he'd leave me alone.

I focused on the narrow, not-quite-pretty face, the yellow eyes given more color and set less closely together by the kindly artist. If there was one feature of Holt that Wu had captured perfectly, I thought, it was the self-absorbed gaze that seemed to extend only a short distance, as if into a mirror, before turning back on itself. In that respect, Wu had captured Holt's overweening narcissism perfectly. I studied the face intently but couldn't for the life of me recall ever meeting him before our recent encounter at A Different Light.

I gave up on the painting and crossed the expansive living room to a hallway that led to a series of smaller rooms. Most of the furniture was of dark wood and velvet, quite old and expensive looking. The general style was baroque, evoking a more opulent, showy era, which seemed to fit a designer like Silvio Galiano, whose heyday had been in the 1940s and '50s, before Hollywood's so-called golden age began to lose its luster.

I stuck my head into a room that appeared to be a study, a bookcase against one wall and an old, heavy desk in a corner. Facing me from the opposite wall was a fine-looking portrait of Galiano, whom I recognized from the photos that had accompanied his obituaries. It had been painted in his later years, when his dark hair had gone gray, but the artist had captured Galiano's lively dark eyes, genial smile, and Italian good looks, along with his obvious sense of fashion. The painting's depth and luminosity were striking. As I got closer, I was surprised to see that the signature on it was that of Charles Wu, who'd also rendered the less accomplished portrait of Holt that hung in the living room. This painting was distinguished by finer details and richer colors and a strong sense of mood, as if the artist had been deeply immersed in his subject. If I hadn't known the same man had painted both portraits, I would never have guessed it.

The floor-to-ceiling bookcase was heavily stocked with large, illustrated books on Hollywood history, classic architecture, and interior design. On another wall was a gallery of framed photographs, all of which featured Galiano posed and smiling with people I presumed to be his friends and clients, many Hollywood luminaries among them. Judging by Galiano's apparent age in the photos, they seemed to be arranged chronologically through the years, from left to right. Jason Holt appeared in the pictures toward the end, when the friends and clients had apparently become few and Galiano had become wizened and sickly looking, with a drawn, pallid face. As I reached the end of the gallery, I was in for another surprise. In the final few photos, presumably taken near the end of his life, Galiano looked considerably healthier—more flesh on his bones, more color in his face, more sparkle in his eyes—as if he'd suddenly found an elixir for whatever had ailed him. Oddly, it was in these last pictures, when Galiano looked so fit and happy, that Holt's countenance seemed the most strained, with a fixed, camera-ready smile.

The only other photos in the room were arranged along a section of shelf, almost hidden among the books, like an obligation. If my guess was right, these were of Holt and his parents as he grew up, since he was recognizable in some of the later pictures, still as blond as he'd been as a toddler. There weren't many. One photo captured his stiff, dour-looking parents in formal dress, assuming that's who they were. A few more posed them with Holt in a rather ordinary suburban backyard, possibly New England, if the autumn colors were a good indication. In each picture, Holt was perfectly groomed and nattily dressed, his hair slicked down, his smile remarkably self-satisfied for one so young, as he basked in the spotlight. He gave me the impression of a worldly, calculating adult trapped in the body of a little boy. The effect was a bit chilling.

Then I came to a photo apparently taken in his college years, judging by the university sweatshirt he was wearing. It was the same school I'd attended, more evidence that he was telling the truth about having known me. He'd grown a mustache—sparse and blond, barely more than a smudge on his upper lip—but it was unmistakably Holt, looking as self-adoring as ever. I recalled that I'd worn a mustache myself around that time, also blond, though considerably thicker, which I'd shaved off during the wrestling season, as the coach required. It occurred to me that Holt might have grown his to mimic or impress me. I shuddered, thinking about it.

I spent only a minute or two in the first room before moving quickly down the hallway, where I stuck my head into the next door, which opened to a guest bedroom. I saw nothing I considered noteworthy and started up the stairway to the second floor.

As I entered the first door on my left, I flicked on a light switch and was instantly transfixed. The walls were covered with photos—and I was in every one. Each was carefully framed, with all the frames perfectly aligned, not a crooked one in sight. Also framed and on display were dozens of newspaper articles in which I was featured, going back to my seventeenth year, when I'd made the regional newspapers in the Northeast after killing my father.

Like the photos downstairs, these items were also arranged in chronological order. I hadn't seen most of them, and had no idea so much had been written about me, or so many photos taken. Holt had not only found old clippings about my father's death, he'd also searched out local press coverage of my high school wrestling matches. Amid these, in a more ornate frame, was an eight-by-ten blown up from my senior yearbook photo. After that came more clippings, from my college years, followed by photos of me after I'd arrived in Southern California to work for the *Los Angeles Times*. Some of these were candid shots taken on the street, while I was out walking or driving, a few with Jacques at my side. There was even a photo of Jacques and me at a Gay Pride march, cheering as Dykes on Bikes rolled by on their motorcycles, and another, also taken surreptitiously, as I helped him walk slowly down Norma Place in the last months of his life, when he was gaunt and pale and his eyes had lost all hope. Finding these stolen moments in Holt's house was unnerving, to say the least. But it also made me feel horribly violated and more furious with him than ever.

Below the framed photos, on a credenza, lay two scrapbooks. I opened one to find it stuffed with yellowed clippings from the on-slaught of news coverage related to my Pulitzer problems eighteen years ago. The other, only partially filled, contained items from the recent publicity focusing on my book.

I closed the scrapbooks and backed away to the door, trying to digest what I was seeing. The room had been turned into a shrine. Under different circumstances, I might have been flattered. Instead, thinking about the implications, I shivered.

I switched off the light, and moved on down the hall.

It was in the next room that I came across the spiders.

There were at least a hundred of them, maybe twice that number, preserved in jars of formaldehyde and boxes under glass. The specimens ranged from creatures as tiny as an aspirin tablet to furry tarantulas as big as a man's hand, each neatly labeled according to genus, in both English and Latin.

I became so absorbed in what I was seeing that I didn't realize I was no longer alone, until Holt's voice startled me from behind.

"I wasn't aware you had such an interest in Arachnida."

I whirled to find him standing in the doorway, holding up his cell phone so that it faced in my direction.

"That's right," he said. "I'm getting you on video. Starting when you broke into the house and following you from room to room. You must be losing your instincts in your old age, letting me get the drop on you like this. Perhaps I'll send a copy to that detective, to go with the one I sent him earlier."

"The one you also sent to DishtheDirt.com."

"The Internet's such fun, don't you think? I just love digital transmission. The push of a button and—presto!—the images are out there for everyone to see."

I started toward him, but he took a step back, keeping the camera on me. "I've already sent the images to a friend, you know, the ones of you breaking in. I'd think twice if I were you before resorting to violence. Burglary is bad enough, don't you think, without adding an assault charge?"

I froze where I was. I didn't know if video could be transmitted that way, to someone else's cell phone or computer, but I suspected Holt was bluffing. In either case, it wasn't a chance I was comfortable taking. Not at the moment anyway.

Holt waltzed past me to stand over his creature collection, keeping his camera trained on me.

"Spiders are so fascinating, don't you think?"

"I really don't know much about them. Unlike you, I never studied zoology in college."

"Silvio would never let me display them like this when he was alive. I kept them stored away, in the garage. They're beautiful, don't you think?"

"Not exactly the word I'd choose."

"Did you know there are close to forty thousand species?"

"What do you want from me, Holt?"

"They've been around for four hundred million years, adapting to almost every environment, which places them among the most successful carnivores in history. They'll be around long after humans are gone."

He lifted a jar, studying a preserved spider.

"*Micaria romana*," he said. "Like most spiders, it has eight legs and two body segments. But it also resembles the ant, its primary prey. Such genius!" He set the jar down and faced me directly. "You and I are not all that dissimilar, Benjamin. Homosexual, roughly the same age, widowers, as it were, in need of companionship. I don't see why we can't be friends."

"You're much too clever for me, Holt. Spending time with you would only give me an inferiority complex."

"You see? You still mock me, after all these years. But you underestimate me, Benjamin." He glanced fondly at his collection. "It's the same with arachnids. Their brains are quite small, and their nervous systems terribly simple. Most people think of them as ugly and useless, even repulsive. But they're capable of quite complex tasks—procreating, building webs, trapping and killing their prey with their venom."

He paused, fixing me with his eyes.

"Do you know what triggers their instinct to kill, what lets them know that it's the right time?"

"I'm afraid I don't."

"The vibrations they feel through the threads of their web when their trapped prey begins to struggle. Tactile sensation—that's how most spiders know when it's time to strike."

"They sound very sensitive."

"Yes, sensitive. Unlike you, Benjamin."

"I'm sorry you're so lonely, Holt. But I'm not the solution."

"Don't patronize me! You led me on, Benjamin. Back in college, when I was most vulnerable, you used me like a toy. You humiliated me."

He was trembling badly. I thought for a moment that he was going to cry.

"I swear, Holt, I don't recall even speaking to you."

"You didn't! That's just the point. It was the looks you gave me, the sideways glances, stealing my beauty, encouraging my adoration, but giving me nothing in return."

"Maybe in your dreams."

"Selective recollection! Like that so-called memoir of yours!"

My patience was gone. I turned and left the room, striding back down the hallway and down the stairs.

Holt chased after me, crying out, "Where are you going?"

"Away from you, that's for sure."

"You'd better not! I'll file charges against you! I'll send this to the blogs!"

"Do what you have to, Holt."

His tone became plaintive. "Wait! Don't go!"

I reached the first floor and turned into the living room. Holt darted around in front of me, blocking my path. He had his cell phone on me again, as if daring me to show aggression. He glanced at the big painting hanging above the mantelpiece.

"I saw you studying the portrait earlier," he said eagerly. "Are you interested in fine art? I count several prominent artists among my closest friends. Charles Wu painted this one. I'm sure you've heard of him. I could introduce you."

I followed his eyes to the painting while I tried to figure my way out of this without an assault charge.

"Charles started out painting lovely botanicals," Holt said. "Watercolors that Silvio placed in many of the homes he decorated. As Charles became better known, he began painting portraits, specializing in famous and beautiful people, mostly through introductions that Silvio gave him. Not that I consider myself beautiful, of course. I felt humbled when Charles asked me to sit for him."

"It sounds like he owed Silvio quite a lot," I said.

"Only his career! Before Silvio started showing his work no one had ever heard of Charles. He's strictly into abstracts now. But you probably know that, don't you?"

"I'm afraid fine art is out of my league."

Holt couldn't seem to keep his eyes off the painting. "I was nearly forty when this portrait was painted. You wouldn't know it, would you? Silvio always said I looked quite young for my age."

I stepped to the mantelpiece, reaching up. "I believe it's crooked."

"No! It's fine, don't touch it!"

But I'd already tilted it, setting it at a slight angle. Holt stepped quickly to my side, set his cell phone on the mantelpiece, and reached up to straighten the frame. When he turned back to retrieve his phone, I clutched it securely in one hand, closed and shut off.

"I'm leaving now, Holt. Unless you want me to mess up all that plastic surgery, I'd suggest you stay out of my way."

I turned and strode out of the house. Holt followed close on my heels.

"Give me that phone!" I ignored him and stepped down into the yard. "You think you're so smart, don't you?"

I started across the patio, past the empty swimming pool, but suddenly stopped to face him.

"And if you value your creepy collection of spiders, you'll leave me alone. Because if you bother me again, I'll come back and smash every one of your specimens to smithereens."

He looked aghast at that. I pivoted and picked up the path back to the street. Holt stayed right behind, hissing in my ear.

"Maybe you'd like to know how they court and have sex."

"Maybe another time, Holt. Say, in the next millennium."

"Courtship varies among different species, but many web-building spiders communicate through vibration. The male sends out a unique signal along a thread of his web that's connected to the female's web. If she's receptive, she positions herself for sex and lets him know she's ready through a special vibration of her own. If she's unreceptive, she shakes her web or simply crawls away."

I emerged from the dense foliage and continued straight to the Metro, forcing Holt to walk faster.

"But some males are so desperate to mate," he went on, "they go after the unwilling female anyway, knowing that she might sink her fangs into him, killing him with her venom. The impulse to couple with some spiders is that strong. They want the object of their desire so badly they're willing to die for it."

"That's romance for you," I said, and climbed into the Metro.

Holt came around by the driver's door. His chemically plumped lips puckered into an ugly sneer.

"I see you're not driving your Mustang these days. Did something happen to it?"

I switched on the ignition, released the emergency brake, and pulled out, forcing Holt back. He stretched out his arms imploringly.

"I'm sorry, Benjamin! Please, stay! I'll make it up to you!"

I tossed his cell phone into the street ahead of the car, took aim, and crushed it like a bug. I could still hear him behind me as I sped from the cul-de-sac. In the rearview mirror, I saw that his hands were clenched at his sides now, like a brat throwing a tantrum.

"I won't be treated like this, Benjamin! I won't! You'll regret this, I promise you!"

Then I turned the corner and he was out of sight, though hardly out of mind.

NINETEEN

Several days passed without further communication from Jason Holt, and I wanted to believe I'd scared him off.

In the meantime, I braced for my final interview with Cathryn Conroy, set for that Saturday evening. But on Friday morning she called to ask if we could postpone so she could finish up another piece she was writing for *Eye*.

"I'm a notoriously slow writer," she said, "and I like to get my facts right."

"By all means," I said, "take all the time you want."

Later that day, Bruce Steele called to remind me that I was scheduled to conduct a clinic the following afternoon for the West Hollywood Wrestling Club, a commitment I'd completely forgotten. I pretended I hadn't, and promised to be there at 2:00 P.M. sharp.

The West Hollywood Wrestling Club held its weekly workouts each Saturday in the Plummer Park Community Center, on the city's Eastside. When I arrived at the room set aside for the workouts, about two dozen men were already paired up on the mats and going through drills under Steele's supervision.

They ranged in age from late teens to early sixties, some

dressed in standard-issue singlets and lightweight wrestling shoes, others—the neophytes—in more motley outfits comprised of baggy shorts, faded T-shirts, and high-topped sneakers. Most wore knee pads to avoid bruised cartilage and headgear to protect against cauliflower ears. A few looked like they didn't know the difference between a duck-under and a double-leg tackle, but I was surprised by how many showed genuine skill.

Steele told the group to keep going through escape drills and sauntered over, still in great shape at forty-three, packing maximum muscle and minimal body fat into his skintight singlet. As a wrestler at Oklahoma State, he'd gone all the way to the top, at both the collegiate and AAU levels. From what I'd seen of him competing more than twenty years ago—on television, winning his weight class at the NCAA tournament—he would have made an excellent coach. But coaching for a living isn't possible for an openly gay man, certainly not in a sport like wrestling, where the close physical proximity between competitors makes so many people uneasy. Faced with living honestly or in the closet, Steele had forsaken his dream of coaching for a living and started the West Hollywood Wrestling Club as an avocation. It allowed him regular workout partners, competition against other amateur clubs, and the chance to stay in shape for the international Gay Games, where he'd won his weight class every time he'd entered.

He thanked me for coming and agreed to serve as my demonstration partner, since we were roughly the same size, give or take a couple of pounds. The other wrestlers formed a circle around us, standing two or three deep. Steele introduced me and mentioned my collegiate wrestling background, making it sound more impressive than it was. When we stood facing each other and locked up, I realized it was the first time I'd been on a wrestling mat in nearly thirty years.

"You're in pretty good shape for an old man," Steele said, grinning.

As I demonstrated three takedowns, they came to me effortlessly, the moves coded into my body's memory from all those years of drills and competition. I started with a single leg tackle, one of the more basic takedowns; followed it with a fireman's carry, slightly more difficult to perform; and finished with a Japanese hip roll, the most complicated of the three, in which balance, timing, and momentum are crucial.

"Like most sports, wrestling is a kind of dance," I told the group, "sensing the rhythm of the match, getting a feel for your partner, setting him up, timing your move just right. You practice them often enough and the moves become instinctive."

"Kind of like sex, you mean?"

The voice came from the back of the group and sounded familiar, as well as vaguely taunting. There was some laughter, but it was more nervous than lighthearted. The notion of sexuality on the wrestling mat is always a touchy subject among coaches and participants, even in a wrestling club, like this one, that was largely gay. In the heat of competition, the sensuality of the sport is never an issue. It's all about moves, countermoves, strength, stamina, injury, the score, how much time is left—being entirely focused on the extreme mental and physical demands of the match. But outside that competitive framework, the old taboo against men getting too comfortable with one another, touching too intimately, invariably raises its ugly head. For wrestlers, straight or gay, the issue is always there, like the subtext of a conversation between two married strangers who have illicit romance on their mind but can't quite admit it.

I ignored the annoying comment from the back of the room and completed my demonstration. Steele announced that it was time for the wrestlers to pair off for three-minute matches. He asked me if I was game.

"Not against you," I said. "I'll need a partner who's lighter, without biceps the size of melons. Otherwise, you'll have to carry me out on a stretcher."

Steele swept his eyes around the circle. "Any volunteers?"

"I'll face off with him," a voice said.

It was the same voice we'd heard a moment ago, tossing out the impolite remark about sex. All eyes turned toward the back of the circle. Wrestlers stepped aside to let the man through.

It was Lance. He held his motorcycle boots in one hand and a sleeveless leather vest in the other, showing off his hard-plated chest and colorful tattoos. His dome was still clean-shaven, but he'd added a blond Fu Manchu mustache to go with the soul patch.

"You don't have the right gear," Steele said. "I don't believe you're even a member, are you?"

"Maybe I'll join, if the competition's any good. Unless the old guy has a problem squaring off with me."

Steele glanced my way. "Benjamin?"

"No problem," I said, keeping my eyes on Lance.

"Cool," he said. "Let's get it on."

I suddenly realized I hadn't disclosed, not to Steele or the others.

"I'm HIV positive," I said. "There could be blood."

"You looking for a way out?" Lance asked.

"Just being up-front about it."

"I told you before," he said, "I like to take risks."

"You two know each other?" Steele asked.

"After a fashion," I said.

Lance glanced at Steele, then back at me. "Do we do this, or not?"

"You'll need to sign a waiver of liability," Steele said. "In case of injury."

"I already did, when I came in."

"You've wrestled before?"

"Some, back in high school. You got gear for me?"

"Shoe size?"

"Ten."

Lance fixed me with his fierce blue eyes while Steele rustled up shoes, a singlet, and headgear.

"I don't need no headgear," Lance told him. "I'm not that pretty, anyway."

Maybe not, but he was worth looking at as he stripped down to his briefs. Exposed like that, he looked even leaner and more wiry, the kind of man whose tensile strength can fool you if you're not careful. He stepped into the Spandex singlet and pulled it up snugly over his hips and torso, slipping his arms through the shoulder straps. A minute later, he was lacing up his wrestling shoes. Then he was standing, rolling his neck and jogging in place to loosen up, while I did the same.

When he was ready, we faced each other in the middle of the mat.

"You sure you're up to this, old man?"

"I guess we'll find out, won't we?"

"Three minutes," Steele said, and blew his whistle.

Lance came at me like a raging bull. An undisciplined wrestler is often more dangerous than one who's well trained—a flurry of awkward motion and flailing limbs, the kind of frenzied, slam-bang action that comes at you from all angles and makes injuries more likely. Lance was like that, ferocious and unrelenting. Right off, we butted heads painfully, but it didn't slow him down. I felt his fingernails dig into my flesh—face, neck, hands—as he clawed at me like a wild animal. I kept trying to push him off, to put some distance between us so I could measure him and set up a move, but I never got an opening. I quickly realized that trying to execute any conventional moves was futile. I was reduced to nothing but defense, trying to ward him off and minimize the damage. He just kept coming, tearing my flesh, banging my skull, thumbing me in the eye, slamming me every which way, until I began resorting to the same illegal tactics, while Steele exhorted us to get back to wrestling.

Finally, with half a minute remaining, he blew his whistle and stepped between us, pushing us apart.

"That's enough," he said. "That's not wrestling. It's warfare."

Neither Lance nor I had scored a point, although we'd both drawn blood. I was heaving for air and close to throwing up.

"I'm bleeding," I said, looking Lance over for abrasions that might allow transmission. "You need to get cleaned up. Use some antiseptic."

Lance just stared at me in silence. His eyes were hard with fury but also brimming with tears. Steele shoved a towel and a bottle of antiseptic at him. Lance ignored him, turning away to strip off his singlet. Steele grabbed him roughly.

"When you're in this room," Steele said, "you do things my way."

To my surprise, Lance didn't argue. He just stood staring at me, wiping away a tear as Steele cleaned my blood off his face and upper chest.

When he was done, Steele said to the group, "That's enough for today. We need to disinfect this mat."

"Sorry about the blood," I said.

"Don't worry about it. We've got a few members who are positive. We deal with it."

Lance moved to a corner to change back into his street clothes. When I approached him, he looked away, blinking back tears.

"You finally got to me, didn't you? You happy now?"

"Don't worry," he said. "I won't bother you again."

"Is that a promise?"

As he slipped into his vest, he finally met my eyes.

"Count on it, old man. You won't see me again."

He strode from the room, down the corridor, and across the lobby. I followed him from a distance, as far as the exit. Outside, he climbed on his old Harley, kick-started it, and roared out of the parking lot.

I turned as Bruce Steele came up beside me. Both of us watched Lance ride off, heading east on Santa Monica Boulevard, toward Hollywood.

"What the hell was *that* about?" Steele asked.

I had no response for him. I was just happy to have Lance out of my life. At least that was what I told myself as I thought about the tears I'd seen in his conflicted eyes, and the perplexing questions he'd left behind.

TWENTY

August arrived in a wave of dry heat, crackling and dangerous.

It was the kind of climate Southern Californians variously think of as wildfire, earthquake, or riot weather, depending on what part of the region they live in. Rampaging wildfires were a sure bet, about as routine as going to the beach. Major earthquakes and urban riots struck less often, every couple of decades or so. But they were always lurking as possibilities, one below the sun-baked streets and the other above.

I didn't need a change in climate to put me on edge. Lance may have ridden his Harley out of my life, but Jason Holt had decided to stay in touch. One early afternoon, the mail carrier delivered another postcard, similar to the others. Fred, unable to climb the stairs to my apartment, left it on the bottom step with my other mail.

This one was addressed to Benjamin Morgue Justice:

Now that your pretty convertible has been reduced to salvage, perhaps you should replace it with something more fitting, like a hearse. (Since those toxic medications you take will surely kill you one of these days, if AIDS doesn't get you first.) Got AIDS? Got Milk? Have a nice death, faggot.

That afternoon, I put my Mustang up for sale online through craigslist, a mess of ruined paint, shredded upholstery, and cracked glass. Since it was a '65, which made it a classic, I was able to unload it quickly, selling it to the first bidder for six-hundred bucks just to get it over with. Still, it wasn't easy watching the Mustang being hooked up and towed away, knowing I'd never see it again.

With the arrival of the latest piece of hate mail, Holt let me know he was still around, determined that I not forget him. I decided to go back on the offensive, but less directly. He'd mentioned two people—his aunt, Victoria Faith, and Charles Wu, the artist who'd painted his portrait—who I hoped might tell me more about him, give me an inside angle and advantage on the guy. It was what my old boss, Harry Brofsky, had called going fishing—keep fishing long enough, and in the right spots, Harry had advised me, and a perceptive reporter was bound to come up with a bite, which invariably led to bigger fish.

I contacted Victoria Faith first, calling her at the Motion Picture & Television Country House. I told her I was writing a nostalgia piece about film ingénues of the 1930s and wondered if she'd see me for an interview. Figuring she might not be computer savvy at her age, I made up a mythical Internet magazine as my employer. She sounded pleasantly surprised and eager for the company, and we scheduled an afternoon appointment for the following Wednesday.

I drove out the 101 through the furnace heat of the San Fernando Valley to the northern stretches of the city of Los Angeles.

Bordered by mountains, this end of the triangular valley had been picturesque but largely arid flatland until the early decades of the twentieth century. That's when the city's wealthiest and most powerful figures—businessmen and landholders, almost exclusively white—decided to transform the onetime Mexican pueblo into a thriving metropolis. For that, they needed water. Through legal maneuvering, ingenious engineering, federal intervention, and outright deception, the power elite had acquired far-flung water rights, extending aqueducts hundreds of miles into distant regions, diverting water from rivers, streams, and lakes, and destroying countless ecosystems in the process. With water came great prosperity and growth: The city's population, a mere eleven thousand in 1880, had exploded to more than half a million by 1920. Today, more than four million residents were packed within L.A.'s 465 square miles, a number that was expected to increase by roughly fifty percent over the next four decades.

The "country house" where Victoria Faith resided, opened in 1942, wasn't really out in the country any longer. As I sped along an elevated freeway that would slow to a crawl in a couple of hours, development of every kind extended in all directions: gated communities, tract homes, trailer parks, horse ranches, golf courses, artificial lakes, colleges, movie studios, hospitals, shopping malls, airports, and endless asphalt and concrete grids comprising thousands of miles of streets, connecting suburban neighborhoods like the intersecting tunnels of an ant farm. These days, the Valley was not much different from the rest of L.A., only hotter and with bigger residential lots. A city without boundaries, Mike Davis had written once of Los Angeles—a metropolis devouring the land, driven by the dream of its own infinity.

I took an off-ramp into the affluent suburb of Woodland Hills, where Victoria Faith resided in a comfortable retirement community, waiting to die.

The Motion Picture & Television Country House and Hospital, as it was officially known, sat on forty lushly landscaped acres just off the 101. A guard at the entrance checked a guest list for my name, asked me to sign it, handed me a map and brochure, and waved me through.

The brochure provided a thumbnail description of the place: a full-service retirement complex that included state-of-the-art medical facilities, a modern gym, and myriad other recreational amenities. Although it had once been known as "the Old Actor's Home," where legendary stars spent their last years, it was open to anyone who had worked in the film or TV industry for twenty years, regardless of their occupation or ability to pay. Of the four hundred residents, about half lived there for free, supported by the nonprofit Motion Picture & Television Fund.

Following the map, I drove past acres of walking paths, manicured lawns, and colorful gardens until I reached the Fran and Ray Stark Villa, an independent and assisted living facility. I checked in at the front desk and was escorted to a studio apartment on the first floor.

A nurse was leaving as I arrived. Victoria Faith stood just inside, stooped over a walker but dressed and made up as if she were going out for an afternoon of tea and high-end shopping. She was small and thin, almost birdlike, yet I got a sense of strength and energy about her that must have been more mental than physical, given her frail condition. Even in her late eighties, she was a handsome woman, with luxuriant, wavy white hair nicely cut and swept back along the sides, and pale, pliant skin whose folds and wrinkles seemed a natural part of her ageless beauty.

"Mr. Justice," she said, speaking precisely. "Please do come in."

Her apartment was small but well appointed, with a window looking out to a garden abloom with hundreds of roses.

"That's the Roddy McDowall Rose Garden," she said, following my eyes beyond her small patio. She raised an arthritic finger and pointed in another direction. "The Wasserman Koi Pond is over that way. I enjoy sitting there in the quiet, watching the fish swim about, when I'm up to it." She smiled warmly, without a hint of complaint. "You'll be my project for today, Mr. Justice, as long as I'm able to last."

"Not feeling well?"

"Not for some time, I'm afraid."

She showed me to a sofa and eased herself down from the walker into an upright recliner, waving me off when I offered assistance. On the table next to her were several framed photos of the same two women, apparently taken over several decades. One of the women I recognized as Miss Faith, brunette in her younger years and stunningly beautiful. The other was a heftier woman with dark blond, closely cropped hair, wearing a pants suit, who appeared to be a few years older. In each photo, their heads were touching or they were facing each other, each looking fondly into the other's eyes. I recalled from her Wikipedia entry that Victoria Faith had never married.

Also on the small table was a copy of *Deep Background.* The moment I saw it I knew I'd been busted. Victoria's rheumy gray eyes were watching me carefully.

"I put in an order for your book after we spoke on the phone the other day," she said. "It just arrived this morning. Perhaps you'll be kind enough to sign it for me before you leave."

"Would that be now?"

She smiled benignly. "If I didn't want you here, Mr. Justice, I would have called to cancel. I didn't recognize your name when we first spoke, but it came to me later. I try to keep up with the news, and you've been getting your share of attention lately. That video, you know, the one where you and that young man are fighting in the street. To be honest, I found it rather disturbing. I turned it off, but not before your name and book were mentioned."

"It's not something I'm proud of, that altercation."

"You didn't do it as a publicity stunt?"

"No."

She clucked critically. "I don't know why you men find violence so appealing. I've often said that if women could just run the world for a few years, things would settle down and be so much better. But I don't suppose that's likely to happen, is it?"

"I apologize for lying about having a magazine assignment."

"Why did you, Mr. Justice?"

"I was afraid you wouldn't see me if I was honest about why I wanted to speak with you."

"And what would that reason be?"

"I believe you have a nephew named Jason Holt. Formerly known as Barclay Simpkins."

She tensed noticeably.

"Yes, Jason is my nephew."

"He's been causing me some problems. I'd like to know more about him. Are you and Jason close?"

"Not really."

"When did you see him last?"

"What kind of problems, Mr. Justice?"

I described the harassment I'd been experiencing. I also mentioned my three conversations with Holt—one at the bookstore, two at his house—and how troubled he seemed.

"I'm sorry he's been such a nuisance," she said. "I'm not sure I can be of any help in that regard. I haven't seen him in years. We never got on too well."

"But in a letter to me, written years ago, he said that—"

"I'm afraid my nephew lives in a world of his own fantasies, so deeply that he believes them."

"You knew him when he was a child?"

"Somewhat. My sister and I didn't see as much of each other after she married. Neither she nor her husband approved of me." She glanced at the photos on the table next to her. "I'm an unconventional woman, Mr. Justice. I never married. I had a female companion until a few years ago, when she passed on. Lenore."

"Were you together long?"

"Nearly seventy years. We met in the late thirties, just before the war. I was under studio contract then and still had some promise as a film actress. We tried to be discreet, but there's only so much one can do to keep one's private life secret, and you pay a terrible price for it. The studio demanded that I marry one of their homosexual male stars, so that we'd both have a cover. Lenore was uncomfortable with all the hiding and lying as it was. She was much braver than I. She also had her own business, so it was safer for her. At any rate, I refused to go along with the studio's arrangement. I lost my contract, word got around, and my career suffered considerably."

"That must have been painful for you."

"I would have liked to have had a more fulfilling career, but not at the expense of being honest, and true to the woman I loved. Had I placed my career first, I doubt that Lenore and I would have had so many wonderful years together."

"You said that your sister and brother-in-law didn't approve."

"They were both very much about so-called propriety and status. They liked to live and act as if they were cultured and successful. In truth, they were a rather ordinary couple, without much imagination or accomplishment. They couldn't stand being ordinary, so they kept up the constant pretense that they were better than everyone else. Barclay, whom you know as Jason, grew up in that atmosphere."

"They're still alive?"

"They died twenty-odd years ago, a few months apart. Lived their whole lives in a suburb outside Boston. I learned of their passing through a distant relative. Jason only mentioned them once, quite disrespectfully. He was upset because they died without leaving him money or property. What little they had went for burial expenses and debts."

"What kind of boy was he?"

"An only child. Precocious, needy. Both his parents were rather cold people, emotionally distant. He was desperate for attention, almost pathologically so. To be honest, I felt sorry for him." She paused, and her face darkened. "At least until he arrived here in Los Angeles as a young man, and I got to know him better."

"When was that exactly?"

"Nineteen eighty-five. I remember because it was in December, just before Christmas. It seemed an odd time to unexpectedly turn up."

"Not too long after I arrived," I said, more to myself than to Miss Faith. "He came to see you?"

"He had this mistaken notion, probably from his mother, that I was a successful actress with lots of money and Hollywood connections. I was happy to see him, of course. He was family, after all."

"Apparently, your feelings didn't last."

"It quickly became clear that Barclay was not a very likable young man, or very trustworthy. He could be charming when he needed to be, but it was superficial, and he was very calculating. He had grand notions about what he wanted to do out here. You know, be in the movies as an actor. Write screenplays, produce, become famous, get rich. Hollywood is a magnet for people like that. I suspect that a lot of young people come here looking for the attention and approval they never got from their parents. Sometimes it works out, but more often not."

"You weren't able to help him?"

"I gave him the names of a few friends, but as soon as he found out there was real work involved, he'd lose interest. He wanted everything handed to him on a silver platter. He'd legally changed his name to Jason Holt by then. He had this notion that with his looks and his new name he was virtually assured of an acting career. He used to send me new photos of himself that he had taken for his portfolio, the kind of thing one sends to agents and casting directors. No note of any kind, mind you, no inquiry as to how I was doing. Just a glossy eight-by-ten of himself, preening for the camera. I've still got them, packed away somewhere."

"Not an easy trade," I said, "acting for the movies."

"The truth was that Jason wasn't all that good-looking. Just young and fair, with noticeable flaws the camera never would have forgiven, at least not if he was going to be the leading man he wanted to be. If he'd been willing to learn his craft and take character roles, I suppose he might have had a chance." She turned her head to glance briefly out toward the distant rose garden. "Like Roddy did, for example. He understood his limitations, worked hard at his craft, and had a nice career. I tried to instill some of that same sense into Jason, a work ethic if you will, but he wouldn't hear any of it."

"You gave up on him at some point?"

"More than that, I'm afraid. I felt compelled to call a number of friends to warn them about him, about his deeper motives. He seemed intent on finding a wealthy older man who would take care of him. He wanted to be kept, and kept well."

"He apparently found that with Silvio Galiano," I said.

At the mention of Galiano's name, darkness passed across her face. She folded her hands tightly in her lap.

"Yes, I suppose Jason got what he wanted after all."

"I'm not sure there's much of it left," I said. "I've been up to the house, and it's in a pretty sorry state."

"A shame. It was once quite grand."

"Were you there often?"

"Lenore and I attended dinner parties there before Jason and Silvio took up together. After Silvio died, I was invited for the memorial service, which Jason held at the house with much fanfare. That was the last time I saw or heard from him."

She paused uncomfortably. "Well, there was that one other time. About a year ago, Jason got in touch with me. He needed money. When I told him I wasn't in a position to help him, he threw a terrible fit. He said some absolutely vile things, and I told him I wanted no more contact with him."

"From what I understand, Jason and Galiano were together for quite a few years. There must have been something there, for it to last that long."

"I suppose so."

She dropped her eyes and began to wring her gnarled hands.

"What is it, Miss Faith? You seem distressed."

She sighed deeply, painfully. "It was I who introduced Jason to Silvio. I thought Silvio might help Jason find some honest work." She shook her head slowly, several times. "I still feel guilty that I brought them together."

She looked up and asked carefully, "You mentioned that you've been up to the house?"

"Yes."

"Is that portrait by Charles Wu still hanging above the mantelpiece? The one he painted of Jason?"

I told her it was.

She dropped her eyes again. "I see."

"What about the portrait, Miss Faith?"

She hesitated a long moment, looking more uneasy than ever, and tighter than the proverbial clam.

"Miss Faith?"

She met my eyes fleetingly and said quickly, "I'm afraid I'm not feeling well, Mr. Justice. Perhaps we can chat again another day, when I'm more up to it." She paused, then added, "We might look through those photos of Jason I mentioned. You might find that interesting. Forgive me if I don't get up."

I stood. "You wouldn't mind if I came back then?"

"I enjoy having visitors. It's why I had you out today, even after I suspected you were coming under false pretenses. That, and curiosity, I suppose. You are a rather interesting man." She reached over and tapped my book. "I intend to read your story. I'm quite looking forward to it. You can sign it the next time you come, if you'd be so kind."

"I'd be honored."

I started for the door, but she called after me. When I turned, her eyes were keen with concern.

"You won't tell Jason you came to see me, will you?"

"Of course not."

She smiled uneasily but looked relieved.

"He can be rather frightening," she said, "when he feels crossed."

TWENTY-ONE

My visit with Victoria Faith prompted me to zero in on Charles Wu, the artist who had painted Holt's portrait.

Google led me to Wu's Web site, which was attractive and tasteful, if unexciting. The home page offered the features one would expect: a prominent reproduction of one of his paintings, head shot, biography, link to his agent for purchases, and three links to his pieces offered for sale, categorized by type—watercolor botanicals, portraits in oil, and abstracts in acrylic.

I've never claimed to know much about art, but the abstract Wu had chosen for his home page left me cold. Presumably one of his emblematic pieces, it was stark in the extreme: a large brown triangle set dead center in a white square canvas. If that was brilliant art—sold for high prices, no less—I just didn't get it. To my uncultured eye it was closer to geometry, about as unexpressive and unrevealing an image as an artist could create. Or maybe that was the point.

The head shot showed a fair-skinned, clean-shaven man, stiffly posed, with dark hair that was conservatively cut and combed, mild brown eyes, and bland, square-jawed looks, an image that revealed about as much as the painting did.

The bio went as follows:

Charles Wu was born in Los Angeles in 1962 to parents who had emigrated from Taiwan four years earlier. Raised in a traditional Chinese-American family, he showed an early talent for drawing. At fifteen he was accepted at the Otis College of Art and Design in Los Angeles, and he later studied at the Ecole des Beaux-Arts in Paris.

By the mideighties, Mr. Wu was gaining a reputation for his exquisite watercolor pastels, particularly of flora, inspired by the array of blossoms he had observed as a child in his father's Monterey Park flower shop.

As his prominence grew, he expanded his vocabulary of painting to portraiture, focusing at first on family, friends, and noted collectors who had supported his earlier work. While many portraitists were working from photographs of their subjects, Mr. Wu became known as an exacting artist who demanded long sittings over many days, without exception, a standard he maintains to this day.

Mr. Wu continued to evolve as an artist and today concentrates on abstract forms, inspired by shadows cast by objects and the spaces between architectural elements, which he considers his most important work.

Mr. Wu's first retrospective was in 2002 at the Museum of Modern Art in New York. In 2004, his work was seen in some of the finest art museums in the U.S. in a traveling exhibit organized by the Museum of Contemporary Art in Los Angeles. His work in all three mediums—watercolor, oil, and acrylic—can be found in many of the finest collections in the world, both public and private.

Mr. Wu works from his studio in Santa Monica Canyon near the ocean, where he lives with his wife, Angela, a prominent art patron and philanthropist, and their two children.

Wu's home page also featured a link for a schedule of his upcoming events. I clicked on it to find a major gallery opening in Los Angeles that Friday evening, by invitation only, timed to the publication of a new book, *The Complete Charles Wu Portraits: 1987–2007*.

I called the gallery and told them I represented Ismael Aragon, a prominent collector from Mexico City who was interested in Wu's work. The manager said she was unfamiliar with Aragon and that the reservation list was limited to a select group of collectors, media, family, and close friends. When I told her that Mr. Aragon was in the United States on a "buying trip" and would be happy to spend some of his vast wealth at another gallery, she told me she thought she could squeeze in one more guest.

"Make it two," I told her. "I'm Mr. Aragon's close companion and interpreter."

"Two then," she said. "We accept Visa and American Express."

Anticipating our Friday evening charade, I decided to treat Ismael and me to good haircuts. Not that I had much hair left to cut, but we'd be among the hoi polloi of the art world and I wanted to look my deceptive best. Ismael wasn't keen on misrepresenting himself, but I convinced him it was for a good cause. Namely, my sanity.

"If I don't get to the bottom of this Jason Holt business," I told him, "I'm going to end up back on Prozac."

Anyway, I added, he wouldn't have to utter a single false word. I'd do all the talking, explaining that he spoke only Spanish.

"All you have to do is look rich," I said, "and appropriately pretentious."

We made appointments for our cuts at the Gendarmerie, a neighborhood spa that also offered facials, waxing, manicures, pedicures, massages, a haberdashery, tai chi classes, and enough high-end hair- and skin-care products to keep a pampered celebrity happy for several days. There was also a line of colognes for men and women, personally created by the owner, Topper Schroeder, which he sold at finer stores throughout the country.

All this was out of my range, of course, financially and philosophically. But I'd once done Topper a favor, tracking down an ex-employee of his who'd absconded with the spa's computerized client list, and he'd treated me like a prince ever since. He'd insisted that I drop in any time I was in the mood for a complimentary hot stone or salt scrub massage, or one of the other treatments provided by his cordial staff. He promised me that a good rub with hot stones and warm oil would open up my "energy channels," or something like that, and I told him that maybe I'd take him up on a haircut.

That Wednesday, I called him to cash in my chips, asking if I could get two cuts instead of one.

"Anything you want, Benjamin," Topper said. "Your wish is our command."

He greeted us effusively at the door, offering us wine, which we politely declined, or water with bubbles in it, which we accepted. Topper was a gregarious, upbeat man, with horn-rimmed spectacles, apple cheeks, and a salt-and-pepper mustache and goatee, who liked nothing better than having company in at all hours. His spa, on a side street near the Beverly Hills border, served as something of a neighborhood salon, bringing all kinds of people together, where wine and conversation flowed freely and relationships flourished. It wasn't unusual to find a movie star sharing an expensive cigar on the back patio with a busboy or delivery driver Topper had invited in on an impulse. If they were there it meant they had Topper's stamp of approval, and that was all that mattered to anyone who knew him.

As Ismael and I entered, a TV actor with a flawless face—whose name escaped me—was in the stylist's chair, getting some final clips. Minutes later, he was moving on to a pedicure, while Ismael took his place.

"Don't make him look as pretty as the last guy," I said, as the stylist draped Ismael. "I don't want it to go to his head."

While Ismael got his cut, Topper gave me a tour of the place, which he'd recently remodeled. It included a comfortable sitting room in front, with chairs and couches arranged around a fireplace, a steam room and massage rooms in a separate building out back, and indoor and outdoor lounges for cocktails and smoking. Colorful artwork hung on nearly every wall, with a small title card accompanying each piece. Several bold acrylic abstracts were by Billy Dee Williams, the noted actor once proclaimed the Black Clark Gable, who had studied at the National Academy of Fine Arts as a young man. There were also a couple of abstracts by Pietro Gamino, an up-and-coming neighborhood artist who, like Williams, dropped in at Topper's from time to time. But what really caught my eye were delicate watercolors in more subdued pastels—not so much because of the skillful rendering but rather the artist's signature in the lower right-hand corner.

"I see you collect pieces by Charles Wu," I said.

"I've had these for at least twenty years," Topper told me. "Aren't they lovely?"

"I just discovered Wu myself."

"I didn't know you'd taken an interest in fine art, Benjamin."

"Just Wu," I said. "I'm itching to learn more about him."

Topper leaned close, dropping his voice to a whisper. "Don't tell anyone, but I got these in trade, before Charles really started making money. Today, they're worth a small fortune."

"He was a client back then?"

"Still is, only now he can afford to pay. Comes in regularly for a style, facial, and manicure. His wife as well, though they usually come in separately."

"What a coincidence. Ismael and I are attending Wu's gallery opening on Friday. That's why I asked for the haircuts."

Topper shrugged. "Not such a coincidence, really. You know how certain people run in circles in this town, and how often the circles overlap."

"Especially here, Topper, where the elite meets the street."

"I love that! I'll have to start using it myself. Charles has me on his guest list, by the way. So I imagine I'll see you at the opening."

"Comes in regularly, you said."

"Every Friday, four P.M. Very punctual, Charles. And talented, my goodness!" He lowered his voice again. "Although it's really Angela who runs things in that family." He winked. "The woman behind the man, as it were."

He asked me what I was wearing to the opening. I told him I wasn't sure and that it was a cause of some concern.

"You want to look nice for one of Charles's showings," he said, looking over my faded jeans and sweatshirt. "No offense, Benjamin, but you're not exactly a fashion plate." He put an arm around my shoulders and turned me toward his haberdasher. "I have just the solution. A rather well-known actor who shall remain nameless ordered some summer casuals a few months ago. Alas, he's now in drug rehab for a long, court-ordered stay. I don't think he'll be picking up his new clothes. They'll need some letting out for you and taking in for your friend, but otherwise, they should be a decent fit."

Topper glanced across the room toward the stylist's chair. "Where did you meet Ismael, anyway? He's gorgeous!"

"At church, actually."

"Church!"

"When he was a priest. He took my confession."

"This sounds deliciously kinky!"

"It's a complicated story, Topper. Maybe for another time. By the way, if we should run into you on Friday, you don't know us, okay?"

Topper's eyes narrowed behind his spectacles. "Benjamin, are you up to something again?" He threw up his hands. "Never mind! It's probably better if I don't know."

Topper's tailor measured and pinned me for a shirt cut from fine Thai silk and pleated pants from luxuriant linen. About the time my fitting was complete, the stylist was finished with Ismael and ready for me, so we traded places. Half an hour later, as the stylist completed his work, I tried to tip him, but Topper wouldn't hear of it.

"Your money's no good here, Benjamin. Not to worry, I'll take care of him."

Ismael and I were on our way out as a supermodel type waltzed in, so thin the warm breeze might have knocked her over. Topper greeted her like a sister, turned her over to his aesthetician, and scurried back to see us out the door. He told us we could pick up our tailoring on Friday, any time after lunch.

"You'll need some decent footwear," he said, sneaking a

glance at my grubby running shoes. He handed me his business card, with a personal note and his signature on the back. "Run up to Kenneth Cole on the Strip. Have them call me. I'll arrange something on trade."

We were on the front steps by now, but I couldn't resist the opportunity to do a bit more probing.

"You must have known Silvio Galiano," I said, "since he was so involved in introducing Wu around during his early years as an artist."

"Indeed," Topper said, beaming. "Silvio's the very one who brought us together. He was a wonderful man, generous in so many ways. Did you know Silvio?"

"No," I said carefully, "but I'm acquainted with Jason Holt."

The mention of Holt's name seemed to affect Topper profoundly. He suddenly looked as stiff as an unclaimed corpse at the county morgue. I don't think I'd ever seen Topper out of sorts. But Holt's name had definitely struck a nerve.

"Jason's not one of my favorite people," Topper said, with pronounced diplomacy.

"I'm not particularly fond of him myself. Is he a client?"

"He was, at one time. He used to come around for all the natural treatments, before he underwent all that god-awful facial work. Came in with Charles now and then, when Silvio wasn't feeling well. Silvio paid for everything, of course. I never did understand what he saw in Jason, except perhaps his youth."

"Youth can be a great temptation, especially to an older man with no one special in his life."

Topper sighed grimly. "I suppose."

"Holt and Wu were close?"

"You might say that. Jason introduced Charles to Silvio. Frankly, I think it was all part of Jason's master plan. Help Charles's career, making sure Charles was indebted to him, while playing the role of Silvio's boyfriend."

"A shame," I said, "taking that fall the way he did. Silvio, I mean. It's always worse, isn't it, when it's an accident, coming so unexpectedly?"

"And just when Silvio was starting to get better."

I couldn't miss the irony in Topper's delivery.

"Silvio was ill?"

"Silvio had AIDS when he died. You didn't know that?"

"There was nothing in his obituary about it."

"Of course not. Silvio managed to keep it quiet while he was alive, so he wouldn't lose business. Then his family kept it out of the papers after his passing. But his friends all knew. And Jason, of course. Jason knew from the very beginning, when he first met Silvio in the late eighties." Topper paused, losing what was left of his smile. "I imagine that was part of the attraction."

It was an odd thing to say, given how stigmatized and lethal AIDS had been back then. Or maybe not, when one thought it through.

"Quite a year for shocks," Topper went on. "Silvio dying like that. Then Charles marrying Angela that June, just two months later. I must say, I never saw that one coming."

He suddenly brightened, banishing the cloud hovering around our conversation.

"But enough about the past, Benjamin! Life's too short for that." He pressed complimentary bottles of cologne and skin lotion into our hands and gave us quick hugs, as a gleaming Rolls-Royce pulled into the driveway, dispensing another client. "I'll see you two on Friday, even if I do have to pretend that you're total strangers."

TWENTY-TWO

The gallery showing Charles Wu was on La Brea Avenue, between Melrose and Beverly.

It was one of those L.A. streets that yuppies had discovered late in the last century, transforming it from a funky stretch of greasy spoons and secondhand stores where ordinary folks could find a bargain into a neighborhood where you needed five bucks for a fancy cup of coffee and another five for the guy who parked your car. It had become a playground for spoiled rich kids and their faux hipster parents, along with twentysomething wannabes who were willing to live in tacky little apartments so they could spend their money on the right cars and clothes, plummeting toward bankruptcy as they kept up appearances to run with an Abercrombie & Fitch crowd that made them feel like somebody.

Ismael and I arrived with our makeovers a few minutes past seven, bypassing the valet service to park around the corner, where the gallery's manager wouldn't see Ismael's Toyota Camry.

"So how do I look," Ismael asked, a touch self-consciously, "with my seventy-five-dollar haircut and fine summer threads?"

"Like a million bucks," I said.

I meant it in the best way. Beige linen slacks and creamy silk shirt floating around his trim frame. Tan suede loafers without socks, the way the cool guys wore them. Thick dark hair clipped neatly around the sides but left long on top, falling boyishly across his forehead. Gleaming white smile in a darkly handsome face, with just enough stubble to add a sexy edge. He might have been mistaken for a model or a movie star—or, better yet, a jet-setting art collector out of Mexico City, which was our ticket through the door. But he never would have been pegged as an ex-priest.

The gallery manager checked our names against the guest list— for obvious reasons, I'd used a pseudonym—and welcomed us in. We stepped into a small room packed with well-groomed people chatting earnestly and sipping champagne from plastic flutes. The room opened into two larger spaces, equally crowded with trendy types, who seemed more interested in one another than in Wu's art. It hung pristinely on clean white walls—finely rendered watercolor botanicals in the first space, oil portraits in the second, acrylic abstracts in the third—each painting uniformly framed and gently illuminated by its own overhead spot.

In the center of the first room was a round table where copies of Wu's oversize book were displayed for browsing and sale. I picked one up and glanced at the title: *The Complete Charles Wu Portraits: 1987–2007*. The price—seventy-five dollars—was printed on an inside flap of the dust jacket.

"Not exactly cheap," I said.

"Lasts longer than a haircut," Ismael said.

"Good point."

I leafed through the big, glossy pages, studying the excellent reproductions of Wu's portraits. They were all done in the same style—more representational than impressionistic, with vibrant colors, rich highlights, and deep shadows that helped bring the faces to life and into sharper relief. I was struck by how Wu was able to capture a distinct mood and personality with each subject, bringing a sense of immediacy and intimacy to the portrait. I recognized a number of the faces, many of them Hollywood celebrities who ran in politically liberal circles, the kind who showed up at all the right fund-raising parties before being chauffeured home to their twenty-room mansions and hired help, but a few on the conservative side as well. There were also two former U.S.

presidents—one Republican, one Democrat—reproduced on facing pages, as if to suggest that Wu took no political positions either way.

Halfway through the big book, a portrait of Silvio Galiano in his later years caught my eye. It was a reproduction of the one I'd seen hanging in the house up in Nichols Canyon. Below the portrait was the title and year it had been painted: *Silvio Galiano, 1997*. He'd died early that year—April 14 to be exact. That meant the portrait had to have been completed shortly before his death. That, in turn, suggested he'd had the strength and stamina to sit for hours each day while Wu captured him painstakingly in oil. So Topper had been right: Silvio Galiano *had* been making a comeback from his illness when he'd fallen to his death.

According to the book's title, as well as the preface by Wu, the collection included the reproductions of every portrait he'd painted over two decades, beginning in 1987. The fact that it was so inclusive, leaving nothing out, gave the book more weight, both literally and figuratively, and was probably a useful marketing angle. Yet as I reached the last page, I hadn't come across the portrait of Jason Holt that hung so prominently above his mantelpiece. Thinking I might have overlooked it, I checked the alphabetized index. His name wasn't there.

"I hope that you and Mr. Aragon are enjoying the party."

I turned to find myself facing a trim woman of medium height who appeared to be in her midforties. She introduced herself as Angela Wu, the artist's wife. She was a flawlessly groomed woman with longish auburn hair swept dramatically to one side and a smile that was fixed but not particularly warm. Attractive, I suppose, if you like the brittle type who dresses and carries herself like a Saks mannequin, without a hair or speck of makeup out of place. There was a requisite touch of artiness about her—a colorful silk scarf loose about her neck, large earrings dangling flashily—but otherwise she would have fit in nicely at just about any hoity-toity gathering in San Marino or Newport Beach.

"We just got here, actually," I said. "Only minutes ago."

"Yes, I know."

She told us she was aware of us from the guest list and my phone call two days earlier, seeking an invitation. I don't know if it was meant to warn us that she stayed on top of things, but it made the point. She studied my face intently, mentioning that I looked familiar. I told her I must have a local doppelganger, since I spent most of my time with Mr. Aragon in Mexico City, where we shared a house together. I slipped my arm through his as I said it, getting the desired result. She stiffened, as if it was more information than she needed to hear, and the subject of my identity and relationship to Ismael didn't come up again. I reminded her that he spoke almost no English, and she brushed it off as unimportant.

"Art is a universal language," she said, in a cultured manner that suggested upper-crust breeding. "I've always felt that a piece by a brilliant artist has more to say than a million mundane words."

A waiter approached with a tray of bubbling flutes. Mrs. Wu and I declined, but Ismael took one.

"And what is it that your husband's paintings say?" I asked.

"That would be in the eye of the beholder, wouldn't it? After all, fine art is to be experienced by each individual, just like great music or great writing." She lifted the corners of her mouth, as if to soften her next comment. "That is, if one's senses are open and attuned." She glanced toward the door, where a well-dressed couple was arriving. "I hope you and Mr. Aragon will take your time and fully appreciate Charles's work. All the paintings are for sale except the portraits, which are on loan from private collections. I'm sure you're aware that Charles's work is constantly appreciating in value."

"It's probably gotten more expensive since we walked in the door," I said, and she laughed lightly. "Speaking of portraits, I looked through the book, but I didn't find one of Jason Holt."

Her smile never faltered, but her eyes gave her away. It was obvious that hearing Holt's name was not something she'd expected or that pleased her very much. It seemed to have that effect on a lot of people.

"I'm afraid I don't know anyone by that name." She tried

hard but couldn't quite sell the lie. "Now, you'll have to excuse me." She turned to Ismael, bowing slightly. "Mr. Aragon."

As we passed from the first room to the second, a few heads turned, both male and female. Possibly because they recognized me, I thought, but just as possibly because Ismael looked so damned good. I spotted Topper Schroeder among the guests, waving across the room to someone, but if he saw us, he didn't let on.

In the middle room, framed portraits were spaced evenly around the walls, each the same size and in identical frames. Hanging right in front of us like this, they were even more impressive. Keeping his voice low, Ismael commented on the deeply layered brushstrokes, intricate detail, and dimensions of shading and color that reminded him of the Old Masters he'd admired as a young seminary student.

"The painting I saw of Holt seemed vastly inferior to these," I said. "I suppose that explains why Wu didn't include it in his published collection. He must have been having a bad day when he painted it."

Standing alone in a far corner was an elderly Chinese couple, dressed formally in grays and blacks, as if they might be going to church, or a funeral. Their posture was rigid, their faces strained. The old man glanced at his watch, but the woman pushed his wrist down, scolding him with her eyes.

"The artist's parents," I said to Ismael. "I saw their portraits in the book."

"They look like they just landed on Mars."

"They don't seem very comfortable, do they?"

"Very traditional." It was Topper, sidling up to us and whispering, as he pretended to study the nearest portrait, peering over his lowered spectacles. "The older Wus are quite straitlaced and proper," he went on. "I was introduced to them once, years ago. I did my best to make chitchat, but it was a challenge. They speak English but pretend they don't. I'm afraid the art scene, and all that connotes, simply isn't their world."

"Awfully loyal of them then," I said, "to make an appearance."

"Charles is the only child, and male at that. In traditional Chinese families, that carries enormous weight. He's absolutely devoted to them, and vice versa. Though the old man is rather stern, from what I gather."

"And Charles works hard to be the perfect son?"

Topper nodded. "He's in the next room, by the way, chatting up his abstracts with the checkbook crowd."

He slipped away, back into the party, as surreptitiously as he'd arrived. I turned my eye to another portrait, this one of an imperial-looking African-American woman, whose name I recognized from the opera world.

"Magnificent, isn't it? His influences are obvious. Rembrandt, Caravaggio, Vermeer."

I glanced over to find a young man standing at my left elbow, looking dapper and cool in a nicely cut vanilla suit. I put his age in the midtwenties and saw in his blond, clean-shaven looks a vague resemblance to a young Jason Holt, although considerably more attractive. He introduced himself as Steven Reigns, personal assistant to Charles Wu, and asked if there was anything he might do for us. I thought of one or two things right off, but they were beyond the limits of good taste, so I kept them to myself.

"We were just admiring the remarkable quality in these portraits," I said. "Wu obviously doesn't knock them out quickly."

"Charles is nothing if not meticulous," Reigns said, with unabashed admiration. "He stretches all his own canvases, you know. Most artists use pre-stretched, commercial canvases, but not Charles. And of course he only paints with the finest oils. He's quite fond of Windsor & Newton, for its consistency of color. Although he uses Holbein for its French Vermillion, because it's so effective for getting the flesh tones just right."

"You sound like you might be an artist yourself," I said.

He dropped his eyes modestly. "Aspiring. I have an awful lot to learn. Working for Charles is the opportunity of a lifetime."

"He does have a way with color and texture," I said. "What's his secret?"

"The glazing has a lot to do with it. Honestly, I believe Charles uses glazing better than the Old Masters themselves."

"Glazing?"

"Methodically adding layer upon layer of transparent color with oil and medium. Paintings built up in glazes tend to be more rich and luminous. Of course, Charles mixes his own. He would never touch a premixed glazing medium."

"Of course," I said.

"His recipe is one part linseed oil, one part turpentine, and one part Damar varnish." He grimaced mildly. "I probably shouldn't be telling you all this."

I raised my fingers to my mouth and twisted them like a key. "My lips are sealed. But it must take forever to dry."

"Oh, yes. Each layer of glaze has to dry before the next layer can be added. But it's worth it, believe me. When the painting's done, the light strikes each layer, resulting in especially deep color and radiant highlights."

"Mr. Wu's subjects must be incredibly patient."

"A number of Charles's subjects have had to sit for a hundred hours or more," Reigns confided, "sometimes for weeks at a stretch. It's the only way he works. But they don't seem to mind. After all, sitting for a Charles Wu portrait is considered a privilege, not an ordeal."

"I believe I saw your portrait in his new book."

Reigns blushed. "He was very kind to allow me to sit for him. I considered it a great honor."

"Perhaps you could introduce him to us."

"I'd be happy to. I'm sorry, I didn't ask your name."

I gave him the phony name I'd checked in with—Howard Thayer, a bail bondsman I'd known for years—and then indicated Ismael. "And I'm sure you've heard of Ismael Aragon, the noted art collector from Mexico City. I'm afraid he doesn't speak English."

"Not a problem, Mr. Thayer," Reigns said. "I'm fluent in Spanish."

I leaned close, whispering in his ear, "He has a terrible stutter. Very shy with strangers. I'm sure you understand."

"Of course," Reigns whispered back. "I'll let you do the talking."

He led us into the next room, where we saw Wu surrounded by his abstracts, speaking with a large woman draped in a colorful caftan, an oversize handbag looped over one arm. Peeking from the handbag was a miniature Chihuahua, its ears pricked up and its bulbous eyes roving nervously. Cute dog, I thought, if you're fond of rodents.

"Charles still paints the occasional portrait," Reigns said, "but he's concentrating more and more on his abstracts."

The ones displayed here were much like the brown triangle painting I'd glimpsed on the home page of Wu's Web site, merely different in shape and color—a red circle, yellow square, blue rectangle, green isosceles triangle, and so on—painted in acrylic against a white square background. A few visitors moved quickly from painting to painting, barely glancing at them before moving on uneasily, as if they felt lacking in the insight needed to appreciate something so profound. Others stood back at a distance, absorbed in Wu's work, studying each painting as if it was filled with unfathomable mystery and meaning.

I stepped over to the isosceles triangle and checked the title and price printed on the title card: *Green Isosceles Triangle Number Three.* $180,000.

"Personally," I said to Reigns, "I'm much more taken with the yellow square. But I certainly find this one intriguing."

"I think it's pure genius," Reigns said, with apparent sincerity. "He's taken the concept of minimalism to its finite level."

"Not in his prices, he hasn't."

I smiled and Reigns laughed uneasily. He glanced toward Wu, who was shaking hands with the large woman in the caftan.

"Let's grab Charles now, Mr. Thayer, before someone else gets him."

Reigns raised a slender hand to beckon Wu. He responded and we met him in the center of the room. He was taller than I expected, with a solid chest and shoulders, but just as clean-cut and nondescript as in his Web site photo, the kind of man who takes pains to blend in and avoid attention. I introduced Ismael, Reigns explained discreetly about the language problem, and I told Wu that we found his abstracts fascinating.

"Unless I'm wrong," I said, "they're all about anonymity, the need for privacy in a clamorous and intrusive world."

"That might be one interpretation," Wu said amiably. "Certainly an interesting one."

"We're also intrigued by your portraits," I said.

"I'm afraid those aren't for sale," Reigns said.

I kept my eye on Wu. "An academic interest, actually."

"And what would that be, Mr. Thayer?"

"You've made the claim that your book is the complete collection of your portraits, over a twenty-year period."

"That's right."

"But there's one missing."

Wu regarded me curiously. "I don't think so, Mr. Thayer."

"The portrait you painted of Jason Holt."

Once more, Holt's name worked its dark magic. Wu reacted visibly, looking petrified.

"You did paint a portrait of Holt, didn't you?"

Wu's smooth Adam's apple bobbed as he swallowed with effort. I glanced at Reigns, who looked innocently confused. My eyes returned to Wu.

"Mr. Wu?"

"I consider that painting inferior," he said, working to keep the anxiety from his voice, with only partial success. "I chose not to include it in the collection."

"Were there other portraits you excluded?"

"No, just that one." He cleared his throat audibly. "I intended to mention it in the preface, but I guess I forgot. It's not really important. The painting you mention—it's nothing."

"Not to Jason Holt," I said. "He's got it hanging prominently above his mantelpiece, in the house he once shared with Silvio Galiano. He apparently places great value on it."

"I wouldn't know anything about that," Wu said. "I haven't

seen Holt in more than a decade, not since—since he sat as a subject in my studio."

"What was the reason you chose Holt?"

"No reason, really." Wu hesitated, searching for his next words. "I . . . I suppose I thought he had an interesting face."

"What exactly went wrong with that particular portrait, anyway? As a collector, I'm always interested in the process."

I watched the sweat bead up on Wu's forehead. His eyes slid away with seeming relief toward his briskly approaching wife.

"Even the most accomplished artists have an off day, Mr. Justice." Angela Wu's voice was controlled but chilly. "That's right, I know who you are. There are a number of art writers here tonight, including one from the *Los Angeles Times*. He recognized you and mentioned your real name. I suppose I should have recognized you myself when you arrived, but I don't really keep up on all the scandalous and sordid aspects of mainstream culture. I prefer to focus on the aesthetics of art and beauty."

She turned her steely eyes on Ismael. "I don't know who this imposter is. But neither of you is welcome here."

"Because I'm so curious about Jason Holt?"

She shifted her steely eyes back to me. "I told you, I've never heard of that person."

"But your husband has, Mrs. Wu." I turned to him. "In fact, Charles and Jason were quite close at one time. Weren't you, Charles?"

"Either you leave now," Angela Wu said, "or I'll have you thrown out."

"Can't your husband speak for himself, Mrs. Wu?"

Ismael grabbed my arm. "We need to go, Benjamin."

His voice was plaintive but firm. I felt bad that I'd gotten him into this, but the damage was done. I wasn't sure what I'd stumbled into, but it was something significant enough to have shaken up Wu and his wife and flummoxed his bright young assistant, Steven Reigns.

Angela Wu moved to stand between me and her husband.

"Charles was never close to Silvio Galiano, you know. And certainly not to Jason Holt."

"I thought you'd never heard of him."

She ignored that. "It was strictly a business arrangement." She pointed a long, painted nail toward the exit. "There's the door, Mr. Justice. It's the last time I'll ask."

I maneuvered my eyes, trying to search out her husband, but couldn't quite find him behind her.

"Perhaps we'll talk again," I told him.

"I don't think so," Angela Wu said, as Ismael pulled me from the gallery.

TWENTY-THREE

Ismael was quietly angry about what had happened at the gallery, and told me never to ask him to do something like that again. I felt lousy about it, and promised I wouldn't.

Needless to say, it didn't make for a romantic evening. Ismael dropped me off out front of the house, declining an invitation to come up to my apartment. I read for a couple of hours, grew sleepy, and was thinking about hitting the pillow when the phone rang. It was Jason Holt.

"I see you've taken an interest in art," he said. "I guess that portrait in my living room piqued your curiosity about Charles Wu. Or maybe it was your new boyfriend who dragged you to the gallery tonight. Although I highly doubt it. Mexicans are more into velvet Elvis paintings, aren't they?"

"Listen, Holt—"

"I would have gone to the gallery with you, Benjamin. All you had to do was ask. I'm personally acquainted with Charles Wu, as you're well aware, and I'm extremely knowledgeable about fine art in general. I doubt that your boyfriend knows the difference between a Pollock and a de Kooning."

"I'm tired, Holt. I'm going to hang up now."

He went on quickly. "I followed him home, you know."

That kept me on the line.

"All the way to that hovel he lives in," Holt went on, "across the river in East Los Angeles. Is he here illegally or just slumming with the wetbacks? Maybe I'll stop by sometime and ask him."

"Holt, if you go near him—"

"Maybe I'll tell him about your feelings for me, how you've never really gotten over your college crush."

"You're a sick man, Holt."

"If you think you can ignore me, Benjamin, you're sadly mistaken. You might treat others that way, but it doesn't play with me."

I couldn't listen to any more and hung up. The phone immediately rang and my caller ID told me it was Holt again. It rang four times until my voice mail picked up the call. I heard a click but no recorded message. Seconds later, he called again. And again and again, for several minutes, until he finally gave up.

The next day, still seething, I worked out at the gym more furiously than ever, adding ten pounds and several reps to every set. When you're pushing iron, next to injected testosterone, anger is an excellent motivator.

That night, Ismael and I joined Fred and Maurice for dinner down at the house. If Ismael was feeling any lingering resentment from the previous evening, he didn't show it. He'd expressed his feelings firmly but without rancor, and that seemed to have taken care of the matter. He and Maurice cooked, getting along famously in the kitchen, after banishing Fred and me to the living room so we wouldn't be in the way.

We sat in front of the television, watching a mixed martial arts fight broadcast live from Las Vegas. MMA, as the sport was known, was the hot new attraction, combining boxing, wrestling, and martial arts into the most violent man-to-man sporting event ever televised: two well-trained men in a caged arena, wearing nothing but shorts and light gloves to protect their knuckles, trying to pound, kick, slam, twist, break, and choke each other into submission or unconsciousness. Not only was MMA the most brutal and bloody sport on television, it was also the most homoerotic—the sexual implications were unavoidable. It wasn't uncommon to see two muscular opponents locked in intimate clinches that lasted for minutes, their sweaty bodies intertwined like two lover-warriors grappling for glory in ancient Greece. One could only wonder how far cage fighting could go and what the next phase would be as the promoters tried to both whet and satisfy the public's seemingly insatiable appetite for violence. I was certainly getting off on it that night, although Fred, who had always been an avid boxing fan, had quickly dozed off.

"He's mounting him from behind!" cried the announcer, as one fighter took his opponent's back, straddling him around the waist, pelvis against tailbone, on the blood-spattered floor of the arena. "He's going for the rear naked choke!"

Ismael appeared behind me, wiping his hands on a dish towel and staring with a troubled look as one opponent choked the other into unconsciousness.

"How can you watch that?" he asked. "Please tell me this is staged, like pro wrestling."

I grabbed the remote and hit the power button, shutting it off.

"If it bothers you," I said, "I don't need to see it."

He looked incredulous. "You've watched this before? I assumed you'd stumbled across it just now."

I shrugged. "I watch it now and then, when Fred has it on."

"Why?"

He asked the question with such directness and sincerity, it took me aback. I'm not sure I had an answer for him, at least not one I wanted to hear. What was I going to tell him? That I got a vicarious thrill from seeing two nearly naked men locked in bloody combat, beating the hell out of each other? That it caused my heart to race and my saliva to sluice? That I sometimes got an erection when the best-looking combatants were having at it, flesh against flesh?

It was possible I didn't need to tell Ismael anything. He studied my face like he'd already figured things out, like he was seeing me in a completely different light.

"Dinner's ready," Maurice said, coming from the kitchen to rouse Fred. "Bring your appetites, dear ones."

We adjourned to the dining table, but Ismael didn't say much as we ate, and rarely looked my way.

I'd hoped to lure Ismael upstairs at the end of the evening. I had fresh linens on the new bed and condoms and lubricant handy in the nightstand, should our lovemaking progress that far. But after we'd cleared the table and helped with the dishes, he begged off, claiming he had a long day ahead of him tomorrow. When we hugged, he made sure it was perfunctory.

It felt as if a small crack had opened in our friendship, like a hairline fracture in a bone that threatens to widen and split with too much pressure. It made me realize how different we were, in so many ways. Little by little he was seeing who I really was, and I think it troubled him, maybe even scared him a little.

I understood. Sometimes it scared me.

I woke in the morning to find the *Los Angeles Times* outside my door. Attached was a note from Maurice, alerting me to look for Templeton's book excerpt beginning on the front page. I boiled water, stirred a cup of instant coffee, and sat down on the top step with Section A in my lap.

The editors had condensed a section from Templeton's forthcoming book, *The Terror Within,* that focused on one domestic terrorist group in particular, an extreme, right-wing Christian group that called itself the Timothy McVeigh Crusade. The TMC, as it was known, was named in honor of the ex-soldier who had masterminded the bombing of the Alfred P. Murrah Federal Building in Oklahoma City in 1995, which had left 168 people dead, 19 of them children—the most deadly domestic terrorist act in U.S. history to that time. According to its secret manifesto, which Templeton had obtained, the group was committed to terrorizing Jews, Muslims, African Americans, and others who "dilute and pollute the white race," as well as leftists, abortionists, feminists, homosexuals, and other "parasites, pariahs, and enemies of a pure Christian nation." The article was long, thorough, well sourced, and chilling. If her book was even half as powerful in its entirety, I thought, it was certain to make a big impact upon publication. She'd clearly moved to a new level as a journalist, light-years from the cub reporter I'd met when she was starting out at the *Los Angeles Sun* twelve years ago, fresh out of J-school with her master's degree.

I was happy for her, but ambivalent. I'd written some strong pieces in my time, but never anything that came close to this in significance, and I never would. Every dream I'd ever had as a journalist was behind me, while Templeton's future couldn't have been brighter. She was headed for glory, and I was on my way to nowhere, and I had no one to blame but myself.

I reached for the phone and dialed her number to congratulate her. Lawrence Kase picked up. When I asked for Templeton, he told me she was in New York, getting ready to tape a segment for *60 Minutes* before embarking on a twenty-city book tour.

"Already?" I asked. "She didn't even call to let me know."

"I guess she doesn't feel like she has to check in with you, Justice."

I gritted my teeth. "When you talk to her, tell her I called to congratulate her, will you?"

"Sure, I can do that. By the way, I had someone dig up the case file on the Silvio Galiano death, back in 1997. You still interested?"

"As a matter of fact, I am."

Kase told me he didn't want to be seen handing me documents and didn't want me coming by the house. He said he was planning to attend a baseball game the next day and we agreed to meet down the hill from Dodger Stadium, at the lotus pond in Echo Park.

The next afternoon, I drove east on Sunset Boulevard through Hollywood until it swung south through Silver Lake and into the land of taquerias and *vendedores* known as Echo Park.

I left the Nash Metro on Park Avenue near Angelus Temple, the former Foursquare Gospel Church where the lusty evangelist Aimee Semple McPherson had preached in the 1920s. The park sat across the street in a canyon that had been dammed up as a reservoir in 1868, creating what was now Echo Park Lake, an elongated body of water that covered about fifteen acres. Out on the placid water, ducks drifted lazily, along with visitors in rented paddle-wheel boats. In summers past, thousands of lotus blossoms had bloomed at the north end, the product of seeds brought from China by missionaries in the 1920s. There was rich history in the park, and an aura of tranquillity, a sense that time had slowed down decades ago and never quite caught up.

Looking south across the water through the eucalyptus, willows, and palms, I could see the distant downtown skyscrapers. In front of me, dark-skinned mothers sat on the grass chatting, while their small children ran happily about and Latin music played on radios in the background. I loped down a slope to the edge of the lake, where thousands of magnificent pink and cream-colored lotus blossoms ordinarily floated on the murky water and spilled onto the shore. But not this year. The lotus plants had always thrived in brackish water, rooted down among the turtles and the muck. But now the water was so polluted with contaminants and man-made debris that only a scattering of sickly leaves had sprung up. The coots that usually nested in the big leaves were nowhere to be seen, and a foul stench rose up from the lake.

Lawrence Kase was leaning against the rough trunk of a palm, clutching a large manila envelope in one hand. He was dressed comfortably for the baseball game but still looked well put together, about what you'd expect of a middle-aged prosecutor who lived in Hancock Park and could afford to buy his casual wear at Banana Republic.

"It's been years since I've been in this park," Kase said. "I see the lotus have finally died."

Before I could reply, the *whack-whack-whack* of a helicopter's rotary blades cut the air. We looked up to see an LAPD chopper circling overhead. A moment later, sirens sounded up in the hills. The chopper swung in that direction and disappeared, taking its noise with it. A few mothers glanced around but without alarm and then went back to chatting and watching their kids.

"Just an illusion, this park," Kase went on, sweeping it with his eyes. "Just like the rest of the city. Beneath the surface, there's a lot of hot." His eyes came back to mine and stayed there. "Not a place Alex and I care to raise a family."

"You're thinking of moving?"

"Planning, not thinking. As soon as I get my twenty-five years in, we're gone. Three more years. We hope to have our second child by then."

Once again, I recalled something Templeton had said weeks ago, when we'd talked about the nesting doves: *They must feel safe here. It's like the Realtors say—location is everything.* Maybe she'd been trying to tell me something.

"She hadn't mentioned that," I said. "That the two of you intend to leave the city."

"I'm sure she would have gotten around to it."

"There's a lot she hasn't shared lately."

"She's had a lot on her mind, Justice. The book, the wedding, the baby."

"Alex and I go way back, Kase. We've been through a lot together."

"People grow, change. They discover they want something different. She's moving on, leaving her old life behind."

"Leaving me behind, you mean?"

He managed to clamp down an incipient smile, but the smugness was unmistakable.

"I'm sure she'll stay in touch."

"You're really enjoying this, aren't you?"

He ignored it and glanced at his heavy gold wristwatch. "Game starts in half an hour. I should get going. You know how the parking is up there." He held up the big envelope. "I brought copies of the reports you wanted. It seemed important to Alex, so I went out on a limb."

"Anything interesting?"

"Not that I can see. Silvio Galiano was found dead on his own property. Took a sixty-foot fall over a low wall, onto solid rock. Something that might happen to an older man suffering from age and infirmity. Nothing to suggest foul play or suicide. The coroner ruled it a probable accident."

"Galiano had a younger lover," I said. "A man named Jason Holt."

"He's mentioned in the detective's report. Holt was Galiano's primary beneficiary. Got the house, the car, most of the liquid assets."

"He was investigated?"

Kase nodded. "The detectives questioned a number of witnesses, looked at the evidence. Holt's alibi was airtight. You can take a look for yourself."

He handed me the envelope.

"I appreciate your help on this," I said.

"You didn't get it from me. Understood?"

I nodded. He turned and started up the slope.

I called after him. "Give my best to Alex, will you, the next time she checks in? Tell her I thought her article was fantastic."

He waved without looking back, the kind of halfhearted gesture that confirmed he heard me, but not much more than that.

I returned home to find Fred at the end of the driveway, digging into the mailbox for the day's deliveries. He handed me a couple of bills and an envelope bearing the return address of the sheriff's West Hollywood substation.

Upstairs, I tossed the clasped envelope Kase had given me on the kitchen table and tore open the smaller one from the Sheriff's Department. Inside was a photocopy of the police report I'd requested weeks ago, dated late June, when I'd had my confrontation with the ex-Marine named Lance.

The first thing I noticed was a few thick, dark lines drawn with an ink marker. Someone had blacked out Lance's address, phone number, and Social Security number, a nod toward personal privacy that seemed reasonable. But they hadn't blacked out his last name, and it riveted my eye.

Zarimba.

It was an unusual last name, too unusual to be a coincidence. Cheryl Zarimba was the last woman I'd been involved with, during my final heterosexual fling in college. She'd supposedly been on the pill, and AIDS was still unknown, so we'd never used protection. Lance was too young to be her brother, and my gut told me he wasn't her nephew. There could only be one explanation, I thought, and it left me reeling.

Lance Zarimba was our child, the son I never knew I had.

All the crazy things he'd done in recent weeks suddenly made sense. Tracking me down after my memoir appeared. Climbing into his old man's Mustang to play make-believe behind the wheel. Getting a thrashing for it, like the beatings I'd taken so often from my own father for the slightest offense. Touching me tenderly the way he had, tricking me into embracing him, if only for a moment, the way every boy longs to be held by an absent or unaffectionate parent. Watching me from a distance, seeing how I lived, trying to figure me out, get a sense of who I was. Luring me down side streets to Kings Road Park so he could talk to me in private, reach out to me again, even as his anger and resentment conflicted with his need to get close. Then showing up unexpectedly at the wrestling clinic to flex his muscles and let me know how tough he was and to even the score, before roaring off on his big bike with a final show of bravado, to let me know he didn't need me.

The explanation seemed as plain as the tattoos on his wiry body: Lance had been acting out the stages so many boys go through with detached or violent fathers. The only difference was that he'd had to wait a decade or two to do it and then stage it all very carefully, playing me like a puppet so he could act out his deepest needs.

I had a son.

The shock of it was immense, overwhelming. I sat down on the nearest chair, clutching the police report, staring dumbfounded at his printed name: Lance Zarimba.

I had a son. A fatherless boy shaped by abandonment and alienation, an ex-soldier forged and scarred by combat, a troubled man I didn't really know.

I had a son.

And I had no idea where he was, or if I'd ever see him again.

TWENTY-FOUR

Jason Holt no longer seemed so important, and I left the big envelope from Lawrence Kase sitting unopened on my kitchen table. Finding Lance was all that mattered to me now. I had to at least talk to him once more, acknowledge that I knew who he was, get a sense of what he wanted from me, if anything. Not finding him was unthinkable.

I spent the rest of that day and most of the night driving the streets of West Hollywood, searching for him. It seemed improbable that I'd run into him, but I couldn't sit still and do nothing. When once he'd been always lurking about, always watching me, now he was nowhere to be found.

I got on the phone to the Veterans Administration, was put on hold forever, was transferred from department to department, finally got somebody who sounded like she might be able to help, but never got a call back. I phoned Detective Haukness and left a message, telling him that I'd discovered I was Lance Zarimba's father, needed more details so I could find him, and would appreciate his help. I kept waiting for his call.

On an outside chance, I called Bruce Steele to ask if Lance had shown up at any of the Saturday wrestling workouts. He hadn't, but Steele reminded me that we'd last seen Lance roaring off on his hog in the direction of Hollywood, which meant due east.

Over the next few days, I got in the Metro and hit every biker bar I could find between West Hollywood and Montebello, where I stopped at the edge of the Rio Hondo, looking across the narrow channel. Beyond the concrete-encased river lay more suburbs and then Riverside County and then the vast desert that stretched all the way to the Mexican border. Lance could have been anywhere out there, I thought, or even long gone and out of the country by now.

It must have been a strange sight as I pulled up to a tough-guy biker bar and parked next to a row of big choppers in Maurice's stubby little turquoise convertible, but I was so intent and focused on finding Lance that it never occurred to me. Most of the bars smelled and sounded the same—cheap beer and stale urine, with the *clack* of billiard balls in the background, along with jukebox music that pounded like angry fists—and every stop was pretty much like the last one. I'd start with the bartender, asking about an ex-Marine named Lance Zarimba, with a shaved head and a Semper Fi tattoo on one biceps, who rode a 1984 Harley FXST Softail. Then I'd move on to the drinkers along the bar and around the pool table, explaining that I was the man's father and needed to talk to him. Just hearing those words—"I'm looking for my son"—coming out of my mouth was a strange sensation. Until I got used to it, it felt like I was hearing them spoken by someone else. I found a few sympathetic listeners, but most of the barflies took me for a cop and clammed up or cleared out fast.

As the days passed with no solid leads and my frustration mounted, I was tempted more than once to slide onto a bar stool and order a shot of Cuervo Gold and throw it down and wait for the alcohol to hit and then order another one, and more after that, into oblivion. But something in me wouldn't let me return to that place, where you see salvation in the golden inch of a shot glass and a full bottle fools you into thinking it will last forever. I came close to caving in, so close I found myself staring at the gleaming fifths behind a bar out in Pico Rivera, hearing the bartender ask me if he could get me something in a voice that sounded muffled and distant, while the saliva sluiced in my mouth and the old hunger seized me. I almost crossed the line, almost ordered a shot, but then I realized if I did I'd never find Lance, never see my son again. Or, if I did, I'd be no good to him because I'd be a pathetic drunk drooling sentimental bullshit or looking for a fight, one or the other. I fled the bar like it was on fire, realizing how close I'd come to detonating my life one more time.

Finding Lance consumed me. I left another message for Haukness, then started hitting motorcycle shops the way I'd scoured the bars. I barely ate, didn't shave, even missed a few doses of my medications, which I'd always taken like clockwork. Ismael left several messages for me that I didn't return and he finally stopped calling. My mail piled up, unopened. I tossed it on the kitchen table, atop the envelope Kase had given me. I always seemed to be going out the door, on my way to somewhere, anywhere, where I might run into Lance.

Finding my son became my mission, my obsession.

"Benjamin, you don't look well. What on earth is going on?"

It was Maurice, who hadn't seen me for nearly a week, bringing Fred back by taxi from a doctor's appointment. I was about to get in the Metro for a trip to North Hollywood to scope out the motorcycle shops there. Fred checked the rainbow mailbox, as always, but no mail had been delivered that day. Then he struggled up the steps and into the house while Maurice lingered behind. He demanded that I explain myself, so I told him about Lance, all of it.

"A son? You're certain he's yours?"

"As certain as I can be, without a blood test to confirm it."

"That's fabulous!" I was silent. Maurice stared at me quizzically. "Isn't it?"

"I'm not sure."

"But you want to find him?"

"Of course."

"Have you spoken to Ismael about this?"

"To be honest, I haven't talked to Ismael for a while."

"Benjamin, what's gotten into you?"

"I have a son, Maurice. It's a bit of a shock."

"That's no excuse not to share it with your boyfriend."

"Is that what Ismael is?"

"Isn't it?"

"I'm not too sure about that, either."

I mentioned Ismael's calls that I hadn't returned and my concern that maybe we weren't right for each other, that Ismael needed someone kinder and gentler, instead of a hothead loaded down with all kinds of bad history and emotional baggage.

"Balderdash, Benjamin! Haven't you ever heard of yin and yang? Oppposites attracting? What's more boring than a symphony composed of only the most melodious and perfectly blended notes? And if you're trying to place Ismael on a pedestal, as if he has no personal issues of his own, think again, dear boy. He was a Catholic priest, after all. Need I say more?"

"I get your point, Maurice."

"You care about him, don't you?"

I didn't have to think about it. "Very much."

"And he happens to be crazy about you, even if he finds your flaws bewildering at times. He deserves to know what you're going through. And you need all the support you can get right now, if you'd just find the courage to admit it."

Frankly, except for Lance, there was no one I would rather have seen just then than Ismael.

"I suppose you're right," I said.

"Of course I'm right! Now turn around and go upstairs and call him! Then get yourself cleaned up and come down for a good lunch. Why is it that you big, burly men always fall to pieces at times like this and need a tough old queen to step in and straighten you out?"

I raised my hands and shrugged. "Yin and yang?"

He rolled his eyes, then shooed me up the driveway.

"Go on, now! I expect to see you cleaned up, decently dressed, and down in the kitchen in thirty minutes flat. And don't forget to floss!"

It took less time than that. I'd reached Ismael at his office and told him I needed to see him, that I had something important to talk about that couldn't wait. He agreed to meet me at his hotel in Boyle Heights. Just hearing the concern and compassion in his voice reminded me why he meant so much to me. I ached fiercely to see him again.

Maurice had fixed me a tuna sandwich on whole wheat to go, and gave me a bottle of juice to wash it down. I gobbled the sandwich and then my meds as I drove.

The fastest way to Ismael's place was straight out Beverly all the way downtown, where it turned into First Street and carried me across one of the fourteen historic, ornate bridges spanning the Los Angeles River and into Boyle Heights.

Ismael had a room in the Boyle Hotel, a four-story redbrick structure built in 1889 that for decades had housed mariachis who ventured out every night with their horns and guitars to perform in restaurants and clubs around the city. The old hotel was located across from the faded bandstand *quiosco* on Mariachi Plaza, a few blocks south of Cesar Chavez Boulevard. I parked on the street and hurried through the musty lobby, past a group of costumed mariachis carrying their instrument cases in one hand and their big, embroidered sombreros in the other.

Ismael's room was on the third floor toward the back, away from the street. The long hallway was empty, although a few doors were open, probably to let the air circulate. I could hear a Spanish-language radio station playing in one of the rooms and residents tuning their instruments in others. I tapped eagerly on Ismael's door. There was no answer, so I knocked louder.

When he still didn't come, I pounded with the meaty part of my fist, remembering what Jason Holt had said to me the last time he'd called: *I followed him home, you know. All the way to that hovel he lives in, across the river in East Los Angeles.* I had no idea what Holt was capable of, but I grew frantic thinking about it, and pounded my fist harder.

"Ismael!"

"I'm right here, Benjamin."

I turned to see him coming from the bathroom at the end of the hall, shirtless and freshly shaved, with a towel draped over his bare shoulders and a grooming kit in one hand. A weave of fine, dark hair spread lightly across his upper chest, still moist from his shower. The sight of him like that sent a bolt of lust through me; I wanted desperately to touch him. Along the hallway, several men poked their heads out of doorways, eyeing me closely.

"Esta bien, es un amigo," Ismael said.

I knew just enough Spanish to understand: *It's okay. He's a friend.*

Ismael opened his unlocked door and I followed him in. It was a small room, with creaking floorboards and a single window open on the far side, looking out on what had once been a bucolic community of gardens, parks, and lovely neighborhoods until the freeway system had cut it up into gritty sections whose residents now lived with the constant din of traffic noise and a cloud of poisonous pollution. Distantly, I could hear the rush of cars, that unsettling sound of humanity surging at high speed past neighborhoods grown impoverished and forgotten in the shadows of the elevated freeways, the kind of places relegated to the grateful poor.

"Welcome to my humble abode," Ismael said, closing the door behind us.

There was a narrow bed, a dresser, a small writing table, and a wooden chair. Nothing else, except for a crucifix hanging over the bed and a framed picture of the Virgin Mary above the table.

I grabbed Ismael and kissed him fiercely. By then, I'd stopped trying to analyze our relationship, looking for reasons to end it because the pieces didn't fit together perfectly. Maurice had told me once that the heart knows no logic, that falling in love is not a rational process. It's a mysterious and crazy thing, he'd advised me, a force beyond comprehending or controlling that makes not a shred of sense. But it's also the spark that brings two people together, he'd said, the start of something that might work out. And one had to take the risk if it was ever to have a chance at all.

"I've missed you, Ismael. I've acted like a fool." I smiled awkwardly. "Nothing new in that, I'm afraid."

"You confuse me, Benjamin. I don't really understand what's going on."

"I keep forgetting, it's your first time at this."

"I'm glad you finally called. I've been concerned." He reached up, touched my face. "It's good to see you again. But you seem a bit frantic. What's happened?"

We sat on the edge of the bed and I told him about Lance. Everything, from our initial confrontation to the police report when I'd become aware of his full name for the first time.

Ismael took my hand. "How do you feel about all this?"

"Frankly, it scares me a little. Suddenly finding out I have a kid."

"Understandable."

"It's driving me crazy that I can't find him."

Ismael stared thoughtfully at the floor a moment. Then he said softly, "If you'd like, we could pray."

"Pray?"

I hadn't spoken a prayer since I was fourteen, and that had been with Father Blackley, our parish priest, who'd made me his "special friend" when I was twelve. We'd always prayed together, kneeling by his bed in his rectory back in Buffalo, just before he undressed me and used me for his pleasure. Ismael knew all about that—I'd spilled it out, sobbing, along with various other dark episodes from my past, when he'd taken my confession five years ago. Looking back, I realized that Father Blackley had inadvertently brought Ismael and me together, that something good had come from my insidious relationship with the long dead priest. But praying—it felt utterly alien to me now.

"Only if you truly feel comfortable with it," Ismael said.

I decided to at least go through the motions, for his sake if not for mine. And so, after several decades, I found myself on my knees again beside a man of God, as the figures of Christ the Savior and the Virgin Mother looked on. I clasped my hands and closed my eyes, asking God's help in reuniting me with my prodigal son. I wasn't completely sold on the prayer business and let Ismael take the lead. But I moved my lips just the same, mumbling a few plaintive words. My desire to find Lance was fervent and sincere, which seemed the most important thing.

When we were done but still on our knees, Ismael reached over and stroked my head, as if to thank me for indulging him. It was a small gesture, but it meant the world to me. Little by little we were getting closer again. Little by little I felt bound to another person, and less alone.

He left his hand on the back of my scruffy neck. Our eyes were locked, inches apart. I could detect the faint scent of shaving cream coming off him, and sensed the moist warmth. I rose and brought him up with me, then pulled him down on top of me on the bed. We slipped easily into each other's arms, and kissed as if we'd known each other forever. Our kisses grew more urgent, finding their natural rhythm, each one building on the last. I let my hands wander, to his face, his hair, his chest, hearing his breath quicken. I was rock hard by then and could feel him pressing against me just as stiffly. But when my hand strayed below his belt, he caught my wrist and stopped me.

"It's too soon, Benjamin. I'm not ready for that."

"I love you, Ismael."

"I know you do, as much as anyone can so soon. But we're just beginning to know each other."

"You don't trust me?" He averted his eyes. "I've told you I'm HIV positive. I'd never do anything to put you at risk."

"It's not that," he said, looking at me again. "I know this sounds hopelessly old-fashioned. But when I make love for the first time, I want it to be part of something deeper, something lasting."

"Then it is a matter of trust."

He touched my face and looked into my eyes. "I placed my trust in the Church for nearly forty years, Benjamin, before I realized how seriously it had betrayed me, betrayed so many of us. It's going to take some time before I'm able to trust like that again. Does that make any sense?"

I remembered what it had felt like at the age of fourteen, when

I'd reached puberty and Father Blackley was finished with me, making me promise to keep our special friendship and what we'd done together a secret. I remembered how forsaken I'd felt and, as I grew older and understood the truth, how deceived and used.

"If you need more time, Ismael, then I'll just have to be more patient."

He embraced me, holding me close. At that moment, with everything I was going through, it felt better than sex. I fell asleep in his arms, the first good sleep I'd had in many days, as guitar melodies drifted down the hall and into the room.

TWENTY-FIVE

The next morning, Judith Zeitler called from Chicago, the current stop on the latest book tour she'd organized. I was naked, still damp from my shower and about to stick a hypodermic in my thigh. The day was already shimmering with heat, and I had the door and both windows in the apartment wide open.

"It's about *Jerry Rivers Live,*" she said, sounding excited. "You ready?"

I carried the phone back into the bathroom, where I'd just uncapped and filled a syringe with 200 cc of testosterone. I squirted a drop from the hair-thin needle into the sink and flicked the syringe with my finger to expunge the air bubble.

"With bated breath, Judith."

"It's confirmed! You're booked on *Jerry Rivers Live!*"

I swabbed a fleshy spot on my thigh with alcohol. "That's terrific."

I lifted my right leg slightly off the floor, letting the muscles relax, then stuck the needle quickly, pushing it in almost to the hilt.

"Benjamin, this is awesome news! Do you realize how many books you'll sell because of this?"

"Believe me, I'm grateful," I said. "If I sound less than enthusiastic, it's because I'm preoccupied at the moment."

"Oh, dear. In bed with someone who stayed over?"

"Not exactly. Keep talking, Judith."

I pressed firmly on the plunger, forcing the chemical out. It stung for a moment as the testosterone entered what fatty tissue I had left on my withered thigh. While the syringe slowly emptied, she filled me in on the details.

I was booked for late September, on a Tuesday, three days after Templeton's wedding. I was to fly to New York the day before, at my publisher's expense. The producers had scheduled me for the full hour of the show. To coincide with my appearance, my publisher was planning another printing of twenty-five thousand copies, roughly doubling the number already in print. Not a blockbuster yet, I thought, but edging toward respectability, especially if the new printing sold through. If my appearance on *Jerry Rivers Live* had the desired effect, Zeitler said, and enough viewers ran out to buy *Deep Background* the next day, the concentrated sales would catapult my book onto the *New York Times* Best Seller List.

I knew how it worked from there: Getting on that list gave a book incredible visibility and created its own momentum, generating even more sales, further printings, special media attention, and sometimes prominent displays in the bookstores and other venues where books were sold. Once the hardcover reached bestseller status, solid paperback sales were virtually guaranteed and foreign publication was a strong possibility. Used-book sales on the Internet would erode much of my eventual tally, robbing me of royalties and credit for books sold, something that was killing the careers of countless midlist authors. But if I could reach bestseller status, I realized, hitting the big numbers, I'd have enough cushion to withstand that insidious Internet enterprise. If my official sales were substantial enough, I might earn back my advance, maybe even the offer of another book contract, and the chance to have a future as a writer. Maybe I could become the new Clifford Irving, whose Howard Hughes autobiography hoax paved the way for his downfall but also his later comeback as a fiction writer. For the first time, I allowed myself to get excited about the possibilities.

"It was the video that sealed the Jerry Rivers deal," Zeitler said. "It's a great hook, and it gives them something visual for the promos and teases."

The video—I'd completely forgotten it. It suddenly occurred to me that I could use it to find Lance. I didn't like the idea of millions more people watching me beat up my kid, but the video was already out there, beyond my control. I couldn't stop it now, I thought, so I might as well use it to my advantage. I'd contact DishtheDirt.com, let them know it was my son in the video, a son I hadn't been aware of, an Iraq war veteran no less. It was a great angle, sure to be picked up by the mainstream media after the blog ran with it. The coverage might even force the Veterans Administration to help me track Lance down. And if I still hadn't found him by late September, I thought, I'd use my appearance on *Jerry Rivers Live* to spur the search. Someone watching was bound to spot him and urge him to get in contact with me. The producers could even set up an 800 number, where viewers could call in with tips. TV shows loved to do that, to reinforce their image of compassion and altruism after they'd milked a poignant story for all it was worth.

I withdrew the needle from my thigh, blotted the bloody spot with a cotton ball, and spoke into the phone as I carried it back to my desk.

"Judith, you're a genius."

Or maybe it was my communion with God, I thought. Maybe there was something to this praying business, after all.

I filled Zeitler in about Lance. She screeched so loudly over the phone that I had to hold it away from my ear.

"Benjamin, this is fantastic! It's a publicist's dream!"

She told me I'd be hearing soon from a producer for *Jerry Rivers Live* and could give her all the details about Lance. Zeitler also reminded me that I was scheduled for a final interview on Wednesday with Cathryn Conroy, the writer for *Eye*. As Zeitler hung up, I was already sitting at my computer, logged on to the Internet. I saw a new message in my mailbox from my editor, Jan Long, congratulating me on the TV booking and the new printing.

I sent her a hasty reply and then logged on to DishtheDirt.com. When I got the blog's home page, I clicked on a special link for news tips and filled out a form, identifying myself, providing the basic facts about Lance and me, and letting the editors know they had an exclusive, if they acted fast. An exchange of e-mails quickly followed, along with a phone call, as the managing editor confirmed my identity and got more information.

Within the hour, my story had broken on the Internet. By late morning, the local TV news shows had picked it up, along with CNN and FOX News nationally. A producer called from *Jerry Rivers Live* to say that because of the Lance angle they were trying to juggle their schedule to get me on at an earlier date, but it wouldn't be easy in an election year with November looming.

Then Detective Haukness called. His wife had just seen the story on a local TV news show and phoned him about it. Haukness said he needed to talk to me.

"I've been leaving messages for you for more than a week," I said. "Why the sudden interest?"

"I need to discuss Lance."

"So discuss."

"Face-to-face, if you don't mind."

I asked him where and when. He said he'd just finished a witness interview in Mount Washington, a cold case he was working on his days off. He could meet me for a bite in Chinatown, he said, if I didn't mind driving that far. He added that lunch was on him.

"How can I turn down a free lunch from a cop?"

He gave me the name and location of a café he liked and said he'd meet me at the adjoining bar in an hour.

Knowing that Haukness was working a cold case on his own time made me like him a little better, and when I saw the place he'd chosen for lunch I liked him a little more.

It was an unpretentious joint on a slightly grubby side street away from the main drag, not yet overrun with outsiders or the new development that was encroaching on Chinatown from all sides. There was no big neon sign out front with a dragon breathing fire or any of the other flashy electronic claptrap designed to lure in tourists. Just modest gold lettering in the center of one window, proclaiming it the Golden Pearl Restaurant and Bar in Chinese, with the smaller English translation underneath.

I entered the little café, which took up one side of the business, and was shown to a doorway covered by heavy curtains. I parted the curtains and stepped into the dimness of the adjoining tavern, where a few old Chinese men perched on stools along the bar, nursing beers and highballs. Sinatra was playing on the jukebox—"Summer Wind"—which was perfect for a place that looked and smelled like it hadn't changed in half a century or more.

Haukness entered a moment later in his usual western-style garb but with his jacket off to accommodate the heat, coming in through the door off the street. He asked me if I wanted a drink. I told him I'd better not and he ordered a martini with an olive for himself. The bartender was a small Chinese man with slumped shoulders and heavy bags under his sad eyes. He mixed the martini and placed a stemmed glass in front of Haukness, full to the brim, and wandered off. As the detective raised the glass to his lips he stopped short of taking a sip, his eyes fixed on the cocktail's surface.

"Excuse me, bartender."

The bartender shuffled back, regarding Haukness listlessly.

"I'm afraid there's a cockroach in my drink," the detective said.

I squinted to see a fat, brown cockroach floating upside down in the martini, doing the backstroke. Without a word, the bartender took the glass, removed the toothpick and olive, laid them on a cocktail napkin, tossed the drink into a sink, mixed a new martini in a fresh glass, placed it on the bar in front of Haukness, then picked up the toothpick and placed the same olive back in the drink.

"Cockroach no on olive," he explained matter-of-factly, and shuffled off again.

Haukness took a sip, smacked his lips appreciatively, and said, "Let's get some grub."

He strode to the draped doorway in his fancy boots, parted the curtains, and I followed him through.

"You're sure he's your kid?"

Haukness and I sat at a deuce near the back, with platters of chicken chop suey and almond green beans and a pot of hot green tea on the table between us.

"It all adds up," I said, and laid the details out for him.

"Unless you've had the blood test, you can't be certain."

"I don't see it going any other way, Detective."

"You never know until you know, do you?"

"I won't know unless I find him."

"Maybe that won't happen," Haukness said, his Texas drawl starting to take on a tougher tone. "Maybe it's better if it doesn't."

"What are you getting at?"

He drained his martini, ate the olive, set the glass down, and reached for the pot. He poured himself a cup of tea, blew across it a few times to cool it, and took a sip.

"Lance Zarimba is a troubled individual," he said.

"I got that impression some time ago."

"No—I mean *seriously* troubled."

"You care to expand on that?"

He piled chop suey and green beans onto his plate, started eating, then resumed talking.

"You already know he was in the Corps, that he served three tours in Iraq. What you might not know is that he came back with two Purple Hearts and a Bronze Star. Got himself involved in some pretty horrific stuff over there. Besides the physical wounds, which include brain trauma, he's suffering from PTSD."

"Post-traumatic stress disorder."

Haukness nodded, and went on. "Marines don't like to complain. It's considered weak, not in keeping with the manly tradition of the Corps. Zarimba let it go a long time, without telling anybody about the hell raging inside his head." Haukness cleared his throat and sipped more tea, looking less comfortable. "I'm getting into dicey territory here, Justice. Medical information that's confidential, that kind of thing."

"Either you're going to tell me or you're not, Detective. I have a feeling you're going to tell me, or you wouldn't have brought it up."

Haukness set his little cup down, spun it slowly several times between his long fingers, then looked up straight into my eyes.

"Lance is on meds. He was taking his meds as directed when we arrested him after that skirmish the two of you had. We counted his pills against the prescription date when we had him at the hospital."

"What kind of meds?"

"Psychoactive drugs, mood stabilizers—substances that act on the central nervous system to alter brain function. Because of patient privacy issues, the VA wouldn't get too specific about his various diagnoses, and Lance didn't have much to say on the subject. But I still have sources within the Corps. I learned a few things."

He paused again to warm his tea and stare at the cup when he put it down. I scooped food onto my plate and dug in. Across the small restaurant, a fly buzzed near a window. A Chinese woman honed in on it and smacked it with a flyswatter. Haukness continued to stare silently at his cup.

"You want to share, Detective? Or do we play Twenty Questions?"

"Don't be such a smart-ass. This isn't easy for me."

"Because he's a jarhead like you?"

"That's part of it, yes."

"It's not easy for me, either, Detective. He's my son. But I want to know who he is and what makes him tick and if he wants me to be part of his life. If you can help me along those lines, I'm willing to listen."

Haukness considered this a moment, then started up again.

"This war's been different from any other our guys ever had to fight. The roadside bombs, the suicide bombers, the hit-and-run, the different factions we're chasing over there who disappear back into the city like phantoms, blending in with the rest of the population. We knew all about this before we ever went in, the intelligence was there, the warnings, but we ignored them and now we're up to our eyeballs in it."

"Include me out, Detective. I wasn't among those waving the flag and beating my chest to invade and occupy."

"Just shut the fuck up and listen, will you?"

I gave him a small salute and he continued.

"They're seeing a lot of what they call silent injuries over there—brain trauma but no visible wounds, from all the IEDs, the improvised explosive devices. When they explode, they rattle a soldier's brain around inside his skull like a yolk inside an egg. The brain's intact afterward, but it no longer functions the way it should. There's thousands of soldiers suffering from these silent injuries, tens of thousands, only they don't show up on any casualty list. The government likes to keep as many names off those lists as possible."

"Lance is one of them?"

Haukness nodded. "There were three dozen men in his platoon. Nearly two dozen came back from their last tour, but only about half can think straight or can get through a night without nightmares that cause them to wake up screaming. And those are the ones who are pretending to be okay, who aren't telling anyone but their wives or girlfriends about it."

"Or their boyfriends," I said.

"I don't need to hear a gay rights speech right now, if it's all the same."

"Continue, Detective."

"Lance was one of those who kept it to himself. Then some sergeant said the wrong thing at the wrong time and Lance almost killed him with his bare hands. Went absolutely berserk. So the psychiatrists finally checked him out. The Corps gave him a medical discharge and twenty-five hundred a month in military disability. They tell me that some of these guys get better with time, lead normal lives. But not all of them."

"I appreciate the information."

"Do you? Are you sure you're the one this kid needs in his life? With your history?"

"I guess that would be up to him, wouldn't it?"

"You think that all this publicity you're putting him through right now is in his best interest? Or is it something you're doing out of guilt, because you plugged some broad back in college without using latex and now your son shows up and you suddenly want to do the right thing and play daddy?"

"I'm not sure, Detective. I can't answer that."

"Well, you better be damn sure, because you could be messing with a time bomb. Who knows what might set him off? You really want to put this kid in a pressure cooker right now?"

"He came looking for me, remember?"

"Yeah, but can you give him what he needs? From what I know about you, you aren't exactly a role model of emotional stability."

"I'm working on it."

"You're fifty fucking years old! Isn't it a little late to be working on it?"

I pushed my plate away and swallowed some lukewarm tea. "What are you suggesting? That I forget about him? That I pretend he doesn't exist?"

"All I'm asking is that you think this through and proceed with his best interest in mind. There are organizations that help vets in trouble. Maybe they're better equipped to handle a situation like this. My wife and I could help in that department. We've done it before, for other soldiers."

"I'm still his father. That's not going to change."

Haukness seemed to soften a little, maybe looking for a compromise. "This video—can you do anything to get it off the air?"

"It's a hot story now. It's out there, on the airwaves, in cyberspace. There's no way to stop it."

I told him about my booking on *Jerry Rivers Live*, how Lance was sure to be a focal point of the hour.

"Jesus damned Christ," he muttered, looking away as if I disgusted him.

"Maybe we'll find him before then," I said. "Maybe it doesn't have to go that far. Who knows, maybe he'll get back in touch with you, you being a fellow Marine and all."

Haukness studied me keenly. "You're not going to leave him alone, are you?"

"Not unless he asks me to."

"Hasn't he already done that? Didn't he tell you that he was splitting and you wouldn't see him around anymore?"

"He said that, yes."

"So leave him be, Justice. Do the right thing for once in your goddamned life." He pushed his chair back and stood, grabbing his jacket. "He's got enough problems to worry about, without adding you to them."

I watched him weave through the tables and settle the bill near the front door, before he stepped back out into the stifling August heat.

I drove away from Chinatown feeling like my life had just been turned inside out. I couldn't get my head around it, couldn't figure out how to proceed.

Maybe Haukness was right, I thought. My past was littered with all kinds of bad choices and trouble. Maybe it would be better if I just butted out. I heard Haukness's words echo in my head: *He's got enough problems to worry about, without adding you to them.*

Then I thought of all the people I'd abandoned in my life, all the challenges I'd run away from. My mother, after the business with my old man. My sister, who got hooked on junk after my mother died, checking out at nineteen. Jacques, in his last days, when he was dying and needed me most and I detached emotionally to blunt the pain. How was I supposed to live with myself if I didn't at least try to be there for Lance?

Only hours before, everything had seemed under control. Now I felt like a mobile on a string, twisting in the wind. If there was anyone I needed right then, I thought, it was Ismael. Ismael would listen to me. Ismael would help me sort things out.

The Boyle Hotel was less than three miles east.

I scooted out of Chinatown in the Metro and reached Mariachi Plaza in fifteen minutes flat. A minute later, I was crossing the lobby, past a group of brown-skinned men playing cards and polishing their trumpets. I took the stairs to the third floor, too impatient to wait for the lumbering old elevator. But as I reached the landing and turned the corner, I suddenly pulled back, pressing against the wall.

Halfway down the hall, a woman was knocking on Ismael's door. She carried a decent-sized handbag, big enough to hold a couple of reporter's notebooks and a portable recorder in case she should need them. She had no reason to be there, not that I could imagine, but there she was.

I peered around the corner to see Ismael open the door and welcome Cathryn Conroy in like an old friend.

TWENTY-SIX

I drove home trapped in a maelstrom of emotions. Along the way, dozens of bars beckoned, offering me the easy way out.

It had been years since I'd anesthetized myself with alcohol. I wasn't one of those ex-drinkers who kept count, looking for gold stars and applause, so I'm not sure exactly how many years, days, hours, and minutes it had been. But I could still remember the taste as the first couple of shots went down, the warm, reassuring feeling that came with blessed relief. I could still recall the wonderful calm that settled over me as the alcohol hit my bloodstream and then my brain, the calm before the storm. It was the storm I couldn't abide, the rage and violence that rose up as the level in the bottle dropped, and the ruination that always followed. So every time I saw the word *cocktails* in neon that afternoon, I fixed my eyes straight ahead, hitting the accelerator instead of the brake.

I reached my apartment, locked myself in, pulled the shades, and took my phone off the hook. There were fourteen messages waiting for me on my voice mail, all from reporters or producers wanting to interview me about Lance and the video. I saved the messages without returning the calls.

For hours, I wracked my brain trying to figure things out, trying to decide if reuniting with Lance was a good or bad idea, trying to find some explanation for Conroy's meeting with Ismael that for some reason he hadn't told me about. But the harder I tried the more dead ends I ran into, the more questions filled my head. I was on an emotional roller-coaster ride, and the wheels were close to coming off the tracks.

At dusk, Maurice tapped on my door, probably to invite me down to dinner. I pretended I wasn't home until I heard his footsteps turn back down the stairs. I stood behind a curtain at the kitchen window, watching him cross the patio and enter the house, wondering what the hell I was going to do.

Cathryn Conroy called the next morning to ask if we could meet for lunch in Koreatown.

Chinatown one day, Koreatown the next. Thai Town, Filipino-town, Little Russia, Little Armenia, Little Ethiopia, Little Tokyo, Little Persia, Little India—we could have met anywhere in polyglot L.A.; I didn't care. I just wanted to get the interview over with and not see Conroy again, or think about her clandestine visit with Ismael, which I couldn't get out of my mind. What the hell, I thought. Facing a few more of her hard questions couldn't make my life any more complicated than it already was.

I said Koreatown was fine. We set a time and place.

With her usual strategic savvy, she'd picked a barbecue place on Western Avenue, in the heart of what had become the city's most commercially vibrant ethnic neighborhood. Half the signs were in Hangul, Korean-style restaurants and nightclubs were crammed into every nook and cranny, and there seemed to be a Korean bank on every other corner. There was money down here, lots of it, which meant the residents had to contend with the growing threat of gangsters from within and other predators from outside, who descended on the bustling streets after dark looking for a quick score.

I'd always liked Korean barbecue—the grills built right into the tables, the little side dishes that got refilled the moment they were empty, the spicy flavors that sometimes scorched your throat, the big bottles of OB beer to wash it down and put out the fire. There was decorum to the service that bordered on ceremony, but it never got in the way of the conversation or the joie de vivre, never crossed into the realm of stiff formality that could ruin a good meal and a good time, the way it did when Westerners tried too hard to put on a fancy dinner. Unlike some Asian groups, Koreans tended to be demonstrative with their passions, sometimes hot-headed, sometimes quick to tears, closer in temperament to Italians. In Koreatown, a meal out was as much about lively talk and fervent companionship as it was about eating and making nice. Maybe that was why Conroy had picked this part of town, I thought—to make me feel more comfortable, to loosen me up while she guided the conversation where she wanted it to go.

"You get down here much anymore?" she asked, when we were seated across from each other in a booth.

"Anymore?"

She reached into her handbag, withdrew her little recorder, and placed it in the middle of the table, with the mic pointed in my direction.

"As I recall," she said, "you had a boyfriend who used to live down here. Jin Jai-Sik."

I'd mentioned Jin Jai-Sik in the epilogue of *Deep Background*, because he'd played a role in the murder case twelve years ago that had brought Templeton and me together for the first time. Sleek, slim, darkly handsome, not unlike the waiter who'd just arrived at our table to take our order.

I let Conroy handle it. She ordered cuts of chicken and beef for the grill, plenty of side dishes, a large bottle of OB, and two glasses.

"No beer for me," I said, weary of her repeated attempts to ply me with alcohol.

"I'm sure you can handle a glass or two," Conroy said, "a big, strong man like you."

I glanced away from her to the waiter. "Iced tea, thanks."

"Afraid I'll take advantage of you?" Conroy asked, purring like a puma.

I ignored it and repeated my beverage order, and the waiter wrote it down. He leaned across the table and fired up the grill. He had beautiful hands—long and slender, as smooth and pale as ivory—just like Jin Jai-Sik's.

"So," Conroy continued, "do you ever see your Korean friend?"

"Why the sudden interest in Jin?"

"You mentioned him in your book, which I'm writing about."

"Not for a long time."

"Another one of those people you let drift out of your life?"

The clever segue, I thought—Koreatown, Jin Jai-Sik, people I've abandoned. Conroy had made her first moves.

"Jin walked out of my life," I said. "It wasn't my choice."

"But you didn't fight to keep him. You let him go, didn't you?"

"He was free to leave or stay."

"People seem to come and go in your life, don't they? Your son, Lance, for example."

Ah, Lance. Of course—she'd seen the story on the Internet and the TV news shows, like everyone else. At least now I knew where she was headed. Or thought I did.

"You said you were writing about *Deep Background*. Lance wasn't mentioned. We had no relationship when I wrote it. There's no reason for us to talk about him."

"You, your book—it's all fair game in a profile, isn't it?"

"Next question."

"You won't discuss your own son? Whose mother, your ex-fiancée, committed suicide?"

"Move on, Cathryn."

The waiter returned with our beverages, setting his tray on the end of the table. I watched him pour frothy beer into a frosty glass and then caught Conroy watching me.

"Sure you won't change your mind?" she asked. "That beer looks awfully tasty."

The waiter placed the full glass and half-empty bottle in front of Conroy and an iced tea with a slice of lemon in front of me, and went away again.

"Since Jin is such a difficult subject for you to discuss," she said, "maybe we should talk about your father. He's fair game, I hope."

"Go on."

"According to your book, you admired a lot about him."

"From all accounts he was a first-rate detective, who closed a lot of homicide cases. He was a good provider. And he could be a decent father, when he wasn't drinking."

"You had a genuine rapport with him?"

"We had some good times together."

"When he wasn't drinking?"

I nodded. "He was a different person when he drank. Some people can handle it. He couldn't."

"Is that why you're so intent on staying sober? Now that you've got a son of your own?"

"I've told you, Lance is off-limits. Don't push it, Cathryn."

"Let's talk more about your father then."

"If you want to."

The waiter came back with a platter loaded with choice pieces of beef and chicken, which he tossed on the hot grill using tongs. He pushed the pieces around, causing them to sizzle, then laid the tongs at the edge of the grill and made another departure. Conroy picked up the tongs and rearranged the meat to her satisfaction. Flames flared up. The aroma of sizzling meat filled the air.

"Did you love him?" she asked.

"It's difficult to use that word, in light of what he did to my little sister, and the way he sometimes treated all of us."

"But you felt love for him, up to the point when you found out what he'd been doing to Elizabeth Jane? The molestation, I mean."

"I suppose there was some love in there, along with other feelings. Love's obligatory, isn't it, between parents and children?"

"Anger, because of the beatings you'd endured?"

"That's all in the book. You can quote or paraphrase from it as you wish."

"You never used the word *hate* in your book. Not when discussing your feelings for him." When I didn't say anything, she asked, "Is that a question you're uncomfortable with?"

"I didn't hear a question."

She smirked. "Let me put it this way: Did you at any time harbor feelings of hatred toward your father?"

"I've covered all that in my book."

"I'd prefer to hear it directly from you."

"And I'd prefer to let my book speak for itself."

"You're saying that your book is a complete and accurate account of what happened between you and your father?"

I shot another glance at her recorder. Then I said very precisely, "I wrote my memoir as accurately and honestly as I was able, based on my personal recollections."

"And that includes your description of the day you killed your father, the details leading up to and including his death?"

I swallowed dryly, took a sip of iced tea. "It includes everything in the book."

"That day, you caught your father molesting your little sister."

"I prefer the term *rape*."

"You pulled him off her."

"Yes."

"The two of you fought."

"Correct."

"Your mother picked up the phone to call the police."

"Yes."

"He began beating her and you were unable to stop him."

"That's right."

"You ran into their bedroom and got his .38 Detective Special, which was loaded."

"Yes."

"You returned and shot him."

"Correct."

"You kept shooting, until the gun was empty."

"Just as I wrote in the book."

"Then you beat him savagely with the butt of the gun, more or less mutilating his face."

I nodded.

"Overkill, wouldn't you say?"

"I was protecting Mom and Elizabeth Jane. I didn't stop to assess the damage."

"The killing strikes me as an act of pure rage, well beyond what the situation demanded. After all, you had the gun."

"If that's how you see it, Cathryn."

"You were never charged. Your father's death was ruled a justifiable homicide."

"That's right."

"But that's not what really happened, is it? It wasn't a justifiable homicide, was it, Justice?"

The waiter returned with a tray filled with small side dishes, mostly little bowls, which he set one by one at the end of the table. Fried green peppers, kimchi, seasoned spinach, mung bean curd, crispy seaweed, seasoned eggplant, red pepper broccoli, one or two others. He also set two covered bowls of sticky rice on the table, one near each of us, and plates in front of us. He stretched across, grabbed the tongs, and turned the meat, causing it to sizzle and flame again. The air had become pungent from our little feast, but I wasn't enjoying it much. I was fixed on Conroy's last words: *But that's not what really happened, is it? It wasn't a justifiable homicide, was it, Justice?*

The waiter asked if there was anything else we needed. I remained silent, staring across at Conroy, who busied herself with the food. She told him everything was fine and he left us.

"It's a funny thing about memoirs," she said, using chopsticks to lift some dried anchovy onto her plate. "They've fallen into such disrepute of late. The James Frey scandal. The hoax involving Laura Albert and JT LeRoy. The debunking of Norma Khouri's *Forbidden Love*. The unmasking of Margaret Seltzer and Misha Defonseca. Any number of authors who've gotten caught exaggerating certain aspects of their lives, covering up important facts to present a false picture of what really happened, or fabricating whole cloth."

Conroy glanced over as she placed some pickled garlic on her plate. "You haven't lost your appetite, have you, Justice?"

I'd written hundreds of articles in my time, so it wasn't difficult to envision the way her profile would take shape. Koreatown as a colorful backdrop leading to Jin Jai-Sik, a clever segue to other people I'd abandoned in my life, my refusal to talk about my own son, then a neat transition to father-son relationships and how I'd killed my old man. Along the way, she'd use the meal to structure this section of her story and punctuate it with certain points—my problem with alcohol, my attention to the handsome waiter, my loss of appetite in the face of troubling questions. It was the way many articles were crafted for structure and pace, the way character was revealed through action and detail, the way a story was built toward its big payoff. Conroy had honed her craft well, and had her strategy down cold.

She turned the meat one more time, let it cook another minute, then used the tongs to place steaming chunks of beef and chicken onto her plate.

"One tries to remember exactly what happened," I said carefully. "But that's not always possible. We can only write from fragments of memory, and we have fewer and fewer fragments as time goes by. In the end, a memoirist can only do his best."

"Are you saying that you no longer stand by everything in your book?"

"I wrote what I remembered, to the best of my recollection."

"Did you?" She paused with her chopsticks in midair, a sliver of sautéed zucchini trapped between the tips. Her eyes were steady, penetrating.

"Or did you write what you *wanted* to remember?"

"Is that your mission, Cathryn—to discredit *Deep Background*? Turn me into another James Frey? Get yourself some attention, booked on the talk shows?"

"You still haven't answered my central question, Justice. Your father's death was ruled a justifiable homicide."

She set her chopsticks aside, placed her elbows on the table, propped her chin on her hands, and looked me straight in the eye.

"But it was actually murder, wasn't it?"

I worked hard to show her a sturdy front.

"The police investigated," I said. "The district attorney evaluated the evidence. The ruling was justifiable homicide."

Her smile was small, taunting. "Of course, a homicide case is never closed, is it? New evidence can always surface, causing an old case to be reexamined."

"That hasn't happened."

"I have an extremely credible source," she said, "who tells me that you confessed to murdering your father."

There it was. The whole game wrapped up in that one line. It hit me like a stun grenade. But she wasn't finished.

"I'm told that when you went into your father's bedroom and got his gun that day, you did it with the full intention of killing him. Not threatening him. Not warning him to back off. Not holding him at gunpoint until the police arrived. But pulling the trigger and making sure he was stone-cold dead. What happened to your little sister was horrible, but it was also the opportunity for which you'd been waiting a long time. It was a chance to kill him and get away with it, and you seized it."

I removed my trembling hands from the table and hid them in my lap.

"And your source says I admitted to this?"

"That's right."

Ismael. He'd heard my confession five years ago when I was a lost and broken man, spilling my guts, baring my soul.

"There's no statute of limitations on murder, Justice. You of all people know that."

My face was hot, my stomach roiling.

"You're really going to use this?"

"I'm in the truth business, Justice. Like you were at one time, before you decided that truth was dispensable. Of course I'm going to use it."

I turned to stare out across the main floor of the big restaurant.

It was a weekday, and most of the diners were Korean men in business suits. There was a lot of animated talk, punctuated now and then by laughter. On Saturday, it would be mostly couples. Sunday, families. Living in the moment, enjoying one another, making pleasant memories. I'd been down here on Sundays before, just to see families together like that, the way it should be.

Conroy reached over to adjust the position of her tape recorder.

"Is there anything more you'd like to say, Justice? In the interest of complete disclosure? Now would be the time."

I barely heard her. I was deep inside my own head, and far away.

"As a courtesy," she went on, drawing me back, "I'll call you before the story runs. Perhaps by then you'll change your mind and have something more to offer, something pithy I can insert into the finished piece without too much trouble."

"Something pithy," I said.

She smiled and nodded. "As you know, I write in-depth pieces for *Eye,* and I'm not the fastest writer. I like to take my time and get it right. So you've still got a little time if you decide you want to respond. All things considered, you'd look better if you did, more forthcoming, and I'd have a more complete story. Your choice, of course."

I slid from the booth and stumbled numbly from the restaurant, back into the glare of sunlight and the din of traffic, feeling as if my life had just imploded, like a detonated building collapsing in on itself.

I hadn't been this low or this lost in eighteen years. I laughed bitterly, thinking that now—finally—things couldn't get any worse.

But I was wrong.

TWENTY-SEVEN

There was certain to be collateral damage when Conroy's article was published, and I decided to alert Jan Long and Judith Zeitler immediately. It seemed the least I could do.

In my e-mails, I didn't spell out exactly what Conroy had on me. I needed more time to weigh all the legal ramifications before I incriminated myself any further. My single message, copied to both Jan and Judith, went like this:

> It's my unfortunate duty to alert you that Cathryn Conroy has uncovered something from my past that could place me in serious legal jeopardy and will also trigger new questions about my credibility.
>
> Her upcoming article for *Eye* will specifically discredit *Deep Background,* characterizing it as the latest in a string of fraudulent memoirs. Her information only pertains to one section of the book, no more than a scene, really, but an important one. Conroy claims to have a credible source who has essentially debunked my version of that particularly violent moment in my life.
>
> For legal reasons, I'm unable to tell you more at this time. I'm deeply sorry for the regrettable situation I've caused, and accept full responsibility for whatever ensues.

When I'd sent the messages, I shut down the computer and washed my face in cold water, trying to clear my head. Then I stood at the front window, looking out to the street, as I'd done so many times over the years since taking over the small apartment where Jacques had once lived. I thought about how far I'd come in the eighteen years since he'd died. Not far by the standards of many people, perhaps, but further than I'd ever hoped when I'd started the long crawl back with the help of Maurice and Fred and, later, Harry Brofsky and Alexandra Templeton.

Now, with the publication of one magazine article, it would all be gone.

Even worse, I could face murder charges, for a crime I committed more than thirty years ago. The truth was, if it came to that, if charges were filed and I was arrested, I wouldn't fight them. I'd own up to what I'd done—that I'd killed my father with hatred in my heart and premeditation in my mind, that it wasn't the spontaneous and necessary act of self-defense I'd made it out to be. It was the final ugly secret, the last great lie of my life, that I'd hoped would never surface. I'd spent much of my life unearthing the lies and secrets of others. There was no reason for me to expect some special grace.

My greatest regret was how this would affect Lance if he ever found out—that I'd murdered his grandfather in cold blood. *He's got enough problems to worry about, without adding you to them.* Haukness had been right about that, I thought, clearing up any conflict on that point.

It occurred to me that if I hadn't written my memoir, if I'd just been able to resist the money and the chance to tell my story, none of this would have happened. I could have plodded on in relative anonymity, unscathed. What was happening now was karmic, I told myself, old debts coming due.

Be careful what you wish for.

From the window, I watched Fred emerge from the back of the house and move slowly down the drive toward the mailbox, repeating the nearly daily routine that had been going on for weeks now. Maurice appeared at the back door and quietly followed, waiting at the corner of the house and watching Fred plod slowly toward the street, hunched and gasping for oxygen, putting one foot in front of the other like a high-altitude climber struggling up a summit one step at a time.

It seemed like an eternity before he reached the mailbox. One more mail delivery, one more day. I didn't understand how he found the will or desire to go on. He lifted a palsied hand, tugged until the mailbox door came open, then reached in to collect whatever parcels were inside. He leaned forward a little and stuck his hand in deeper, apparently to get to the letters at the back.

Then something strange and frightening happened.

He jerked his hand out and stepped back unsteadily, dropping the mail and shaking the hand like he'd burned it. With his other hand, he slammed the mailbox shut. He started hollering, making an awful racket for so diminished a man. Maurice was down the driveway in seconds, while I dashed down the stairs to join them.

When I got there Maurice said, "Fred thinks something stung him. I suppose it was a bee or a wasp."

"I didn't say I'd been stung," Fred grumbled.

"Let's get him into the house," Maurice said.

I gathered up the spilled mail and we each took one of Fred's arms. He fended us off, insisting he could walk on his own.

"I said something *bit* me," he muttered, making his way to the steps. "Probably a damn spider."

"In the mailbox?" Maurice asked, hovering close.

"My hand wasn't down your pants, was it?"

"It's not like I haven't been available, sweetheart."

Fred scowled and mounted the steps, gripping the handrail purposefully. Inside, he eased himself onto the couch, while the two cats stirred from their naps at the other end. Maurice plumped a pillow, placed it behind Fred's back, and went to the kitchen for a glass of water. I took Fred's big paw to inspect it. He pulled away.

"Stop fussing over me! It's a little spider bite, that's all."

"Stop being such a grump," Maurice said, pushing the glass at him. "Drink this. It's a warm day and you've just suffered a trauma."

"Trauma," Fred said, making it sound silly, but took a few sips.

Maurice inspected Fred's hand.

"I see a red mark." He put his hand to Fred's forehead. "How do you feel?"

"Put upon!"

Against Maurice's protestations, Fred started to rise, but wobbled badly as he reached his feet, and sat back down.

"Dizzy," he admitted. He rubbed his hand. "It stings like hell."

"We're taking you to the emergency room," Maurice said. "Benjamin, get the car ready."

Ten minutes later, as we pulled into the emergency room parking area of the nearest medical center, Fred was breathing with difficulty and feeling nauseated. By the time we got him signed in and two orderlies had him in a wheelchair, he was complaining of blurred vision.

Maurice kissed him on the forehead and told him not to give the doctors any trouble. He held Fred's good hand until the last possible moment, giving it a final squeeze as one of the orderlies turned the wheelchair toward the ER.

"My baby," Maurice said, as we watched Fred being wheeled away.

I reminded him that Fred was in a first-rate hospital and assured him that everything was going to be okay.

Fewer than fifteen minutes had passed when a doctor named Kaplan found us in the waiting room.

"It's definitely a spider bite," he said. "There's a bull's-eye wound at the puncture site. Given his symptoms, it's almost certainly one of the more venomous spiders—black widow, possibly, or a recluse."

"Is this common?" Maurice asked. "A bite like this?"

"We're seeing more bites this year," Dr. Kaplan said, "because of the early heat and humidity. It's been a very active spider season."

"What's being done for Fred?" I asked.

"We've iced the wound and we'd like to inject antivenom. It would help if we knew what kind of spider bit him. Did either of you see it?"

We shook our heads. I'd never dealt with a spider bite situation before. It hadn't occurred to me until now to capture the spider and bring it with us.

"It was in the mailbox," I said. "It might still be there."

"We have an entomologist available," Dr. Kaplan said. "If we could see the actual spider, it would be of great value. But we need to move quickly."

"Are you saying this is serious?" Maurice asked.

"Most spider bites are relatively harmless. But given the patient's age and general condition, there's concern." The doctor turned to me. "If you feel it's safer to kill the spider than capture it, that's fine. But the abdomen—the main body mass—needs to be relatively intact. That's how we'll make the identification."

As I sped home, I went over in my mind what I'd need: a flashlight, heavy gloves, a long, narrow tool of some kind, and a glass jar with a lid. Or a Tupperware container; that would do. Maurice had plenty of those—Tupperware collecting was one of his last remaining vices.

In the kitchen, I found a clean Mason jar and lid on a shelf and a pair of salad tongs in a drawer. I found the other two items on the back porch.

Fully gloved, I opened the mailbox door slowly and peered in. Between the glare outside and the dark interior I couldn't make out any unusual shapes. But when I searched the deeper recesses with the flashlight, the beam fell on a bulbous brown spider, hunkered down in a far corner. It was tawny in color, with fine hairs covering its eight legs and body. I switched the flashlight to my left hand, keeping the beam on the spider. As I reached in with the tongs, the spider began to stir. At the first touch of the tongs it wriggled, pressing against the metal walls. If possible, I wanted to take it alive, but as I closed the tongs it managed to scramble away to the other corner, where I followed it with my light. As I squinted with my one good eye, I could just make out two small fangs protruding from the creature's head, coming together like pincers. Above the fangs were six tiny eyes, arranged in pairs of two each, with one anterior pair and one lateral pair on each side. The spider definitely had the advantage on me in the vision department.

I took a deep breath, steadied my hand, and moved in with the tongs opened wide, expecting the spider to scramble away again. But it remained where it was, counting on its fangs for protection. A moment later, I closed the tongs around it, trapping but not crushing it. Its hairy legs flailed as I drew it out, but I had a firm grip on its body and was able to drop it into the Mason jar and screw on the lid.

I jumped in the Metro and headed back to the hospital.

When I reached the ER reception area, Maurice was speaking quietly with Dr. Kaplan. As I joined them, he informed us that Fred was suffering from muscle rigidity and a spiking fever but that his vital signs were stable. I handed him the Mason jar and he disappeared with it into the bowels of the big hospital.

We heard nothing more for nearly an hour. Finally, Dr. Kaplan reappeared, carrying the Mason jar with the spider still inside. He held the jar up high enough for us to see the spider from below.

"It's a brown recluse—*Loxosceles reclusa*—also known as a violin spider," he said. "If you look closely, you'll see a darkened violin pattern on its abdomen. After the black widow, this is probably the most common dangerous spider we see in Southern California. They prefer to hide in dark places, often under houses. But they venture out at night, which sometimes brings them into contact with humans."

"But Fred was bitten in broad daylight," I said, "reaching into an enclosed mailbox."

"This recluse must have crawled inside during the night. Perhaps the mailbox had been left partially open. They only bite if they feel threatened, or if something brushes up against them."

"How dangerous?" Maurice asked.

"Most bites from *Loxosceles* range from localized, requiring little or no care, to dermonecrotic, in which tissue damage occurs around the wound and supportive care might be needed. But if the venom spreads quickly through the system, it's much more serious."

"*How* serious?" Maurice demanded.

"Your friend's symptoms concern us. We're not seeing necrosis, the localized tissue damage I spoke of. Early symptoms such as fever and nausea without necrosis often indicate a systemic reaction. Full systemic effects may not show themselves for twenty-four to seventy-two hours after the bite."

Maurice raised his voice. "How serious, doctor?"

"*Loxosceles* systemic syndrome is uncommon but not unknown, especially with immune-depressed individuals." Dr. Kaplan placed a hand on Maurice's shoulder. "He's an elderly man, in extremely frail condition."

Maurice searched the doctor's face with stricken eyes. "Are you telling us that Fred could die from this?"

"We've injected your friend with antivenom and placed him in the ICU," the doctor said. "He's getting excellent care."

"He's not my 'friend,'" Maurice said, sounding more bewildered than angry. "He's—we've been together as a couple fifty-seven years. We were married in June. Legally—at least for now."

"I understand." The doctor smiled sympathetically. "Believe me, we're going to do everything humanly possible to save him."

The doctor asked if he could turn the brown recluse over to the hospital's entomologist for medical purposes, and we consented. As he walked away with the Mason jar, I realized he might have another reason for hanging on to it. If Fred were to die and the coroner to investigate, they'd want the spider as evidence. A bite from a venomous spider trapped in a mailbox wasn't something that happened every day.

It was then that I thought of Jason Holt and his fascination with arachnids. At first, it seemed a stretch to connect the two—Holt and Fred's injury. Holt was a troubled man, I told myself, but he'd never intentionally conceal a dangerous spider in a place where it might seriously harm someone. He'd never take his twisted feelings for me to that extreme.

Then I thought about all the harassment and intimidation that had been directed at me through the summer, how it had escalated and become more sinister. And there was that strange phone call, the precursor to everything that followed: *I've killed before, just like you. So, you see, we have more in common than you might realize.*

When I looked at it that way, it didn't seem like such a stretch after all.

TWENTY-EIGHT

Within twenty-four hours, Fred had developed a rash over much of his body, and he began to suffer seizures soon after that. The cause was determined to be loxoscelism, the systemic syndrome Dr. Kaplan had warned us about.

Maurice and I sat vigil in the hospital waiting room, although I found it increasingly difficult to be there. Everything about the place reminded me of Jacques' futile hospital stays in the last year of his life—the medicinal smells; the dutiful nurses padding efficiently about in their soft-soled shoes; the look of despair on the faces of gaunt patients who occasionally appeared in the corridors like wandering ghosts, dragging their IV hookups behind them like giant pull toys; the sight of an empty bed in a silent room after a corpse had been removed; the sound of quiet weeping in distant corners of the waiting area, as friends and family members reacted to bad news, or sensed that it was coming. I understood that hospitals could be sanctuaries of hope and healing, where compassion was common and lives were often saved. But I couldn't shake their connection in my mind with Jacques' long decline and suffering. To me, they were nightmarish places, haunted by death.

"He's going to be fine," I told Maurice, holding his hand the way he'd so often held mine in rough times.

He smiled bravely, the kind of cover one chooses when the only other option is despair.

Toward the end of the second day, after Maurice and I had eaten yet another bland cafeteria meal, I urged him to come home with me and get a good night's rest. We'd purchased toothbrushes and toothpaste in the hospital pharmacy, but that was as close as we'd gotten to personal hygiene. I needed badly to get out of there for my own selfish reasons, though I kept them to myself. Maurice said he was staying put.

"You'll be no good to Fred if you end up sick yourself," I said. "We can come back first thing in the morning."

He still wouldn't budge, so I suggested we go home for showers, shaves, and fresh clothes, and return that night.

"You go, Benjamin. I know it isn't easy for you, being around a hospital like this."

"I wish I was as strong as you, Maurice."

He patted my knee. "You've been wonderful support. Go on, now. You need a break. I'll see you in the morning."

So I went, with feelings of guilt and the understanding that he call me on my cell the moment there was a change, or if he needed me for any reason.

I got home around ten, gave the cats fresh dry food and water, cleaned their litter box, and climbed the stairs to my apartment. I showered and checked my voice mail messages—mostly calls from reporters, but no concrete leads that might put me in touch with Lance, and nothing from Lance himself, which was just as well. There were also several messages from Ismael, asking where I was and why I hadn't been in touch. And one from Jan Long in New York, responding to my e-mail about the likely fallout from Cathryn Conroy's *Eye* profile when it was published.

Jan's message was typically stalwart and succinct: "Don't give up all hope, Benjamin. There might be a way out of this. Let me work on it."

As I was erasing the messages, the phone rang. I took the call and heard the smug voice of Jason Holt.

"Checked your mail lately, Benjamin?"

He hung up without waiting for a reply. I went to look out the window. He must be out there, I thought, watching me, to be able to time his call like this, when I've just come home. But what game was he playing this time?

Checked your mail lately, Benjamin?

It occurred to me that he might not even know Fred had been bitten by the brown recluse. Holt might have assumed the spider was still in the mailbox, hunkered down and hiding, having yet to bite anyone. Maybe Holt was impatient, I thought, wanting me to find the spider and respond in some way. Or maybe there was a new piece of hate mail down there, waiting to be retrieved. Maybe that was it and Holt had nothing to do with the spider at all.

I pulled the shade, climbed into bed, and closed my eyes, determined to not let him manipulate my every move. An hour passed and then another, but I was still wide awake, thinking about his call. I got up, pulled on a pair of sweatpants, grabbed a flashlight, and padded barefoot down the stairs to the mailbox.

I hadn't worn gloves, but I didn't intend to reach in, only to look. Still, I opened the mailbox cautiously. When I aimed the beam inside, all I could see were a few bills laying flat on the metal floor. No spider in sight. I left the mail for the next day, closed the door tight, and stepped to the middle of the street, glancing both ways, on the off chance that Holt might still be around.

Norma Place was still and quiet, not even a dog barking. Somewhere high above me, in the night sky, a plane droned. I didn't hear much else. I stood there for a minute or two, in case Holt was lurking in the shadows and might be tempted to step out and make himself visible. I was turning back to the house when headlights appeared at the end of the street, coming in my direction. Holt?

I stood where I was, unwilling to give any ground. Let him come, I thought. Let him try to run me down, if that's his plan. Let him finally cross the line and get caught red-handed in a criminal act, something I can pin on him. It was foolhardy, but I felt like I had nothing to lose at this point. Let's just get this over with, I thought.

I stayed where I was, blinded by the approaching headlights. If it was Holt behind the wheel, I figured, he could swerve around me and keep going, run me down, or stop and climb from the car to confront me, man-to-man. Not likely, that last possibility, given how scheming and cowardly he was. Still, I thought: Come and get me. I'm ready for whatever you bring. At that moment, I appreciated more than ever the testosterone I'd been replacing in my system, the muscle it had helped me rebuild, the primal male drive it had induced that I could feel torquing inside me.

Bring it on, Holt. Let's get this settled.

The car slowed as it drew closer. I felt my rage building to a fine edge. The driver pulled to the curb and shut off his headlights.

That's when I recognized the car and then the driver, as he stepped out.

It wasn't Jason Holt at all. It was Ismael.

TWENTY-NINE

As he approached, Ismael looked as open-faced as ever, almost wide-eyed with innocence. He'd always seemed too good to be true. If I hadn't seen Cathryn Conroy entering his apartment that day, I never would have suspected otherwise.

"Benjamin, what are you doing out here?"

He was wearing a striped crew-neck shirt and lightweight jeans and colorful, low-cut canvas shoes that accentuated the youthful look. He could have fit right in with the Boys Town crowd, I thought, all those fine-looking men in their casual fashions, trading on their attractive faces and bodies, hopping from club to club looking for the same. I wondered for a moment if that was where Ismael would end up, down on the boulevard with all the others, desperately seeking someone, until he got too old to compete and moved to Palm Springs to sit poolside with a drink in his hand, while he traded gossip with other Boys Town exiles and withered in the sun like a lizard. It wasn't a fair assessment of gay men in either city, but I wasn't in a benevolent mood just then.

"Waiting for someone," I said.

He glanced at his watch and cocked his head curiously. "It's half past twelve."

"So?"

"Who were you waiting for at this hour?"

"You'll do."

He grinned, looking both pleased and perplexed. Maybe it was the flatness in my voice, the hardness, that had him confused.

"I've been calling," he said. "When I didn't hear back, I got worried. I decided to drive over."

"Aren't you sweet?"

I told him perfunctorily about Fred—about the spider, the bite, the vigil at the hospital, the break I was taking before returning in the morning. I didn't mention Jason Holt and his fixation with spiders; too complicated. Ismael appeared genuinely distressed at the news, but he could have been faking. He volunteered to stay the night and accompany me to the hospital at daybreak, but I figured that for some kind of ruse as well. I no longer knew what to believe about him, what was behind his sensitive manner, what he wanted with me, what his deal with Conroy was.

He stepped close and took me in his arms. It felt good, feeling him close against me, holding me, while the warm winds buffeted our bodies. But it was different now. It felt good in a dark, crazy way, with my rage mixed in with my lust and my confusion about who he really was and what his real intentions were. It was the first time he'd touched me when my shirt was off. He didn't seem inhibited in the slightest.

I placed one of his hands on my chest, pressing his fingers into the thick mat of dark blond hair. He didn't resist and his eyes looked expectant, like he was finally ready to follow my lead.

"Let's go upstairs," I said.

When we were in the darkened apartment, he asked to use the bathroom. While he was in there, I found a condom and lube in my nightstand and tossed them onto the bed. I hated him at that moment, but not enough to infect him with the virus. I could hear him pissing on the other side of the door, a long, full stream. Then it was quiet. I envisioned him shaking off, zipping up, glancing momentarily at his beautiful face in the mirror for no particular reason, or maybe to calculate what his next move would be. Whatever it was, I planned to stay a step ahead.

As he came out, he turned out the light behind him.

"Leave it on," I said. "I want to be able to see you."

He gave me a curious look. I was tempted to tell him his act was getting old. He reached back and flicked the switch. It left the outer room in diffused light, the kind that allows you to see the finer details of a naked man but also leaves a little mystery, a sense of the hidden, the unexplored.

As he came around the end of the bed, I touched his face. He hadn't shaved for a day or two and the grate of his dark beard sharpened my sense of him, of his maleness, of the reason I wanted him so badly. I wasn't wearing briefs under the sweatpants and my erection strained against the loose cotton. I took Ismael's hand and placed it below my belly where I was hard.

"Trust is important to you, isn't it, Ismael?"

He nodded earnestly, his brown eyes inquisitive and maybe a little scared.

"Very much," he said. "We discussed it the other day, in my room at the hotel."

"Yes, I remember."

I ran my hand through his thick, black hair, then pulled his face to mine and kissed him forcefully on the mouth. Just as he responded, I pulled away.

"Without trust," I said, "a relationship never feels right, does it?"

"I'm not that experienced, but—"

"It's either there, or it isn't, wouldn't you say? It's something you can feel in your gut. Not something to be discussed. Because words lie, don't they, Ismael? Words can detour around the truth as easily as they can express it."

"Benjamin, what's going on? What's the matter?"

I reached down to the hem of his T-shirt, pulled it up and over his head, and tossed it aside, into the shadows of the room. I clawed at his chest, through the dark hair until I found his hardening nipples. I bent to seize one in my teeth until he cried out.

"Without trust," I said, "it never feels healthy and complete, does it? Never feels real. There's always an unspoken tension, an invisible component that keeps the private moments between two people artificial and just a bit off-kilter. Because they don't really know each other, not truly and profoundly, and they know they don't. But they don't want to talk about it, either, to get at it, to root out the causes of the uncomfortable moments and awkward silences. Because that would be too intimate, too frightening. They each have their shameful secrets, their endless deceptions, their unspoken feelings. That's how most couples live out their lives, isn't it, Ismael? Not so much trusting and loving as pretending."

"Why are you talking like this? What's gotten into you, Benjamin?"

I ignored him and went on. "So they settle into their rhythms and routines, into their imitation of life. They make the best of it, content to have a stranger beside them, because the alternative—loneliness—is unbearable. How many marriages have you known like that, unions between breeders blessed by church and state? How many relationships based more on appearance than reality, designed to fool as many people as possible?"

"Benjamin, I know your parents didn't have a model marriage, but—"

I cut him off, softening my voice. "Maybe none of us can ever truly know another person. Maybe that's the final truth—that we're all connected yet ultimately alone, destined to live among strangers, going through the motions, getting through this illusory life."

He started to speak again, but I put a finger on his lips.

"Do you feel you know me, Ismael? Do you trust me? Are you ready to prove it?"

I found his belt buckle, unfastened it, unhitched and unzipped his pants, and let them drop around his ankles. I ran my hands along the sides of his solid torso.

"Should I trust you, Ismael?"

"Yes, of course."

I kneeled to pull off his shoes, then his jeans, which I tossed aside. I ran my hands up his hairy legs, up the lean, strong calves, the firm thighs. Then I explored with my tongue. Then with my teeth, biting his flesh, tasting him, feasting on his beauty. He grabbed my head on both sides, forcing me to look up at him.

"Benjamin, please. We talked about this. You said you'd give me more time."

"You'd never betray me, would you, Ismael?"

"Of course I wouldn't."

I gripped his hips to hold him steady and buried my tongue in the trail of dark hair that ran down his belly. I heard him gasp, short and sharp. Then I pressed my face against his crotch and he moaned, long and low. Beneath his briefs he was as hard as I was. I pinched the waistband and pulled them down and off him so that he was naked, exposed to me in a way that he'd never been with a woman or another man, if what he'd told me about him-self was true.

I looked up into his face.

"So do you trust me or not? Which is it, Ismael? Because it's either one or the other. The time to decide is now."

His eyes were a confusion of fear and desire. He parted his lips, but no words came out. His silence told me all I needed to know. I took him in my mouth, all of him, right down to the nest of thick hair and firm muscles of his abdomen. He grabbed my head with both hands, digging in with his nails like a man holding on for the ride of his life. I reached around to grip his buttocks, one in each hand, kneading the soft parts until I found the muscle beneath, as he clenched up like every other homosexual virgin facing his first time. He could have reached back to push my hands away or ordered me to stop. He didn't.

I pulled back, coming off him quickly, and pressed the flat of my hand against his chest, pushing him back on the bed and kick-ing off my sweatpants at the same time.

"I'm glad to hear you say that, Ismael—that you'd never betray me. It tells me so much about you."

I reached for the condom, tore the package open with my teeth, and rolled on the latex, watching his conflicted eyes move from my face to my cock and back again. I lathered myself with gel until I was slick, then pushed his legs high and used a finger to lube him for safer passage.

"Trust me," I said. "Trust me the way I trusted you."

I took my position between his legs, his ankles up over my shoulders. I turned to kiss his muscular calves, to run my tongue over his hairiness, to nibble at his flesh. I bit harder until he cried out. His stiff cock jerked and quivered.

"I saw you with Cathryn Conroy," I said.

"Oh." His voice was small, surprised.

I parted the cheeks of his ass and placed the tip of my cock where I wanted it to be. His breathing was shallow, hesitant.

"The other day, at the door to your room, when you invited her in."

"I was going to tell you about that."

"I bet you were."

I thrust my hips forward slightly, opening him just a little. He cried out and clinched against the pressure, keeping me out.

"Benjamin, please! Stop! It's not the right time. It feels wrong."

"It feels wrong?"

"Yes!"

I grabbed his throat with my right hand, pinning him down.

"It felt wrong when I saw Conroy going into your apartment."

"Why?"

I gripped tighter, choking him.

"You told Conroy about what happened between me and my father, the day I killed him. You repeated what I'd confessed to you five years ago."

"No!"

"Did you think because you left the priesthood you no longer had to honor your vow of confidentiality?"

"Benjamin, you don't understand—"

"I trusted you, Ismael. I opened my heart to you, bared my soul, confessed my worst sins. And you betrayed me."

"That's not true!"

I pressed down with my right hand, cutting off his air, and thrust forward again with my hips. He pushed and flailed at me with both hands, trying to keep me from penetrating any deeper while fighting desperately for air. I was about to plunge into him, to hurt him and shame him and make him feel my anger in a way he'd never forget, when I heard someone pounding on the door. Then I heard Maurice's voice, alarmed and shrill.

"Benjamin! What's going on? Are you all right?"

He pounded harder and kept calling my name. I stared at Ismael's reddening face, and into his terrified eyes.

"Benjamin! Open this door!"

I loosened my hold on Ismael's throat and withdrew from his rectum, where I'd only started to penetrate, not yet drawing blood. He fell back on the pillow, coughing and rubbing his neck. Tears flooded his face.

I turned my head toward the door.

"It's all right, Maurice. Everything's okay."

"Are you sure? I heard an awful commotion."

"We're fine, Maurice. Don't worry."

Through the door, he explained that he'd changed his mind and decided to come home after all, heeding my advice. He'd taken a taxi, he said, and heard loud voices through the open window as he walked up the drive.

"Get some sleep, Maurice. I'll see you in the morning."

I heard his footsteps treading lightly down the stairs. Then it was quiet. Ismael and I were alone, and I was faced with what I'd done, and almost done.

At times, the line between rape and consensual sex can be a fine one, not always clearly drawn, as some would have it. But the distinction rarely matters, because the heart knows.

If Maurice hadn't arrived when he did that night, I would have raped Ismael Aragon. I knew that. We both knew.

The moment I was off him, he grabbed the bedsheet and drew it up around him, covering himself. I climbed off the bed and pulled on my sweatpants, unable to let him see my face, my eyes. I spoke over my shoulder, barely turning my head.

"You can use the shower if you want."

It was the only thing I could think of to say, the only thing I had the courage to say. He dragged the sheet from the bed, keeping it around him, and gathered up his clothes from the floor. He ducked into the bathroom for a minute and I heard him sobbing behind the locked door. After a while, he grew quiet. I heard him blow his nose, then run the tap in the sink.

When he came out, dressed, he kept his eyes on me. I kept mine moving.

"Cathryn Conroy called me," he said, with surprising calm, "because she wanted to ask a few questions about you. I don't know how she got my number. I assumed you'd given it to her."

I spoke quietly, barely whispering. "I didn't."

"I suppose I should have called you," he went on, "and asked about it first, but she said she was in my neighborhood and was in a hurry, so I told her to come up. She turned on her recorder and began asking questions. I told her that you and I were dating and that I liked you very much, and that you'd been a tremendous source of support as I'd faced sexual identity issues. I told her that I considered you my closest friend, that despite all the trouble you've had, there was another side of you that many people didn't know. That deep down, I felt you had a good heart, that you were a good person. She seemed disappointed in my responses and tried to get me to say more, or to say something different, but I didn't. The subject of your father never came up. That's the simple truth, Benjamin. You can believe it or not."

"Ismael—"

I stepped toward him, but he put up a hand and backed away, toward the door. "If Miss Conroy knows something about your father's death, something you've kept private, she didn't hear it from me. Do you remember what I told you five years ago, when I took your confession?"

"Some of it."

"I reminded you that when you took your father's life, you were seventeen. That you acted in the heat of the moment when your father was a genuine threat. I doubt that you really know what your feelings were when you pulled that trigger, Benjamin. Time and guilt have a way of warping memory, of blurring reality. Whatever might have happened that day, God is a forgiving Lord. He has surely forgiven you, Benjamin. But you still need to forgive yourself. You need to forgive yourself for so many things."

"But she knows," I said. "She knows that I'd thought about killing my father long before I did it. She *knows*, Ismael."

"Then you must have revealed that to someone else as well. Because I never betrayed you, Benjamin, and I never would."

Then you must have revealed that to someone else as well. Because I never betrayed you, Benjamin, and I never would.

There *was* someone else, whom I'd completely forgotten until now. Alexandra Templeton. Years ago, in a moment of anguish, I'd told her. Templeton, who was as ambitious as she was accomplished. Templeton, who was friendly with Cathryn Conroy, who'd helped Templeton land her big-shot agent and get her book deal.

Ismael opened the door. I reached out for him, but he kept his hand up to keep me away.

"Please, Benjamin. Just leave me alone."

He stepped out and closed the door softly behind him, like a gentle but firm good-bye. From the window, I watched him walk down the driveway. He never looked back before he turned into the street. I saw his headlights come on and watched him drive away.

I don't know how long I stood there, staring out. An hour maybe. I'd like to say that I felt empty and numb inside. The truth is I only wished I felt that way.

I was my father's son. I'd been haunted by the fact of it for years but never more than now. He lived inside me as surely as the heart that beat within my chest. I was less than two weeks from my fiftieth birthday, and he continued to cleave to me like a shadow. I was still trying to please him, mimic him, elude him, kill him. At what point does the son free himself from the father? I wondered. At what point does the son exert his own will, become his own man, breathe his own air? Is it even possible?

I turned from the window, suddenly nauseated, and dashed to the bathroom to throw up. As I rinsed my mouth and washed up at the sink, I saw my vial of testosterone nearby, next to several packaged syringes bound together by a rubber band. At what cost, I asked myself, had I replenished my youthful vigor, my depleted manhood? What constituted manhood? What did it mean to be a real man? At that moment, I knew that Ismael was a more complete man than I could ever hope to be, more dependable, more self-aware, more courageous. All my muscles and libido and rage didn't make me more of a man at all.

I turned to glimpse my face in the mirror and what I saw was a fool, a fraud, a pathetic imposter.

The vial had one dose left, with three refills marked on the label. I stroked a hard biceps, remembering what the testosterone had done for me. Then I shut my eyes, trying to blot out the image of what I'd done to Ismael, turning a sexual act that should have been infused with tenderness and pleasure into something rapacious and reprehensible. I didn't blame the steroid for what I'd done; that was all on me. But the testosterone boost was part of it—part of my desperate quest to measure up to a perverted standard of manhood that caused more grief than good.

I grabbed the vial and syringes, tossed them into the waste can, pulled on some fresh clothes, and left the apartment.

I drove the freeways for hours, without a destination. I sped anonymously through cities and suburbs, past millions of buildings, darkened windows, silent rooms. Through a borderless landscape of asphalt and concrete, brick and mortar, metal and glass, neon and billboards, commerce run amok, endless miles of crackling transmission lines that connected everyone yet connected no one at all. Through the dark early morning hours I glided, a man alone among millions, with no idea why I was here, no sense of belonging, no purpose other than to propagate. Which I'd managed to do, but I'd even screwed that up. Thousands of drivers sped past me, nameless, faceless, locked in their steel compartments, a rush of hard metal and power.

It was nearly 5:00 A.M. when I finally stopped. I was somewhere off the 101 in the Santa Monica Mountains. A wildfire had flared up, moving quickly, an orange glow coming up over a nearby ridge. Burning embers danced about like fireflies. Fire trucks were all around me, their big engines groaning as they carried firefighters in yellow helmets and heavy protective jackets into the hills, toward the advancing flames. Coming out was a stream of civilian vehicles, packed with people, pets, belongings. A lone woman walked on foot beside the road, leading two horses by their reins. Behind her, across an open field, a gray mare galloped through the drifting smoke, eyes wide in terror, nostrils flaring.

Two cops pulled a barricade across my side of the road, blocking traffic going in. One of them ordered me to turn around and get out.

I returned to West Hollywood just before dawn, coming down through Laurel Canyon and turning west on Santa Monica Boulevard. It had been years since I'd been on the boulevard in the early morning hours, and it seemed spookily quiet. The only people I saw were one or two young men passed out on the sidewalk in their vomit and weary, brown-skinned workers from the clubs, waiting at bus stops for their communal transportation home.

The light was green as I approached San Vicente Boulevard, but I slowed for two scrawny coyotes pausing in the middle of the intersection. In recent years, we'd begun to see more of them in the city, as far south as the Fairfax District and the Grove, sometimes in broad daylight, driven down from the hills by drought and hunger and diminishing space. The light turned red, but they remained where they were, alert but indecisive. Finally, one trotted south, toward the Pacific Design Center and West Hollywood Park. The other followed. They passed beneath a banner stretched across the street, promoting the seventh annual West Hollywood Book Fair. Then I couldn't see them anymore.

The light changed again and I drove on to Hilldale, where I turned right and continued up the hill to Norma Place.

Maurice was sitting alone on the front porch swing, as if waiting for me so we could return to the hospital. He was in fresh clothes and his long, white hair looked clean, pulled back and secured behind his head. At first, I was heartened. But as I climbed from the Metro and approached the house, I got a closer glimpse of his drawn face, and the bereft look in his eyes.

He sat waiting in the swing, which Fred had built with his own hands long before Jacques or I had known them. The cats were there, half-asleep on Maurice's lap as he rubbed them around the ears. They barely looked up as I slid onto the swing beside him.

"Fred's gone," Maurice said. "The hospital called a few minutes ago. I tried to reach you, but there was no answer."

"I forgot to take my phone. I'm sorry."

"His heart was too weak. I'm sure they did their best."

I had no words, so I just let him talk. Mostly, he recalled milestones in his life with Fred, the good times, alternately laughing and crying. He told me that it all felt unreal, that it didn't seem possible that Fred was actually gone from his life.

Then he said, "Benjamin, there's something you should know."

"What's that, Maurice?"

"Years ago, Fred and I decided to leave this property to you. I know it's an old house, not that big and nothing fancy. But we've kept it up fairly well, and it's all paid off. And with the apartment and the yard, and this being West Hollywood, well, it's worth a good bit of money, at least by our standards."

"Maurice, that's very generous. But let's not talk about that now."

"No, I want to say this. At some point, you and I will exchange places. If I'm still able to get up and down stairs, I'll move into the apartment and you'll come down here to live."

"Maurice—"

He shushed me, and continued. "Our hope was always that you would make a good life for yourself in this house, maybe settle down with someone special. Maybe that nice young man, Ismael, who Fred and I like so much. You see a future with him, don't you?"

Shame gripped me. I couldn't bear to tell him what had happened up in the apartment a few hours earlier. Not just then, maybe not ever.

"I'm not so sure Ismael and I are meant to be together."

Maurice patted my knee, as he had so often over the years.

"You'll learn soon enough," he said, "if you haven't already, that companionship with someone you respect and care deeply about is what makes life bearable, even worthwhile. Loneliness is the great burden we all face, Benjamin. But how we face it and meet its challenge, how it shapes and transforms us, all that is within our power. And the power of two is infinitely greater than the power of one."

The cats shifted to get more comfortable, molding themselves into each other like a spooning couple. To the east, through the trees, the sky was pink. The early sunlight found its way to the street and began to gently baste the house.

"If you could drive me to the hospital in a few minutes, I'd appreciate it. They promised not to move Fred until I come to see him. And his wedding band—I told them I'd prefer to remove that myself."

"Of course," I said. "We can go whenever you like."

"Where have you been, anyway? Coming in at such a late hour."

"Just out," I said. "Out driving."

He searched my face. "Is there something you need to tell me, Benjamin?"

"No. Things are okay."

"You're sure?"

I nodded vaguely and reached over to take his hand. It was withered but soft, and I noticed that he'd removed all his jewelry, the bracelets and rings he was so fond of wearing. Except for his gold wedding band, the one that matched Fred's. I couldn't imagine Maurice ever removing that.

"How are you holding up, Maurice?"

"I've had better days." He smiled self-consciously. "But you're with me, Benjamin. That helps." He squeezed my hand. "You and the cats."

THIRTY

With September came blistering Santa Ana winds and more wild-fires. The sound of sirens became routine. White ash drifted down on the neighborhood like a fine mist.

Amid all the news coverage of the fires, Fred's death briefly got some attention, as spider bite fatalities in urban areas some-times do. If Jason Holt hadn't known about Fred's contact with the brown recluse, I thought, he surely did now. Maybe he real-ized he'd finally gone too far, because I heard nothing from him in the ensuing days. I was in a quandary about what to tell the au-thorities, whether I should raise questions that would trigger a coroner's investigation. Since I had no proof, I hadn't mentioned my suspicions to Dr. Kaplan. With nothing to indicate foul play, he was likely to declare Fred's death natural when he signed the death certificate. To be on the safe side, though, he'd ordered tox-icology tests. The tox report would take several days, probably longer, which bought me some time to make a decision.

As much as I dreaded it, I felt compelled to talk to Maurice about the possible connection between Holt and Fred's death. I worried that Dr. Kaplan might decide on his own to get the coro-ner involved, and I didn't want Maurice to hear about it first from someone else. But I procrastinated, fearing his reaction.

At week's end, on a Saturday, Maurice held a memorial service behind the house. It seemed too soon to me, the timing more appropriate for a funeral than a festive celebration of Fred's life that one might have expected from Maurice. I'd anticipated music, dancing, laughter, but the service turned out to be a modest and somber affair, with only Maurice's closest friends in attendance. When he stood up before us to speak, his voice and manner lacked any sign of vigor. He commented that each year his circle of friends grew smaller, as age or disease took them one by one, and how grateful he was for those who remained. He briefly reminisced about Fred, becoming emotional when he spoke of Fred's devotion and essential decency, which was often lost on others beneath his gruff exterior. Maurice also spoke about the various causes they'd been involved in over the decades—civil rights, women's rights, gay rights, workers' rights, the environment—and how he saw them all connected, inseparable from one another. It troubled him, he said, that the younger gay generation, by and large, didn't seem too concerned about the issues shaping its future, that too many young queers had grown dangerously complacent, focused on their own immediate comfort and pleasure, while forces that would oppress them grew stronger and bolder with each passing day.

For all his sincerity, Maurice's words lacked the energy and passion for which he'd always been known in the community. He'd been understandably subdued since Fred's passing, unwilling to be away from home for any length of time, and preferring to spend long hours alone with the cats, rather than have friends in or accept their invitations to go out. He'd always been the most resourceful and dependable man I'd known. But he wasn't the same now that he'd spent a week of nights alone in the bed he and Fred had shared for so long. The reality of Fred's death, I think, had finally sunk in. Maurice seemed detached, less engaged with the outer world, and simply worn-out, as if all of his eighty-three years had suddenly caught up with him.

Toward the end, when it was time to spread Fred's ashes, Maurice carried the urn out into the rear yard and removed the lid, while we stood around him. But he was quickly overcome with feelings and asked me to do it for him. I used my bare hand, tossing handfuls into the garden they'd tended together for so long, saving the final ashes for spreading on the grave where they'd buried the baby dove in the shade of the blue hydrangea.

When the service was over and everyone was gone, the cats reappeared on the patio, taking their usual places on the cushions, while Maurice and I cleaned up.

"Your friend Ismael didn't come," Maurice said. "Didn't you want him here?"

"We haven't spoken recently," I said.

He waited for more, but when I wasn't forthcoming, he said, "I see."

I dumped paper plates in the trash cans beside the garage while he carried a tray of glasses into the house. We met again on the patio. Maurice picked up a broom and began sweeping.

"Alexandra called yesterday from Seattle," he said, "expressing her apologies that she couldn't be here today."

"I guess her book tour is pretty tightly scheduled."

Templeton had been profiled on *60 Minutes* the previous week, and interviewed on several talk shows, looking gorgeous, sounding articulate, and demonstrating an impressive grasp of her extremely serious subject. *The Terror Within* was climbing all the big bestseller lists and would probably win an important award or two. It seemed likely that she'd become a media star, grabbed up by one of the network news departments or at least turned into a staple on the gab shows, where the male experts could be fat, bald, and frumpy, but their female counterparts had to be trim and attractive, as well as smart and well-spoken. In that sense, Templeton was just what the networks and cable news shows were looking for. She was due in San Francisco today for more interviews, then back in Los Angeles on Monday, just in time to help her parents make the final preparations for her Saturday wedding.

"She asked me to wish you a happy—" Maurice broke off, mildly alarmed. "Oh, my goodness. It's your birthday, isn't it? Where's my mind, Benjamin? I completely forgot."

"That's all right, Maurice. I've been trying to forget, myself."

"But fifty, Benjamin. It's such a milestone. I should have at least made a nice cake." Distress crossed his face like a cloud. He placed a withered hand to his cheek. "Everything's been so—I don't know, so out of sync."

Our eyes met and he burst into tears. I thought he might collapse and took him in my arms.

"What's happening to me, Benjamin? I'm behaving like such an old Nellie."

"You've earned the right," I said.

He cried on my shoulder for a minute or two, then pulled himself together.

"Let's finish cleaning up," he said. "It's funny how much cleaning I've done this past week. I haven't been able to stop. The house has never been so spic-and-span."

He began rearranging patio furniture, which didn't really need it.

"Won't it be wonderful," he said, "seeing Alexandra get married next week?" He looked over. "You are planning on attending, aren't you?"

I smiled for his benefit. "Of course. I wouldn't miss it."

I hadn't told him about my suspicions regarding Templeton and Cathryn Conroy, and what Conroy planned to write about my father's death. Maurice didn't even know about my secret; I'd never discussed it with anyone but Ismael and Alexandra. Conroy surely would have filed her piece by now, I thought, and it would have been scheduled for the next available issue. With biweeklies like *Eye*, that usually required several weeks' lead time, even if the story warranted a fast break. So I still had a little time before I needed to prepare Maurice for what was coming.

What couldn't wait, however, were my suspicions regarding Jason Holt. The thought of broaching it with Maurice sickened me, and not just for his sake. If Holt had put that spider in our mailbox, it had surely been meant for me, not Fred. That made me culpable, if only indirectly. All my life, I'd been a magnet for trouble that had ended up hurting others. But never more than this time.

"Maurice, there's something I need to talk to you about."

"What is it, Benjamin?"

He paused in his work to face me.

"Do you remember the hate mail I was getting earlier this summer? The nasty phone calls and other harassment?"

"From that strange man, Jason something-or-other?"

"Jason Holt."

"Is he bothering you again?"

I told Maurice about my two visits to Holt, about his implied threats and his fascination with spiders.

"He does sound awfully strange," Maurice said, still not getting it.

"I have no way of proving it," I said, "and I could be over-reacting. It's just that—" I broke off, avoiding his eyes.

"What is it, Benjamin? What is it you're trying to tell me?"

I laid a hand on his shoulder, and forced myself to meet his eyes.

"I'm concerned that Holt might have been involved in Fred's death."

Maurice drew back as if repulsed, causing my hand to drop. "What?"

"The spider, the mailbox, Holt's vengeful behavior toward me. It raises certain questions."

He turned away, using the broom for support. When he faced me again, he shook his head resolutely.

"That's not possible, Benjamin. Fred's death was an accident."

"I suppose it was. But still—"

"No!" He shook a bony finger at me, his eyes sparking. "It was a terrible but unavoidable accident. That's all it was."

"If it was homicide," I said gently, "it wouldn't diminish our memories of Fred. And you'd want to know the truth, wouldn't you? If Holt was involved, you'd want him to answer for it."

Maurice sat down heavily in a folding chair, his eyes downcast.

"I'm not sure that I would." When he looked up, tears brimmed. "That someone had intended that spider for you, and Fred had died because of it? That Fred and I had been robbed of whatever time we had left together by such a thoughtless, danger-ous prank?"

He shook his head again, and stared out across the yard, where the flowers he'd planted in the late spring were fading.

"I don't know if I could live with that, Benjamin. I truly don't."

THIRTY-ONE

In the days that followed, I saw and heard nothing from Jason Holt. Yet the specter of Fred's death and Holt's possible involvement in it continued to hover darkly over my life, temporarily casting Lance Zarimba to its fringes. My appearance on *Jerry Rivers Live* was growing near—the producers had called twice to ask questions and prep me—and I knew Lance would be a focal point of the hour. But at the moment, it was Fred's passing and the way he'd died that loomed largest.

Several times I picked up the phone to contact Detective Haukness, feeling compelled to trigger a homicide investigation. But each time I hung up before completing the call.

I didn't know for sure that Holt was responsible for Fred's death or if I could ever prove it. It's one thing to become obsessed with someone, I thought, harassing and punishing him because he won't pay attention to you, as Holt had done to me. It's quite another to cross the line to homicide. Had Holt placed that spider in the mailbox simply to frighten me, to remind me that he was still capable of annoying and intimidating me? Or had he, knowing that I was immune depressed, placed it there hoping it would bite me and make me seriously ill, maybe even kill me? Was Holt merely a petty sociopath and self-deluding narcissist, or was he capable of murder?

I still craved more clues about him and about his past. In my mind, I went over the three key people in his life that he'd mentioned: Silvio Galiano, Charles Wu, and Victoria Faith.

I hadn't thought about Victoria Faith in weeks, but I remembered something she'd said toward the end of our visit—that she had some photographs that might interest me, which she'd show me when I came to visit again. At the time, I'd figured it for a possible ploy to get me to return and give a lonely old lady some company for a while. But I'd also sensed there were things she hadn't told me, things she was holding back. She'd all but conceded as much as we'd parted that day.

On Thursday morning, I called the Motion Picture & Television Country House and asked to be connected to her room. Instead, my call was forwarded to the administrative office. When I inquired again about the retired actress, the woman on the line asked what my relationship was to her.

"Just a friend," I said.

"Your name, sir?"

"Benjamin Justice."

"Mr. Justice, I'm sorry to have to tell you that Miss Faith passed away earlier this week. As you probably know, she'd been in declining health for some time. If it's any comfort to you, I can tell you that she died peacefully in her sleep."

"We should all be so lucky."

The administrator gave me information about the funeral arrangements. I thanked her for her help and hung up, cursing myself for not going back while Miss Faith was alive to probe more deeply into the man who had once been known as Barclay Simpkins.

My regret was short-lived. That afternoon, the postal carrier arrived on schedule, and I went down to meet her. She knew about the spider that had killed Fred and eyed the mailbox suspiciously.

"After I found out about that spider," she said, "I cleaned out every cobweb in my house. Every night before we go to bed I make my husband shake out the sheets. I don't ever want no spider to surprise me!"

She laughed nervously, handed me a large envelope, and proceeded to the next house. The envelope was addressed to me in handwriting that was old-fashioned and graceful. In the upper left-hand corner was Victoria Faith's name, followed by a return address for the Motion Picture & Television Country House. I carried the envelope upstairs and opened it in the kitchen.

Inside was a single photograph. It was a glossy eight-by-ten of Jason Holt, one of those professional head shots aspiring actors routinely have taken to send around to casting directors or leave with producers and directors at auditions. In the photo, Holt appeared to be in his late twenties, with blond highlights and an effete, self-satisfied look. It was an image I immediately recognized, surprisingly similar to the portrait Charles Wu had painted that hung above Holt's mantelpiece. Even the color and style of the shirt collar was identical.

Victoria Faith had waited until she was dying to send me the photo. Even then, she hadn't clearly stated her suspicions, remaining discreet to the end. There was no note, nothing of any kind written. But there was a message here, and she'd apparently had confidence in me to decipher it.

I cleared a pile of old mail and papers to one side and placed the photograph in front of me, studying it as I also recalled Wu's portrait. There had to be more to them than just their similarity, some deeper meaning that Miss Faith had wanted me to see.

As I pondered that, the edge of a manila envelope caught my eye. It was buried under a mass of mail that I'd tossed onto the table, unopened, during the previous chaotic weeks. I lifted it from the pile—the same envelope Lawrence Kase had handed over when we'd met at the polluted lotus pond in Echo Park. My eye went from the envelope to the photo and back to the envelope again. I grabbed it and tore it open, and began scanning the old LAPD reports inside.

It wasn't long before I found what I was looking for. Kase had mentioned to me that following Silvio Galiano's death, the investigating detectives had cleared Jason Holt as a suspect, because he'd had an airtight alibi. The final detective's report provided more details: During the days before and for several hours after

Galiano had taken his deadly fall, Holt had been sitting patiently as Charles Wu had painstakingly painted his portrait in oil, staying the entire time in a guest room of the house Wu was then renting in Venice Beach. The final sitting—more than nine hours, by Wu's account—had overlapped and exceeded the period of time when Galiano had tumbled roughly six stories, dying within minutes of his fall. The coroner had been able to estimate the time of death by taking the temperature of the body. In addition, Galiano's wristwatch had been crushed in the fall, with the hands frozen in place, confirming the coroner's approximation. There seemed to be no doubt about the hour that Galiano had died.

According to the police report, both Charles Wu and Angela Wainwright, his fiancée, had given statements supporting Holt's account of his whereabouts at the time. It was Angela who'd received a call from Holt after he'd returned home hours later to discover his elderly lover's body on the rocks. She'd described him to police as distraught and nearly hysterical.

I scanned that section of the report a second time, then studied the photograph again. Crucial pieces of the puzzle seemed to be right in front of me. Still, I had to be sure. I couldn't move forward on suspicion alone.

First, there was Maurice to consider. I'd never seen him so fragile, so vulnerable. I didn't want to involve him in a murder investigation, at least not while his grief was so raw. Maybe in time, I figured, when he was stronger, he'd be able to accept the reality of how Fred had died—that fate had put him in my place, at that moment, at that mailbox, where he'd intersected with evil. When that time came, I had to be absolutely certain of what had happened.

Then there was the matter of my credibility, or lack of it. I belonged to that small but shameful club of journalists—Walter Duranty, Janet Cooke, Stephen Glass, Jayson Blair, et al.—who, over the decades, had been exposed as frauds, tarnishing an otherwise honorable trade. We were not writers who'd gotten the facts wrong because of faulty memories—a forgivable human failing—or selected certain incidents or facts and ignored others to develop a theme or make a point, which was a natural part of putting together a story with a point of view. No, we were nonfiction writers who had deliberately deceived, creating outright fabrications and presenting them as fact—blatant misinformation, sources that didn't exist, quotes that were never spoken, interviews that never took place. We were a disreputable group, never again to be trusted or believed, however we might try to rationalize and explain away our actions.

So my suspicions about Holt were not enough. I had to nail down the facts tighter than the lid on a rich man's coffin.

It was time to have another chat with Charles Wu, whether he liked it or not.

THIRTY-TWO

I couldn't find a business number for Charles Wu in the phone book or on his Web site. I did find one for his representative, who declined to put me directly in touch with his client. When I called the gallery where I'd attended Wu's exhibit and asked for his personal number, the manager recognized my voice, told me as much, and hung up.

Then I remembered a conversation I'd had with Topper Schroeder, the affable owner of the Gendarmerie. Topper had mentioned that Wu kept a regular afternoon appointment at the spa, every Friday afternoon, 4:00 P.M. sharp. That would be tomorrow.

At a quarter to four the next afternoon, I parked the Metro in an alley across the street, close to a wall that gave me some cover. The convertible top was up, providing more camouflage, and I lowered the visor as I hunkered down. Within ten minutes, Wu arrived in a black Lexus, driven by Steven Reigns, his young assistant. As Reigns crossed the bricks out front, I was struck again by his general resemblance to a younger Jason Holt—slim, dark blond, boyish, but better looking, without the butchered face or prissy pretension. As Reigns held open the door and Wu stepped inside, Reigns briefly laid a hand on Wu's back and followed him in.

I didn't want to confront Wu in Topper's place of business, so I settled back in my seat, closed my eyes, and caught a nap. At half past four, I woke with a start to the sound of a rumbling motorcycle, unsure if I'd actually heard it or it was part of a dream. There were no motorcycles in sight, but Wu's gleaming Lexus was still parked in front of the spa. With time to kill, I took out a notebook and pen and began sketching a rough time line of events in the Barclay Simpkins/Jason Holt saga, trying to better sort things out:

1980—My last year in college (Barclay Simpkins's fifth year)
1983—I arrive in L.A. to work for L.A. Times
1984—Simpkins arrives in L.A., changes name to Jason Holt
1989—Holt becomes Silvio Galiano's lover (Galiano ill with AIDS)
1990—Jacques dies, Pulitzer scandal, Holt writes rambling letter to me
April 14, 1997—Galiano dies from fall, Wu completes Holt's portrait
June 1997—Charles Wu and Angela marry
Early June 2008—Deep Background published
Late June 2008—Harassment begins with phone call, hate mail
Mid-July 2008—I confront Holt, he denies harassment
Early August 2008—I discover Holt's spider collection
Late August 2008—As harassment continues, Fred dies from spider bite
Early September 2008—Victoria Faith sends me photo of Holt as younger man

I glanced over the time line, satisfied at first that all the dots were connected, that everything had fallen into place. But as I studied it, I realized it was incomplete. I'd neglected to add the year 1996, a life-affirming, milestone year for millions but a setback and dark turning point for Holt. For me, it was the intangible but crucial element that explained so much.

Just as I finished making the insert, my attention was drawn across the street.

Wu and Reigns were emerging from the Gendarmerie, each sporting a fresh haircut and probably a new manicure as well. Topper stood on the front steps, looking jocular as he bid them goodbye. They climbed into the Lexus and Reigns pulled out, working his way out of the neighborhood and over to Santa Monica Boulevard. I followed as he turned west into Beverly Hills.

It was half past five, well into the Friday rush hour. The eastward flow, always the worst at workday's end, was already moribund, while our west-moving lanes were merely sluggish. We crept along at fifteen miles per hour while the drivers pointed east glanced at us with envy. To my right, the joggers and power walkers were out in force, pounding the trail through Beverly Gardens Park. To pass the time, I tuned in NPR and got the news. It was pretty much what you'd expect: election campaign evasion and double-talk, political corruption, corporate greed, the Iraq war, international terrorism, nuclear proliferation, global warming, third-world poverty, ethnic genocide. It seemed that nothing much was changing, except the styles of running shoes worn by the joggers passing through the pretty park.

The Lexus turned right at Wilshire, cutting through the vast Los Angeles Country Club, where the wealthy golfers played through on their private manicured greens as if the horrors of the world could never touch them. We continued past the towering condo and office buildings of Westwood, with Little Persia to the south and UCLA to the north. Then we were crawling past the Los Angeles National Cemetery, where thousands of veterans were buried under thousands of identical white headstones and the streets were named for famous generals who had led the ill-fated soldiers to battle. On the left, I saw a sign for the Veterans Administration medical center, and I thought about Lance, wondering where he was and if he was okay. Thinking about Lance led me to Ismael, which stirred all kinds of emotions. Perhaps I still had a chance at one day finding my son, I thought, especially with my upcoming appearance on *Jerry Rivers Live* and the attention it would focus on him. But Ismael—he was almost surely out of my life for good and better off without me for all that.

Still, I ached for him, in a way I hadn't for a man since Jacques had passed.

A mile or so later, on busy San Vicente Boulevard, the air began to cool as we crossed from Brentwood into Santa Monica, getting closer to the ocean. With the megalopolis behind us and the end of civilization just ahead, traffic finally unlocked and drivers hit their accelerators like prisoners making a jailbreak. Reigns turned right at Nineteenth Street and right again on La Mesa Drive, which comprised about half a mile of extremely pricey real estate running along the southern rim of Santa Monica Canyon. The architecture here tended toward classic Spanish, with homes dating from the 1920s and a sprinkling of more modern styles that had begun popping up in the thirties. It seemed a world apart, caught in a pleasant time warp from a period when the future looked nothing but promising. Despite the continuing drought and a request by city officials to cut back on water usage, the landscaping here was Technicolor lush, with immaculate lawns and gardens and venerable Moreton Bay figs lining the parkways on both sides of the street, and the occasional ornamental fountain burbling with precious water.

Half a block ahead, Reigns pulled into a circular driveway behind a Cadillac Escalade, in front of a two-story home on the north side of the street, at the canyon's edge. I swung to the curb and stopped as Reigns and Wu climbed from the car. Just then Angela Wu emerged from the house, dressed tastefully but comfortably, as if she might be going out for an early dinner and a movie. It was an idealized Spanish house with traditional adobe walls and a red-tiled roof, whose understated elegance blended in nicely with the surrounding architecture. Two children emerged from the house behind her, a girl and a boy of roughly seven or eight years, who looked faintly Chinese and greeted their father respectfully. Angela Wu turned her cheek to accept a chaste kiss from her husband.

I'd observed more than a few marriages between straight women and gay men in my time, and had come to recognize a few basic types among the wives. There was the unworldly and blissfully naïve wife, who married a gay man out of ignorance and innocence, so blinded by love and devotion—and perhaps a touch of comforting denial—that she never recognized the telltale signs. Then there was the more experienced and astute type, who suspected her husband might be homo or bisexual but figured she could change him, that his homosexuality was just an itch or a phase that would pass now that they'd exchanged marriage vows and were about to begin a family. There was the classic marriage of convenience, prevalent in Hollywood but also in the world at large, in which a lesbian married a gay man as a beard, and vice versa. There were also unconventional women who coupled enthusiastically with gay men, even preferring homosexual husbands, happy to share them with other men for the rewards it might provide while keeping up the hetero charade for propriety's sake.

Angela Wu seemed to fit this latter mold: shrewd, calculating, manipulative, someone who knew exactly what she was getting when she married her husband—control, the emotional dependence of a weak man, social and financial security, and the certainty that he'd never leave her for another woman. These weren't marriages on the "down low," in which wives were used and deceived by men who cheated with other men. They were mutual pacts, based on loyalty and commitment, and more likely to last than many heterosexual unions, since each partner was getting exactly what he or she wanted without unrealistic expectations, a carefully constructed deceit based on almost naked honesty. Passionless relationships, perhaps, like so many straight unions that are based less on deep feelings than on need and convenience, but far more common than many people realized.

Reigns laid a hand fondly on each of the children's heads, and then proceeded alone through a side gate. Wu lingered to chat briefly with his wife, then kneeled to hug the kids. Mrs. Wu ushered them into the luxurious SUV, and her husband stood waving until she'd driven off, passing the Metro while I kept my head down. When she was out of sight, Wu turned and disappeared through the same gate Reigns had used, picking up his pace as he went.

I hopped from the Metro and scurried across to the house,

and followed the same route. Behind the house, the stone path led past a broad terrace built into the hillside, overlooking the lush greens of the Riviera Country Club, where a few foursomes were playing through the final holes, trying to beat the encroaching dusk. From the terrace, looking down the canyon, one had a post-card view all the way to the ocean, where the sun was setting through the smoky sky, creating a dreamy golden light. Some-where down there, closer to the ocean in another hillside house, the noted artist Don Bachardy had spent most of his life with the late iconic writer Christopher Isherwood. It was a canyon with bohemian history that was now an enclave of the very rich, at least up here where the congestion of business and traffic along the coast highway was distant and the views more serene.

The stone path twisted downward through a series of terraced gardens until it reached a small, one-story building on the right, constructed to match the main house. A door was open and I looked in to find an art studio, with large west- and north-facing windows and a skylight that flooded the room with gentle light. Large abstract paintings done in Wu's trademark geometric style took up much of the space. They hung on walls or were propped on easels, or stacked on the floor against a paint-spattered worktable, where a box cutter lay among several open cardboard containers filled with cans of acrylic paint. Judging by the price tags I'd seen in Wu's gallery exhibit, the paintings here must have cumulatively been worth a small fortune.

Neither Wu nor Reigns was there, so I stepped out and sur-veyed the property. The paths and terraces were likewise empty, and it occurred to me that the two men might have entered the rear of the main house and that I'd overshot my mark. Then I no-ticed another set of stone steps, just beyond the studio, leading steeply down, and decided to proceed farther. Past the steps, the path angled sharply to the right. I stayed on it for another hun-dred feet or so until I found myself blocked by a wooden fence covered by a tangle of thorny bougainvillea, and a sturdy, latched gate. On the gate was a sign in bold red letters: *PRIVATE—DO NOT ENTER.*

Beyond the gate, up against the east side of the property, was a small cottage situated out of sight of the main house and the studio. I lifted the latch quietly and entered. The front door of the small house was closed, so I went exploring and found a rear window with the curtains open. I raised myself up and peeked in. Reigns and Wu were in deep embrace, the artist smothering his younger assistant with kisses, the kind of unbridled passion Wu's public demeanor and lifeless abstracts worked so hard to conceal. Reigns maneuvered Wu to the edge of a bed and began unbuttoning his shirt to expose a smooth, well-developed chest. Reigns sat on the bed, worked Wu's pants and shorts down, and proceeded to give his boss one of the more creative blow jobs I'd ever been privileged to witness. When Reigns was finished and Wu fully satiated, they fell together onto the bed in each other's arms, kissing ardently like two men who were truly in love and whose stolen moments together—clandestine, hurried, a bit desperate—only enhanced the experience.

A minute later, Wu unbuttoned and unzipped Reigns, exposing a lithe body sprinkled deliciously with fine, blond hair, and returned the favor. With a final, tender kiss, Wu got to his feet and put himself back together. Reigns remained where he was, lighting a cigarette, reclining on satin pillows, and looking blissfully content. I ducked down and waited behind the house until Wu emerged. He closed the door behind him, and started back up the path. As he reached his studio and stepped inside, I climbed the path after him, stopping when I reached the doorway.

He was standing across the room before an easel, intently studying a large white canvas with a black square in the center.

"Maybe you could call it *Death,*" I said. "That has a nice ring to it."

He spun at the sound of my voice. When he recognized me, he became as taut as one of his expertly stretched canvases.

"No one gave you permission to be here," he said. "What do you want?"

I sauntered in, brushing past him to study the black square.

"What's the price tag on this one, Wu? A couple hundred thousand?"

"Some of my paintings are priceless." He glanced around the studio. "These are my most personal pieces. Only a few of these are for sale."

I gave up trying to understand this particular style of abstract art, and moved on to a more practical subject.

"So tell me, Wu, how long were you and Jason Holt lovers?"

He feigned effrontery. "I beg your pardon?"

"I'll give you credit. Steven Reigns is a big improvement."

Wu stepped toward me, but not too close. "I want you off my property, now."

"You've got everything arranged as neatly as one of your paintings, don't you? The smart, attractive wife and two well-behaved kids up at the house. And your nice-looking assistant down here, staying in the guesthouse, so close when you need him."

Wu reached into his pants pocket, pulled out a small cell phone. "If you don't go now, I'm going to call the police."

He raised his other hand, his finger poised as if he was about to press the speed dial number for 911.

"Go ahead, Wu. Call the police. When they get here, you can tell them why you excluded Holt's portrait from your otherwise complete collection. Not the PR version, but the truth."

He stared at me with widening eyes.

"You can tell them why Holt's portrait didn't measure up to the standard of the others," I went on, "because you painted it so quickly, without your usual meticulous layering, and because it was the only one you painted from a photograph."

"I don't know how you came up with that," Wu said.

"I have a copy of the photograph you used. It's almost identical to the portrait, right down to the blond highlights, which Holt had for only a short time."

"Please go." Wu's voice quavered. He lowered his cell phone. "Please. Just go."

"Holt brought you the photograph just after he pushed Silvio Galiano to his death."

Wu shook his head furiously. "No."

"You worked fast, nonstop, painting the portrait to create an alibi for Holt, who was about to tell the police he'd been sitting for you at the time of Galiano's death. After he did, you and Angela backed up his story."

Wu stood motionless in shocked silence, blood bringing color to his pale face.

"Why, Wu? Did he blackmail you? Threaten to expose you as a closet queen? Threaten to implicate you in Galiano's murder?"

"You don't know what you're talking about. You don't!"

"Then why? I need the truth, Wu."

He shoved me forcefully toward the door. I slipped away and around him and grabbed the box cutter lying on his workbench. The razor's edge was exposed. When he saw the sharp tool in my hand, he backed away.

"I'm tired of waiting, Wu. I want the truth."

When he said nothing, I stepped over to the painting of the black square, raised the box cutter to the upper right corner of the canvas, and sliced downward, dissecting the square neatly in half.

"Dear God, no!"

Wu threw up his hands, rushing to the mutilated canvas.

"Now you've got two black triangles," I said. "I think I like it better this way."

He ran his hands over the mutilated canvas the way a father might touch his dead child. Small, agonized moans escaped his throat. I stepped across the room to another large white canvas, this one with a cobalt blue circle in the center.

"Let's see what we can do to improve this one."

He dashed toward me as I sliced diagonally through the canvas, halving the blue circle. As he reached it, I was already on the move with my weapon, heading toward more of his paintings. He darted frantically around his studio, putting himself between me and his cherished creations.

"All right, all right!" He choked back sobs, imploring with his outstretched hands. "I'll tell you. If you'll just stop."

"It better be good, because I'm really enjoying this."

"It's true," he said, "Jason and I were seeing each other in secret. I don't know why I got involved with him. He was charming and I found him attractive. I was shy, introverted, inexperienced. He was the first man I'd ever been with. I thought I loved him. Later, I realized I just couldn't see beyond him, to the possibility of anyone else."

"The portrait, Wu. Galiano's death." I held up the box cutter, showing him the blade. "Let's cut to the chase, so to speak."

"Jason came to me that night with the photograph. He told me that Silvio had fallen to his death. He claimed it was an accident. He convinced me that if he didn't have an alibi, the police were certain to suspect him, since he was set to inherit Silvio's estate. He suggested that I might even become a suspect, since Jason and I were"—he paused to swallow dryly—"were romantically involved. At the very least, Jason said, our relationship was certain to be exposed and get into the newspapers." Wu broke off again, looking mortified. "It would have seemed so sordid, the two of us having an affair while Jason was living off an older man like Silvio. I couldn't bear that. My parents—"

He stopped, seemingly horrified by his own words.

"He wanted you to work fast," I said helpfully, "nonstop, painting a portrait from the photograph, so you could tell the police he'd been sitting for you at the time Galiano died."

Wu nodded pathetically. "Yes."

"Why couldn't Holt sit for you, like all your other subjects? Why did you need the photograph?"

"He hadn't come up with his plan for an alibi right away. Several hours had passed after Silvio's death before Jason came to me about it. To avoid suspicion, he felt he needed to return home and appear to discover Silvio's body himself. The plan was for me to be painting the portrait from the photograph while Jason dealt with the authorities. By the time the police questioned me, the portrait would be finished."

"And when the police got around to you, you told them you'd completed the painting the previous day, while Holt was sitting for you in your studio. Holt worked it out so that it amply covered the approximate time of death the coroner would establish after examining Galiano's body."

Wu sagged hopelessly, nodding again.

"And your wife agreed to help you back up Holt's story."

"Angela and I weren't married yet."

"Of course—that would happen a few months later."

"We'd been discussing marriage. She'd been—she'd been pressuring me."

"I assume she knew about your secret life, your relationship with Holt."

"Angela had become my confidante, my closest friend. It was such a relief, to be able to reveal certain things to her."

"Let me guess. She proposed a deal. She agreed to back you up, providing a stronger alibi for Holt. In exchange, you agreed to marry her and start a family. She got what she wanted—a noted artist as a husband and companion, with complete control over him. And you got the cover you needed, so no one would suspect that you and Holt had been lovers."

"I love Angela very much."

"I'm sure you do."

"She saved me!" Wu's outcry seemed as sincere as it was anguished. "She took an enormous risk to help me when I needed it."

"She also joined you as an accessory to murder."

"We believed that Silvio died exactly as Jason told us he did—accidentally."

"But you must have had doubts."

"Angela said we had no choice but to believe Jason. That I was in a bad spot, and the only way out was to provide Jason with the alibi he needed. Otherwise—"

"The lie you were living would be exposed. You'd bring shame upon your family. You'd be a pariah in the eyes of your unforgiving father."

Wu clasped his hands in front of him, prayerlike, beseeching me to believe him.

"I swear, I never thought Jason was responsible for Silvio's death."

"All this doesn't exactly square with the neat and tidy image you and your wife have so carefully cultivated, does it?"

Wu stared dully at me, or perhaps beyond me to something only he could see, within himself. Then he turned away to wander among his hand-stretched canvases with their perfect geometric images, which revealed far more about him than I'd previously realized. Maybe that was their genius, I thought, the way they exposed so much while working so masterfully to conceal it.

I tossed the box cutter onto the table and made my exit, pleased that Wu had corroborated much of what I'd suspected, but still unsatisfied. He'd only disclosed what Holt had told him years ago—that Silvio Galiano had fallen accidentally to his death and that Wu and Holt had needed to allay any suspicions. It was cowardly and conniving—nothing new for Holt—and probably untrue. But what I'd heard from Wu didn't necessarily add up to murder, or the final confirmation of it.

And if Holt had killed Galiano, did that also suggest he'd killed Fred, even inadvertently? Probably. But with so much hanging in the balance, including Maurice's vulnerable emotional state, probably wasn't good enough.

THIRTY-THREE

I was awakened at dawn by a phone call from Jan Long in New York. She'd never called on the weekend, and never contacted me so early in the day, so I knew it must be important.

"Sorry to rouse you from a deep sleep, Benjamin."

"Not so deep, actually."

"Cathryn Conroy have you tossing and turning?"

"Conroy and a few others."

"You've made some new acquaintances recently, I gather."

"Crawling out of the proverbial woodwork, I'm afraid."

"Books can do that, when they're provocative. So you're not the first. Take some pride in it, Benjamin."

"If it's all the same, I'd rather have a good night's sleep."

I yawned; she laughed.

"I might be able to help in that department," she said. "I have some interesting news regarding Conroy."

Since our last conversation, Jan said, she'd consulted with two of her other authors, both well-respected journalists with hundreds of articles and a slew of books between them. It seems they'd been jointly working up a lawsuit that would accuse Conroy of plagiarizing their work. In their meticulous research, they'd turned up flagrant examples in which Conroy had copied lines or passages from more than a dozen published texts by as many different writers, almost word for word. Most of the victimized writers had agreed to join the lawsuit or at least support it and to issue public statements when the time was right.

"Speculation has circulated for years about the originality of some of her work," Jan said. "Especially recently, when her drinking has become excessive and she's had increasing trouble meeting deadlines."

"What's the timing on all this?"

"A sympathetic source at *Eye* tells me that Conroy filed the first draft of her profile eight days ago. She's doing some cutting and making other revisions now. It's due back to her editor on Monday. *Eye* plans to publish it in two weeks. Unfortunately, the plaintiffs and their lawyer won't be ready to file a lawsuit until next month."

"By then it would be too late," I said.

"Any ideas?"

"Have you got enough to break a story now?"

"More than enough."

"Well organized and documented?"

"Very. Several of the aggrieved authors are prepared to issue statements immediately."

I suggested she have a trusted third party leak the story to DishtheDirt.com, keeping it as distant from me as possible, and to do it quickly.

"I'll do what I can," Jan said. "No guarantees, though. I'm entering uncharted waters here."

Her tone was somber. Neither of us took any joy in seeing another capable journalist crash and burn. Like most editors, Jan lived to help build literary careers and publish the best writing she could find. We both realized what Conroy was about to face, if the plagiarism scandal broke with the impact we hoped it would. In the past, a number of noted writers had survived plagiarism accusations, but their transgressions had generally been incidental, often explained away as sloppy transcription or note taking during the research process, or short passages inadvertently pasted into rough drafts but never rewritten during hurried work accelerated by the speed of computer technology. But Conroy's offenses appeared to be frequent, deliberate, and of considerably greater magnitude. It was surprising that she'd gotten away with it as long as she had.

"I'd ask you what it is that Conroy has on you," Jan said, "but I have a feeling I'm better off not knowing."

"Maybe I'll reveal it in a future memoir," I said, only half-kidding, "to be published posthumously."

She wished me luck with my appearance on *Jerry Rivers Live,* which was only three days away, and we bid each other good-bye.

Maurice and I met down at the house at 2:00 P.M., planning to drive out to Malibu together for Templeton's wedding.

"The big day has finally arrived," he said. His smile seemed forced. "At long last, our Alexandra is about to become a bride."

He'd opted for gender blur in a shimmering white caftan and tasteful sandals, with lots of exotic jewelry and colorful scarves and white hair flowing to his shoulders, an old man who'd always lived his life as if it was really his, decent to a fault yet unconcerned about the judgments of others. I was considerably more traditional in a blue blazer and necktie that made me feel like a performing monkey.

"You look awfully tense, Benjamin. Feeling okay?"

"I've got a few things on my mind."

"I can commiserate."

He seemed distracted and disengaged, but I attributed it to his mourning process and didn't probe. We climbed into the Metro and I drove off with the top down, Maurice's hair trailing in the warm air.

I took Sunset all the way, past the grandiose mansions of Beverly Hills and the pompous gates of Bel-Air, and across the 405 Freeway into the flats of Brentwood. A mile or two later, Sunset suddenly twisted right and descended into a series of canyons dense with oak, eucalyptus, and sycamore. I hadn't been out this way in a couple of years and when I glimpsed the street sign for Rockingham

Avenue it gave me a jolt. North Rockingham was where the grisly murders of Nicole Simpson and Ron Goldman had gone down, putting O. J. Simpson on the front page and forever changing our naïve perception of celebrity charm. I was suddenly reminded how thin the line is between normalcy and insanity, between control and deadly rage. That got me to thinking about Jason Holt, of the kind of sociopath who can lurk behind the camera-ready smile. From Holt my mind jumped to Fred, and how he'd died, and then to how Maurice was suffering for it, and I felt my blood begin to boil. At some point the image of my father, lying bloody and lifeless on the kitchen floor of my childhood home, worked its way into the mix, and I couldn't separate my rage from my shame. By the time I reached Will Rogers State Historic Park, it was all mixed in with the perplexing problems I had with Templeton and Conroy and my brain felt like it was about to explode.

I passed through respectable Pacific Palisades until I glimpsed a shimmer of silvery blue in the distance, just before Sunset swung hard to the right and descended steeply toward Pacific Coast Highway. Then the ocean was right in front of us, vast and sparkling. I could see triangles of white sails riding across the whitecaps, and gulls and pelicans gliding on outstretched wings. As we joined the northward traffic, I glimpsed surfers cutting up the waves with their short, pointy boards. They looked almost like birds, riding on cascading water instead of currents of air, wonderfully free.

When I'd first come to Southern California, at twenty-five, I'd promised myself that I'd learn to surf, or at least give it a try. Now, suddenly, I was fifty. And I knew it would never happen, like so many other things I'd planned to do but never would.

"Lovely day for a wedding," Maurice said, and we rode the rest of the way in silence.

Templeton's embossed invitation provided an address on Malibu Mesa Drive, along with instructions to park at a designated lot near Pacific Coast Highway, from which shuttle buses would ferry guests up the hill to the house.

I pulled into the lot with ten minutes to spare, and a young valet took the old Metro, looking at it like he'd never seen one before. Maurice and I climbed aboard a shuttle bus with several others and it whisked us up the hill and through an ornate gate to an enormous house that looked like an ancient Roman villa. It belonged to one of Lawrence Kase's brothers, a producer who'd gotten rich making bad movies, but might just as easily have served as a museum. Because of the hour, we were escorted quickly through the antique-filled house and out to a large courtyard, where a long reflecting pool stretched toward the edge of a bluff and the ocean beyond. Huge bouquets of fresh flowers were all around the pool, along with small tables and folding chairs under colorful umbrellas. Among the Roman columns supporting the second-story terraces were replicas of classical Greek and Roman sculptures.

"If I didn't know better," Maurice said, "I'd swear we were attending a gay soiree thrown by some closeted Hollywood CEO."

On either side of the house was a wide lawn, manicured like a fine putting green. Chairs were set up on the north lawn for the ceremony. On the south lawn, a huge tent had been erected for the reception and a portable parquet floor laid out for dancing. There appeared to be several hundred in attendance, and almost all the chairs on the north side were filled, but we found two empty ones near the back. Looking around, I spotted Cathryn Conroy across the aisle several rows ahead. Seeing her set my teeth on edge, so I tried to concentrate on the nice view of the mountains, even though a few of the hilltops were charred black from the recent wildfires.

I glanced at my watch a couple of times before a small orchestra finally struck up the wedding march. Lawrence Kase appeared behind us, accompanied by his best man. Kase looked properly dignified, if a bit full of himself, in a gray, pin-striped morning suit, the tails trailing pompously at the end of the cutaway jacket, with a large white carnation in the lapel. Then Templeton emerged on the arm of her father, a man not much older than Kase and equally handsome, but without the silly tails. Templeton had never looked more lovely. Her elegant gown was silk, the color of creamy coffee, and draped to midcalf. Her long hair was upswept and pulled together with a small bunch of pale green cymbidiums. More of the delicate orchids were weaved into the braided hair cascading down her back. She carried a small bouquet of the same flowers, and wore a string of pearls around her slender neck. Otherwise, she was unadorned—no flashy jewelry—letting her flawless, dark-skinned beauty speak for itself.

As if on cue, a pleasant breeze swept across the property from the ocean and gently ruffled the soft folds of her gown. For a moment, I was truly happy for her, until the Conroy matter popped into my head, with all its attendant questions, and I wasn't sure exactly how I felt about Templeton just then.

Up front, two ministers waited for the bride and groom—a Baptist for Templeton, a rabbi for Kase. Templeton's parents, both African American and stuffy liberals, had always been opposed to her marrying outside her race. Apparently, they'd worked things out, because her father was beaming as he escorted her down the aisle. Then again, Alexandra was in her late thirties, her biological clock ticking fast. So maybe he was just thankful she'd finally gotten hitched and that his first grandchild was in the oven.

The bifurcated rituals, both Jewish and Baptist, were mercifully brief. I'm sure it was a touching ceremony. I heard a good deal of sniffling among the guests, Maurice included. Thankfully, the whole thing was over fairly quickly.

As the bride and groom made their exit and the chairs gradually emptied around us, Maurice stayed put. Despite his momentary tears, he was unusually quiet, and I didn't try to hurry him.

Finally, without looking over, he said, "I'm truly happy for Alexandra and Mr. Kase. But I can't help feeling just a little bitter. Fred and I were together nearly sixty years. No two people have ever been more devoted or supportive of each other. Yet voters will decide if our union is worthy and valid. And they may very well rule against us, as if what we had together didn't matter. As if we ourselves didn't matter."

He looked over, his eyes finally coming to life after weeks of sadness.

"That's just not right, Benjamin, and it makes me so damn angry."

Outside the tent, Maurice excused himself to find a bathroom and I went wandering. I ran into Conroy at the edge of the bluff as she removed a flute of champagne from the tray of a passing waiter. She downed it in one gulp and looked around for more.

"They're not serving hard liquor," she muttered under her breath. "If I'd known, I would have brought a flask."

Given what I'd recently learned about her serial plagiarism, I now saw Conroy and her tough-gal act in a different light. At that moment, as she fortified herself with alcohol, I actually felt sorry for her. I'd been there, after all.

"Your story should be out soon," I said. "I'm waiting with bated breath."

"Which piece would that be? I'm juggling several assignments."

"That's right," I said. "You stay so busy, don't you?"

"Oh, you must be referring to the profile I'm writing on you." She waved at a nearby waiter, who approached with his tray. She exchanged her empty flute for a full one. "I've got it down to length and turned in the final draft. You won't have long to wait, Justice."

"You have to know it's going to end any chance I have of ever writing for money again."

"It seems to me that's the least of your worries."

"I've got to hand it to you, Cathryn. Like a lot of hard-nosed reporters, you've taken all that anger and insecurity of yours and channeled it well."

"Is that what made you such a good journalist, Justice?"

"I imagine that was part of it."

"What a shame, all that potential. And look what you did with it."

"And now you get to feast on the carcass."

She raised the flute in a mock toast.

"No hard feelings. Just doing my job."

She tipped back her head and drained the bubbly.

Eventually, suitably plied with alcohol, the guests assembled in the main tent for the cutting of the multitiered cake and the requisite toasts. The speeches were alternately poignant, silly, and long-winded. Then they were over, the music started, and Kase led Templeton to the dance floor for a waltz. Maurice and I got some food and I bided my time while she danced with her father and each of Kase's three brothers, until I finally saw an opportunity to cut in.

I told her how beautiful she looked and wished her a long and fulfilling marriage.

"You and the hubby certainly have a lot of friends," I said. "There must be five hundred people here."

She laughed, embarrassed. "It's kind of crazy, isn't it?"

"Whatever makes you happy, Alex."

"Larry makes me happy. He wanted a big wedding. My parents are thrilled. It will all be over quickly enough."

"Your book's a big hit. Congratulations."

"There's a good deal of you in it, you know. Everything you taught me. You helped me get where I am, Benjamin. I won't ever forget that."

I allowed a moment to pass. Then I said pointedly, "I see you invited Cathryn Conroy."

"We're friends. Why not?"

"As I recall, she helped you get your agent, the one that put together that great deal on your book."

"Let's not talk shop now, Justice. It's my wedding day."

We bumped into another dancing couple, so I led Templeton to an open space on the parquet floor.

"The thing is," I said, "I've been wondering what Conroy got in return."

"I'm not sure I follow."

"Conroy's tough as nails, or likes to think so, and about as warm as frozen pizza. She doesn't strike me as someone who goes out of her way to help a rival writer. Not unless there's something in it for her."

Kase's best man, who appeared to be drunk, tried to cut in.

"Later," I said. "The bride and I are talking."

He looked offended but went away. I whisked Templeton back toward the middle of the floor.

"Can't we just dance," she asked, "and enjoy ourselves?"

"Conroy knows about me and my father," I said. "She's using it as the hook for her profile."

Templeton regarded me curiously. "What about you and your father?"

"That when I killed him, it wasn't entirely in defense of my mother and sister. That it was more like murder."

"She's writing that?"

I nodded. "She's basing it on something I revealed to you, in confidence, several years ago. Something I've only told one other person, who swears he never uttered a word about it to Conroy or anyone else."

Templeton stopped dancing and disengaged from me. The music kept playing and the other couples continued dancing around us.

"Cathryn's using that in her story?"

"That *is* her story, Templeton. At least it's the hook, the bombshell that's going to make her piece a national sensation."

Templeton put a hand to her mouth. "Oh, my God."

"You understand the legal ramifications, don't you?"

She reached out, seized my arm. "Benjamin, I never meant for her to find that out."

"But she did, Templeton. And you told her, didn't you?"

Templeton's words began tumbling out, her voice quavering. "She invited me to dinner to celebrate my book deal. I had a glass of wine. You know how I am with alcohol, Benjamin. One glass and I'm a babbling idiot. She kept refilling my glass, urging me to drink up. She turned it into a girls' night out, even refrained from drinking herself, making herself the designated driver. After a few glasses—"

"You just blurted it out."

Templeton nodded, tears spilling over. "It was out of my mouth before I realized what I'd said. I tried to put it into context, explaining that it was only your impression of what had happened and that you tend to be extremely hard on yourself. Then I told her I didn't really mean it. I tried to take it back, but I only made it worse."

"And she ended up with something even more sensational than she'd hoped for when she poured you that first glass of wine."

"I told her it was strictly between us, totally off-the-record."

"But you told her after the fact, which doesn't really count."

"She didn't record it, Benjamin. She didn't even take notes."

"That never stopped a determined reporter, did it? I'm sure she jotted your words down the moment she was alone. Probably on a cocktail napkin in the powder room."

"Oh, my God. She's really going to use it? You're sure?"

"The article's been scheduled. It's a done deal."

"I'll talk to her, Benjamin. I'll contact the magazine and deny that I ever said those things."

"I think it's a little late for that, Alex."

She burst into tears and I realized the couples around us had stopped dancing. Then Lawrence Kase was striding across the floor. The music went silent behind him. When he reached us, he put an arm protectively around his bride.

"What is it, Alex? What's the matter?"

"Nothing much," I said. "Just a little betrayal between friends."

"What the hell's going on?" Kase demanded.

"Oh, God." Templeton broke away and ran across the dance floor, her pretty braids and baby orchids trailing.

Kase turned his fury on me. "What the hell have you done now?"

"Fuck you, Kase."

He motioned to his brothers and they were on me like bouncers at a Sunset Strip club. They grabbed me by both arms and hustled me out of the tent. Maurice rushed to my side, trying to keep pace as the three brothers kept me moving.

"Benjamin, what on earth is happening? What did you say to Alexandra?"

The three Kases dragged me past the reflecting pool as guests stepped aside, staring. Then we were passing through the opulent house and down the drive to the street, where they dumped me near the curb to wait with other departing guests for the next shuttle.

Maurice caught up a moment later, as I stood and brushed myself off.

"Benjamin, what have you done? Alexandra was in tears."

"Screwed up again, I'm afraid."

"You haven't been drinking, have you?"

"I wish the explanation was that easy."

A bus finally arrived but filled up quickly, and we had to wait for the next one. Before it came, Conroy appeared, weaving in her high heels down the sloping drive. She had a champagne bottle that was half-empty in one hand and an iPhone in the other. When she reached the end of the drive, she plopped down on the curb and guzzled straight from the bottle. As she lowered it to come up for air she noticed me standing nearby.

"My agent just called," she said. "Someone put together a rather unflattering story about me, claiming that I've been plagiarizing other writers. Apparently, it's all over the Internet. It'll be in all the newspapers tomorrow. My agent tells me it's loaded with examples, documented to a fucking farthing."

"You should be pleased," I said. "So much of what you see on the Web is pure crap."

"Forgive me if I don't laugh. I don't suppose you know anything about it, do you?"

"Sorry, no comment."

"You know what this means, don't you?"

"That it's time to find a new agent?"

Conroy showed me a sour face. "The editors at *Eye* will kill my piece. No respectable publication will ever touch it. Or anything else I write. The blogs won't even be interested in what I've dug up about you. They'll zero in on the plagiarism angle like buzzards on roadkill."

"Tough break," I said.

She suddenly grew weary of the sparring. Her bravado evaporated like bubbles from dead champagne.

"Yeah, tough," she said, staring straight ahead at nothing in particular.

A shuttle bus pulled up and I helped Maurice climb aboard, then followed after him. Conroy stayed behind, plopped forlornly on the curb. As the shuttle pulled away I looked back to see her tilt the bottle, guzzling like there was no tomorrow.

THIRTY-FOUR

Dusk was approaching as I turned off Sunset Boulevard and cruised down the hill to Norma Place.

By then, I'd filled Maurice in on what had transpired between Templeton and me at the wedding, including, reluctantly, the details surrounding my father's death. Maurice was seriously put out, running out of patience with me after years of watching me leave wreckage in my wake. In a strange way, though, it was good to see him so angry, to see the old spark flaring up, even if I happened to be the fuel. By the time we reached the house, he'd vented his unhappiness with me and was leavening it with his characteristic kindness and understanding.

"Perhaps your father's death was as you described it, Benjamin. Perhaps not. Memory is a slippery thing. Each of us perceives certain events in our lives through the prism of our own needs."

I pulled into the driveway, switched off the ignition, set the brake. Birds and crickets chirped in the gloaming.

"You've always looked for the dark side in life and in people," he went on. "Don't you think it's possible that you've done the same with yourself? Imagined the worst and then remembered it that way until it calcified in your mind as something you now see as fact?"

I said nothing. He squeezed my hand.

"Give yourself a break, Benjamin. If not for yourself, dearest, then the rest of us. Because you're driving all of us crazy."

I smiled, despite myself. So did Maurice. He's back, I thought. Or at least slowly returning, from that cold, remote place to which grief had taken him.

Then his smile faded and he said very pointedly, "Sometimes, one never knows the real truth about certain things." His eyes drilled into mine, making his message unmistakable. "And maybe that's just as well, Benjamin. Maybe it's necessary at times, because it allows us to survive emotionally and keep going."

Maurice went into the house to lie down, suggesting we meet up later for dinner, maybe even go out for a hearty meal at Boy Meets Grill.

I headed up to my apartment, where I found a single message waiting for me on my landline. It was from Judith Zeitler, asking me to call her immediately.

I erased it, went to the kitchen for a glass of water, took a leak after that, and was about to phone Zeitler when a call came in. The caller ID told me it was Jason Holt. I considered letting my voice mail take it, thought better of it, and picked up the receiver.

"I've been waiting for you, Benjamin. Waiting for you to come back and see me."

"Have you now?"

"Such a shame about Fred," he went on. "I read about it in the newspaper. A spider bite, imagine that. Tsk, tsk, tsk. Of course, he was quite old, wasn't he? How's Maurice holding up, by the way?"

"I wouldn't try to make light of it, Holt. Not after what you've done."

"Am I supposed to be afraid, Benjamin? Of what? That you'll report me to the police? Do you really think I'm worried about that?"

"Apparently not."

"You should have stayed in touch, Benjamin. All I asked for was your friendship. A little consideration. Some quality time."

"You'd better tell me something interesting, Holt, because I'm about to hang up."

"Did I mention that I have a gift for Maurice?"

That kept me listening.

"No, I don't think you did."

"I'm not sure when I'll deliver it. I think I'll surprise him. Surprises are so much fun, don't you think?"

"I think he's had enough surprises recently."

"I went to a great deal of trouble to get it, you know. I imported it all the way from Australia."

Except for my father on that fateful day when I was seventeen, I'm not sure I'd ever loathed anyone as much as I did Jason Holt at that moment. But I feared him just as much, feared what he might do to Maurice.

"Maybe I could come up and get it for him," I said.

Holt perked up.

"You'd really do that?"

"I'd get a chance to see you as well," I said, "to spend a little of that quality time you mentioned. Maybe you and I could be buddies, after all."

"You don't mean that, Benjamin. I don't believe it for a second."

"I've been lonely, Jason. It's finished between Ismael and me, you know."

"Is that true?" He sounded pliant, hopeful. "I wasn't aware of that."

"For all I know, he already has another boyfriend."

"Good riddance, I say. You deserve so much better, Benjamin."

"Maybe you were right, Jason. Maybe you and I were meant to be together."

"Do you really mean that? Because I won't be toyed with, Benjamin. I won't have you playing with my emotions. Not ever again."

"We go back a long way, you and I. We have some history together. That means a lot as one grows older and finds himself alone."

His words came urgently now. "Fred's death really was an accident, Benjamin. The spider wasn't meant for him."

"For me then?"

"I just wanted you to pay attention to me, that's all!"

"I'm paying attention now, Jason."

"You're serious? You really want to see me?"

"I've never been more serious in my life."

"Oh, Benjamin!"

"Are you at home?"

"Standing on the terrace, looking out at the city. The light's lovely up here in the early evening. Maybe we could go out for a nice dinner and catch up. I know the most divine little café in Larchmont Village."

"I'm on my way, Jason."

I lost the blazer, necktie, and slacks and slipped into jeans, a T-shirt, and running shoes. Then I rinsed my face in cold water, taking my time, determined to think this through and not rush things. When I felt ready, I left quietly, hoping not to disturb Maurice. I shifted the Metro into neutral and pushed it down the drive and out to the street before switching on the ignition. Then I climbed behind the wheel and headed toward the Hollywood Hills.

I wasn't sure exactly what I was going to do when I got to Holt's place, but I had a general idea. He had to be stopped, but I didn't think there was enough hard evidence to connect him to anyone's death. Anyway, police investigations can sometimes drag on for months, and there was no telling what Holt might do in that time. I wouldn't be able to live with myself if something happened to Maurice. Someone had to deal with Holt in a permanent way, and I seemed to be as good a candidate as any. At this point, I figured, I didn't have a whole lot to lose.

The dusk was deepening as I approached Nichols Canyon Terrace. I parked on a turnout, hiding the Metro in the shadows of an oleander grove, and hiked up Nichols Canyon Road from there. As I turned into Holt's street, I heard a few dogs bark in the canyon behind me, aroused by the sound of a passing motorcycle heading up toward Mulholland Drive. The engine's rumble gradually faded and with it the yapping of the dogs. The cul-de-sac was empty as I made my way quietly to the end. I saw one or two lights in windows that turned living rooms into dioramas with live figures moving about, but they didn't appear to notice as I crept past. Holt's bloodred 1953 Ferrari sat in the driveway where I'd seen it the first time I was up here. A *FOR SALE* was displayed in a side window.

I walked directly along the stone path around the north side of the house. As I rounded the corner, I saw Holt standing on the terrace with his back to me, silhouetted against the city lights. The patio had recently been swept clean; a broom leaned against a wall of the house, next to a pile of sweepings. With no leaves underfoot, I was able to cross the patio soundlessly, past the empty swimming pool.

As I got closer, I saw the machete lying flat atop the low wall, near the heavy stand of bamboo Holt had been thinning the first time I was here. Closer to where Holt stood, the morning-glory vines entangling the wall were still untouched, entwined around the columns and stretching out unchecked toward Runyon Canyon.

When I was only a few steps behind him he turned to face me, as if he'd been aware of my approach all along. He was wearing a heavy gardening glove on his right hand, which was loosely closed. The other glove lay atop the wall next to him.

"Hello, Benjamin. I can't tell you how pleased I am that you've returned."

"How could I not, after all that's happened?"

I stepped over next to him, my thighs pressed against the upper edge of the wall, calculating the effort it would take to push a man of Holt's size over. Not much, I thought. He was slightly built and not very tall. I remembered the look of his soft torso when he'd had his shirt off, the undeveloped muscles. I figured it would depend on how much fight he put up. Maybe none at all, I thought, if I struck quickly and unexpectedly.

"It took a bit of doing," he said, almost whimsically, "but you've finally taken me seriously."

"It's always about you, isn't it, Jason?"

"Not a very nice thing to say, for someone who wants to be my friend."

"You didn't really believe that, did you? That I'd ever want to be close to someone like you."

"But we are close, Benjamin. We're together now. Two people who have so much in common."

"Because we both know what it is to kill someone?"

He stepped toward me, laying his ungloved hand on my upper arm, stroking it, looking into my eyes. The feel of his hand made my skin crawl, but I let it stay, biding my time.

"How I've longed to touch you, Benjamin. It seems like forever, and now you're here."

"At the very spot," I said, "where you pushed Silvio Galiano to his death."

I glanced over the low wall to the rocks. They were faintly illuminated by light from the big front windows of the house. Otherwise, this side of the property was secluded and deep in shadow. It was unlikely anyone could see us.

Holt raised his bleached brows playfully. "Is that what you think happened, Benjamin? That I'm responsible for Silvio's unfortunate death?"

"There's not a doubt in my mind."

"Why would I kill Silvio? He provided everything I needed."

"Because you wanted it all for yourself, without the responsibility of being his companion. You hooked up with him in 1989, when he was already old and sick with AIDS. It was still considered a death sentence then. Gay men were dying by the thousands. You figured he'd be gone in a year or two, like all the others. Only he managed to hang on. His doctors and his strong spirit kept him alive. Then the protease inhibitors showed such promise in '95 and came on the market the next year, the so-called AIDS cocktail that suddenly offered new hope for people like Silvio. He started getting better, like so many others who were infected."

"On the contrary, I was thrilled about the protease cocktail. I'd lost friends, you know. There were others who were infected for whom I cared deeply."

"Yes, it was great news for them. But not for you, Jason. It ruined your scheme to get your hands on Silvio's assets. You were stuck with an old man who might live on for years and possibly disinherit you if he discovered your affair with Charles Wu. So you pushed him over this wall, down to those rocks."

"Pure speculation, from a man without a shred of credibility. Anyway, the police investigated. My alibi was airtight."

"I have a copy of the photograph Wu used to paint your portrait. Before she died, your aunt, Victoria Faith, made sure I would get it. I've spoken with Wu. He's admitted everything."

To my surprise, the tone of Holt's voice grew increasingly smug.

"I knew you couldn't resist playing detective. I spun my web. You took the bait. And here we are, together at last."

"You've killed two people, Holt. That's all you've accomplished."

Holt laughed brightly.

"Don't tell me you're wired up with a hidden microphone, like in the movies? Trying to get me to say something incriminating." He ran his ungloved hand up and down my sides, then patted my chest. "Mmmm, still in good shape for a man your age. What a shame I won't be able to enjoy you in the flesh."

He spun me suddenly so that I was pinned between him and the wall, and brought his gloved hand up to within an inch of my face. Cushioned in his gloved fingers was a large, dark spider— four to five centimeters long, if I had to guess—with hair covering its stubby body and thick, jointed legs.

Holt was grinning. "Maybe you'll tolerate spider venom better than Fred, even with your compromised immune system. But I wouldn't count on it."

I started to slide away, but Holt kept me penned in, pressing the spider close to my mouth.

"I wouldn't move if I were you. He's very aggressive. Doesn't scurry away and hide, like the black widow or the brown recluse. This is the deadly Australian funnel-web spider—*Atrax robustus*. Only twenty-seven species of spider are known to have caused human fatalities, and the male funnel-web ranks right up there at the top. This one comes from the Sydney area—the most dangerous of all the southern Australian funnel-webs. Cost me a pretty penny to have him smuggled in. I'm selling the Ferrari to cover it. They like moist climates, you know. I keep him in the spare bathroom. He has his own humidifier."

"He must hate this dry heat," I said. "Maybe you should take him inside, put him to bed."

Holt laughed archly. "It's always nice when one can make jokes in the face of death."

"Wouldn't it look suspicious if I died of a spider bite, so soon after Fred?"

"I doubt they'll ever know the cause. Even if they do, they'd have a good deal of trouble proving I was responsible. I know how to cover my tracks, you know. And if they do figure things out and arrest me—"

"You'll finally be a media darling, grabbing the spotlight for your fifteen minutes of fame. And I will have been punished, for never giving you the attention you demanded."

He smirked. "Nicely put—very succinct."

I tried to draw back from the spider, but Holt followed, keeping him close.

"The onset of symptoms occurs almost immediately," Holt said, "and they're quite unpleasant. For small children and others with weak immune systems death can come within hours, even minutes. Even if you remained conscious long enough to tell someone what kind of spider bit you, I doubt there's any funnel-web antivenom around here. By the time they flew in a vial from Australia, you'd be long gone."

He pressed the spider toward my lower lip until it was only millimeters away.

"Oh, look! It's showing its fangs. They're rather large for a spider, you know. It's one reason the funnel-web can inject a large dose of venom so quickly."

Behind Holt, I noticed a crouched figure slipping quietly through the shadows, across the leafless patio. He moved with practiced stealth, like someone who'd been trained for it. Even before he got close, I recognized him as Lance.

I raised my voice, hoping he'd hear. "I suppose striking quickly would be the best course, wouldn't it?"

Before Holt could respond, Lance grabbed him by the back of his shirt and yanked him away. Holt's eyes widened and he cried out, stumbling backward. His gloved fingers opened, losing the spider. Lance slipped his left arm around Holt's neck, and used his right to reach down and seize Holt firmly between the legs. Holt screamed, but not for long. Before I could stop Lance, or even think about trying, he raised Holt off his feet and flung him face-first over the wall. Holt's arms flailed in a frantic windmill motion as he dropped through space. His scream died in his throat in the second or two before he struck the rocks.

I looked over to see him sprawled facedown, blood pooling beneath his cracked skull. His legs were twisted awkwardly beneath him, still twitching. They kept on like that for the better part of a minute. Then the movements ceased and the pool of blood stopped spreading, a sure sign the pumping heart had been stilled.

I turned away to look for the funnel-web but couldn't find it. It had crawled into the darkness of the untended yard and I wasn't about to go searching around for him in the weeds. In this parched environment, I figured, he wouldn't last long.

As I returned to the wall, Lance was drawing a cigarette and staring out at the city lights like someone having a smoke after sex. As he turned toward me, I could see by the brightness in his eyes and the flush in his face that he'd enjoyed the thrill of what he'd just done. It was a feeling I knew all too well. Like father, like son, I thought, and so on, into eternity. Lance was still at war, but now the war was inside his head. I knew that feeling too. At that moment, I didn't need a paternity test to know that Lance Zarimba came from my seed, from my genes.

"I owe you my life," I said.

"You gave me mine," he said, exhaling a stream of smoke. "That makes us even."

"You saw the news reports that I've been searching for you?"

"Yeah, I saw 'em."

It was nearly dark. A few dogs had barked up and down the nearby canyons for a minute or two after the commotion but had grown quiet again.

"The spider's gone," I said. "We've got nothing to prove that Holt threatened me."

"I guess we don't."

He took another drag, unhurried, unruffled.

"With our backgrounds," I said, "and my problems with Holt, I doubt the cops or the D.A. would believe us. They'd probably see this as pure revenge."

"I suppose you're right."

"You need to get out of here. We both do."

He said nothing to that, just looked steadily into my eyes.

"If questions ever come up," I went on, "and they somehow put us together up here on the night this happened, I'll take full responsibility. I'll tell the truth leading up to the moment Holt went over the wall, but I'll claim that I did it myself, that you tried to stop me but couldn't. I'll stick to that story, no matter what. Understood?"

He considered it a moment, took another hit of nicotine, and said, "If that's how you want it."

Distantly, behind him, a light came on in a hilltop house. Several other houses around the canyon that had been dark were now brightly lit.

"Lance, you really need to go."

"Not just yet."

He crushed his cigarette in his callused palm and slipped the butt into a pocket of his jeans. Then he surveyed the patio and the yard. He grabbed the glove off the wall, shoved his left hand into it, and took hold of the machete by the handle. He returned to the spot where he'd tossed Holt over and where the morning-glory vines had spread. Gripping the machete tightly, he leaned out and hacked away at the farthest branches, letting them fall near Holt's body but not atop it. Then he dropped the machete over the side so it landed in the same general area. It clattered on the rocks and skidded away a few feet before it stopped. A couple of dogs barked briefly at the noise and then the stillness returned.

"That might help us a little," he said.

He removed the glove and laid it back on top of the wall where he'd found it. Then he faced me, standing close.

"I guess it's time I hit the road," he said, but didn't move.

"Where will you go?"

"I got a wife waiting for me in Mexico, name of Paca. Down in Jalisco, little town called Purificación. We got a restaurant there and a little house I built. Things are simpler down there, the way I like 'em. With my disability check, we live pretty good."

"You'll need to keep taking your meds."

"You know about that, huh?"

"Detective Haukness filled me in. He's concerned about you."

"Tell him I'll be okay. I get my meds sent down."

"What about therapy, regular appointments to monitor your progress?"

"What I got down there is better than anything the doctors can do. I got a woman who loves and needs me. I got a family."

"A family?"

"We got a daughter, born last year. Estrellita, we call her. Little Star."

"I have a granddaughter?"

He nodded. "Looks a little like me, which means she looks a little like you. The blue eyes mostly. Otherwise, she's dark and pretty like her mom."

I stared out at the city, letting it sink in. When I turned to Lance again, I said quickly, "I swear, I never knew about you. Your mother never contacted me, never let on that she was pregnant."

"But if you'd known," he said, "you would have been gone just the same. She told me how you left her cold, without so much as a good-bye."

"I was scared, Lance."

"She told me she loved you, man."

"I was running. Running from a life I couldn't live. Running from myself mostly."

He smiled with faint derision and shook his head slightly.

"Sounds like something a writer would say."

"Look, I've made plenty of mistakes. I know that. But you weren't one of them. You might not believe that, but that's how I feel. You're my son. Do you have any idea what that means to me?"

He dropped his eyes, shuffled his feet.

"I got to get going," he said. "I want to be across the border in a couple of hours."

"Try not to stop until you're well out of L.A. Avoid surveillance cameras if you can. If you have to get gas, pay cash, no credit cards."

"Yeah, I know the drill."

Still, we stood there, no more than two feet separating us. But we were men, a father and son who didn't know how to communicate or reach out or touch, like so many fathers and sons. The gap between us might as well have been a mile, a continent.

Lance finally broke the silence.

"Take it easy, man."

He crossed the patio and disappeared around the side of the house. I glanced over a last time to make sure Holt hadn't moved. He hadn't.

As I followed the same path Lance had taken, I heard him start the big engine on his Harley. When I got to the street he was rolling quietly toward Nichols Canyon Road, keeping his throttle low. I saw his brake light briefly flash. Only when he'd turned the corner and started up the hill did he hit the gas and set the dogs to barking again.

THIRTY-FIVE

It was nearly nine when I pulled the Metro into the driveway. As I climbed out, I saw a figure sitting on the darkened porch.

Maurice, I thought, waiting for me to make dinner plans. But as I climbed from the car and the man stood, I saw that it was Ismael. He came down the steps as I approached up the front walk. We didn't say a word, just walked into each other's arms and held on.

"I don't deserve another chance," I said. "Not after what I did."

"Without forgiveness, Benjamin, love is impossible. Because none of us is perfect."

"You have so much faith, Ismael."

"My life is based on faith. It's taken a different form, but I haven't lost it."

"You've got your whole life ahead of you. You could do so much better than me."

He disengaged from me and took my face in his hands, looking into my eyes.

"Shouldn't I be the one to decide that?" The self-assurance in his voice surprised me. "I'm not as naïve as you think, Benjamin. When you give up nearly forty years of your life to a religion based on fear and guilt, and finally come to realize the truth, and decide to break free and start over, you're not weaker for it, but stronger."

"I never thought of you as weak, Ismael. Quite the opposite. You have to believe that."

He took my hand and led me up the drive.

"We have some unfinished business," he said.

Upstairs, in the muted light of a window, we kissed the way millions of other men do who understand what love is and have the freedom to express it with another man.

We undressed slowly, taking our time as we rediscovered each other in a different way. How two people relate physically, how and where they touch each other, the balance of tenderness and passion, the pleasure they take but also give unselfishly, can reveal a multitude about their true feelings for each other, about the depth of their intimacy. In those first minutes back together, Ismael and I bridged the last gap between us, crossed the final barrier. It was our souls connecting, not just our bodies.

When it came time to make love, I rolled a condom onto him, lubed him properly, and lay back on the bed, waiting. He was hesitant at first but let me show him the way. I guided him deep inside me, helping him explore another man in a way he never had. As we fell into rhythm with each other, I watched the play of sensation and emotion on his face as he watched mine, the incomparable beauty of one person's love for another, two people letting go and joining, all at once.

Afterward, we lay naked and entwined on the bed. I told him about my reunion with Lance, what I'd learned about his life in Mexico, although I never mentioned where we'd met or what had happened to Jason Holt. I hoped I'd never have to, that Holt's body would be discovered and the cause of death attributed to an accident, the way Lance had arranged it to appear. I hoped that would be the end of it, for everyone's sake, including Maurice. But you never know.

"He's on his way to Mexico?" Ismael asked.

I glanced at the clock on the nightstand. "He's probably approaching the border, if he planned to cross at Tijuana. Maybe he's already across, knowing how fast a Harley can move on the open road."

"How soon are you going down to see him?"

"Down to Mexico?"

"You're planning to follow him, aren't you? To meet his wife? To meet your granddaughter?"

I turned my eyes to the ceiling, silent.

"Benjamin, he's your son, your flesh and blood." Ismael reached over, took hold of my chin, forced me to meet his eyes. "Are you listening?"

I tried to look away, but he wouldn't let me.

"I figure I'll try to contact him at some point," I said, hoping that would end it.

But Ismael wouldn't give it up.

"You're afraid to go down, aren't you?"

"You're saying I should go now?"

"If you wait, the distance will only grow wider. The days and weeks will stretch into years."

I shifted my eyes uneasily.

"You're frightened of the responsibility," he said, "frightened that it might not work out."

"My life is littered with things that didn't work out."

"So you're giving up? Is that what you'll do when we hit our first bump in the road?"

"We've already hit some of those," I said. "I'm still here, aren't I?"

"We're a couple now, Benjamin. Now is when it starts to mean something, right?" His eyes stayed on mine. He wouldn't let me escape. "If you don't take the risk, you'll never know what might have been. You'll be haunted by questions and regrets the rest of your life. What's keeping you here?"

I placed my hand on his chest. "You don't know?"

"I'll go with you. I'm on a leave of absence from work. My

passport's in the car. I've got my credit card. I can buy whatever I need down there."

"Go, right this minute?"

"Right this minute, before something gets in the way, before it's too late."

"And you'll go with me?"

He laughed lightly, as if it was a silly question.

"Of course I'll go with you."

We showered and dressed quickly, and threw some essentials together. Since we both had passports, getting visas in Mexico wouldn't be a problem. All it would take would be some cash for the *mordida,* slipped secretly to the clerk when we handed in our applications for new ones, claiming ours had been lost or stolen.

As I locked up the apartment, a siren wailed down near the boulevard. I froze, my key still in the door. Ismael noticed.

"What's wrong, Benjamin?"

I listened to the siren. It seemed to be turning south, away from us, instead of coming up the hill toward the house.

"Nothing," I said. "Everything's fine."

Below, at the house, I knocked on the kitchen door. Through a window, I could see Maurice in the living room, sitting with the cats. Candles were burning, and I could hear Billie Holiday on his old turntable. He got up slowly and shuffled through the kitchen and opened the door. The aroma of incense wafted out.

He perked up at the sight of us. "Benjamin! Ismael! What a nice surprise, seeing you together."

He asked us in, suggesting we go out for dinner. After declining, I explained about Lance and told Maurice about our plans. Tears welled up in his eyes.

"Oh, Benjamin, this is the best news I could ever ask for!"

I told him we were leaving immediately in Ismael's dependable Toyota. I'd parked the Metro in the garage, and handed Maurice the keys.

"Will you be all right, Maurice? Here by yourself?"

"You've known me a long time, Benjamin. I'm having a rough

spell, but you didn't really think I'd fall apart and become help-less, did you?"

I laughed. "If I did, I deserve to be punished."

Maurice winked. "I'll leave that to Ismael. He seems to know how to handle you. Anyway, I still have some wonderful friends left. I won't be alone. And with Fred gone, I'll have more time to devote to the gay marriage campaign. We're planning a big rally for November, just before the election. There's always something to do, Benjamin—something positive and important."

While I loaded my bags into Ismael's car, Maurice fixed us a Thermos of hot coffee. He brought it out to the street, where he hugged Ismael and said good-bye. Then it was my turn. We held each other for a minute or two. I promised I'd stay in touch along the road.

"I love you as if you were my own son," Maurice said. "Don't you ever forget that."

As Ismael drove off, I looked back to see Maurice waving with one hand and wiping away tears with the other.

Over the next few hours, sitting on the passenger side, I dozed. I woke to find us speeding across the Arizona desert, through hun-dreds of miles of cities, suburbs, and small towns, then through arid forests of rugged yucca and towering saguaro. Just before dawn, the gas and fast-food stops and cheap motels appeared more often along the highway, neon and fluorescent bright in the darkness.

Just as dawn was breaking, the border checkpoint at Nogales came into view. We passed through without a hitch; all the inspec-tion was being done on the other side, where hundreds of cars were lined up, going north, filled with Mexicans showing their pa-pers to cross legally as day workers, before returning that night.

We stopped to fill the tank on the Mexican side, where the gas was cheaper. Ismael chatted in Spanish with the attendant, and pur-chased a travel map of Mexico. I took over the driving as we left Nogales behind, taking a two-lane highway into the vast Sonoran desert. Ahead of us, an old pickup lurched and belched its way south. In the bed were crates of chickens and two small children. One of them, a wide-eyed, dark-skinned girl, waved at me with a gap-toothed grin.

As I waved back, my cell phone rang. I glanced at my caller ID. It was Judith Zeitler. Until that moment, I'd completely forgotten about *Jerry Rivers Live.*

"Judith," I said.

"Benjamin, didn't you get my message asking you to call?"

"I'm sorry. Things have been hectic."

"I'm afraid I have bad news."

"I'm listening."

"It's about *Jerry Rivers Live.* They've scratched you from the schedule. When I tell you why, you're not going to be very happy."

"Try me."

"You've been replaced by Alexandra Templeton. Her new book has gotten really hot. They want her on right away."

I smiled at the irony.

"But she doesn't have video," I said.

"You're angry, aren't you?"

"No, Judith, I'm not angry. I'm completely okay with it."

"Seriously?"

"Templeton's book deserves the exposure. It's a lot more important than mine. If I were the producer of *Jerry Rivers Live,* I'd book her too."

"I'm afraid your publisher's canceled the new printing."

"I understand."

She suddenly brightened. "There's always the West Hollywood Book Fair!"

"I'm afraid I'll have to miss the book fair, Judith. Give them my apologies, will you?"

"But why?"

"I'm taking a vacation, and I don't know when I'll be back."

Our signal broke up, and I closed my phone and set it aside. The pickup turned off onto a side road, raising dust, and the little girl waved to me again. I waved back and continued on the highway. As the miles passed, my thoughts drifted to Templeton and her best-selling book. To my surprise, I felt no envy or bitterness but only happiness for her. I realized that in these last few hours a sense of peace had settled over me, unlike I'd ever known.

In the east, the sun was rising, flooding the flat landscape of sagebrush and cactus with golden light. Ismael shifted in his seat to get more comfortable, and took my hand in his. Before long he fell asleep with his head on my shoulder.

I understood now that I'd never fully escape my past, the history that I carried in my blood and in the darker recesses of my heart. When I'd been a young reporter, Harry Brofsky had told me that the past is always with us, always infused in the present, shaping who we are and what we do, holding us back in some ways even as it pushes us ahead in others. In facing what was behind me, I thought, and embracing it, perhaps I'd find a way to finally move forward, whatever the future might hold.

And so I drove on, with Ismael beside me, in search of my son, my family, myself.